Other books by Mark Farrer

Dirty Barry
Where Seagulls Dare
A Fistful Of Collars

THE GOOD
THE BAD
&
THE RUGBY

mark farrer

funny business press

THE GOOD, THE BAD & THE RUGBY

ISBN: 978-1-9164892-3-3

Published by Funny Business Press

To Alice
For giving her everything to everything.

This is a work of fiction.
Names, characters, places and incidents either are products of the author's imagination or are used fictitiously.
Any resemblance to actual events or locales or persons, living or dead, is entirely coincidental.
Except for Big Paul.

CONTENTS

FOREWORD

This is a tale of two towns. Two very different towns: Galashiels and Melrose, nestling cheek-by-jowl in the Scottish Borders.

Galashiels is like the Jeremy Kyle green room. On a bad day. Badly-tweezered, orange, single mums parade their multi-coloured babies in top-of-the-line strollers through a forest of satellite dishes. Their ex-boyfriends (looking like lower league footballers who have been tattooed and pushed through Sports Direct) vape and let their dangerous dogs shit on the pavement.

Melrose isn't like that. At all. Sir Walter Scott had a home there; it is said that King Arthur is buried there. It is the home of Rugby Sevens, has a 14th Century abbey, an annual literary festival, and a cheese shop. And money.

Lots of money.

If Melrose was a person, it would be Angela Lansbury in a two-piece heather mixture and pearls cycling home from the local butchers in the sunshine with a juicy fillet steak in the basket for her pet Pekinese. If Galashiels was a person, it would be helping police with their enquiries.

The two towns are only four miles apart, geographically, but light years apart in terms of almost everything else. Why does such a low-rent place like Galashiels lie so inelegantly juxtaposed next to the sleepy, leafy market-town pleasantness of Melrose?

This book, alas, does not answer that question.

PART ONE

IN COURT: GLORIA

"Can you tell us, Mrs Ingoglia, what happened on the night of the 26th December last year?"

The Procurator Fiscal stood tapping her elegant nails on the lectern. She adjusted one shoulder of her gown and glanced down at her notebook, scribbling a comment now and then, while Gloria spoke. Gloria shifted nervously from one foot to another in the cramped witness box and tried to remember the line she had agreed to tread with Duffy. They had talked this trial over and over until she was sick to death of the whole thing - what had happened, what she should say happened, what she shouldn't mention, words she shouldn't use. Her head buzzed with confusion and over-concentration. The Procurator Fiscal was looking at her in a strange way and Gloria wondered if the mental effort was showing on her face. She looked across at the jury to steady her nerves, but that didn't work - fifteen strangers staring at her as she struggled with her English.

"I watch TV in house-"

"In your living room?"

"Yes. Living woom. Love Island. Catchup. Vewy much I like." She squeezed out a smile and a titter ran through the jury.

"What time was this?"

"All night."

"I understand, Mrs Ingoglia. Between what times?" The Fiscal turned towards the Sheriff. "My Lord, Mrs

Ingoglia is not a native English speaker."

"I understand." The Sheriff scribbled and looked kindly at Gloria. "Take your time, Mrs Ingoglia. If you are unsure how to reply, Ms Whittaker will rephrase the question for you."

"Between what times, Mrs Ingoglia?"

"Fwom six to… maybe ten?"

"I see. Go on."

"Well, there was sudden shake and bang - like earthquake. Vewy loud. House wobbled and wall fell down. Vewy dusty. I scweamed and it was a van."

"A van?"

"Yes. Large blue van."

"You're sure it was blue?"

"Yes."

"So the van crashed into your living room. Around ten?" Gloria gave a series of small nods as the Fiscal helped her limp through her story. "Can you describe the damage?"

"Wall had big hole, bwicks and powder on floor and dust evewywhere. All surfaces needed good clean afterwards." She shook her head, displeased, and the jurors tittered again. "Many things on sideboard bwoken."

"And the ceiling?" The Fiscal seemed not to be interested in Gloria's treasured collection of porcelain figures depicting shepherdesses and sheepdogs. Gloria was thrown off her stride as she recalled the damage to her precious ornaments and the fact that she'd had to brush them up and scrape them into bin bags. Her eyes pricked with tears.

"Ceiling was hanging down."

"So you could see through a hole in the ceiling?"

"Yes."

"My Lord, I would draw your attention to exhibits 12 through 17 - photographs taken by Mr Ingoglia the morning after the event." The Clerk of the Court distributed copies to each of the jurors while the Sheriff flicked through his own sheaf of photos. "Go on, Ms Whittaker."

"Mrs Ingoglia. Did you see the driver of the van?"

"Yes. It was Dewek."

"Objection, my Lord!" The counsel for the Defence, Darren Patterson, was on his feet. "The witness's written statement indicates quite clearly that she was unable to see anyone at the wheel at the time of the crash."

"Ms Whittaker?" The Sheriff nodded. "Perhaps you would refrain from leading the witness and rephrase your question?"

"Yes, my Lord. Mrs Ingoglia, could you see who was at the wheel *at the time* of the collision?"

"No."

"Did you see anyone shortly after?"

"Yes. Dewek."

"Derek Marshall?"

"Yes."

"And where was he - when you saw him?"

"He was staggewing down the twack. Away from house. I looked out of window and saw him."

"And you are sure it was Mr Marshall?"

"Yes."

"Mrs Ingoglia. Do you have any idea why Mr Marshall drove the van into your property that night?"

"Objection, My Lord." Patterson rose to his feet again. "My learned friend is calling for conjecture from the witness."

"My Lord, I wish to establish motive." The Fiscal

retorted. "Mrs Ingoglia has important evidence which will show motive in this case."

"Then perhaps you can ask the questions in such a way as to avoid conjecture on the part of the witness, Ms Whittaker?"

"As you wish, my Lord." The Fiscal sighed and looked down at her notes for several moments, gathering her thoughts, before looking back up at Gloria. "Mrs Ingoglia, was that the first time you had ever seen Mr Marshall?"

Gloria felt her knees weaken and she bit her lip. "No."

"When had you seen him before?"

"Many time."

"Often?"

"Yes."

"Why?"

"He is my bwother-in-law."

"Your brother-in-law?"

"My husband bwother-in-law. Not weally mine."

"I see."

"Dewek used to be mawwied to Duffy's sister."

"Duffy being your husband?"

"Yes."

"So, you knew Mr Marshall well?"

Gloria swallowed hard. "Yes."

"Had, in fact, seen him many times."

"Yes."

"So had no problem identifying him when you saw him staggering away from the van?"

"Yes."

"You had a problem?"

"No."

"You didn't have a problem?"

"No."

"I'm sorry, Mrs Ingoglia. So the jury is clear: were you sure that it was Mr Marshall you saw immediately after the collision with your house?"

"Yes."

"Thank you." The Fiscal caught Gloria's eye and held it briefly, in silence, before continuing. Gloria knew what was coming. "Mrs Ingoglia, why had you been seeing Mr Marshall so frequently?"

There was something about the tone and the phrasing of the question that made the court collectively hold its breath. One of the jurors unconsciously leant forward in his seat and the air seemed to crackle with expectation. Gloria looked down at her hands pressed together at her lap and squeezed her eyes tight shut.

"For sex." She managed, quietly.

"Pardon me?"

Gloria hung her head, ashamed.

"I'm sorry, Mrs Ingoglia. But could you answer please, for the record." The courtroom hush was palpable.

"For sex." Gloria kept her head bowed, unable to look at anyone.

"You and Mr Marshall had been having sex?"

"Yes."

"For how long?"

"Not long." Gloria looked up and glared at Derek in the dock. "He not last long. He have issue."

At least one juror sniggered and Derek looked up at the ceiling in despair.

"I meant, for how long had you been having sex with Mr Marshall." The prosecutor said, patiently.

"Few months."

"A few months?"

"Yes." Gloria lowered her face to the floor again,

shame burning her cheeks.

"Where you still having sex when Mr Marshall drove the van into your house?"

"No." Gloria looked up at the Fiscal as if she was an idiot. "I was on sofa. He was in van."

"Mrs Ingoglia." Whittaker sighed, fiddling with the pen in her hand. "This affair, with Mr Marshall-"

"Was not affair." Gloria blurted. "Was... awwangement."

"This arrangement - let's come back to that. For now, were you still seeing Mr Marshall for sex around the time of Boxing Day or had you stopped seeing him for sex?"

"Stopped."

"And why was that?"

"Duffy told him to stop."

"Your husband knew about it?"

"Yes." Gloria traced the cracks between the floorboards of the witness box, unable to meet anyone's eye.

"And he told Mr Marshall to stop having sex with you, his wife?"

"Yes."

"Not you?"

"No, I'm his wife."

"I mean, your husband didn't tell *you* to stop having sex, he told Mr Marshall?"

"Yes."

"Why was that, Mrs Ingoglia?"

"I didn't want to stop." Gloria shook her head slowly.

"You wanted to continue having sex with Mr Marshall?"

Gloria threw her head up and glared at the Procurator Fiscal, her face wet with tears. "Yes!"

GLORIA

Derek's body was rough-hewn and scarred. Wounds from god-knows-what inflicted by god-knows-who, tattoos which had been inexpertly done, blotches on his legs, and old track marks on his forearms. He was tall and rangy, good upper-body definition but it looked like he had skipped leg day. Gloria hadn't expected to get this close a look at his nakedness quite so suddenly, but his idea of how to conduct himself was clearly different to hers. He had opened his front door wearing nothing except a far-too-small polyester kimono, wide open, and a pair of towelling slippers that looked like they'd been stolen from a cheap hotel. (They had).

He didn't try to kiss her on the cheek, but just smiled broadly and innocently at her. He was hung like a Hoover.

"Gloria, babe. Come in."

Gloria tried to stride confidently past him into the hallway but couldn't avoid inhaling an almighty lungful of horrible aftershave. She imagined him following behind, leering over her backside as she swayed towards the lounge. But she needn't have. From behind her, he silently reached out to grab her shoulder and steer her sharply left towards the stairs and an entirely different room to the one she'd been heading for.

The bedroom.

Derek's room was a bad parody of a bachelor pad - if the bachelor in question had been a tasteless, poor, uncultured layabout with a history of failed relationships and a long gap since his last romantic liaison. Derek ticked all those boxes, and more.

The mood board was predominantly black. Black metal bedframe adorned by a black Playboy quilt cover and pillows. Bedside tables, wardrobe and a chest of drawers all made from black fibreboard; their doors and drawers with black plastic handles. A chrome lamp on the bedside table and a floor-standing chrome uplighter in the corner of the room were both on dim. The lighting was the only thing about the room that was discrete. Gloria felt as if the thin carpet should be sticky.

She watched as he boldly let his kimono fall to the floor and swung himself into bed. As he did so Gloria couldn't help registering a new entry in her catalogue of "dicks I have seen", adding it to the super-heavyweight section.

Which made the actual event a terrible let-down. She had felt her libido momentarily rise when she saw his pendulum swing and curiosity got much the better of her nervousness and modesty. She shyly undressed while he looked at her, unashamedly, although there seemed no lust on his face. Naked, she slid into bed and found his clammy hands silently all over her.

She pictured his dick again and imagined the heft and girth of the thing, in her hand and inside her. But a minute later, when he was rising from the bed and reassuming the pointless mantel of the kimono, she realised that her imagination was going to have to do. By his departure from the bed, he was signalling that the act was done.

Gloria remembered reading once about mosquitoes - when you lived in the tropics, you did well to know as much about the disease-carrying pests as you could - but, after all this time, about the only fact she could recall about them was that they were amongst the fastest animals on the planet to have sex. From gun to tape, it was all over in a few seconds. The key phrase here, she now realised, was amongst the fastest. *Amongst.* She had just met the title-holder.

Gloria lay in bed, feeling like she had been used as a basic, functional receptacle. An empty shell to be watched and handled and then summarily injected. She stared at the ceiling in silent disgust - the incident more painful and humiliating in its brevity and one-sidedness than she could articulate.

She dressed hurriedly, shame in her eyes, and padded down the stairs, high heels in her hand. She couldn't bring herself to say Goodbye, wanting to just slip away and pretend none of this had happened.

As she softly turned the latch, Derek called to her down the hallway: "Same time again tomorrow!"

Gloria Phatipatanawong had grown up in the hilly countryside around Phetchaburi, in northern Thailand. She had two brothers and five sisters - in such a heavily agricultural economy, most families were like hers: large and poor. It was a tradition, and not one to be ashamed of. Family pride and family ties were strongest where food and money were rarest. And her parents had drilled it into her from an early age: the duty of a child, above all else, was to take care of the family - especially to provide for your parents in old age.

When large families don't have enough money to go around, one of the first decisions made was to withdraw their daughters from school and send them out to work. What money that existed was prioritised for educating the boys. So Gloria and her sisters helped in the rice fields and then graduated to small factory work when she turned eleven, bringing home much valuable income, while the boys studied hard so they could make their way out in the big wide world.

Her childhood was happy even if it was not care-free, and money doesn't really mean much when you've never had any. She was a healthy, happy, and energetic child with a broad smile and a generous heart who would help others and show them kindness and consideration as naturally as breathing air. She even had a boyfriend, Worrawut, whom she adored and who adored her. After work and school, they would walk in the hills and plan their future - nearly always involving hordes of beautiful, smiling children and a life of joy and happiness.

Gloria's dreams came to a sudden end when she turned sixteen. Her father had always drunk a lot - many fathers did, and their wives just accepted it - but it got worse and worse. What little money came in was squandered or gambled away, so more money was borrowed at usurious interest to make ends meet. (Her parents, not educated, couldn't tell a percentage from a porcupine). But the family shame which would result if they lost their struggling farm or their meagre livestock? Gloria didn't need a picture drawing for her when, as the eldest, her tearful mother had confided all to her.

So she had decided what she needed to do, had just as tearfully told Worrawut that now it was her turn to show how strong and powerful was her intention to do her daughterly duty. Everyone in her village knew other young women who had left home to make good money in the tourist meccas of Bangkok, Phuket and Pattaya. Working in hotels or restaurants, Gloria herself knew a friend who was sending home 2,000 baht a week! Imagine such wealth, when her entire family subsisted on little more than 3,000 baht each month.

She left home with a heavy heart but a clear belief that she was embarking on an enormous adventure and would, one day, return to lift her family out of poverty and marry Worrawut just as they had dreamed, living in a big house in the hills with a swathe of giggling children.

The day she left was during the rainy season. The huge leaves on the plantation trees glistened between downpours. The dark brown earth steamed and sighed in the tropical afternoon, sending shivers of delightful breath into the air in replenishing wonder. She could smell the musk of the buffalo and hogs sweating in the heat, and hear the scratch of the chickens as they pecked under the shade of the family house, raised on stilts.

Her parents embraced her, her sisters kissed her and waved and waved (her brothers were both at school) and stood waving until the oxcart she was riding sauntered out of view and gave her the sight of the gleaming river as it wound its way beneath the blistering sun.

She didn't know then that she would never, ever, go back.

Her friend from the village had paid for her flight and Gloria had spent her first twelve hours in wonder at the city, the airport, the bustle and crush, the noise and stink of the crowds. Whizzed through chaotic traffic in a tuk-tuk, she found herself in a noisy, neon bar with dozens of girls dancing up on tables and small stages, all dressed (if that was the word) in skimpy outfits - many little more than bras and pants.

Gloria was overwhelmed. This was nothing like anything she had ever known, heard or dreamt of. That night she went to bed and couldn't sleep. Excitement, wonder, fear, homesickness, disorientation - all played hopscotch through her head and the thickness of the noise and the closeness of her friend's tiny apartment were all too much for her. After little more than an hour's sleep she was staring broad daylight in the face and wondering what on earth today held for her.

Five years later, she was the toast of Phuket's riotous nightlife. The Banana Girl.

The memories had bled into a blur of regret, denial and accomplished numbness. She saw what she'd been through and what it had done to her as if it was all nothing. Perfectly understandable and the result of a nineteenth century upbringing in the backwoods of beyond. But in the shining citadel of 21st century grime and greed and cash, she could see herself for what she truly had become.

A whore.

Even as she had adapted to life away from home, the idea of becoming a bar girl had been a bitter pill for Gloria to swallow and she seriously believed that, if it hadn't been for her sense of duty and devotion to her parents she couldn't have done it. Raelyn, her friend, told her that her parents would know - deep down - what Gloria was doing to earn the sort of money she was sending home. They might be far away but they weren't deluded. Young, attractive women earned good money in only one way and they knew it. You could be sure, though, that they wouldn't be sharing their suspicions with the other villagers. It would all be a jointly persistent front of pride and gratitude in their eldest daughter and the status she had acquired through leaving to support her family and build a future for herself. The tears they shed inside when, or if, they thought of what Gloria was actually doing, would be known only to themselves and their souls.

When she'd first understood the implications of the work required of her, Gloria had been shaken to the core and strode out of the bar. Eventually she persuaded herself to work there just serving drinks, but she soon became aware that the dancers earned more money - a lot more. She had worked tables, endured drunken groping and leering customers and slowly watched and learnt.

Reluctantly, she agreed to become a dancer. For the first month, the bar owner allowed her a full salary, regardless of her performance. She had been very nervous, that first time, up on stage, but the other girls had taken her under their wings and Gloria had been determined to earn her money, degradation or not. But after that first month, she had been taken to one side and told in no uncertain terms that her wages would be cut and she would need to make them up by throwing in some extras. "However you want to do it" the owner had said. Consulting again with the other girls she began the transition from showing more flesh, to private dances, to handjobs.

From there, it didn't seem much of a stretch - or much of a surprise - a month or two later when the owner told her she had to meet a quota of at least twenty customers a month or she would be out. Gloria had almost been expecting it.

Her first customer was a westerner - most customers were. He'd been fairly young and kind to her but it had still been scary and disgusting. It hadn't lasted long and she had really not participated at all, just wanting it to be over and thinking about the money. She couldn't wait for him to leave, and when he did she showered for a very,

very long time. She had started crying when she got back to the bar and the owner had taken her aside and told her to buck her ideas up. Customers came in for a good time and a girl, not to see some mopey tearful mannequin with all the allure of a dead seal. These weren't the word he used but she knew what he meant.

By the end of that week she was already becoming numb to the whole thing: the process of smiling and giving the come-on to strangers, allowing them to touch her and then later, enter her, whilst maintaining this facade of pleasure and sexiness. She found the way to manage was to tune out, regard herself as some kind of disembodied spirit occupying a physical vehicle for male pleasure temporarily each night. None of her customers ever asked about her life; they didn't care. One time a man had asked her if she was okay, but Gloria hadn't known what to say and had just looked away.

But the hours she worked left her a lot of time to herself. Time to forget about what she did and enjoy some of the money she made. She worked six days a week, but only 8pm to 2am. She'd wake each day around noon and have achingly long hours to herself before she needed to be back at work. One weekend a month, she was free to do whatever she wanted for an entire 48 hours. She would travel to Bangkok, visiting the red light area there, checking out the bars and venues of the capital. She made friends with other girls there and within a year, what she did for a living didn't seem so bad. She continued to study what went on in the bar, look at what the other girls did, tried to see if there was a way to embellish her role, earn more money, find a route out of this life. An exit strategy.

That was where the bananas came in.

Inspired by her trips to Bangkok, she proposed some

changes to the bar owner. He had agreed and she had started an act that blew the other bars in Phuket out of the water. One which had the punters queueing up around the block and prepared to pay top-dollar for the watered-down drinks on offer. The owner had been delighted, and so had Gloria - her money and share in the business idea grew and grew. She could see her way out!

Generating such huge business through her stage antics, she was no longer required to have sex with strangers, even if she did allow them to caress her and kiss her. She had become a show-woman, a temptress, a star attraction.

It had required training and lots and lots of practice but, boy, when she perfected it she was gold. And the punters couldn't get enough. She watched them as they stood, or sat, entranced as she fed a banana into herself and then performed one, or both, of her party pieces: either she would fire the banana across the room, aiming it at whichever drunk was prepared to pay the most (usually for her to aim it at someone else). The bidding could be furious, mostly because the resulting stains were difficult to get out. Sometimes she inserted the banana before she went on stage. This not only added extra juiciness to the final projectile but also had the inadvertent bonus of starting a rumour that the bananas were inserted with the skin on and that one of her unsung skills was peeling the banana inside her before firing it across the room. This rumour alone, the owner had calculated, doubled her trade during high season.

Her other trick was to carefully control the extrusion of a peeled banana so that it appeared a couple of inches at a time. She would leave a biteable portion of banana protruding from between her legs and invite favoured (i.e., top-paying) customers to take a bite. This latter trick required exquisite control of her vaginal musculature so she spent half an hour each day practising and flexing her genitalia in front of a mirror, first with a dildo to develop control, then later with a real fruit once she realised her muscles were so strong that she could squish the bananas into a pulp just trying to push them out.

No-one had seen anything like it. It blew the ping-pong ball trick into a cocked hat - another variation of her banana routine she had tried and abandoned. When the ever-eager owner inevitably asked her if she would be willing to repeat her party tricks with her other orifice she politely pointed out that the first trick would result in much more mess (although probably higher bidding to avoid being targeted) and that no-one in their right mind would want to be force-fed an excreted banana. He took her point and never mentioned it again.

So, all had looked really bright until the owner had had a sudden heart attack and died, and her share of the business vanished like ice on a hot-plate. She had never signed a contract, never got anything in writing. His widow sold the business to a competitor and Gloria's pleas fell on deaf ears. She was the banana girl, and got paid handsomely for it, and enjoyed more leisure hours than all the other girls. That was enough. She needed to understand and accept it - or another banana girl would be found.

Inured to life on the hard side, she sighed and left her dreams at the kerb. Picking herself up one more time to find a retirement plan, she fell upon a common scheme, harboured by many of the other girls. A favourite fantasy but one rarely achieved: the Hugh Grant strategy.

In her free time, Gloria watched movies - whatever she

could get her hands on. Bootleg DVDs were available on every street corner, and Gloria was able to while away hours and days watching Hollywood movies depicting lives of glamour and wealth she could only dream of.

So dream is what she did.

Of England. Specifically the England of Hugh Grant. An England populated by willowy, elegant, charming men with good hair and pale skin, large houses and expensive cars. Men who would be kind to a woman. Gentlemen. Men who would use the term *lady* without following it with the word *garden.*

So she bought herself a laptop, got an internet connection and a no-nipple selfie. Then spent an entire week carefully crafting a personal profile on a Thai bride internet website. She didn't exactly lie, just omitted certain information she deemed might deter any natural gentleman. She did work in Phuket; she did have many years experience; she had never had a proper boyfriend; she had a rudimentary grasp of English and was only 26 years old and she had, once, won a beauty pageant two years in a row. (The fact that it was called Miss Topless Beer Queen and the final round involved transgender judges licking ice-cold lager off her chest was a detail that no gentleman would surely push her to provide).

Then she waited.

Within a month she had been found.

By Duffy.

Ok, he didn't look much like Hugh Grant, was almost a foot shorter, and that same foot greater in girth. And he was Scottish, not English. But these were mere details in her mind. He was intelligent, endlessly discursive on all manner of subjects that he would rattle off in endless online messages and long, long emails. Her limited English was hardly needed as she found herself able to simply marvel at Duffy's prolixity and energy. He had oodles of hair, a goofy grin and a warm, domestic charm which appealed to her. And when they had transitioned to Skype she had become enchanted with his odd little ways - how he shook his head when he was agitated and couldn't get all his words out in a straight line; how he found the need to quantify things when there really seemed no need to; how he avoided eye contact and twisted the fingers on each hand into rapidly-changing contortions when he was anxious. How could she not fall in love with him?

Gloria put the last of the dishes on the drainer and stared out at the rain. Truly, she thought, Scottish weather must be the worst in the world.

She was no expert, of course. Her life experience after twenty-nine years on the planet, extended exactly as far as Thailand and Scotland. Two more disparate climates she had a tough time imagining. In fact, she'd had a tough time imagining the Scottish climate in the first place. She'd asked Duffy, when they were first communicating online, what Scotland was like and had marvelled at his wonderful descriptions of such alien concepts as snow and sleet.

And ice. When he first told her that lakes (correction: *lochs*; Duffy was very insistent on accuracy) froze in winter because of how cold it got, she hadn't understood. She'd only ever seen ice in drinks, how could a large body of water turn into ice? And how did the fish stay alive when it happened? Did they go into suspended animation until the ice thawed out? No, Duffy had said, the lochs didn't freeze solid! It was only the surface that froze, silly.

They had both laughed, and Gloria had asked him to

tell her more about his home country, so she could marvel at the strangeness and exotic nature of this faraway land.

She wasn't laughing now. Or marvelling. She was just cold. Constantly. She stared out at the sodden landscape, the rain hammering at the window, hard and plentiful enough that a few drops had somehow managed to make their way through the edges of the rickety frame and were starting to pool on the sill above the sink.

They had a word for this cold and wet weather here in Scotland: June.

It wasn't just cold and wet. It was fucking cold. Fucking wet.

Her grasp of English was poor, but her handle on the vernacular was strong - courtesy of years spent in Phuket - and it fitted in well round these parts. The word *fuck* was well-travelled. It may have been born and brought up on these cold, damp Anglo-Saxon shores, but it had spread its wings long ago and wormed its multi-talented way into every corner of the globe. She'd had what she thought was a decent grasp of its scope in Thailand, but two years in Scotland had taught her the amazing versatility of the word. Verb, noun, adjective, interjection. She had yet to find a way to not use it. Duffy found it distasteful, but fuck him! She clung to it - a multi-purpose life-raft which single-handedly kept her ability to communicate with the natives afloat. It had embedded itself into her vocabulary like a tapeworm and shot from her mouth whenever she needed to fill a blank in any sentence. Yes, she got funny looks sometimes, but then she got funny looks anyway since she was clearly not Scottish - she had a clean complexion. What mattered to her was that she was able to make herself understood.

In a shop: *How much are these… fuckers?*

At the bus stop: *When the fuck…?*

In the post office: *How fucking much?*

Almost anywhere: *But… fuck!*

The locals would very hurriedly grasp her meaning, or serve her more swiftly, when her fumbling inarticulacy was embellished with strident obscenity. And how much more weirdly *could* they look at her, anyway? She was dark-skinned, spoke poor English, peppered her speech with expletives and… oh yes, how could she forget … had trouble pronouncing her R's. *Really?* People would question when she told them. *Yes. Wealy.*

Gloria flopped the tea towel on top of the draining dishes and turned her back on the miserable weather. Duffy stood before her with his dirty plate in his hands.

"Sorry. Meant to bring it over. Meant to. Really meant to." He was waggling his head from side to side, avoiding eye contact. She knew he was agitated. Upset with himself for having made a mistake. "Really, really meant to."

She looked at him, softening slightly, despite her annoyance.

"Fuck." She murmured and took the plate from him, turning back to the sink.

WINGNUT

Almost the first things Wingnut did after getting out of prison, was shoot his load into some hooker in the disabled toilets at Abington services.

It took him twenty-seven seconds.

A new personal best.

It had been a get-out-of-jail gift from his eldest, Sam. Eight years of pent-up desire released in under a minute. He didn't know why the woman in the wheelchair had given him a dirty look when he came out of the toilets. It wasn't like she'd had to wait long.

Sam had picked him up outside Hamilton prison, driven him down the M74 to Abington and sat waiting in the car park outside while his father did the deed. Now they were heading across country to Galashiels; a long-forgotten place that Wingnut would unfamiliarly now get to call home. Sean would be there to greet him. He hadn't been there with Sam because he was sitting his first year exam's at Queen Margaret's University, on the outskirts of Edinburgh. Imagine that: him, the father of a University student! His chest swelled with pride at the mere thought.

Wingnut sat contemplatively in the passenger seat, the pair of them largely silent on the drive home. He wasn't much used to conversation. Was too self-conscious of the fact that he was the father to this grown man driving beside him that he hardly knew. Didn't know what to say, where to start. He had so much catching up to do, the enormity of it paralysed him.

"Nice van." He managed, scanning the cabin interior. "Yours?"

"Work's." Sam said, keeping his eyes on the road. "I get to use it whenever I want though."

Wingnut nodded to himself and looked out of the passenger window, at the hills and fields as they sidled by. He was finally a free man once again. He rolled down the window to smell the air, a chill blast that Sam turned to complain about and then, seeing the appreciative smile on his father's face as the wind blew his hair back, fed his face with freshness, he too smiled and said nothing. He pointed the van towards Galashiels and put his foot down.

Derek Marshall looked very much like someone who scowled for a living. Truth was: he didn't; but he was an enthusiast of the form. Two small lines etched his forehead between his eyebrows, gouged into the skin from the almost permanent expression of disapproval he wore. His view of the world was that it was mostly shit, peopled mostly by shitty people, and the best thing to do was make sure that these shitty people didn't get in his way, up his nose or on his case.

Scowling, glaring, frowning, staring: these were the tools on his Swiss Army pen-knife of expressions. They could lend themselves to most tasks, even though there was usually a more specialised tool which would do the job better. But, as photographers were wont to say: the best camera to use is the one you have on you at the time - and Wingnut always had a scowl within easy reach.

Derek had no idea everyone called him Wingnut. But he'd have understood why: his huge ears stood out from his head at an acute angle making him look like the FA

Cup in silhouette. This had been one of his life-long crosses to bear and he had been called names because of his ears throughout his life. In or out of prison, all that ever changed was the nickname used: *jugears, dumbo, shrek, Prince Charles, chimp fucker, Dobbie the house elf.*

In childhood it had hurt and in his teens he had worked hard at body-building and self-defence so that he could take it out on anyone who called him names to his face. Once an adult, people complied. But prison had been another matter. The tactic to use there, was to not let on that a nickname bothered you - that was one sure way to guarantee people would keep using it. But within the first week inside, he'd been given the nickname *knife-drawer*. Wingnut actually thought this was cool and the result of a first-day fight he'd had in the canteen over an evening meal where he'd tried to stab his assailant with a table knife. In reality, they called him that because he clearly wasn't the sharpest knife in the drawer.

Like Irn Bru, Wingnut was an acquired taste. If you take a big bottle and shake it up and then open it, everyone gets it all over them. No-one likes that. And when he was younger, he was so eager to get out of the bottle, fizzing full of energy and life - he didn't stop to think. Just wanted to get out. So he did, and he got all over everyone and in their faces and they hated him as a result.

But the years - decades, in fact - of his life spent in and out of prison had gradually eaten away at this impetuosity. Formerly quick-to-anger he felt he now exhibited much better self-control; was more proportionate in his responses. Whether anyone else shared that view was another matter. Approaching forty, Wingnut was like a Rubik cube: old and tired and no-one could be quite bothered enough to work him out any more.

But he liked to think he was now a more patient, attentive, considerate man. Perhaps that's what being a proud father did to you.

Not that Wingnut had done much fathering. His two boys hadn't seen much of him over the years. And he hadn't seen Sean since he was eleven. Everyone - everyone except Wingnut, that is - had reckoned it was for the best. Keep the young impressionable child away from the bad, bad man. A controlled nature-versus-nurture experiment, if you like. If the fruit really doesn't fall that far from the tree then perhaps if the fruit is cocooned and protected, nurtured and cared for, it will grow up proud and tall, not stunted and bent from growing in the shade of the overarching parental canopy with massive reach.

Well, today, Wingnut was about to find out.

"Alright, Tiny Tears. No need for all this." Wingnut said, hugging his younger son.

And so it started. Or, rather, continued where it left off. Even though it had left off some eight years ago.

The fact was that, whilst Sean was a big lad - not surprising given Wingnut's own large frame - he was a clear two inches shorter than his father and a crucial half an inch shorter than his elder brother. Sam took every chance he got to verbally belittle Sean and, when he and their father were together, they seemed to take it in turns to exaggerate this pathetic difference. Here they both were now, obviously having bonded on the car journey from Hamilton, reminiscing and catching up, so that they could seamlessly pick up as if it was yesterday.

And, yes, Sean was wiping a tear away, and why? He knew not. He hadn't really missed his father, at least that was what he had told himself these past years. Not having a wastrel father-figure to not look up to - well, Sean reckoned he could just as easily not-look-up-to any other bloke he came across and achieve the same amount of guidance. And the fact was that, from the moment his father had been arrested, their Uncle Duffy had taken both boys on as if it was a natural family duty. Duffy had moved into their house and Sean, if not exactly Sam, had benefited from the presence of an actual adult who took parental responsibilities seriously, if misguidedly in their uncle's case. Sure it hadn't been plain sailing, but what had been plain to Sean was that if his father had been around and Duffy hadn't, his own academic ambitions would never have been realised.

But here and now, with his own flesh and blood in front of him for the first time in Sean's adult life, something came over him and he realised that an emotional dam had burst within him and he had no choice but to let it out.

"What about a guided tour then?" His father had said, detaching himself.

Sam whisked their father away while Sean stood motionless. His vision swam as he wrestled with a desire to see his father anew - connect with him all over again - whilst sensing that, deep down, something inside himself didn't really want to.

"This is Sean's room." Sam said. "Where he does all his worrying."

"You mean studying?"

"Same difference." Sam closed the door dismissively. "You know, Dad, you used to live here remember? Like, how much can it have changed since you were last here?"

"Sam. Son. I've been inside so long, so often, I get disoriented easy. Show me somewhere I can go into and out of rooms as I like and I lose my bearings. This place is... palatial. I'm just trying to take it all in."

Sam looked at his father sadly, then reached over and gave him a bear hug. This man whom he hardly knew. Being away for so long, Sam had remembered and dreamed, and wondered if what he recalled was real or imagined. Where there were gaps, he'd filled them in and, as a result, conjured up an image of a father which he had no way of knowing was true or fictional. Here, in front of him now, was the real thing and he would find out if his own creation of a father matched reality.

"This is my room." Sam opened the door onto a large room littered with boxes and a carpet spattered with oil patches. Heaps of packaging had been torn open and strewn messily around, an open toolbox sat on the floor with oily spanners, wrenches and pliers spilling from it, and the centrepiece was a partially-dismantled mountain bike, up-ended, sitting on its handlebars and saddle *sans* rear wheel.

"It needs a bit of a tidy." Sam admitted.

"What is this? Your workshop? Do you work from home?"

"No. But it kinda is my workshop. This is my bike." Sam swept his hand across the room display proudly, like a glamorous assistant caressing first prize on a game show. "I work on it. A lot."

"Why's it still in bits then? Doesn't it work?"

"'Course it works!" Sam was indignant. "It's state of the art, this bike. Built it myself from top-of-the-range components. Cost me thousands, this!"

"Thousands! For a fucking bike? That's in bits?"

"You don't understand, dad. That's not how bikes work these days."

"I know how fucking bikes work, son. You pedal them and the wheels go round. I can't believe cycling technology has advanced so far in eight years that they've reinvented the fucking wheel!"

Sam sighed and decided now was not the time to educate his father in the ways of modern cycling.

"Fancy a pint?"

Wingnut stood back, surprised, and looked at his son. His eyes were brown and clear, his skin stubbled and youthful, his hair buzzcut and fresh. A vision of young manhood he had never seen before. The boy he'd left when he went to jail had been transformed by time into this. This vision of what he himself had once been. True, he didn't quite look like him - Sean was a more accurate, if shorter, version of himself as far as Wingnut was concerned, although when the boys were younger the general sentiment had been that Sam was the spitting image of his father. Roll the clock forward some eight years and, now, well not so much. But nevertheless, his son had become a man and, as if to prove it, was offering to take his father to the pub. Wingnut beamed.

"Seanie? Coming down the pub?" Wingnut yelled downstairs.

"What, now?" Sean's voice filtered up from the living room over the burble of the TV.

"Yes now. Whaddyasay, kiddo?"

"It's a bit early isn't it?"

"Early? It's drink o'clock and the big hand is on beer! Come on."

There was a pause, followed by: "I'm good. I'll come

along later."

"Sean? Come on, son! I haven't had a drink in eight years. That's over fifty in dog beers!"

When there was no answer, Sam looked at his father, shaking his head pitifully. "Wankstain."

"Hey. Give him a break, hmm?" Wingnut tried ruffling Sam's hair but it was like a Brillo pad. "Maybe his brain's hurting from all that studying."

The pair trotted down the stairs to the front door. "We'll be in The Ship!" Sam shouted behind him.

Sean gave no response.

"Christ! How much?" Wingnut watched as the barman tilled up the round of drinks. "How long have I been away?"

He picked up his pint and whisky chaser and moved over to one of the small tables scattered around the lounge bar. He and Sam were the only patrons this early in the day. Wingnut crouched on a stool and sucked the foam head off his pint. A football match was playing on a large TV up on the wall.

"Wow. Look at that." Wingnut marvelled at the size of the screen, the vibrancy of the colours, the resolution, and multiple camera angles. The text scrolling across the bottom of the screen had his eyes swivelling. "Feel like I've been to the fucking moon, coming back to all this. This is going to take some getting used to. You know, when I was younger you used to be able to have a few down the pub, go to the game, get a fish supper on the way home, get a video out and still have change from a tenner."

"Yeah, well. You can't do that now." Sam replied,

sipping his pint and looking around the empty bar. "Too many security cameras."

"Huh." Wingnut downed his whole pint and then swallowed his whisky, slamming it down on the table when he'd finished. He gave a deep sigh of satisfaction. "Missed this. All this." He swept his hand around the scruffy-looking room as if it was Versailles, instead of a velour kingdom where the predominant colour was sewage-outlet brown. He looked at Sam and smiled. "Beer me!"

"Again?"

"Son. I've been away. I'm not going back. And therefore I am celebrating. Simple as that."

"Not going back? Ever?"

"Exact-a-fucking-mundo."

"Dad, no-one says stuff like that anymore. If they ever did."

"They did." Wingnut sniffed.

Sam stood up and returned to the bar. Wingnut watched him all the way and when he sat back on his own stool, presenting his father with two more drinks, Wingnut looked at him intently.

"So, tell me. How's it all been with your Uncle Duff."

By the time Sam had finished, Wingnut had waded his way through another three pint-and-chaser combo's. His gaze was now somewhat askew but no-one had told his brain. When Sean walked in, his father was loudly and confidently pontificating on the finer points of his own particular brand of parenting style. Catching his eye, his father stood up and held his arms wide apart, welcoming Sean into the pub like some noble member of the inebriati accepting a new disciple.

"Sean, my baby. You're here! Come and have a drink.

Come on. Have a drink. A wee drinkie-doo. With your old man. Celebrate his freedom. I'm buying. What'll yer have?"

Sean was glad the place was empty. His father was embarrassing himself. "A lager top."

"A lager fucking top? That's a puff's drink! Come on, have something proper."

"No thanks. That's fine."

"Ach, fuck me. Ok, if that's what you want." Wingnut slurred his way over to the bar, navigating clumsily between the empty stools and tables. Sean sat down under Sam's glare. The pair waited in silence until their father returned with Sean's drink. "Your brother here was just tellin' me all about Duffy and how he's looked after you's both."

"Yes." Sean said. "And we're both really grateful. Without him I don't know where I'd be."

Sam sneered. "Well, he did his job. And that's it, as far as I'm concerned. We're well shut of him now."

Sean said nothing and sipped his drink, unwilling to be goaded into an argument with his brother.

"Aye. He did right by me, he did. Simple as that." Wingnut raised his glass in tribute.

"Dad, you do know he's a nutter?" Sam asked.

"Nutter shmutter. Did he look after you or not?"

"Aye, he did. But we could've looked after ourselves."

"You were thirteen, fuck sake! Seanie was only nine."

"Nearly eleven." Sean corrected him,

"Whatever. Kids! You can't look after yourself at that age. Simple as that. 'Sides, probably illegal."

"Since when did that bother you?" Sam was now sneering at his father; Sean stayed silent.

"Fuck off! I'm your father, show me respect."

"Why?" Sam snarled. "Why the fuck should I? You fucked off and left us in the care of a total nutjob."

"Why?" Wingnut was startled by his son's sudden ferocity.

"Yes. Why? In two words. Go on. Why should we show you any respect?"

"Two words?" Wingnut rallied. "Or else."

He stared Sam down and, when Sam finally looked away, Wingnut glanced at Sean to make sure there was no defiance coming from that direction either. Content he had re-established dominance, Wingnut went for a slash. As he stood to go, Sam took a sideways look at Sean and kicked him under the table. Sean glared back but said nothing.

The following afternoon, Wingnut crossed the A-road and headed up the farm track which slowly wound its way uphill and to the right, curling past a copse and a muddy field of uninterested cows, sadly grazing and contemplating him with slow brown eyes. He wasn't quite dressed for a ramble but a bit of mud wasn't going to hurt him. Sam had given him a few quid and he had skipped happily down to ASDA like a toddler with his first pocket money to see what eight years behind bars had wrought in the way of progress in menswear.

The answer was little and he was grateful for it. Sartorial elegance was very much not his strong suit and anything which fitted would do, as long as it was black. Or navy at a push. Or on the large side. As long as it wasn't too short or too tight.

Wingnut was six feet tall with a large, loping gait. He had broad shoulders and a muscular torso; his legs were perhaps a little spindly to carry his gangling frame but since they were generally enclosed in trousers he didn't bother too much. Anyone likely to see his skinny calves in the shower was either asking for a smack or intimate enough with him to not be looking at his calves. He had a large male appendage - even the prison doctor had commented on this: hence the term male appendage. Wingnut knew it, loved it and used it every chance he got. Which for the past eight years had been nowhere near enough.

Now, striding through the manure and mud in his new jogging bottoms, T-shirt and parka - all black - he felt his dick swinging meatily and freely between his thighs. Happy, strangely, to be outdoors (that was what enforced incarceration did for you, made you pleased to be cold and muddy) he ploughed on until he came to the house. Wingnut stood looking it at in astonishment for several minutes, wondering if perhaps Sam had not made a mistake or that maybe he himself had taken a wrong turning. The place was a total dump.

It was a single storey cottage with a most eccentric extension bolted on to the side, perhaps to get the best of the daylight, given the hills and woods to his right which the sun was already starting to sink behind. A rickety picket fence, with posts and planks missing at irregular intervals, attempted to keep the mess from the muddy track out, or the detritus from the shambolic garden in. At both objectives it failed miserably.

Three small dirty windows looked out at him, grimy net curtains visible and torn in each. A mouldy caravan with a flat tire was parked to the right of the furthest window, blocking his view of the rest of the house. But not the extension. Oh no, this was resplendently splayed out for all to see, acting almost as an advert for the property as a whole. In fact, as Wingnut looked at it, is was as if the extension had grown to become the larger part of the structure, relegating the original brickwork to a forgotten stub - like a new bush growing on an old tree stump, the foundations had been needed, but the rest of the infrastructure was no longer relevant.

But the extension, oh my. It looked like it had been built by a child from flotsam and jetsam that had washed up on the tide of mud which made its way up the hillside. Here, where no-one would ever come, except the farmer, Wingnut assumed. The roof was assorted sheets of plywood, corrugated iron and oddments of timber, piled loosely on top of each other, a large nail here and there sticking out where the solidity of the material had prevented it being hammered all the way in. The protruding ends of these nails had been bent at odd angles, either as a feeble attempt at interesting decor or as a result of a tired arm which had mis-aimed its last hammer swing and then given up, annoyed. Plastic sheeting spooled from beneath the fringes of this delicate roof arrangement and cascaded unevenly down, a grey moulding waterfall of flapping material designed, Wingnut guessed, to provide some protection from the rain and snow. On the whole, it looked like it didn't.

The piece de resistance to the whole affair was the large bay window which formed the centrepiece of the extended cube. This looked for all the world like the sawn-off end of a large static caravan that had been roughly and unevenly inserted into place and was held down with two small pyramids of breeze blocks, one on either side. Several long pieces of four-by-two had been secured as gable ends above the bay window but large gaps were evident everywhere where the wind and the cold and the rain would all too easily gain access. Some of these gaps were closed by rags, more plastic sheeting, or hacked-off sections of corrugated plastic. The finishing touch, like gargoyles added to a cathedral roof, was the intermittent bloom of insulation foam which had been sprayed into the remaining holes and crevices in this whole construction, left to expand then darken with lichen and more mould. Crusty piebald warts on the face of a burns victim who had had too much, and quite inferior, plastic surgery.

Wingnut couldn't bear to look; couldn't tear himself away. It was a magnificently awful creation. How it even remained standing was a complete mystery to him and one he intended to take up with the owner at some point. Shaking his head in admiration, wonder and dismay, he lifted the flimsy gate off its one remaining hinge and walked up what was, no doubt, meant to be a garden path.

The hammering on the door made Duffy jump, and then made him agitated. His normally neat handwriting jerked and he scribbled untidily in his notebook, his orderly thoughts now rattled and disjointed. He ignored the door until it hammered again, a longer rebuke this time. How was he meant to get his theory update down under these conditions? It wasn't good. Not good. Gloria should have been here. Should have been here. Should. Yes she should.

He got up from his desk, unaware he was still in his pyjamas, and pattered to the door, fingers whirling in his palms. When he opened the door he was momentarily stunned into silence.

"No doorbell."

"What?" Duffy found himself unable to change his brain up through the gears this quickly.

"You don't have a doorbell."

"Right. Yes. No. I mean, I know. No, we don't have a doorbell." He struggled to recover his composure, and failed. "What the hell?"

"Oh that's nice. Not Wow, bruv, great to see you! Or Hey, what a surprise. Gimme a hug, you big lump!"

Duffy reached up to give Wingnut the requested hug. "Not brother. Brother in law. In law. Very different. Completely different. Totally different."

"Whatever!" Wingnut laughed and squeezed Duffy round the shoulders. "You gonna invite me in, then?"

He didn't wait for Duffy to do anything of the sort, and pushed past into the hallway. Duffy obediently closed the door and followed him into the house. Wingnut was a good foot taller than Duffy, and his broad frame filled the corridor that led to the living area. Duffy hurried up behind, talking to his back.

"When did you get out? I didn't know you were out? Didn't know. You never said. I could've come. You never said. Never said. I could've come."

"S'all right. Sam picked me up." Wingnut smiled proudly at Duffy. "Great boy, that. We did a good job there, you and me."

"Yes. Um yes. Yes. We did, yes."

Wingnut looked around the open plan arrangement, frowning. "You been burgled?"

"What?" Duffy surveyed his living quarters, panicking. "Really? No. No. No. They mustn't take anything. It's all needed. All important. Vitally important. Vital."

"Hey, man. Calm down. Only joking. Just looks like a bomb's hit it, is all."

Duffy remained deeply concerned and scrutinised the room. All surfaces, and much of the floor, were littered with piles of papers, stacks of books or bundles of newspapers tied with string. He scanned each one, mentally checking his inventory to make sure the contents of each was still intact. While he did this, Wingnut prowled over to a large whiteboard leaning against the far wall. It was burdened with writing in different coloured marker pen, newspaper clippings taped in place, scattered sections of Ordnance Survey maps and strands of coloured ribbons connecting post-it notes here with push-pins in maps there.

"Oh aye. Nerve centre is it? Mission Control?"

Duffy, finally satisfied his stacks of records were still safely intact, looked up at his brother-in-law. He started rubbing his fingers again, sifting imaginary flour onto the unvarnished floorboards. He waggled his head from side to side, awkward and silent.

"It's alright, mate. It's alright. It's the aliens isn't it? That what this is? Aliens?"

Duffy's head swung jerkily as he bent his gaze to the floor, mumbling.

"Still banging on about beings from the stars, hmm?"

"We are all beings from the stars." Duffy's voice rose noticeably, his tone defensive. "We are. They are. All of us. We're all made of star stuff."

"Yeah, so's dogshit. Calm down." Wingnut turned away from the whiteboard, instantly forgetting it. "Any chance of a cuppa? I've got a mouth like Tutankhamen's armpit."

Duffy sloped over to the kitchen and busied himself with mugs and a kettle. The afternoon sun was now streaming in through the French doors, motes of dust jittering in the hazy light. Wingnut looked out onto the overgrown garden and past it to the empty fields and woodland beyond. "Nice view here, mate. Nice and quiet too. Been here long?"

Duffy nodded. "Moved in when…" He faltered and started rubbing his fingers again. "When Sam… No, when I… when, when…" He trailed off and Wingnut stood looking at him expectantly. "Just before I met Gloria. Met Gloria. Yes. Met Gloria." Duffy eventually managed.

"Who's Gloria?"

Duffy shuffled back with two mugs of tea and handed one to Wingnut. "My wife."

"Your wife!" Wingnut's eyebrows shot up and he surveyed the room again, looking for any evidence of a feminine touch. "She real?"

"Yes. Yes. Yes. Real. Yes, real."

"She around?"

"No. Not here. Not right now. No."

"She been taken up by aliens?" Wingnut laughed.

"No!" Duffy whirled around and rapidly scanned the whiteboard, his eyes jumping from place to place. He sloshed some tea onto the floor. "No! They wouldn't! No, not Gloria. No, not my Gloria!"

"Hey, hey! Duff! Look, sorry mate. Sorry. Didn't mean to agitate you. If you say she hasn't, then she hasn't, ok? Look, why don't you call her? Use my phone, hmm? On me?" Wingnut extended his phone to Duffy, a peace offering. Duffy eyed it suspiciously and didn't take it. "Go on. It's ok. Sam gave it me. Nice huh? Didn't have anything like this when I went inside."

Duffy wasn't listening and had wandered back over to the whiteboard, tracing notes and ribbons with his fingers, muttering to himself as he did so. Wingnut hefted the phone in his hand once more, marvelling at its smoothness and grace.

"So this is what happens. This is what you miss."

"What did I miss?" Duffy continued to finger the whiteboard but spoke to Wingnut over his shoulder.

"No, not what you missed. What I missed. This." Wingnut waggled the phone at Duffy's back, gazing at it wistfully. "Technology. Progress. The physical representation of lost time. Time I could've spent outside enjoying this. Life. My boys."

Duffy, finished with his review of all his maps and notes, had calmed noticeably and turned back to Wingnut, his face innocent and enquiring. "What's your plan?"

"Plan!" Wingnut scoffed. "Ha! Schoolboy error."

"You have to have a plan. Must have a plan. Got to plan."

"Is that right?" Wingnut looked at Duffy as if for the first time. He scanned the cherubic face and its scruffy greying curls, the wide brown eyes and grizzled stubble. He considered Duffy's hunched shoulders and flabby paunch, the thick hands with their wildly waggling fingers, their nails badly bitten; the tattered slippers and stained pyjamas: a man-child gone to seed, with the wisdom of a man and the clarity of a child. Out of the mouths of babes, though, didn't they say? "Yeah. Maybe you're right. That's where I've been going wrong all these years. I've been looking on life as if it's a prison sentence: you just gotta get through it. In, out. Hasn't made any difference to me. But I got out yesterday and saw my boys. Man, they're fully grown! What did I miss? More than this phone. And for what?"

"GBH."

"Rhetorical." Wingnut growled. "Eight years I won't

get back. Eight years with psychos and thugs, arse-bandits and rapists. Eight years wasted. No matter what's changed out here, not much changed in there. Not really. Maybe a few less pervs and paedos now than before. But that's only because we've got more progressive. We don't put 'em in jail anymore, we just put them in the Premier League!"

Duffy stood still, watching and wondering. When Wingnut had finished, they both stood in silence for a while, before Duffy's brain jumped the lights.

"What are you going to do then, get a job?"

Wingnut was roused rudely from his contemplation. "Fuck off! It's only called work because all the other four letter words were taken."

"So what are you going to do?"

"Dunno. Spend time with my boys, first off. Try and make up for lost time. Not sure what else."

"Get a plan. Very important to have a plan. Got to have a plan."

"Yeah, I get it. Gimme time. I'm only out a few days. I haven't - fuck ME!"

This last expression was uttered almost involuntarily as Wingnut saw a beautiful, dark-haired woman appear in the doorway. Duffy trotted dutifully over to her and gave her a peck on the cheek and took the shopping bags from her tired grip. "Come in, love. Come in. Visitor. Look visitor."

Wingnut was stunned. This was a woman. A real woman. A young woman. An attractive, shapely, young almost glamorous-looking woman. An oriental woman. With Duffy. Not for the first time since he had been released, Wingnut felt the need to physically pinch himself to see if he would wake up still in his cell.

Gloria wore a bright, beaming smile which revealed a terrific blast of white streamlined teeth. Her hair was long and thick, falling in waves to her shoulders where it rested in a tangled mane. Black irises sparkled in the whites of her eyes and she had long lashes which made her eyes curl and smile at the same time. She was only slightly taller than Duffy but much, much slimmer with tiny hands that fluttered a little - although nothing like as much as his did - and each finger ended with a tiny painted bright pink nail. She wore a pink beret and a dark grey woollen coat, wellington boots which she had stepped out of the moment she walked in through the door which revealed dainty bare feet, again each tiny toenail the same vivid pink.

"You must be Gloria." Wingnut smiled at her then switched his gaze briefly to Duffy, mouthing a silent Wow. "I'm Derek. Duffy's brother-in-law."

"Hello Dewek." She shook his hand, hers lost in his grasp.

Wingnut looked down at her face looking up at him, caught the smallest glimpse of a white bra surrounding a modest cleavage, and thought he was in love.

IN COURT: GLORIA AGAIN

"Mrs Ingoglia, could you please tell the court why you were having regular sex with Mr Marshall." The Procurator Fiscal said.

"I want have baby."

"You wanted to have a baby with Mr Marshall?"

"No. Want baby with Duffy."

"By having sex with Mr Marshall?"

"No. I want have baby with Duffy by have sex with Duffy. Duffy cannot give me baby."

"Why not?"

"His sperm no work."

"Your husband is infertile?"

"Yes."

"So you decided to have sex with Mr Marshall instead?"

"No. Duffy's idea, not mine."

"Your husband suggested you have sex with his brother-in-law so that you could become pregnant?"

"Yes."

"And you agreed?"

"Yes. I want baby."

"I see. And when was this agreement made?"

Gloria thought for a moment. "Summertime. Dewek came out of jail."

"Objection, my Lord!" Patterson sprung to his feet.

"Yes, Mr Patterson." The Sheriff looked sternly at Gloria and the Fiscal and then turned to the jury.

"Members of the jury, please strike from your memory what Mrs Ingoglia has just said. The personal history of Mr Marshall is irrelevant unless it is pertinent to the events in this trial. Until any relevance is so established - and I will confirm with you if that situation arises, so that there is no doubt - please ignore it."

"I am sorry, my Lord." The Fiscal gave a summary nod to the Sheriff.

"I accept that this was not intentional, Ms Whittaker. Nevertheless." The Sheriff returned to admonish Gloria. "Mrs Ingoglia, hard though it may be, please try to confine yourself to only answering the questions asked and not providing extraneous information until asked to do so." He nodded back to the Fiscal to continue.

"So you had been having sex with Mr Marshall since summer least year. A period of several months?"

"Yes."

"How often?"

"Thwee, four time a week."

"You had sex with Mr Marshall three or four times a week for a number of months?"

"Yes."

"Did you become pregnant?"

"No."

"I see. Is that when your husband decided to put an end to the sex?"

"Yes."

"And when was that?"

"Chwistmas."

"Before Christmas?"

"Boxing Day."

"Boxing Day. So, Mr Marshall had been having regular sex with you for several months and then, on Boxing Day, this ended?"

"Yes."

"Against his will?"

"Sowwy?"

"Was Mr Marshall happy to stop having sex with you?"

"I don't know."

"Did he enjoy it?"

"I think so."

"Did you?"

"No."

"But you continued anyway?"

"I wanted baby."

"How did Mr Marshall take this decision by your husband to cease having sex with you?"

"I don't know."

"You don't know?"

"I don't know. Duffy didn't tell me."

"You weren't there when your husband told Mr Marshall?"

"No. I didn't know Duffy had told Dewek to stop until the next day."

"So let me see if I have this straight. Mr Marshall had been having sex with you frequently for four or five months, and enjoying it, until - against his will - the day after Christmas he was told it had to stop. And, later that same evening, he got roaring drunk and crashed his van into your house."

"Objection, my Lord!" Patterson zoomed to his feet.

"I'm eighty-five, you know." The woman cupped her liver-spotted hands around the plastic cup and introduced herself, nodded smiling at the lady next to her. "Marjorie."

"Really?"

"Yes. My grandson's a court officer." She beamed. "In Glasgow."

"Isn't there an upper age limit for serving on a jury?" This was a well-fed, middle-aged man wearing a suit and tie - he had the self-important air of a senior businessman about him.

"Ooh, no!" Said Marjorie. "You can excuse yourself once you're over seventy, I think. But it's up to you." She turned to the woman next to her and confided in a voice everyone else could hear. "I'm quite excited about this. Never been on a jury before. Fancy that!"

"I have." The businessman moaned. "You've not missed anything."

"Ooh, well, you should be the foreman then!" Exclaimed Lorraine, the woman that Marjorie had smiled at.

"Hold on a minute." Interrupted one of the other men, seated directly in front of the window at what looked suspiciously like the head of the table, even though it was circular. "Case hasn't got going yet. Don't you think it's a bit early to be talking about who's the foreman?" He looked around the table seeking moral support. None was forthcoming.

"My husband used to work in a court." Volunteered a smartly-dressed woman, still with her coat buttoned up, the fur collar kissing the bottom of her curled and stiff hairdo. "Used to tell me all kinds of tales. You wouldn't believe!"

"Aren't these things meant to be confidential?" The businessman asked.

"Well, this was in England." The smart woman said by way of an excuse.

"I don't think that matters. The law is the law."

"Scottish law is different from English law." Piped up Marjorie, newly a font of Scots legal wisdom.

"Yes, well… Michael said we are not to discuss this case with anyone, even our partners." The businessman looked authoritatively around the room. "Anyone."

There was disgruntled silence, as if a teacher had just told off the whole class.

"Do you think he did it? I think he did it." Said Val, a small woman with pinched features and a ridiculous beige perm.

"I'm sorry?" Lorraine's face completely failed to disguise her astonishment.

"This chap, Marshall. I think he did it."

"Yes." Lorraine looked askance at Val and tried to weigh her up. She was wearing a thin padded jacket, dirty green, zipped up to a cream scarf, and brown slacks tucked into a pair of Hunter wellies. A fake Chanel handbag was resting on the table in front of her, sitting on a folded newspaper and a gold tube of eye mascara. "I think, perhaps, we should hear more of the evidence before we come to a decision."

Val frowned. "How much more do you think we need to hear?"

"Some of it, certainly."

"But we've already been here a day! My horses won't feed themselves you know."

"Yes, but we've only heard from one witness. There'll be more!"

"Really?"

"Of course! Have you never seen a trial on TV or in a film? There's always lots of witnesses. Usually one of them gives the vital bit of evidence that changes the whole picture after you think it's cut and dried."

"I think it's already cut and dried."

"Yes, but-"

"I mean, why would the police arrest him if he didn't do it?"

"But-"

"He looks like he did it, doesn't he? And if he didn't do this, I bet he did something else."

"Yes, but you see-"

"Why would they bother appointing lawyers and taking up time in the courts if he was innocent? Doesn't make any sense."

"Well, surely you've heard of innocent until proven guilty?"

Val studied Lorraine, like a pigeon might study a turd: unsure quite what it was but unwilling to get any of it on her. "Yes, I know that's what they *say*. They have to say that, though, don't they? These bleeding-heart liberals who read The Guardian and knit their own yoghurt. What they don't realise is prison is about punishment not rehabilitation."

Lorraine raised both eyebrows at the extent of the sudden animation from this previously silent woman. It looked like she had inadvertently tripped Val's *on* switch and would now have to wait until the battery died. Or the cord ran all the way back in. "I'm going to guess that you voted for Brexit?" Lorraine asked, before realising that what she had just done was pour petrol on a flickering flame.

She unconsciously leant back in anticipation.

DUFFY & THE PLAN

The letter would have flopped onto the doormat, if they'd had one. Duffy shuffled into the hallway and stooped to pick it from the cold flagstones. A chill wind whistled in beneath the door. There was an imprint on the envelope which said NHS Scotland. Duffy swallowed hard and started to ripple the letter between the thumb and fingers of each hand, as if trying to bend it like Uri Geller.

"Is it for me?" Gloria shouted from the kitchen.

"No. It's mine. I think it might be my test results. Pretty sure it is. Pretty sure." Duffy padded into the kitchen where Gloria stood with her back to him at the sink. "Results. Yes. 60, 65% sure. Maybe 70%"

She put down the dishcloth before turning to him, smoothing back her hair with still-wet hands. He was agitating the envelope in his hands, waving it this way and that as if wondering which member of an invisible audience to give it to.

"Open it then." She smiled, wiped her hands on her apron and sat down at the table expectantly.

Duffy slit the top of the envelope neatly, pulled out a single folded sheet of paper and read it. He didn't look up. When he'd finished he slid the letter back into the envelope placed it on the table and lowered himself into a chair. He waggled his head from side to side, his fingers drumming on the wooden table top.

"Must be correct. Must be. NHS. Don't make mistakes. Very professional. Very, very professional. Very, very, very professional."

"Well?"

"Must be correct. Technically. Technically correct. The best kind, best kind of correct. Best kind."

Gloria reached out her hand to lay it on top of his. Duffy shot back in his chair, his hands and whole body snatched away from her. His eyes stayed fixed on the table.

"Duff?" He continued shaking his head back and forth, rocking slightly in his chair. "What does it say?"

"Sub-optimum. Sub. Sub. Sub-optimum."

"What does that mean?"

Duffy wasn't listening. "Insufficient progressive motility. Insufficient."

"Duffy please? What does it mean?"

"Low. Scores are low. Very low. Five. 5%." Duffy looked up at her from beneath his brows, his head still waggling this way and that but his eyes staying roughly fixed on her face. "Less than 5%. Very very low."

"Is that bad?" She could see tears forming in his eyes and realised she already had her answer.

They had both been to see a doctor, several times. She'd had tests, he'd had tests. Then they'd been to the clinic and he'd been taking supplements, making dietary changes, even had some injections. Months of this and then he'd been for a final set of tests two months ago. Throughout all this time, they still had regular sex, still tried for a baby. Gloria believing if she couldn't understand the medical words they used then they really didn't count and that, in the end, actual man-on-woman physical sex - if you did it often enough, and well enough - couldn't fail to result in a pregnancy.

Duffy's face said differently and Gloria's own crumpled. "But I want a baby!"

She felt her whole body shake as the words left her, her vocal cords cracking as she reached the last emotive word.

Duffy stood up and began pacing up and down the living room, muttering. "Of course. Of course. Of course. Yes. Of course. Yes. Of course."

"Duff?"

"Need a plan. Got to have a plan. A solution. Needed. Get one. Think. Need to think." He started rooting beneath the coats hanging in the hall, put on his walking boots and grabbed a waterproof jacket. "I must find a plan. Need a plan."

"Duff! Where are you going?" Gloria closed her eyes in despair and tried to stay calm. "Sweetheart please."

But Duffy had already gone.

```
DATE: JUNE 24 2017.
TIME: 1450 HRS
SIGHTINGS (CUMULATIVE): ZERO.
```

Uh-oh. Problem.

Duffy looked around the hillside and saw there were more people here than he had expected. He clutched his camping stool tightly as he wandered agitatedly in a circle, looking at the ground and trying to talk himself into staying here. Here where there were other people.

It's a problem. It's a big problem. A very big problem. Very very big problem.

He was usually here at night. Late at night. No-one came up here then. But the letter had thrown him. He needed to think, relax his mind, seek guidance from the universe.

In his pack he had a rough, thick notebook: heavily thumbed, filled with scribbled notes in tiny, precise green handwriting. He rambled on to himself, stool clutched in his right hand, the fingers on his left madly twisting and twirling the greying curls beneath his baseball cap. He waggled his head from side to side, scanning the ground for an answer only to find himself following his tracks around in a circle, worrying the grass and compressing it into mud. His tatty trainers started to squelch and this brought him up short.

Need a clearing. Empty clearing. Quiet. Don't want to scare them away. Not scare them away. At all. Not at all. No, no.

Up here, on top of Eildon Hill North, he had a panoramic view of this part of the Scottish borders, high above the town of Melrose. The air was fresh and clean, with only a slight breeze blowing. He hustled back in the direction he had come and marched off to the left so that he was out of sight of the strangers on the hilltop and had this view over Melrose to himself. He found a flattish stretch, unfolded his camping stool and plopped himself down on it. He took out his notebook and pen, and took stock of his situation:

```
POST: 15M BELOW PEAK. ABBEY CLEARLY IN
SIGHT.
VISIBILITY: EXCELLENT (10)
WIND: LOW (3).
ACTIVITY: NONE (0)
```

He put down his notebook, pulled out a small pair of binoculars and idly scanned the abbey ruins below. The graceful arches, ruined tower and remains of 14th century stonework had a gloriously gothic feel enhanced by the solitude of their setting. The headstones and statues in the graveyard glistened like diamonds on a carpet in the afternoon sunshine. He heard a barking laugh and tried not to let it distract him. Failing, he picked up his notebook again:

```
DISTURBANCE RATING: HIGH(7.5)
CHANCE OF ENCOUNTER: LOW.
```

He looked at this last entry, hesitating to put a figure on what he meant by low. When he had first started his programme of observations, he had devised a scale from 1 to 10, for the probabilities of an encounter occurring. But as the months and years had passed, he had gradually revised the scale down until he realised his numbers were only getting smaller and smaller with each visit. He couldn't bear the thought of going back and recalibrating all his previous entries onto a new scale, nor could he accept the option of simply not making an assessment of the likelihood of them turning up. Caught between these two stools, and worrying himself afresh each time he made a new entry that he hadn't resolved this particular conundrum, he hovered the pen over his notebook with a sigh.

Duffy looked at the date he had written in his notebook. It had been eight years now. Eight years without a word from the beings who had abducted her; eight years of waiting and waiting, not always observing, not always observing in the same location. But the skies were the same skies, wherever you were, whenever you were. *They* would know. He knew. And they would find him if he made himself available. Accessible. Visible. Alone.

He knew they didn't like crowds, didn't want attention. That wasn't their plan. They had chosen to watch from afar and interfere little. Anything else would be a waste of time. And they were far too intelligent to waste their time.

They had wisdom. Self-control. Patience.

Just like me. Eight years is an eye-blink to the cosmos. A tiny blink. No need to be pessimistic. Something could well happen. Something special. Will they let an opportunity slip on such a clear and sparkling afternoon as this? I don't think so. While I am sitting here, available? Patient. Expectant. Waiting. I don't think so.

Duffy sat upright on his stool and scanned the sky with fresh energy. Looking for the slightest movement, a single thing out of the ordinary. He held his head this way and that, straining to catch any stray sound. Hearing another sharp laugh away up behind him, he twitched, grimaced and scribbled out his disturbance rating of 7.5, replacing it with an angry 8.3.

Patience is required. Patience. I can wait. I am good at waiting. Very good at waiting. Very very good at waiting.

Sitting quietly, high above the lazy town, Duffy waited. For anything which could constitute a warning. A message. A sign.

Duffy had verbal diarrhoea. And it was chronic. A life-long need to mutter and verbalise the riot of ideas ricocheting round his head, day and night. His synapses fired incessantly and, as if connected by some tripwire to his jaw, his mouth chased the tail of his mind as it thrashed and roiled in the pounding surf of uncontrollable thoughts.

There were times when he wished he could switch his brain into neutral and simply coast. When all he wanted was to do was scream: *Somebody, get this thing off me!* But he never did. He had long ago accepted that this was his brain, that was what it did and how it did it, and his job was to hang on for dear life while it did its thing and get to the end of each day in one piece.

He had accepted it. But his friends had not.

Which was why his friend tally, at the last count, had been exactly: zero.

His loved ones endured. Somehow. They loved and they saw and they listened and they gradually learnt to accept it or tune it out. Like some static on low coming from the radio in the room, or the background hum of the refrigerator when you sat at the kitchen table, the white noise from the small appliance that was Duffy became the backdrop to their lives, like the sound of waves lapping on the beach. Always there, sometimes soothing, sometimes nagging away at you.

Ironically, Duffy had been a very quiet baby. Slept long and soundly, cried softly when he woke, didn't ask for much and spent most of his time gazing intently at a space eighteen inches in front of his face, which was usually vacant.

The space, not the gaze.

But, like a Saturn rocket at dawn, the still silence on the launchpad eventually gave way to the clicks and clucks of the pre-flight check, then the hard consonant shakings and tremors of the ignition sequence, before the full blast of vocabulary fired and, with a mighty heave, rose majestically off the ground. Aged about twelve months, MacDuff Angel Ingoglia cleared the tower.

His name was a weird mashup, when you looked at. A Scottish mother and an Italian father accounted for his Christian name and surname respectively. His middle name had been an insistence by his Sicilian grandmother. On the night of his birth, she had had a visitation from an angel. The creature had hovered at her bedpost and held forth for many minutes in an unintelligible tongue, but had been an apparition of such beauty and grace, that his Nana had known from the first - *l'inizio dell'inizio* - that he was blessed. Special. A gift from God and, perhaps, a messenger. His early incessant babbling had confirmed this to her - that he too shared the gift of tongues with the angels - and Duffy was only ever worshipped in her eyes.

Until she passed away when he was barely two.

Because Duffy's mother and father were simply too busy with their own business - literally - to give him the attention he needed to make sense of the world around him. His grandmother and grandfather had moved to Scotland in the sixties and set up an ice cream shop in Hawick. It had been a small family business, generating an income that kept their head above water, and his father, Ricardo, an only child, had been groomed from the beginning to take over the business. When his grandfather died prematurely, Ricardo had taken over with his mother to keep the shop afloat and things had got very sketchy for a while, so Duffy had learnt much later. But, by the time Duffy had come along, his father had married Tessa from Hawick who was an ambitious and vivacious woman who had turned Ricardo's head and embedded her dreams into him. She imagined not just a successful business in Hawick, but a chain of ice cream parlours right across Scotland. High-end: the very term newly-coined, back then. The baby Duffy had been an unexpected bit of grit in the oyster and had taken a back seat as the dowdy shop received a makeover courtesy of a sizable investment from his grandmother's life insurance policy.

The shop was extended, upgraded, rebranded - *Ingoglia's Ices* became *Love Will Find A Wafer* - and his parents poured all their time into it. Duffy sat in a playpen in a backroom behind the counter and slid his abacus beads on the bars back and forth, listening to the burbling chatter which drifted through to him from the clientele. His mother gave him books to keep him quiet and taught him to read - not so much out of maternal devotion so much as being a way to keep the boy occupied and engaged when she was unavailable to spend time with him, which was most of the time. Duffy sucked up the information, mulled it over, feeding on it and playing with it to try and get the maximum amount of nutrients from it he could. Starved of attention and affection from his parents, he absorbed information about the world however he could get it, and his unformed mind cared not which of it was real, imagined, artificial or fictitious. Mixing, spooning and stirring as he went, he would treat each nugget of information as morsels in an ice-cream recipe and soon progressed to constructing his own - formulating marvellous confections from the most innocent and meagre of ingredients.

His incessant chatter, nourished by being alone with no-one to stifle it, became a hindrance at school. Teachers tried, and failed, to quell it. Streaming him away from the talented kids so that they could concentrate without his barrage of gibberish, relegating him to the company of the slovenly, dull-witted or plain violent of his cohorts. From whom he thus retreated further to avoid their braying scorn, ridicule or bullying. His endless curiosity and enthusiasm, undulled by lack of focus, drove him energetically on but, unguided, he bounced from idea to idea. By the time he was sixteen, it was clear he was going to go places.

But not college, just places.

His father found him a position with a local building contractor who took Duffy on as an apprentice electrician and Duffy suddenly found himself useful. And at home. The logic and the systems, colour-coding and circuitry design, all made sense to him. He embraced the structure and order of Health & Safety checklists and procedures to his bosom and clocked on and off with a smiling contentment.

But it didn't challenge him enough to stifle his endless curiosity or quell his restless brain. During the day his mind would wander, occasionally jeopardising the central nervous systems of some of his fellow apprentices; at night he would devour books, magazine articles and the new-fangled developments of online forums and bulletin boards, made accessible by an interminably slow dial-up connection.

And he would watch the heavens.

His interest in the night sky had been sparked initially by the Star Wars movies, and an eleventh birthday present of a telescope. Then Halley's Comet appeared when he was seventeen, shortly followed by comet Halle-Bopp and then topped off with the potentially cosmic implications of Y2K. So, as the end of the millennium neared, Duffy found himself approaching twenty-one, with a comprehensive grasp of the electrician's trade but a total lack of interest in wrangling it into useful practicality.

He handed in his notice, and sat in his parent's flat above the ice cream shop, watching SkyTV by day and the sky by night. Thoughts whizzed and flashed into and out of his consciousness like shooting stars and when he saw a news headline about an impending total eclipse, August 1999, which would last over two minutes in the skies over Romania, Duffy packed a bag, left a note, and headed for the airport.

Ten years later, having chased eclipses from

Madagascar to South Africa, Australia to Peru, Siberia to China, he found himself in Thailand, on the verge of turning thirty with a headful of crackpot theories about ancient civilisations, alien artefacts, cosmic confluences and more - theories expounded by the fellow eclipse-chasers, whacked out hippies and pot-heads that he had shared his travels with. And he had synthesised this into a set of personal theories and beliefs so intertwined, impenetrable and opaque that not even Bletchley Park could have cracked them. But Duffy had.

The angel at his grandmother's bedside all those years ago had not just been a sign, it had been an omen. A foreshadowing. He, and he alone, was meant for greatness and he, and he alone, had managed to acquire and co-opt all the vital clues and gems of information, gleaned from all corners of the world on his quest for meaning and enlightenment. Only he had collated and analysed them, documented them in miniature handwriting crammed into well-thumbed and bursting filofaxes, and tested them in his stream-of-consciousness style to anyone who ever groped within earshot. These folk tended to be either like-minded individuals of the dog-on-a-string persuasion with alternative theories of their own, who would indulge Duffy in a sort of *I'll-show-you-mine-if-you-show-me-yours* mental masturbation play; or those who had managed to retain a healthy grip on their sanity and would, if they came into contact with Duffy, instinctively make the sign of the cross.

And then, after a short while, the sign of the very cross.

But then, tragedy had struck. His beloved sister, Heather, had disappeared. Vanished, leaving two young sons behind when her violent husband had found himself in jail. And Duffy, ever-devoted, ever-loving of his beautiful baby sister did what he knew to be his duty, and he came home. Back to Scotland, to take care of Sean and Sam Marshall.

"She's expecting a baby. Gloria." Duffy confided, shaking his head slowly from side to side.

It was late July and Wingnut had become a regular visitor to the Duffy residence. Possible sightings of the delectable Gloria might have had something to do with it.

"Wow! Congratulations. When's it due?" Wingnut took another swig from his beer and burped. Five weeks out of prison and beer still tasted sweet and new.

"No. Expecting. From me. Expecting a baby from me. She wants a baby."

"Well, man. Give her one! Know what I mean?" Wingnut leered.

"Its… not that simple."

"Mate, it is that simple. It really is. That. Simple."

"I can't… do it. Can't do it." Duffy started pacing up and down, fingers on the move again. "Can't do it."

"No? Hey, here." Wingnut reached into his trouser pocket and pulled out a small plastic tab of 4 blue pills. "Use these. They'll get you stiffer than an arm-wrestlers ruler."

Duffy ignored him. "Had tests. Lot of tests. Lots and lots of tests."

"Tests? Tests my arse. Cheers." Wingnut emptied his beer can, scrunched it up and lobbed it out over the sofa aiming at a small wastepaper basket in the corner of the room. The aluminium meteorite bounced against the wall, off the rim of the basket and onto the floorboards with a clatter. "Bollocks." He announced, reaching over onto the coffee table for the next can in the plastic multipack yoke. Five down, three to go. "Just got to try harder, is all. Woman like that, Christ, hard won't be the problem. Keeping off her'll be the problem." Wingnut whistled and took a swig from his new can.

"Tests say I can't have kids. Everything too low. Count. Motility. Velocity. All low. Very low. Very very low."

"Velocity? Fucking hell. What you trying to do, race her? What else did they measure? 0-60? Torque? Fuck, Duff, not sure any tests are worth jack shit. You just need to give it to her good and keep doin' it. It's that simple."

"Yes, it's simple. Very simple. Very very simple. I cannot have kids. With Gloria or anyone else. Can't be done."

"Well, it's probably for the best. The two of you can just fuck each other's brains out, day and night - Christ I would - and no worries! Johnnies not required. Fill yer boots, mate."

Duffy looked at him, wounded. "Don't you care?"

"Nah. Someone cares. Not me, but someone. Does Gloria care?" Wingnut looked into Duffy's face and saw the answer. "Ok, so Gloria cares. Probably."

"Gloria does care. Not probably. Absolutely. Absolutely she cares. And I do. Because…" Duffy looked around the room and dropped his voice before continuing, his fingers flying in his palms once more. "Gloria will leave me if I do not give her a baby. She will. Yes, she will."

"Man, really? I mean, really?" Wingnut burped and crumpled another empty can.

Duffy looked at his brother-in-law, his face filled with worry and doubt. He hesitated for a moment.

"Is that true, what you just said? That you would - you

know - with Gloria?"

Wingnut gave him a questioning glance. "Seriously? Gloria? Duff, she's hot as fuck. Surely you can see that. You're a lucky man. Me, I'd bone her in a heartbeat."

Duffy swallowed hard and glanced anxiously at the door again. "Would you? For me?"

"What?" Wingnut did a double-take and put his beer down on the coffee table, suddenly all business. "Straight up? Sorry-" He added hastily, seeing the grimace on Duffy's face. "Poor choice of words."

"Yes. Seriously. I'm not suggesting this… lightly. I've been thinking. A lot. Lot of thinking needed."

Wingnut was wide-eyed and felt an erection rising in his pants. "You mean… now?"

"No!" Duffy was indignant. "This needs planning. Got to have a plan. Planning very important."

"Fuck off! What do I need a plan for? Let me at her!" Wingnut stood rather too quickly and his head span. The beers had absolutely nothing to do with it.

"If you're going to take that attitude then I will rescind my proposal. Utterly."

"Re-what?"

"Rescind. Withdraw. Take away." Duffy's fingers fluttered and he shook his head to himself, his eyes cast down onto the bare boards. "Not meant to be enjoyable. Not. Not at all. Meant to be a serious proposition. Business."

"You want me to fuck your wife and NOT enjoy it?"

"Yes. Absolutely. 100%. NOT enjoy it. NOT. That is the deal."

"Well, I'm not sure I can promise that mate. But I'll give it a go!" Wingnut took a huge swig from the can and beamed his delight, even though Duffy wasn't looking at him.

"No. You must promise. Must. Must promise." Duffy started rocking back and forth in his chair

"Ok, ok. I'll try, ok? I promise. I'll try."

"No no no no. Promise. Not promise to try."

"How can I promise that, Duff? Hmm? How?"

"You promise. Or it doesn't happen." Duffy forced himself to lift his face and look Wingnut in the eyes. He was crying. "This is for her. Not for you. Her. Not you."

"Christ, ok! Ok, Duff. I promise NOT to enjoy it, ok?"

Duffy seemed not to hear him. "It is difficult. Very very difficult. To do this. You understand? Difficult. Thinking of you sleeping with my wife. Over and over."

"Look, I know. Ok? Wait, what? Over and over?"

"Yes. I don't know if I can do this. Can't do this. Forget it. No forget it." Duffy tore his tear-stained face away and went back to rocking in his chair, head down.

"Wait, Duff. Over and over? What? You mean, more than once? Fu - Sleep with her more than once?"

"Of course, more than once!" Duffy sobbed. "You think you will get her pregnant first time? It's unlikely. Very very unlikely. 72% unlikely. 74%"

Wingnut finished his beer and cracked another can. He could see Duffy was right on the edge of giving up on this whole idea. But Jesus-suffering-fuck, this was gold! What a chance - give it to this stunner repeatedly until she got pregnant! It was the deal of the century. Who'd have believed it? He wasn't prepared to let this slip. Not now.

"Duff, listen." Wingnut lowered his voice, tried tenderness, and put his arm round Duffy who flinched at the touch but didn't shake it away. "Look. I promise, ok? Let me do this for Gloria. For you. Hmm? After all you did for me? Taking care of my boys while I was gone?

Being a Dad to them? A better Dad than I was. Hmm? This is the least I could do. The very least."

"Yes." Duffy nodded in understanding. "Yes. For Gloria. For me. Yes."

"I promise. Cross my heart."

Duffy snapped his head up and stared into Wingnut's eyes. "And hope to die?"

Wingnut paused, taken aback by this sudden forcefulness from his brother-in-law. "Yes." He swallowed. "And hope to die."

"You fucking did what?" Gloria was used to not understanding what Duffy told her - sometimes it was idioms he used, or words she didn't understand; sometimes he was just obscure and approached topics from unusual angles and she had to mentally zoom out, scan the horizon and see if she could work out which bit of the landscape he was attacking the subject from. Sometimes, though, she was simply dumbfounded by the way his brain worked and the plans he could cook up.

This was one of those times.

Even when Duffy repeated it, she was at a complete loss as to how to respond. Her first emotion was of dizziness and nausea; a flashback to her previous life in Phuket where strange men had used her in strange ways and she had learnt to rise up, out of her body, and watch disinterestedly from above until it was all over. This slingshot back into that time, that world, left her reeling and she had to steady herself on the kitchen counter for a moment, recapture her normal breathing pattern.

She was here, with him, to escape from her past. Create a new future with him, a new family with him. And here he was, stating that the new family would start with a strange man touching her skin, being inside her. Creating a new life. Injecting her with life maybe, but not with love. This was not what she wanted, or had envisaged, and the thought of it made her physically recoil. She gagged. This would not be a new life, this would be her old life rewritten - reinvented here in a cold, cold climate. Another place where she would find no love.

"How could you? What the fuck you think?"

Duffy was largely oblivious. To him the plan made perfect sense. This was a perfectly practical solution to an intractable problem. He could see no reason to object or express - what was she expressing - disbelief?

"I know. I know. It's a great plan, isn't it? Great plan. Thought it up all myself. Just me. It's great to have a plan. And this is a great plan." He beamed at her, rightly pleased with himself for presenting her with a brilliant solution for her appreciation.

"Are you mad!"

"Mad?" Duffy frowned. He hadn't expected brilliance to be mis-diagnosed as insanity. Perhaps this was the way with all brilliant ideas - they were so brilliant it took people some time to see the greatness. The light they gave off was too intense for newcomers to make out their perfect shape. They needed time for their eyes to adjust. "Mad? No. Brilliant? Maybe. Creative? Certainly. Genius? Well, modesty forbids - ha!" He tapped his head several times. "Always thinking. Always. There is no off-position on the genius switch!"

Gloria shivered involuntarily as another wave of revulsion hit her. Her husband was staring at her, eyes wild with enthusiasm, radiating energy at her.

"Absolutely. 100% No." Gloria crossed her arms and

glared at him, setting her jaw.

It took Duffy a while to process her statement as he was still in full spate. "Yes, I know, right! I mean… what?"

"No. Fucking. Way."

"What? Why not? What's wrong?"

"What's wrong?"

"Yes. It's a great plan. An excellent plan. Excellent. Quite, quite excellent."

"Don't you see?"

"See? Yes, I see! Don't you see? How perfect it is? Perfect!"

"You want me to… have a baby with … that fucker!"

"Yes! Now you're getting it." Duffy was relieved. For a moment there he had wondered if perhaps Gloria had got hold of the wrong end of the stick. That would perhaps explain why she had seemed against it.

"No, I not getting it. Neither is he!"

"What?" Duffy's fingers started wildly sifting flour and Gloria could see confusion building behind his eyes. She took a deep breath and tried to take her proven, patient approach with him whenever he got agitated. She reached for his shoulder tenderly and ran her hand around the back of his neck, stroking him slowly.

"Honey. Listen. Ok? Hmm?"

Duffy remained motionless, his eyes swivelling beneath rapidly blinking lids. He was not looking at her but he was not running away either. She had his attention. For now.

"Can you see why I might have some… weservations about it?"

Duffy stole a glance at her, head shyly cocked. "No."

Gloria exhaled slowly and kept her voice low and calm. "I love you. Not - Dewek. I want a baby with you, not him."

"Yes, but I can't! The tests! The tests! I can't do it. He can. He has. Twice. Yes, twice. Both boys!" He threw this little bonus in for her - she had told him of the Thai attitude towards male children.

Gloria ploughed on past his interruption. "But… I don't like him. He's all big and smelly."

Duffy considered the practicalities. "We could make sure he always has a bath first. That would deal with the smell. Not sure what can be done about his size. Really."

"Duffy! You're not listening. There must be other ways." A stray thought occurred to her. "What do you mean, always?"

"Hmm?"

"*Always* have a bath? Always."

"Well, I'm not expecting it to work first time. Will need several goes."

"What! You want me to fuck this stwanger *many* times?"

"He's not a stranger. He's my brother-in-law."

"He stwanger to me. No. No!" Gloria put her hands on her hips, adamant. "What about test-tube babies? Things like that?"

"Yes. I thought of them." Duffy nodded, appreciating the interest she was now showing. "But they take a long time. Waiting lists, you know. Stretching out many months, maybe years. And that's once you've been approved. Suppose we didn't get approval? It's tricky getting approval. Always tricky. Very tricky."

"Are we in a wush?"

And as she uttered the words, she realised that she was.

In the silence surrounding them both now, Gloria could hear her biological clock ticking loudly and she crumpled her face as she tried to consider this outrageous idea of Duffy's with some degree of rationality. What he had said was true, she supposed. Her responses and reactions were all based on emotion and instinct, not on practicality. She wanted a baby didn't she? She had to make a choice: either continue with treatment and go through all the steps of IVF to see if they worked, and who knew how long that would take to work, if it worked at all. What would happen if she got to the end of that process and found that Duffy still couldn't provide a useable sperm sample and she was now three or four years older? How would she look back at this bizarre idea then?

And how bad could it be? Surely it wouldn't require too many attempts? Derek was clearly fertile and fit; so was she. If she worked out the timings and arranged conditions just right perhaps she could limit it to two or three? That wasn't too bad, was it? She'd done much worse in the past. Surely if the end result was a bouncing baby she could overlook the fleeting distaste involved with mating with this man?

"What do you say, Glor? Hmm? What do you say?" Duffy was looking directly at her now, his stress had evaporated.

Gloria looked sadly at her husband. His kind and gentle eyes, his curly grey hair and childlike features. She shook her head in resignation. "Let me think about it."

Once he had sobered up, Wingnut wondered if perhaps there was a downside to this deal of Duffy's that he had agreed to. That downside was his reputation in bed. Because Wingnut had a problem and the name of that problem was premature ejaculation.

Very premature.

In fact, if he was being honest, it might better be termed *immediate* rather than premature. Immediately upon penetration, he would ejaculate. Heather, his ex, had prevailed upon him to seek help during the early days of their relationship and so he had cringingly consulted his GP, a woman for crying out loud, who had suggested sexual techniques he was to practice with Heather - which hadn't worked; then later medication, which hadn't worked, and finally hypnotherapy - which Wingnut decided was never going to work, as he had no intention of allowing some headshrink inside his noggin, thank you very much. But by that time Heather was pregnant with Sam, Wingnut was growing tired of Heather's sarcastic comments about his performance in bed and the whole business became a moot point. A year or so later, when she became pregnant for the second time with Sean, the bloom was long off the rose and the fact that he didn't hang about - romped home by several lengths in the bedroom antic stakes, as Heather would have put it - had become something of a blessing.

But Heather - well, she was long gone.

So Gloria wouldn't help but notice, he thought. And likely she would tell Duffy and then… He pondered what might happen and realised that maybe, just maybe, it would actually be a beneficial upside. Duffy insisted he not enjoy the process. What better way to illustrate it than by demonstrating that it was a purely perfunctory and trivial act - over in a shot, literally. Wingnut could have the time of his life whilst pretending that he was not, Gloria wouldn't be enamoured with him and so wouldn't be led astray, and Duffy would have evidence that this whole arrangement was what he wanted it to be: strictly business.

Result!

Delighted with this bit of cogitation and it's satisfactory conclusion, Wingnut went in search of some paracetamol.

SAM & PAUL

The sun was finally setting across the top of Minch Moor as Cullen and Beep wound their way past the Three Brethren along the Southern Upland Way. Ant and Dec scuffed and noodled in the heather as the two men walked in their shirt sleeves across the moor on this beautiful June evening.

"Smell that?" Cullen stopped and tasted the air. Beep did the same.

"Nope. What you got?"

"That." Cullen pointed to a wisp of smoke rising over the far hill as the path wound its way down towards Innerleithen.

"Spidey senses tingling again? Probably just a camp fire. Or a barbie. Nice night for it."

It was and, although it was almost eleven, the light was still good and the evening was cool without being freezing.

"Huh." Cullen picked up his pace and Beep felt obliged to do the same. As they came round the corner the column of smoke grew thicker and they could see where it originated.

"Bastards!"

Cullen threw himself into a run and started down the hill towards the bothy which was now clearly on fire. Beep stopped and stood, observing from a distance as his friend bounded down the hill only to pull up sharply as a sudden explosion of dazzling orange leapt from the bothy and, a second later, a huge bang as the sound waves hit his ears.

The bothy, which had been burning in one corner up until that point, was now engulfed in flames and clearly beyond help. When Beep caught up with Cullen, the latter was standing staring at the distant building as the fire claimed it.

"What was that?" Beep asked. "That was a bang and a half!"

"Dunno." Cullen lied. "My backpack and sleeping bag were in there."

"What're they made of - nitro-glycerine?"

Cullen ignored him, scouring the hillside for any signs of life. "There." He pointed to a tiny figure standing up in the saddle of a bike, pedalling hard along the forest track which led across the moor and then disappeared down out of sight. "Why would someone do that?" Cullen asked the still evening air.

"Fucktards." Beep spat.

"That's my bed gone for the night."

"I've got a perfectly good floor you can use. Hot and cold running wossname. Well, cold-running wossname anyway. Tea and coffee-making facilities. Complimentary early morning alarm call of smelly dog incursion."

"Tempting." Cullen squinted into the distance, unable to make out the cyclist any longer.

"Please yourself." Beep knew when an offer was being rejected.

Sam had been unable to keep the smile off his face, even as the midgies bit into it. He flew down the cinder track beaming, dirt and grit flying beneath his wheels and out behind him in a hot grey cloud. On long summer evenings like this it was only on his cherished mountain bike that he truly felt alive.

All day his mind had been like a razor-blade: small, sure, but so sharp he could cut himself. Hammering and wrenching in the workshop he had spent all day fantasising about setting fire to the bothy, how and when he would do it, and what it would feel like to see the flames start to lick the building before consuming it in the late summer light.

It was a simple log cabin, made from pine, with a sloping roof and a single "window" at the front with a wooden shutter you could latch closed from the inside. It had a front porch and a stable door and inside it housed a pair of wooden sleeping platforms and a trestle table and bench set into one wall. Basic, dry accommodation for walkers was the theory; the practice was, it was a regular haunt for drugged up or hooked up teenagers with nowhere else to go. The graffiti inside and out told the story to anyone who cared to stop and read it. Most didn't.

In short, the building was 100 per cent soft timber, bone dry and unused. As far as Sam was concerned, the bothy was asking for it.

His bike was a beauty he had built himself. Custom frame, forks, brakes, pedals, grips, gears, saddle, wheels, seals and crank. He'd configured and constructed it painstakingly over the years, saving up to splash out on the next upgraded component, the latest best thing. The frame had been second-hand but was a classic lightweight frame, still much admired. He had got it knock-down from one of the mad bikers over at Glentress who upgraded their frames every year and he had it resprayed and decal'ed in Galashiels Rugby colours - a glossy maroon with polar white flashes.

He pushed himself hard up the rough trail from

Traquair village and leant his bike against the dry stone wall which bounded the bothy. Then he set to work.

Trusty Zippo and lighter fuel was all he needed, and he carried both at all times. The lighter was a gift from his father, donated to him "for safe-keeping" his father had said, before he was arrested. No doubt to keep it away from the other lags who would have whipped it from him before he'd finished his first day inside - or the screws who would have kept it from him to prevent any arson in the jail. Either way, Wingnut had vouchsafed it to Sam with express intention that it be returned to him, in perfect working order, when he was released. Sam, thirteen at the time, had regarded it as a sacred mission and a holy object - one to be cherished and polished. And used. At that early age, Sam was already on the fags and having this snappy, shiny, foreign object which could only have come from America was the height of exoticism. In Galashiels, the Zippo had passed for *objet d'art.*

The lighter fuel was another permanent accessory in Sam's wardrobe. You couldn't always rely on a handy fuel source or starter material. If arson was your game, you had to be ready at a moment's notice. Be prepared, that was Sam's motto. And he had a 125ml refill - Zippo branded, naturally - in his front jeans pocket. Standard issue.

He had moved round the back of the bothy to the furthest corner from view, slewed a lick of lighter fuel onto the wood, bundled a few twigs beneath the exposed corner logs of the building and lit it. The flames crackled and spat, shooting sparks up into the air as the wood quickly caught. Sam stood admiring his handiwork for a moment and then stepped back through the ankle high grass and shot off back down the hill on his bike.

Sam was a bit like one of Google's new cars: completely self-driven but you just knew that eventually he would cause an accident.

As a child he had often been spoilt by his father, who had plied him with toys and gifts - usually stolen from other children, but Wingnut's sentiment was that it was the thought that counted. Either because he knew how his father had come by the toys, or because he consequently developed some wrong sense of self-entitlement, it didn't take long before Sam started half-inching other kids' stuff for himself. Cutting out the middle-man, you might say.

His father had been a very hands-on parent - hands all over Sam, in fact, whenever he stepped out of line, or whenever his father had had too much to drink. So, most of the time. Wingnut saw this as a good way to bring up a son to be strong, masculine and able to stand up for himself; Sam saw it as a driver to be tougher, harder, meaner - this would either prove to his father that he was strong enough not to deserve a beating, or that he was strong enough to withstand the next one. Win-win, as they say.

But Sam never felt like a winner. The elation that followed from bullying a classmate, or nicking someone's dinner money, didn't last long. Too often, in fact, it was supplanted by the displeasure of a teacher at his behaviour or general demeanour. So the cycle would repeat and Sam would tell himself that he was growing up to be a tough guy, able to handle himself.

As he grew, his father's absences became more frequent or lengthier, until aged thirteen the defining moment of his young life arrived. Wingnut had found Sam's mother, Heather, in bed with another man. A huge fight ensued and the other man was beaten half to death. His mother had fled from Wingnut's rage, never to return, and his father had been arrested, found guilty and given twelve years for GBH (the judge had considered more). Sam and his younger brother Sean were left alone, whereupon his Uncle Duffy had stepped up and moved in with them, looking after them until Sam reached maturity.

So Sam's view of his father was constantly balanced on a knife-edge, veering from true devotion and hero-worship for his creator, and petulant fury that this was the same man who had taken his mother from him and ruined his childhood. Nevertheless, Sam had treasured his father's Zippo gift and seen it almost as a prompt. It never left his possession and, as he became a more troublesome and aggressive teen, he became a walking arson-in-waiting - his firestarter kit of lighter and fuel burning a hole in his pocket. He just *had* to use it, so use it he did, at every opportunity. There were murmurings and circumstantial evidence, but never any proof or witnesses.

So Sam got in plenty of practice and, over the years, progressed up a steady career incline - starting with putting bangers in exhaust pipes or tying them to cat's tails, graduating on to bus shelters, public toilets, and then abandoned or derelict buildings.

He had tried to get Sean interested in summer fires in the fields and woodland surrounding Galashiels, initiating a giant game of tic-tac-toe where a 3x3 grid of fields was their board and you marked an X or an O by setting fire to a haybale in that particular field. That had failed when the farmer in question had taken his bales in for the winter so Sam had burnt down the whole barn: his equivalent of upturning the board when he was losing the game. Everyone knew Sam had burnt down the barn but no-one could prove it. And thus emboldened, Sam pursued a relentless and ever-growing campaign of arson.

There was fuck all to do in Galashiels of an evening anyway.

"I know this is a silly question." Beep started, the following evening.

"Go on."

"But is this legal?"

"There's the law. And there's what's right."

"And this is?"

Cullen didn't answer but instead raised the binoculars to his face again. "Is it 10:45?"

Beep checked his phone. "Eight minutes to."

Cullen tutted quietly. "Sloppy."

"What makes you think he'll come back at exactly the same time as he did last night?"

Cullen shrugged. "Habit."

"We're not all like you, you know."

Cullen kept looking through the binoculars. "Since when did you become interested in legality, anyway?"

"Thinking of turning over a new wossname."

"Really?" Cullen dropped his binoculars and raised his eyebrows at his friend.

"Straight up. Shirley's a stabilising influence on me. She says."

"*She* says?"

"Aye, well I'm saying so'n'all."

"Right. And what does this new leaf look like?"

Beep sighed. "Well, it doesn't look like two men sitting in foliage, spying on a third man, with intent to inflict serious injury."

Cullen gave his friend the look. This, Beep knew, was just how it was. He sighed again. "Guess I can start turning over my new leaf tomorrow."

Cullen went back to his binoculars. "Good plan. And we're not spying. We are observing."

"Right."

Beep knew well enough to leave it there, for now. Realising that in the need-to-know scheme of things which Cullen liked to operate, Beep had been given all he needed to know, he busied himself with studying his surroundings - in case a speedy exit might be required of him.

"The drive up here was something of an experience." Beep paused, waiting for a sign that Cullen was interested in conversation. When none occurred, he ploughed on in solo mode. "Potholes everywhere, man. Shocking state, these roads. Council should do something. 'Stead of shutting down pubs they should be filling in these fecking holes. My van's suspension's already on its arse. Three cheers for Wanksy, I say."

Cullen had tried to not listen to Beep's rambling but found there was simply too much in there to unpack for him to resist commenting. He put down his binoculars and faltered, working out where to start.

"You know council's don't shut down pubs, don't you?"

"Tell that to Davy!" Beep snorted. "Feckers have clamped down on his extended licenses - too much aggro and shenanigans going on late into the night. Allegedly. Davy reckons that's his profit margins in the toilet. He's put the For Sale sign up."

"The Lamb & Flag, I take it?"

"Aye. Been drinking there, man and boy, for… well, doesn't matter does it? That's my pub they're closing."

"Hmm. And what's this got to do with potholes?"

"Well, if they spent their time mending the roads instead of putting valuable infrastructure out of business, we'd all be better off."

Cullen ignored the fact that the Lamb & Flag couldn't strictly be classified as valuable infrastructure. "And is this where Wanksy comes in?"

"Too right. Top bloke. Doing vital work for the community." Beep gave an affirming thumbs-up.

"Enlighten me."

"Well, these fecking potholes. Getting out of hand. See I know Micky - used to work in Planning & Transport. He says the council always fiddles their budget. Every year. 'Cos if you spend it all too soon they give you less next year. Or summat. Anyway, what this means is that they wait until the end of the financial year and then splurge what they've got left on road repairs an' all that. 'Swhy the roads are in a shocking state all year and, then come March, there's roadworks left, right and bleeding centre. So these potholes build up and you end up like one of those old games where you've got to stop the ball-bearing falling down the holes. Never mind driving on the left; you're driving on what's left!"

"And Wanksy?" Cullen was now wishing he'd left this particular line of questioning untouched.

"Right. Well you must've seen the bright orange dick'n'balls been appearing all over the place?"

"Well, I wouldn't say *all over the place*. But I have seen them, yes."

"Aye, well round potholes any road. So, it's genius. Some bloke has been going round drawing great big hairy dick and balls, in bright orange spray paint, round any pothole he sees. Right-thinking people, with kiddies prob'ly, phone to complain. Council comes round, fills in the hole and covers up the paint. Voila! Potholes fixed."

"Inventive." Cullen mused.

"Aye. And, since no-one knows who it is, they call him Wanksy. Like Banksy! Good, eh?"

"Marvellous." Cullen returned to his binoculars. Being with Beep sometimes was like verbal waterboarding. "Glad we got all that cleared up."

"Right. So, how much longer do we wait for our man here?"

Cullen suddenly stood up and brushed the pine needles from his trousers. "He's here."

Beep was short for BP, which was short for Big Paul.

As far as Paul could remember, he had always been called Big Paul and had always found his height and girth an advantage. In school, he had towered effortlessly over his classmates, flattened them on the rugby pitch, and grown jet black body hair almost at will whilst his pals were still straining to push through the merest dusting of blonde fuzz. A healthy - if sometimes disturbing - 6'5" and eighteen stone or more, he had never had trouble getting to the bar or holding his drink once he got there. His laidback manner and easy-going charm had also worked wonders with the ladies and Paul had found no shortage of girls keen to establish whether what they said about men with big hands was true.

In Paul's case, it most certainly was.

Word spread - Peebles being a small town - but, as his reputation grew, so too did Paul's waistline. A beard had been cultivated to disguise his chins, and loose fitting T-shirts and jogging bottoms (the humble attire of a joiner-at-large) served a dual purpose of covering up some of the body fat which accumulated. Never ambitious, any ready money earned (cash in hand, natch) found its way quickly into the tills of pubs and bookies or, through some marvellous alchemy, transformed itself into drugs of various hardnesses which were voraciously consumed.

Somehow, he had woken up one day to find himself magically married and much-needed stability and security resulted. Paul embraced it - just a little too heartily - until, one day, without warning, his wife walked out on him and he was on his uppers again. On his birthday, at the wrong end of his forties without a coin to his name, he woke up on a friend's floor, saw himself in the mirror and decided it was time to change. When the birthday fug had finally dispersed, he trimmed up, knuckled down, and started building himself a new home.

Not entirely legally.

But then legality wasn't Paul's forte any more than those other idiosyncrasies: subtlety, punctuality, reliability. An unholy trinity of shortcomings which his current girlfriend, Shirley, had made a point of articulating to him - several times in fact, he now recalled - but in a loving way (her words). Shortcomings which, she felt, he needed to work on - over time, of course. None of them were deal-breakers in their relationship, Shirley assured him.

And Big Paul was keen to remain in this relationship with Big Shirl. They were, he felt, a tremendous match. Both big-hearted, life-loving, happy-go-lucky types who had found soulmates in each other, wondrously given that they had been based in the same town all their lives, known each other but never, well, clicked.

Now they clicked every chance they got. Which, for Paul, was still not enough. He and Shirley were working on that. Just as he was working on his trinity of shortcomings, with Shirley's love and support. Subtlety: well that was a tricky one, involving constantly counting to ten before saying anything and trying to put himself in Shirley's shoes when he did speak. It was still very much a work in progress.

Punctuality: ah, now that had been a life-long failing. Something his ex-wife had harangued him about many times, to no effect. Let's start on the nursery slopes before we tackle the black runs, shall we?

But reliability: now here, Paul felt he could make some in-roads. Especially when it came down to being trustworthy amongst those whose relationships he valued. Well, ok, valued was perhaps a bit strong. But there were some - all men - who had helped Paul out when he needed it. Given him a lifeline or a vital second chance when life was threatening to piss in his Pot Noodle. And Cullen was one of those. So, when Cullen called, Big Paul responded.

Plus, right now, he was interested. Because when Cullen had "something on", things tended to escalate very quickly indeed.

"Fuck me, he's fast!" Paul, out of breath, careered to a halt on the forest track and bent over, hands on his knees. Cullen stood beside him, looking through his binoculars at the receding cyclist.

"Should have thought this through." Cullen winced, dropped his binoculars and looked at his friend, panting in the heat. "You're a big man, but you're out of shape."

"Cheers, mate. Nothing like sugar-coating the criticism."

"If I sugar-coated it, you'd eat that too."

Paul's dogs trotted back, they too had been beaten by the speed of the vanishing rider.

"So, what do we have?" Paul stood and took some deep breaths, slowly recovering from the exertion.

"Maroon and white mountain bike, maroon top, jeans, white cycle helmet. Young fella. Wouldn't recognise him again if I saw him. Could be anyone."

Paul considered this for a moment. "Anyone who's got a thing for Gala."

"Huh?"

"Gala. RFC?" Paul looked at Cullen's blank face. "Rugby? That's their colours, maroon and white."

"Does that help us?"

"Maybe." Paul mulled on this for a moment, wondering if - for perhaps the first time ever - he had something on his friend. "The smart money would be on Sam Marshall."

Cullen did a quick mental reconnoitre and came up empty. "Nope."

"One of Derek Marshall's boys?"

"Still nope."

"Sam Marshall. Derek Marshall."

"Yep. Say it twice, that'll help me remember people I've never heard of."

"Derek Marshall? Wingnut? Notorious jailbird and all-round bad chap of this parish?"

"You're forgetting. I'm not really from these parts."

"You're not really from any parts, are you?"

"I am always out and about." Cullen protested.

"Yeah. Physically. But mentally? You're always in your own little comfort zone."

"It's comfortable there. That's why it's called a comfort zone."

"Well, anyway. That's my guess. Local tearaway, big Gala rugby fan."

"Hmm." Cullen considered this lead. "It's thin."

"Not when you consider his nickname."

"Which is?"

"Fireman Sam."

"Cuppa tea?" Paul put a pan of water on the stove and lit it.

Paul had brought Cullen back to his cabin in his van, still keen to see if he would accept a floor for the night after his temporary bothy residence had been destroyed. For his part, Cullen still showed no sign of accepting it, but had accepted the lift gracefully enough.

"Not for me. Water."

"Right you are." Paul filled a glass from the tap and passed it to Cullen who looked at it suspiciously.

"It's a bit cloudy."

"Aye, but it's clean."

"What about all these bits floating in it?"

"Ah, they're dirty. The water's clean. Let it settle."

Cullen put the glass down on the worktop and stooped to pick up a pack of letters rubber-banded together on the floor. "How can you possibly have post? This place doesn't officially exist. Does it?"

"Nah. Although might change that, too, with my new citizen status." Paul looked at his friend's face trying, with difficulty due to unfamiliarity, to register astonishment. "I think the word you're searching for is *Blimey*."

"You're not wrong." Cullen waggled the wodge of letters in his hand. "So?"

"Ah, well. Have a sort of unofficial redirect going on.

Scott the postie keeps an eye out. Letters to my old address 'n' that. Puts 'em to one side. When he has a stack he pops by. Voila!"

The two men were standing in what passed for the living room of the cabin that passed for Paul's home. It was a work in progress which, given Paul's natural work rate, was on schedule to be completed sometime shortly before the death of the sun. To be fair to him, it was now watertight and offered warmth (in summer) and intermittent power, courtesy of a surreptitious tap into his neighbour's generator. A rainbutt on the deck outside provided water which wasn't drinkable without boiling first. Paul drank it anyway, when he ran out of beer.

The interior was remarkably tidy and suspiciously clean. There were even two scatter cushions on the dilapidated sofa. Cullen figured this was almost entirely due to the ministrations of the elusive Shirley that Paul frequently mentioned, but Cullen had never seen.

"Scott?"

"Yeah. Pub quiz team mate. Specialist subject: The Clash."

"Right." Cullen responded absently as he riffled through Paul's post. "This new leaf thing. Does it stretch to stuff like paying taxes, perhaps? Not stealing electricity from your neighbour. That kind of thing?"

Paul spat out his tea. "Steady on. I'm not morphing into Mother fucking Theresa."

"Uh-oh. Who's been a naughty boy then?" Cullen plucked one envelope from the pack and brandished it at Paul's frown. "Sheriff Court."

"Oh man! Fuck sake, I haven't done anything. Lately." Paul grimaced. "Can you open it? I daren't look."

Cullen tore the envelope neatly and removed a single

folded sheet of A4. He studied it silently for a few moments and then smiled broadly.

"Just the thing for Mr New Citizen!"

"Huh?" Paul was nonplussed.

"It's a letter of citation. For jury service!"

IN COURT: THE BOUNCER

The courtroom at Selkirk Sheriff Courthouse is high-ceilinged and echoey, tall windows filter weak spring sunlight through at the back and along one side. The painted walls bear minimal decoration, save three enormous portraits in gilt frames; veneration of the court considered substitute enough for any finery they could think of to display. At the front, a raised platform with panelled hoardings shoulder-high contains a high-backed leather chair waiting for the Sheriff.

From the courtroom entrance, steps lead up the side of tiered pews of patina'd wood, the varnish scratched and shiny in places by the backsides and elbows of observers who have sat in the public gallery through the years. Aged burgundy carpet lies wall-to-wall across the courtroom floor, with a couple of mahogany desks plonked in the middle for the counsels, a small dock in the centre of the floor with knee-high railings around it, a mahogany handrail atop bars painted red. Within this is a trap door with scuffed painted steps leading down to the cells. From there, the bowels of the courthouse give onto a car park where waiting police or prison vans dispatch the convicted to their due destinations.

The first morning of the trial, all was nervous whisper and hush: those summoned fidgeting or fiddling with their citation letters. The Clerk of the Court - a bustling, busy lady in a black gown - conversed at a table in front of the judge's platform. The Procurator Fiscal, counsel for the prosecution, and the counsel for the Defence sat similarly gowned on separate tables nearby. This trio engaged in murmured conversation as the courtroom assistant placed folded pieces of paper into a huge goldfish bowl. A man in black trousers and a white shirt, ticked off entries on his clipboard as she did so. When both were happy that everything was ready, the man paced over to the courtroom door, closed it with some finality, and then stood with his back to it, arms crossed clutching his clipboard to his chest. The woman looked up at the serried rows of whispering strangers and waited for silence to fall.

"Court!" The clerk intoned. The players at the front stood, which was sufficient prompt for the people in the gallery to also rise, as the door to the Sheriff's chambers was opened and the Lord Sheriff presiding swept in and climbed the steps to his waiting throne. He settled and nodded to the clerk who acknowledged the nod and turned to face the gallery. Everyone rustled back down in their seats.

"Good Morning, Ladies and Gentleman. Thank you for coming to the court today. My name is Carol and I am the Clerk of the Sheriff's Court here in Selkirk. You should all have with you your letter summoning you to jury duty today. At the top of it you will see a number in bold. This is your juror number. In this bowl I have placed a piece of paper with all the numbers on it." She looked over at the man by the door who nodded summarily back. "I will draw fifteen numbers from the bowl. If I read out the number on your letter, I would like you to stand up and come down to the front here and take a seat in the jury box over there." She indicated the two rows of tiered wooden benches lined up on the far wall to her right. "If you can fill the seats starting from the back row first, just go along it as far as you can and take the furthest available seat. We are trying only one case this week so I will only call names for one jury. The trial is expected to last between three and five days, so you should assume that you will be unavailable for work for the whole of this week if you are selected for jury service today."

The Clerk trotted through her overview, scanning the full pews in the gallery - over a hundred people seated, most of them still with their coats on.

"The name of the accused is Derek Arthur Marshall of Galashiels and it is alleged that the accused caused criminal damage, whilst driving under the influence of alcohol, to the property of MacDuff Ingoglia and his wife Gloria, who are both resident in the Housebyres area. If you know any of these names, or have any knowledge of the incident in question you must indicate that fact to me now so that I may determine whether you need to be excused jury duty in this case. Anyone?"

No-one raised their hands or made any movement.

"If, for any reason, your number is called and then a reason is identified which prevents you from being on the jury, I will draw another number. And so on, until we have a complete jury of fifteen people. You will then be asked to swear the oath or take an affirmation. If there is anyone who wishes to take the affirmation, can you please raise your hand and tell me your number."

A few scattered hands went up and the clerk asked each for their number and her assistant made a note of them.

"If your number is not called, please remain seated where you are until the jury selection process is over. Once the jury has been sworn in, if your number has not been called you will be free to go. Your name will be re-entered for jury duty and you may be selected at some future date, but your service for this week will be at an end. Are there any questions?"

No-one spoke, so the officer approached the glass bowl and dipped her hand in for the first number.

Cullen sat watching the proceedings from his perch up high in the gallery. The citation letter hidden on his lap - beneath the cowboy hat which the courtroom officer had insisted he remove - bore the name *Paul McInnes* and the number *86*.

"Oh, come on Mungo! I'd do the same for you." Paul only used Cullen's Christian name when in dire straits as he knew that Cullen resented it being used - by anyone. But he was desperate.

"Would you?"

"'Course!" Paul was outraged at the very idea of non-reciprocity. "Look, it's not for me. It's for Shirl."

"The letter has your name on it."

"I know that. What I mean is, my reasons for not wanting to do jury duty *at this time* is so that I can get this job done and use the money to treat her! I've got plans. It's not that I object to serving-"

"Isn't it?"

"God no. Sitting in a comfy chair all day, lunch included, getting paid, to judge people? Give me a few cold beers and my life would be complete." Paul held both palms upwards as if offering to be struck down if he was lying. "It's a timing thing. This job in Melrose. It's huge! Not only does it earn me good money now, but it gets me on a list, doesn't it?"

"You're already on plenty of lists."

"I mean a list of approved craftsmen, sarky." Paul

grimaced. "These developers, they're all cliquey like. Use the same team over and over. You get in their good books, you're set. They'll use you again and again."

"Almost like having a proper job." Cullen observed drily.

"Yeah, yeah. Look, it could be my big break. Any other time…" Paul swigged from a mug of cold tea, pulled a face but swallowed it anyway. "And it's all part of my plans, isn't it?"

"It is?"

"Yes! Move the relationship along with Shirl. Turn over a new wossname. Be more reliable."

"Don't over-reach."

Paul ignored him. He was on a roll. "Get some good money in my pocket. Take her away somewhere nice! Show her a good time. Get this place finished." He swept his hands around the partially decorated interior of his cabin.

"Save up for a proper home." Cullen smiled.

"This is a proper home!" Paul was offended. "Lick of paint. Sort the plumbing. Couple of nice doors. Double-glazing. It'd be dead cosy in the winter."

"Well, save up anyway."

"I'm already saving." Paul objected. "But this'll allow me to save more."

"You could save more if you spent less on beer."

"If I saved the money I spend on beer, I'd only spend it on beer!" Paul noted, not unreasonably. "And, since beer in the future will cost more - due to inflation - I'm actually saving money by buying beer now!"

"Yes, well. Let's not wander off into macro-economics shall we?"

"Macro-what?"

"Doesn't matter." Cullen eyed his friend carefully, assaying the extent of the genuine amongst the bullshit. "So, I'd be doing this for Shirley - not you?"

"Exactly!" Paul beamed. "What do you say?"

86 was the fifteenth and final number called. Cullen sighed, stood and made his way down to the jury box.

The Clerk of the Court read out the indictment in full and handed it to the Sheriff, who then addressed the jury.

"Ladies and Gentlemen, you have been selected for the jury and heard the indictment. Do any of you know the accused directly or indirectly? Do you know any of the people mentioned in the indictment or are aware of this case other than through media reports? Do you know any possible witnesses or are you unable, for any other reason, to serve on this jury for the duration of this trial?"

None of the jurors moved so the Sheriff nodded to the Clerk to administer the oath and, when that was complete, he said:

"Ladies and gentlemen, we're going to adjourn briefly to allow you to get comfortable in the jury room. Michael is your jury attendant…" He indicated to the white-shirted man who now stepped up alongside the handrail. "And he will guide you to and from the jury room, and accompany you at mealtimes to ensure you do not accidentally come into contact with anyone involved with this case. Please direct any questions about this case, or your jury duty, to Michael in the first instance. He will pass them to me or the Clerk if he cannot answer them himself. Michael?"

"Would you all come this way please?" Michael waved them towards a wooden door in the corner of the room, to one side of the jury box. The seven women and eight men rose and trooped out of the box and through the door. The room was circular, no more than five yards in diameter, with two large windows facing north and east. A large round table and fifteen chairs dominated the room, leaving only just enough room around it for people to sidle past behind chairs and take a seat.

To the left of the door was another, smaller door, which led to a compact and cramped toilet cubicle. To the right of the east window was a hot drinks machine and a water cooler. On the table, in front of each chair, was a clipboard loaded with a few sheets of paper and a biro.

The jury wallowed slowly in and sat down around the table. When they were all seated, Michael closed the door and rubbed his hands together.

"Right. Before we get started. Who'd like tea or coffee?" He pointed to the drinks machine. "Help yourselves. I'm just going to get your jury forms and some other bits and pieces for you and I'll be right back. On no account are you allowed to leave this room when I am not here. Is that clear? If you need anything, either wait for me to come back or, if it is urgent, please knock loudly on the door. Ok?"

Heads bobbed silently and one elderly women closest to the machine stood up and looked around the table. "Shall I be mother?"

The Procurator Fiscal wore a black gown and looked like a female Snape. Black dress, black tights, black hair, black eyes, black shoes. A single gold brooch the only item which glistened amongst the raven smoothness. Her hair was swept back and pinned in a bun and you would imagine her, after a long day in court, removing the pin and letting her hair tumble down like a shampoo advert.

She faced the Sheriff, scooping up a folder and some notes from the desk in front of her. "My Lord, the prosecution would like to call Timothy Hawthorne as a witness." The Sheriff nodded to the court officer at the closed door, standing in his G4S short-sleeved white shirt and black trousers. The officer, went through the door and motioned to someone seated outside. Timothy Hawthorne walked in, stepped up into the witness box and took the oath. The Fiscal walked gaminely over to a lectern at the far end of the jury box, directly in front of Cullen. In facing the witness box, she had the jury behind her and the Sheriff to her left, the public gallery to her right.

"Mr Hawthorne, would you give your full name and occupation to the court?"

"Timothy Hawthorne. Doorman."

"Mr Hawthorne, where do you work?"

"The Ship Inn in Gala."

"Gala being Galashiels, correct?"

"Aye."

"And were you working there the night of the 26th December, last year?"

"Yes."

"And did you witness the accused in your pub at any time during that evening?"

"I did, yes."

"Could you tell the court what you recall of that night?"

"Well, there was a big crowd of Melrose supporters in, celebrating their victory like."

"This was a victory over Galashiels?"

"Aye. They'd hammered Gala and were all out celebrating. Nothing too bad, like, just lots of singing and drinking an' that."

"So this was a typical Boxing Day occurrence was it?"

"Pretty much. If the match is played at Netherdale, any road."

"Netherdale?"

"The home ground for Gala."

"I see. So this rugby match between Galashiels and Melrose is an annual event?"

"Aye, every Boxing Day."

"And it alternates venue? One year at Melrose, the next at Galashiels, and so on?"

"Aye."

"So, this last Boxing Day, the match had taken place at Galashiels, Melrose had won and Galashiels had lost, and the supporters of both teams were in your pub?"

"Aye, well we always have Gala supporters in. This Melrose gang were on some kind of pub-crawl, how it looked anyway, and when I let 'em in I was on the alert in case anything kicked off. Rugby fans are usually a lot better than footie fans, though, so I wasn't too bothered. But you never know when they've had a few, do you know what I mean?"

Timothy Hawthorne had a haircut of rough, blonde spikes atop a bulky torso, his belly overhanging his belt, his stocky arms swollen in a rather tight-fitting dark jacket, beneath which he wore a shirt and tie his employer had forced on him the night before. If he was going to represent The Ship, he needed to look respectable and not like an overweight toilet brush. The effort at dressing him up had not entirely succeeded.

"And Derek Marshall was in the pub at this time?"

"Yes. He were in there, I reckon, from early doors - maybe six, six-thirty - through until I had to chuck him out - gone eleven."

"You threw him out?"

"Aye."

"Objection, my Lord." Patterson rose to his feet, it seemed to Cullen more in hope than expectation. "There is no relevance here to what my client may or may not have done prior to the alleged incidents at Mr Ingoglia's residence."

"My Lord, I am seeking to establish the state of Mr Marshall's sobriety and state of mind." The Fiscal retorted, haughtily. "One of the charges in the indictment relates to intoxication. Mr Hawthorne can provide eye-witness evidence as to the capacity of Mr Marshall in the lead-up to the events in question."

"Yes, yes." The Sheriff waved a weary hand. "Mr Patterson, if we get off-topic I shall be the first to stop the particular line of questioning. For now, I see no question of irrelevance in this case." He looked over his glasses at the bouncer. "You may answer the question Mr Hawthorne."

"What was the question again?"

"Could you describe the events which led up to you ejecting Derek Marshall from The Ship?"

"Oh aye. Well, there were a kerfuffle between these Melrose supporters and him and his sons." Hawthorne nodded over to where Derek Marshall was sitting, a lonely figure hunched forward with his elbows on his knees, staring at the stairs in front of him which led down to the cells below the courtroom.

"Mr Marshall's sons?"

"Aye. Two of them - Sam and Sean. One of these Melrose lads said summat and it all kinda kicked off."

"Do you know what was said?"

"Objection, my Lord."

"Mr Patterson." The Sheriff screwed his face up at the solicitor and rolled his eyes at the Procurator Fiscal. "On you go."

"Did you hear what was said, Mr Hawthorne?" The Fiscal repeated.

"I didn't hear the whole thing - conversation were getting louder and rowdier, and there were more people coming in all the time. But I did hear one of the lads call one of them a Pail."

"A pail?"

"Aye."

"Could you explain - for the benefit of the jury - what a pail is?"

"And me." Smirked the Sheriff. "I am unfamiliar with the phrase, unless it refers to a bucket?"

"Och, well it does your honour. Refer to a bucket. A pail's a metal bucket, right enough. But it's an insult, yer see. Quite a bad 'un if you're from Gala."

"Why?" Said the Fiscal.

"Well it's short for pailmerk. And a pailmerk is the mark you get on your, er, backside, if you squat bare-arsed - sorry, your honour - on a metal bucket. A pail."

"I'm not with you, Mr Hawthorne."

"Well, see in years gone by all o' the towns in the Borders - long ago, mind, all this - people used to have outside toilets an' that and at some point each town was given indoor plumbing and outside toilets became a thing o' the past. Well, 'cos Gala was the last town to get indoor plumbing, people from outside Gala, if they wanted to insult you, would call you a pailmerk - like someone who still has to shit - er, sorry your honour - go to the toilet in a bucket."

"I see." The Fiscal paused for effect and cast an eye

across the back row of the jury to make sure they had taken note of this salient fact. "So Mr Marshall was insulted - badly - by a supporter of the rugby team who had defeated his own team, Galashiels. And this caused him to - what, exactly?"

"Well it all kicked off an' that, didn't it?"

"So it was a fight?"

"Well, it were a drunken scrap, yer know. Not a fight as such."

"Objection, your honour. The witness can't speak for the sobriety of my client."

The Sheriff sighed. "Mr Hawthorne. Can you describe what it was about Mr Marshall that led you to conclude that he was drunk?"

"Well, it weren't just him. Everyone were drinking. But he seemed the most belligerent like. He were swaying and shouting and he threw a full pint into the group of Melrose supporters."

"Were any punches thrown?"

"A few. None of 'em landed mind. That's when I grabbed hold of him and pulled him out of the crowd and muscled him out into the street."

"And what happened after you ejected Mr Marshall?"

"Well, I went back inside and… it were all kind of quietened down."

"The fight had stopped?"

"Aye. I think some of the Melrose lads had separated the scufflers and taken them off to one end of the bar, and some of the Gala boys had done likewise. There was some old bloke shouting at them, telling 'em to behave 'emselves. It kinda blew itself out."

"Did you eject anyone else?"

"Didn't see the need. The Marshall boys stormed out

after their Dad and they'd been the main troublemakers from what I could see."

"So, Mr Marshall - the accused - was visibly drunk in The Ship that night, got involved in some kind of altercation and you ejected him from the pub."

"Correct."

"Did he struggle when you ejected him?"

"Not once he were outside. On his own like."

"And could you tell what time this was?"

"Aye, it were bang on eleven o'clock. Church clock were actually goin' off as I was standing there watchin' him wander off down the street."

"Bang on eleven. 11pm?"

"Aye."

The prosecutor made a note and glanced sideways at the jury.

"Where did he go - Mr Marshall?"

"Dunno. I went back inside and he never came back in."

"Thank-you, Mr Hawthorne." The Procurator Fiscal swept up her folder and notes and strode back to her seat. Patterson stood and sauntered over to the same lectern the Fiscal had just left.

"Long story short: it was a chairlift."

Lorraine and Carol came into the jury room together, their bus having been unexpectedly early. Only Marjorie was there, at the drinks machine. "Morning both." she trilled.

"Morning." Lorraine rejoined, absently.

"Like a Stannah chairlift? Like Thora Hird off the telly?" asked Carol.

"Yes! Although I think Thora Hird's dead now."

"Is she?"

"Ooh, yes. Years ago, I think."

"Gosh. That's awful." Carol mulled this dreadful fact over for a moment before re-finding her place in the conversation. "I thought you said you lived in a flat?"

"We do."

"Well, what's he doing bidding on a chairlift?"

"I don't know!" Lorraine's short grey hair was neatly trimmed and she wore tiny pearl studs in her ears, although she barely had the lobes in which to put them. She took no nonsense from anyone - apart from the fact that she had a husband who appeared to be a loose cannon on a rocking ship. Lorraine had thin lips painted bruised plum, held tight in a pasty set-in-her-ways face, which made her look a little like a cherry bakewell which had been damaged in transit. "I think maybe he's getting Alzheimer's or something? Doesn't know what he's doing half the time."

"Does he need a chairlift?" Marjorie came over to the table stirring sugar into her tea. "I don't need a chairlift - and I'm eighty-three you know."

"No, he doesn't need a bloody chairlift. Needs his bloody head examined, is what he needs. He can't stop - he's addicted. Ever since our Pauline got him that iPad, he's got an app for this, an app for that. He's on eBay night and day."

"Oh dear." Carol hmm'ed and aah'ed. "Still, look on the bright side. For the next few hours we've got the Trial of the Century to engross ourselves in. Getting right good, isn't it?"

"Is it? Waste of time if you ask me."

"Ooh, come on! All this sex-for-a-baby malarkey, eh?

That's good isn't it? It's like wife-swapping - people throwing their car keys into a bowl and having a good old gander at each other's privates. You know, you read about these things in the paper but you don't ever think they're real do you? Then bingo! It's shoved right in your face." She reddened. "So to speak."

"Red herring is what it is. Why are they going on about it? I feel for the poor woman. Standing up there, having her private life picked over. What's that got to do with the price of fish?"

"Motive isn't it." Said Marjorie. "The Fiscal said it yesterday. Establishing motive. Why did he do it? To get his own back? Own back for what? For no longer being able to have it away with someone else's missus. Why was he having it away with her? 'Cos she wanted a baby and couldn't have one with her own hubby." She sniffed conclusively. "All makes sense to me."

Slowly the rest of the jurors started arriving, handing out reluctant greetings, queueing at the drinks machine and then taking the same seats around the table they'd originally been given. Michael appeared through the open door.

"There's going to be a small delay. One of the witnesses isn't here yet." He looked at his watch. "I'll give you another update in fifteen minutes." He smiled and closed the door on them. There was a general look of what-now around the table.

"Is it too early to do a show of hands?" Carol piped up.

"The trial's not got going yet!" protested Lorraine.

"Aye, but surely we can get some feel for where each of us is at? It'll save time at the end if we know where we stand."

There was a general hubbub of murmuring and vague

assent.

"Alright then. It's not like we've got anything better to do while we're waiting. Let's have a show of hands." The businessman raised his voice for attention. "Everyone? Just so we can see where we all are, right now. Raise your hand if you think Marshall did it."

Seven hands went up - five straight away, a further two more slowly. Jerry, running his eye down the runners and riders for the meeting at Carlisle, came to rest on *14: Guilty As Charged*. He raised his hand to make it eight.

"Really?" Said the businessman, astonished.

BOXING DAY: PART I

"You're enjoying this!"

"No. That is the *last* thing I am doing."

"Oh you are. You must be." Duffy was pacing furiously up and down in front of his whiteboard, fingers flying like a touch-typist after an adrenalin shot. "Must be. The evidence is clear. 100% clear. Totally clear."

"Why must I?" Gloria was crying. She was angry and confused, hurt and dejected by Duffy's accusations. He'd been flinging them now for many minutes and she really just wanted to run away and sob her heart out. But this man and his wounding comments - she needed to set him straight first. "Why you say this howwid thing?"

"Because…" Duffy stopped pacing and faced her, although he didn't look her in the eye - that was too confrontational, too raw for him to do. But when he kind of looked at you over your shoulder, his eyes off to one side with his head shaking slightly, that was when you knew he was at his most provoked, most distressed, most strung out. "It's been five months! Five months. One hundred and forty six days. Three or four times each week. Almost eighty times! Eighty! No pregnancy. No baby."

"But I don't enjoy it!" She protested, wondering momentarily just how true her protest was. Since this programme with Wingnut had started, she and Duffy had not had sex. At all. They hadn't even slept in the same bed. He had slept on the sofa and then, after the first month, found himself a blow-up mattress and put it in their spare room. Duffy had been unable to desire her, unable even to touch her or show her any physical affection. It was if, until this was over, she was impure - infected and only a pregnancy would cure her. And him.

"Really? Really? You expect me to believe that?"

"It's true! I hate it. I hate… fucking him." *But it's the only sex I'm getting,* she thought. *And I have needs. Why should I feel bad about it? Why should I feel guilty?* "This was your idea, wemember."

At this, Duffy started slapping himself about the head, the heels of his palms smacking into his temples.

"Duff! Stop it! Please, stop it!" Gloria rushed over to hug him but he stepped back and away, unwilling to have her near him. She stood there, shoulders sagging, tears clouding her vision. She had had plenty of low points in her life, she knew, but this was starting to feel like one of the worst. Duffy, for now at least, had stopped hitting himself and stood rigidly apart from her.

"If you hate it. Really hate it. Why do you keep doing it?" He spoke slowly, defeated, his fists clenched at his side, eyes on the floor.

"Because I want a baby!" Gloria pleaded. "Don't you?"

Duffy looked up and over her shoulder again, his eyes wet and red. She realised as she looked at him, that this was the first time ever she had seen him completely still and motionless.

"Not this much." He said.

"Cheer up, it's your birthday!" Wingnut planted the three pint glasses down on the table, along with the two bags of pork scratchings he was carrying in his mouth.

Sean looked at the bags forlornly. "There's three of us."

"S'all they had left. Must have been a run on 'em." Wingnut sniffed. "You too, Sammie! Fuckin' hell, it's Christmas, his birthday, and you're both sitting there with a face tripping you up."

"We just go shat on by Melrose, Dad." Sam sulked. "Perhaps you weren't at the same game as us?"

"Jesus, it's only a fucking game Sam! It's not life or death. Just a game. Simple as that. Happy Birthday, son" He lifted up his glass to salute Sean and took a long swig from his pint, wiping the foam from his lips when he finished. "You're a proper man now, eh?"

"What?" Sean squinted at his father, his pint untouched.

"Got your end away didn't yer? Well done, son. Good on yer." Wingnut dropped a heavy wink and took another swig from his glass. Sam smiled thinly at his brother.

"How did you-?"

"Walls are fucking paper thin, son. Couldn't help but overhear. You know." Wingnut waggled his eyebrows. "She's a bonnie lass 'n' all. I bloody would if I had the chance."

Sean sat in silence, caught somewhere between shame and mortification. Belittlement and jokes at his expense, that was what your pals did, not your father. Salivating over his girlfriend merely added insult to injury. He toyed gingerly with the chain around his neck and thought of Janine.

"Don't put it in there!" She had wriggled underneath Sean's bulk earlier that day, giggling.

Ah, right. Sean had made a mental note. The only words of wisdom Sam had been able to impart to him had been *"it's lower down than you think."* Sean had been keeping this in mind all day, if only to fend off his impending climax. Clearly, his aim was too low.

Sean would have been all fingers-and-thumbs if it had been those extremities which were being called upon to do their duty at this particular moment. Alas, it was not, since he was altogether more dexterous with his hands than he clearly was with his penis. Fortunately, with the curtains drawn, Janine hadn't see him blushing but Sean had been unhappily torn between the incredible urge to ejaculate forcibly *right there* and the recognition that in doing so he would both disappoint her and potentially reveal that he was a virgin and his *bragga* was actually one hundred per cent *docio.*

Janine had rolled and bucked in his hands like a well-used bar of soap and Sean hadn't been able to gain any purchase on her. Her curves and softness kept yielding - delightfully, it had to be said - when he really needed something solid to steady himself on. He'd felt like he was playing one of those games where you have to thread the hook all the way along the wiggly wire without setting the buzzer off. In the dark. In an air pocket.

"Oh!" She had gasped and pulled herself forward, clutching his neck as he managed to locate the correct point of entry. "Oh. My. God."

"You ok?"

"Fuck." Janine bit her lip. "Just keep doing that."

Doing what? Thought Sean. I *haven't started yet. Have I? Although if she carries on like this, I'll soon be finished.*

He had hunkered down on top of her, carrying his weight on his shoulders, pretending he was leaning into the scrum and started to thrust in and out. All the time whilst trying to do his seventeen times table. This seemed to do the trick, as far as both he and Janine were concerned.

"Yes. Yes. There. Do it!"

Her clutch had turned into a grasp and then a grab. Her hands were everywhere, tugging his hair, scratching his back, pulling his shoulders down onto her, holding onto him with everything she had. Sean had felt himself start to unravel. His mind busying itself getting past eight seventeens and worrying about the noise Janine was making and whether they could be overheard and whether what he was doing was how it was supposed to be done. On this last point he decided that it probably didn't really matter, since Janine clearly thought so. He was just forcing his brain to add on another seventeen, when Janine wrapped her legs around his waist and it was all too much for him.

He felt his insides liquefy and then explode while she writhed and rode him, now grabbing onto his necklace and pulling it until it dug into the flesh at the back of his neck. And this was where, once more, the conflict in his brain helped him out. He'd read advice for young lovers online, which had all been about making sure she got satisfaction, not just seeing your partner as a means to a personal end. Be considerate, hold her, kiss her, cuddle her afterwards. Show tenderness and attention to your partner, not *wham-bam-thank-you-mam.* So, when Sean came he had the stinging sensation in his neck to remind him that, whilst his train might have pulled into the station and was discharging passengers, Janine's was still taking the bends like a Pendolino running full tilt to beat the London-to-Edinburgh speed record. He decided to keep steaming on and see if he could get her to ride the rails to the terminus. Gritting his teeth, he stoked the boiler and pile-drived onward as Janine's exclamations became louder and closer together, a high-pitched whistle piercing the countryside alerting all around to the fact that this locomotive was approaching a tunnel.

That was when his necklace snapped.

Sean stopped in his tracks and Janine coasted into the station on the last of the power, shuddering to a stop, her breath ragged and raw. Sean had looked down at his girlfriend, eyes wide with wonder and then sudden disappointment as he saw the sparkling gold circle resting on the pillow next to her. The face-up *H* engraved in the centre of the disc glinted at him and caught him unawares. Sean saw his mother and how much he missed her. The boy she had left eight years ago was now a man and his heart suddenly ached out through his chest.

Janine took a long, slow breath as she felt Sean shudder slightly on top of her. When she opened her eyes, she could see he was crying and she pulled him down to her, cradled his head and shhh'ed him until they had both fallen asleep.

Janine Crombie was a right handful. And a left handful too. In fact, Sean could have done with a spare pair of hands just to capture the main points, so to speak. And Sean had big hands.

She usually looked like she'd been poured into her dress and most of it had spilt. Eyebrows plucked to oblivion and replaced with painted scouse-brow substitutes, fingernails embedded with glitter and rhinestones and a back-combed hairstyle of whipped candyfloss. She was an economy-size Barbie made from pink balloons.

They had met at a rugby match in the queue for a pie and Bovril. Janine had been there to accompany a pal, not being a big rugby fan herself. But she had taken one look at this hunky blonde figure in front of her, given her friend a massive nudge in the ribs and then sidled up behind him, bold as brass, and asked for his number - just as he was being served.

Sean had forgotten his order and dropped his change.

Hunky he may have been, but he was essentially a shy teenager, still clumsily coming to terms with a magnificent body. A meaty, muscly fifteen stone seven, he had short, tufty, blonde scrub for hair, a belter of a broken nose, and two close-set eyes of the most piercing blue shining out beneath a proud brow. His arms were like thick rope, coated with blonde fuzz and freckles, and his chest struggled to burst from whatever shirt or jersey he wore. Sweaters didn't work on him - they just made him look like a woollen wall. As far as Janine was concerned, he could be Thor's younger brother.

And it was rugby that had made him. That, plus nature and hours in the gym. But mostly rugby.

His dad had first taken him and Sam to rugby games down at Netherdale and, even in the prolonged periods of his father's absence, they had both developed a deep love of the game. Sean threw himself into rugby as he progressed into manhood. Both he and Sam had the build, power and appetite for the game. Six foot clear, the pair of them, broad-chested and thick-necked, muscular, athletic and strong. They played as centre-backs - Sean had the better rugby brain and so played inside-centre; Sam with the slightly superior bulk and pace played outside-centre. Both used to seeing a lot of the ball, even if not necessarily doing a lot with it, other than passing it on to those that did. Sam in particular liked nothing more than spending an evening in the bar after a game explaining how he had broken tackles and come close to scoring a try, while those around him nodded sympathetically and reserved their praise for the winger who had actually put the points on the board. Sean preferred to keep his thoughts to himself and focus on minor improvements he could make next time he ran onto the pitch.

But Janine - ah, his Janine! She was a pocket Venus of unbridled energy and life. A bustling dental receptionist in Peebles, she was short and curvaceous, her torso went in and out in all the right places, more or less as far as it was possible to go. She too was blonde, with glinting brown eyes, and a bee-stung mouth. She had a small tattoo of a butterfly on the back of her neck and anyone not drawn in by the tractor beam of her cleavage would have seen a small emerald stone dangling dangerously from a dainty silver chain.

Sean himself wore a gold necklace chain on which hung a small spinning disc which bore the legend "S <space> S" on one side, and a central "H" on the other. When you spun it, it read SHS. A gift from his mother to represent Heather in the middle of her two sons Sam and Sean. She had had three of them made and they had each worn one every day since his mother had given it to them. He hoped that, wherever she was, she was still wearing hers too.

So the fact that he had now damaged his, hurt him deeply. It still just about fastened but the clasp was fragile and easily came apart. He couldn't determine whether the fact that it had happened in the throes of passion made it better or worse. And, since he was at college, he wasn't exactly flush enough to be able to consider repairing it immediately. He'd have to save a wee bit. Janine was pulling down a full-time wage, but he didn't want to ask her for money. Any more than he had wanted to consummate their relationship in his own bedroom with the chances of Sam listening in on the other side of the wall. How much more embarrassing was it knowing, now, that his father had been silently applauding as well. But Janine still lived at home with a Victorian father and obedient mother, so the list of "potential places we could *do it*" as Janine urged him, was a very short one. And she had been very insistent and persistent.

With a body like hers, and teenage hormones like his, there had only been so long Sean had been able to hold out.

Gloria was walking in the jungle high above the winding Chao Phraya river, brown and sluggish below her. Beads of sweat clustered round her hairline and stained the back of her vest - a ribboned spine of grey on a tiny floodplain of white. The only part of her that was cool were her feet, slapping through the moist undergrowth in battered leather thongs. Mosquitoes squatted and were casually swatted as she strode along the scruffy trail. A shrill cacophony of shrieking, whistling and calling rent the air, stale sunlight winnowing through the canopy and spattering stripes across her delicate frame.

Suddenly, silently, Worrawut appeared before her. He was wearing only his ceremonial skirt - a black silk cloth wrapped around his legs and hips, tucked in and secured at the waist with a bone broach shaped like a tusk. His torso and calves were brown and smooth and slick. A large beetle crawled across his right foot, a blithe pedestrian traversing a human crossing on its way home.

His smile was broad and genuine and she could see the love in his eyes and he extended both arms towards her. *Come to me, my darling. Come to me. Be my betrothed as I undertake the journey into manhood, under the proud eyes of my village elders. Come. Let us sit together as I take my pledge.*

Gloria made a move towards him and found herself struggling against a mighty force, a web of lianas wrapped invisibly around her limbs and held her back as she strained forward. Inches of progress were all that resulted from the sweat and the effort on her face. She opened her mouth wide to shout his name and the air choked her, stifling her words, vocal cords quivering but silent.

Worrawut kept smiling and beaming, entreating her to reach out to him while he remained stubbornly where he was. Gloria put her head down and heaved with everything she had, focussing every muscle into pulling against this creeping tide, managing to move each foot only a few more inches in the process. Determined, she gritted her teeth and strained her shoulders into the fight, wrestling herself forward inch by sweating inch. When she looked up again, Worrawut was even further away. Arms still outstretched, he was now standing further down the trail, a smaller distant figure in a collage of vibrant greens. She put her head down once more and gave a mighty pull and the effort broke her free. She almost fell on her face, but managed to transfer the unexpected forward motion into an upright stance, only to bundle into the bare chest of Derek Marshall.

She recognised the smell of him, his close warmth detectable even in this humidity. He was right there in front of her now, blocking out any view she might have had of Worrawut. Scared and suddenly angry, she beat her small fists against his chest but the soundless thumps bounced harmlessly off and when she steeled herself to look up to him, he was laughing at her and moving his hands down to his groin. Through the audible havoc she heard the unmistakable sound of a man unzipping his flies. The chirping static was briefly shattered by a Tarzan-like howl somewhere away to her left. Gloria jerked her head towards the sound and saw a hairy figure swinging through the trees, from branch to branch, calling wildly and enthusiastically as it went.

It was Duffy, smirking through the branches, howling and jabbering, protesting as he swung. Capering like a mad fiend, he ploughed through the trees and leapt down onto the jungle floor a few metres behind Derek. The pair wheeled to face each other and their respective stances and builds created an eerie tableau: Derek tall and broad, tattooed and muscly, half an arse in his jeans but well-defined shoulders and abs; Duffy like a short-tailed barrel organ, all bristling and hairy, swarthy neck and hairy shoulders, squat and solid, hugging the ground. They stood looking at each other, Derek silent, Duffy hooting like a gibbon - each eyeing the other, waiting for the right moment to pounce.

Out of nowhere, Worrawut materialised between them, as if dropped from a plane. Between these two savages he shimmered like a mirage, smooth and sleek as a polished penknife, open and ready to wound. The two men drew back and looked at him in surprise: Duffy momentarily silenced, Derek considering whether this interloper was a threat or a prize.

Gloria couldn't move. Out of the corner of her eye, a silent tiger trod softly into view, its teeth bared glistening in the dark light. It had eyes only for Worrawut, the glistening prize embedded between two statues. The tiger leapt, the two men crunched and Worrawut disappeared.

Gloria woke and found herself staring at a ceiling dripping with condensation, alone in her bed.

"This place is like a fucking morgue." Wingnut looked around the public bar of The Ship. "Don't know why they've got a bouncer on, it's dead!"

There was a huge surly doorman standing just inside the main entrance, wearing a black polo shirt that revealed bulging biceps and a blonde cut which said "fuck off" in hair. He turned to glance at Wingnut as he heard himself referred to and Wingnut quickly found something immensely interesting in his pint glass.

"Fuck." Wingnut was looking down at his phone which had just whistled at him. It was a text from Duffy which said simply: `ITS OVER. LEAVE GLORIA ALONE.`

"Get 'em in then, Sean." Wingnut rose and ambled over to the toilets. "I'm just gonna deal with this knobhead."

The aesthetic of the Gents' lavatory at The Ship would come as a surprise only to a woman who had either never been in a men's lavatory, or never been in the Ladies'. The dominant theme was prison-chic grim with a strong motif of broken tiles and manky lino. The walls were riddled with misspelled graffiti, adulterated posters in glass frames above the urinals and a lone condom machine covered with pornographic Sharpie drawings. The acrid tang of stale urine wrapped itself around you the minute you walked in and the place had the ambient temperature of a Monday-morning concrete floor in an Aberdeen fish market.

Its saving grace, for Wingnut at least, was that it was

currently empty and quiet. He'd missed a number of texts from Duffy in the last ten minutes or so and he scrolled up to read them and consider his response. Duffy, via text, was enormously more concise then he ever was in person. Wingnut leant against the separating porcelain of one of the urinals and unzipped his fly with one hand while he punched a reply to Duffy into his phone:

`MAYBE. MAYBE NOT.`

He wasn't letting Duffy put an end to his funbag funtime, especially not over Christmas. He'd been looking forward to getting his end away a couple of times more over the festive period and this was an unnecessary and unwelcome development. Duffy could swing.

Up on Eildon hill, Duffy was jabbering to himself and fuming with frustration at his inability to text as fluently as he felt he could verbalise. He hated mobile phones. They were dangerous and unsecure. But it was either deal with his brother-in-law face-to-face or this. Bad enough that he had to remove his gloves to get his touchscreen keyboard to work - it was freezing cold up here and his precipitous departure after rowing with Gloria had meant he had omitted to make a flask of anything hot. He'd only realised this on the ascent and his options of skulking briefly back home versus defiantly sticking it out on the hill had been an easy choice when he asked himself what Heather would have wanted.

The problem was his fingers: they were stubby and chubby and he couldn't for the life of him seem to manage to tap one key at a time. And, if by some magic he did, the phone would maddeningly interpret his successful stab as a selection of one of the five keys surrounding the one he thought he'd hit. The process was infuriating and compounded by the fact that his whirring mind and whizzing thoughts would fly this way and that a thousand times in the duration it took him to type out a coherent sentence. And no way was he going to press send on an incoherent, misspelled or badly punctuated text. *Oh no. That would be bad. Very bad. Very very bad.*

This icy torture made him even more unable to text evenly and, with Wingnut's irascible and unreasonable replies - well, Duffy considered himself massively provoked. The sole benefit was that his core temperature was rising as his anger grew so he was at least missing the flask less than would otherwise have been the case. His phone vibrated now - he never had it on ring, always silent vibrate - and he looked down at Wingnut's response: `LETS SEE WHAT GLORIA HAS TO SAY ABOUT THAT, SHALL WE:)`

Duffy was stunned. He got up from his camping stool and strode madly about the hillside, rolling his head from side to side as he talked to himself. His anger and frustration bore down on him, compressing him. The very weight of the words made them harder to come. He texted again.

`STAY AWAY.`

The response from Wingnut was swift.

`WHY?`

Duffy punched himself on the side of the head, wanting this madness to end, unable to continue and wondering why Wingnut was being so difficult.

`IT'S TOO HARD.` Was all he could manage. Wingnut's response made him gasp.

`THATS WHAT SHE SAID:)`

Duffy hurled his phone onto the frosty ground and then immediately regretted it and scrabbled to pick it up, checking to make sure it wasn't broken. Unable to face a phonecall with Wingnut and unwilling to leave this conversation without closure, Duffy couldn't understand why Wingnut wouldn't just leave it alone.

STOP THIS. I MEAN IT. THIS IS THE END.

There was no response and, after the silence extended to several minutes, Duffy started to breathe more easily. It was done.

Then his phone vibrated.

I AGREED TO DO THIS TO GIVE YOU BOTH A BABY. I INTEND TO CONTINUE UNTIL I HAVE DONE THAT. I DO NOT RENEGE ON MY DEALS.

And again: WE'RE NEARLY THERE.

Duffy stabbed, frustrated, at his keypad: NO. I CAN'T TAKE THIS ANYMORE.

THATS WHAT SHE SAID:)

Duffy almost sobbed into his phone and began pacing frantically up and down, unable to think of what else to say. In the end, he collapsed back onto his chair and sent a final plea.

STOP. PLEASE. NO MORE.

Sam had been livid when his father came out of the toilets and sidled up to him at the bar, saying: "Gimme the Zippo, Sammie."

"What?"

"You heard. Hand it over."

"What for?"

"I want to give it to Sean. For his birthday."

"But it's mine!"

"No, it's not. It's mine." Wingnut prodded him in the chest. "I gave it to you for safe-keeping, while I was … away." His father didn't like to say *inside* or *in prison* - both terms reminded him of his mistakes. "And now I'm giving it to him on his birthday."

"But you've already given him a present." Sam protested. He was damned if his father was going to take it from him. If he then turned around and gave it to Sean that was, well, intolerable. He was the eldest, he was the adult here. Sean might have turned nineteen, but he was still a bloody baby and it was Sam who'd taken care of him while his father was inside. Alright, Duffy had too, but Sam had turfed him out once he himself had reached the age of majority and taken on the role of man of the house and surrogate father to Sean. The precious lighter meant something, indicated this adult status he had taken on voluntarily. Removing it now felt like a deep punch in the gut.

"That was for *this* birthday." Wingnut said. "But I missed his eighteenth, last year. When he became a man. Least I can do is give him this, to show him he's reached manhood. C'mon, he can use it to light his cigars!"

"He doesn't even like cigars. Can't you see him splutter and gag when he takes a drag?"

"Ooh, you're a poet! Look, it's not the point. Give me the fucking Zippo."

Sam bristled. "No."

"Sammie. Give it to me. It's mine."

"Dad!" Sam whined and grimaced, hoping to change his father's mind. But Wingnut simply stood there with his hand out and waited. Sam reluctantly reached into his pocket and pulled out the smooth, polished lighter and slapped it into his father's hand.

"Thank you."

"Same again, Keith." Wingnut motioned to the barman. "And two more shots of vodka in the last one."

"Dad, what are you doing? Sean can't really handle his drink."

"Fuck off!" Wingnut waved Sam's protest away. "Son of mine can't handle his drink? He's no fucking son of mine. Time he fucking learnt then, innit?" He nodded to Keith who had paused with the pint glass up to the optic, waiting for this father-son altercation to resolve itself. Keith pushed the glass upwards, twice.

Sam shuffled back to their table and took his seat, scowling around the bar willing any of the other drinkers to make eye contact with him. None did.

"Happy Birthday, son." Wingnut toasted and all three took a drink from their glasses. Sean's eyes were starting to feel uncontrollably mobile while he himself felt sluggish. He didn't drink as a rule, but his father's birthday insistence, and Sam's urge that they blot out the pain of the 37-9 defeat by their bitter rivals by abusing alcohol and smoking some birthday cigars, had caused him to go along. Sean had gagged and choked on the nasty things but persisted under peril of ridicule from the pair of them.

"Present for you, Seanie. An overdue gift for your eighteenth." Wingnut opened his palm in front of Sean to reveal the gleaming metal block.

"Wow. Really?"

"Yes, son. You're a man now. This is for you. From me." Wingnut caught Sam's glare out of the corner of his eye. "From us."

Sean plucked it from his father's palm, flipped the lid back and ran his thumb down the wheel. It lit smoothly. "Thanks, Dad. Sam." He smiled tearfully and nodded at both of them. Sam managed a flicker of a grim smile in return. "I'll take massive care of it. I promise." Sean closed the lighter and tucked it into his pocket just as Wingnut's phone whistled again.

Wingnut was getting angrier and angrier. He caught the increasing note of desperation in Duffy's texts but realised that continuing to simply refuse to comply wasn't actually getting him anywhere or bringing this conversation to a conclusion. It was time to replace words with action - show Duffy that this was a mutual agreement and you just didn't unilaterally end it, especially when he was having such a fine time of it.

What he should really do, he thought, was send Duffy a message he could not ignore and show him that it wasn't actually up to him to end it. Like doing the deed in Duffy's own bed? While Duffy looked on! That'd show who was in charge here.

Wingnut cracked a lecherous grin. Christmas celebratory shag or farewell shag? Who cared. Let's give the hairy little cuckold hobbit something to really get steamed up about. He tried to tell the time on his watch, failed, and decided it didn't matter anyway.

"Going to call it a night, boys." Wingnut announced when he returned to the table. His sons were staring gloomily at the bottom of their drinks.

"Wha'?" Sam slurred and frowned at his father. "Still early."

"Is it?"

"Aye. It's…" Sam looked around the pub for a clock but couldn't see one. He decided it didn't matter. "Still early. Let me get 'em in." He stood and headed towards the bar. Wingnut sat reluctantly down and looked at Sean who was close to nodding off on the other side of the table. Between them was Sam's chair with his coat draped over it. Wingnut's eyes landed on the coat pocket nearest to him.

"Tell your brother I've got to go. Mercy dash, if you will." Wingnut jerked his thumb towards the door and nodded at Sean to make sure he'd heard him. When Sean returned the nod vacantly, Wingnut stood and put his own coat on, turned towards the bar only to see Sam's broad back as he chatted to the barmaid. He meandered out of the pub, shuffling past the bouncer as a group of rowdy men barged in singing loudly.

The singing was loud and lusty and one of the newcomers to the pub brushed awkwardly past Sam to get to the bar.

"Watch it, pal." Sam grizzled as he picked the three pint glasses off the bar. He looked up into the eyes of a very large man with a bright red face and a black and gold scarf around his neck. The lyrics being chanted filtered through to his brain and Sam realised that he was face-to-face with a group of bevvied-up Melrose supporters, most of whom were considerably larger than him.

"Be fookin' careful yersel'" was the response from this monster closest to him.

Sam dropped his eyes and muttered "Wankers" under his breath.

He thought.

"Wha'dya say?"

"Nothin'"

The red-faced man thrust his face into Sam's, his eyes narrowed and crazy. "What did you say, pail?"

Sam felt the hairs on his neck rise and the unfamiliar flight-or-fight adrenalin rush hit him in his chest.

"What did you call me?"

The man drew himself up to his full height and scowled at him. "I called you a fookin' pail. You are a fookin' pail aint'cha? Pailmerk."

The bouncer reached Sam just as the full pint was smashed against the bar and the glass was being raised to the Melrose fan's face. Sam felt himself lifted bodily off the ground and carried on air, away from the bar and the jostling group. No-one was singing any more. Next thing he knew he was sitting on the cold pavement, damp seeping into the arse of his jeans and Sean gazing woozily down at him, tears in his eyes.

Sam snapped to.

"What're you crying for?"

"We've been barred."

"What?"

"Thrown out and barred."

Sam struggled to his feet, shivering. "Where's me coat? Hey!" he shouted at the bouncer who was standing, arms folded, outside the pub entrance, an impassive gatekeeper. "I've left me coat in there."

"Unlucky."

"I want me coat." Sam hurled himself at the bouncer but the giant just stood his ground with a bored expression on his face that said: *really? this fucking shit again.*

"Come back tomorrow and get it."

"But I want it now. It's freezing!"

"Tough. Fuck off." The bouncer jerked a thumb down the street.

"But it's got me car keys in it."

"You're in no state to drive, pal. Bog off. I'm doing you

a favour."

"What favour?" Sam was indignant. "This is a fucking Gala pub for Gala folk. What've you let some Melrose fuckers in for?"

The bouncer shrugged, already bored of the conversation. This was as much talking as he did all week. Christ, it was like having a girlfriend - all these fucking questions.

"Their money's as good as anyone's."

"Fuck you."

"Yeah, yeah. Merry fucking Christmas. On yer way."

Sean wrapped his arm around his brother's shoulder. "Come on, Sammie. It's late. Dad's gone home. We should too."

Sam let himself be led away, casting a backward glance at the bouncer until they were at the end of the street and he turned and went back inside the pub. Sam looked at his brother, his face dark and menacing.

"No fucking way."

"What?"

"You heard. Do you think I'm goin' to take this lyin' down?"

"Take what? Come on, let's go home."

"Fuck no." Sam muscled up to his brother, snorting beery breath in his face. "Today has been a complete fucking disaster. And I am not havin' it."

"Sammie. Come on. It's Christmas!"

"Christmas, my arse." Sam snarled. "We've been fucking creamed by Melrose, some twat has called me a pail - to my face - and got me thrown out of me own fuckin' pub. I've lost my bloody coat and my fucking keys." Not to mention my fucking useless cretin of a father has taken my fucking Zippo and passed it to my sissie brother like some kind of fucking baton passing in the race of life, he thought. "You and me. We're goin' to teach those fucking Melrose clowns a lesson."

"What sort of lesson?"

Sam leered at his brother, his face a mask of anger in the sodium streetlight. "A history lesson."

PART TWO

IN COURT: THE BOUNCER AGAIN

Waiting for Michael to call them through to the jury box, Cullen scanned his fellow jurors around the table recalling the adage: *If you're the smartest person in the room, you're in the wrong room.* Clockwise around the table, starting at the window seat, there was the businessman - Cullen had overheard him at lunch yesterday introducing himself to Lorraine as Malcolm. There was no doubt in Cullen's mind that this man would be the jury foreman - and he strongly suspected Malcolm shared this view.

His potential alpha-male rival for the position, Frank, sat glaring at the opposite end of the table. He was dishevelled with a day or two's stubble and the acrid tang of cigarette smoke wafted across the room from him whenever he shifted in his chair.

Next to Malcolm was Jean. She was a wee nervous bird of a woman, with a greying perm and a wafer-thin raincoat which she never removed. Jean seemed to possess an instant eye for who was in charge and a need to be close to that authority. She huddled up to Malcolm and kept casting furtive glances in his direction as if seeking constant reassurance that he was still there.

The old woman, Marjorie, was nattering to a well-dressed lady, Moira, in a fur-trimmed collar. She had a well-coiffed head of thick blonde hair, painted nails, patent leather shoes and a matching handbag. There was clearly money there.

Lorraine - the eBay widow - was sitting uneasily, arms

folded, next to Val, who was immersed in her Daily Mail. Next to Val was a spindly young man listening with his eyes closed to some nasty tinny sounds emanating from his earphones. He inserted them every time they came into the jury room and clearly didn't wish to engage with anyone. The only time he seemed to contribute was when there was a show of hands. Val would nudge him and he would dumbly put his hand up. In all likelihood, Malcolm would be having words with him at some point.

Then there were three elderly gentlemen who seemed to appear and disappear together, spent most of their time in close quiet conversation only with each other and, as the trial progressed, had taken to even dressing alike in three-button grey cardigans. The man seated in the middle of the three was distinguishable mainly by a very trim pencil-thin moustache which may or may not have been treated with Grecian Formula and, if ever any contribution from the three was required, it would usually be him that supplied it. The vocal chords of this superannuated hive mind.

Next to him was Jerry who seemed to spend all his time, and mental energy, on the contents of his Racing Post. And next to him was a short, pretty girl with long brown hair framing a heart-shaped face. She had yet to speak. Between the girl and Cullen was Carol, the final member of the fifteen. Whatever the question or situation, Carol was unhappy and wanted to share her misery with those around her.

"This rooms freezing. Don't they have any heating in this bloody place?" She sniped.

"Old buildin's." Said Frank. "All wossname... buggered up the wossname, 'scuse my, erm... pipes clanking. I heard 'em. When I was out having a crafty, erm,

…on the erm…. thing. I was out talking to erm… Marvin. Mitchell. The guy with the badge? Maxwell. They may not build 'em like they used to but they also don't… erm… Michael. That's it."

"Well I wish they'd turn it up. Or turn it on and leave it on. There's a real draft coming under that window." Carol hunkered down in her woollen coat, inching her scarf up around her chin and crossed her arms stiffly to keep hold of every last ounce of body heat she had. She glared accusingly at the window frame and the grey scenery beyond.

"It's like him… thing. In the box… dock. The Accused. You can see he's freezin' n' all. That big trap door down to the cells an' that. Wind'll be whipping right up 'im from there. S'alright for the judge innit? Sheriff. Big ol' wig, heavy cloak. He ain't goin' to feel cold. Me Laddo, though. Not only is he goin' to feel the cold. He'll be feelin' the cold hand o' justice n' all."

While Frank chuckled at his own wordplay, Carol was oblivious to it.

"They're all the same aren't they, these professional classes."

"Huh?"

"The lawyers, the judge."

"Sheriff."

"Sheriff, right. They're making loads of money, wrapped up warm. We're freezing cold and getting paid a pittance for doing our civic duty. It's alright for them. I think it's a bloody disgrace."

"You do get erm… thing. For loss of earnings."

"I'm on a widow's pension. All I'm getting is my bus fare."

"Ah. Well." Frank gave a cross between a shake of the

head and a shrug, unsure how to respond. The wind in his word-blind sails was being swallowed up a towering wall of negativity emanating from this woman.

"And when they all knock off early. Like yesterday? Don't make me laugh. And the Sheriff says: *I'm sure the members of the jury have had a tiring day. Court will reconvene tomorrow at 10am.* Where's he working! Never mind us. It's four o'clock and he's off to the bloody golf course. I've got to stand at a freezing cold bus stop for half an hour waiting for a seat 'cos all the busses are full of schoolkids gobbing on you out of the windows. It's alright for some, s'what I say."

Cullen sighed and stared out of the window until Michael opened the door and led them out into the courtroom.

Counsel for the Defence, Darren Patterson, looked like he had an Honours Degree in smarm. A smooth-shaven peacock, thumbs tucked into the pockets of a pale grey waistcoat beneath his flowing black gown, he strutted and preened - the very model of a young man thrusting with ambition to make his name in the Scottish legal system. He worked for a law firm in Edinburgh and the Sheriff's court in Selkirk was a poor stage for his talents - poor but necessary, if he was to climb smoothly to the heights he considered appropriate to his abilities. He intended to ascend the greasy pole as smoothly as his clients slid inexorably down the razor blade of their own lives. Today Selkirk, tomorrow the Old Bailey.

But, yes alas, today: Selkirk.

Standing at the lectern, he swept his eyes over the jurors arraigned in the box next to him, mentally projecting a message to them all: look at me; do I not represent reasoned argument, success, status? Behold and compare me and this witness, for instance. Look at him - leaning on the lip of the witness box with both hands, flexing his biceps like some demented steroid abuser, his knuckles adorned with homemade tattoos: the fingers of the bouncer's left hand bore the letters P-L-A-N; on his right the letters A-H-E-A.

In terms of who to believe, surely this was no contest. Patterson's job was just to show the jury how right he was and how wrong this witness was. How hard could that be? He addressed the pub bouncer.

"Mr Hawthorne. Do you know - not guess, but know - exactly how much my client, Derek Marshall, had had to drink in The Ship that night?"

"Not exactly-"

"Could it have been merely a reasonable amount?"

"Not really, no."

"Oh, on what grounds do you say that?"

"He was staggering and slurring."

"Signs that you believed him to be drunk?"

"Signs he was drunk."

"Or that he has an underlying medical condition?"

"What?"

"Staggering and slurring. Both recognised symptoms associated with someone who suffers from dysarthria perhaps?"

"What?" The bouncer screwed up his features as if he was squinting into the sun. Patterson took this as a compliment: the sign of a man staring into dazzling brilliance and accepting his inferiority. He glanced down at the list of medical conditions on his notebook and continued.

"Or labyrynthitis - an ear infection?"

"You what?"

"Or early signs of a stroke or a heart condition or hemlytic anaemia… or simply the onset of dehydration-"

"He was dehydrated all right!" The bouncer recovered himself enough to throw this quip in.

"Mr Patterson." The Sheriff tangled with Patterson's momentum. "I trust there is good reason for regurgitating the contents of the BMA's medical dictionary?"

"Yes, my Lord."

"Which is…?"

"I am merely trying to show that the witness cannot necessarily be relied upon as to the state of my client's sobriety and that there may, indeed, be an explanation for his observations that he is unaware of."

"And you intend to refer to your client's medical history at some point to tie this altogether?"

"Indeed, my Lord." Patterson lied smoothly.

"Well, see that you do." The Sheriff made a note in his own notebook, presumably to remind himself to chastise Patterson when the time came. Patterson smoothed imaginary crumbs from his waistcoat to conceal his irritation and then returned to the man in the witness box.

"Mr. Hawthorne, are you sure it was my client who was the ringleader in the kerfuffle at The Ship, that night?"

"Aye."

"Really? Because wasn't it the case that the pub was very crowded by this time. The time when it all *kicked off*?" Patterson put everything he had into belittling the bouncer's own words.

"It were busy, yeah."

"Yes. It was very busy. And the Melrose supporters were rowdy and there was a crush at the bar I imagine.

Boxing Day evening presumably a busy night in the pub?"

"Yes. Always busy."

"And your station was, as you explained, over at the main entrance to the pub?"

"'Sright."

"And, in The Ship, how far would you say that is from the bar area where Mr Marshall was?"

The bouncer looked up onto the wall, seeking some reference measurement.

"Five, six yards maybe?"

"How about ten yards, Mr Hawthorne."

"Nah. It's never ten." The bouncer shook his head.

"Well, ok. You are quite correct." Hawthorne smiled victoriously and looked at the jury for acknowledgement. Patterson pressed on. "It is actually 9.6 yards, but I assume you will allow me to round up that extra foot or so?"

"Eh?"

"Yes, I measured it myself last week. 9.6 yards from door to bar." Patterson was the one smiling now. "9.6 yards across which were many bodies, people passing between you and my client with drinks, loud conversations, jostling and laughing. Perhaps a juke box blaring? Am I painting an accurate picture?"

The bouncer shuffled uneasily in the witness box.

"Mr Hawthorne?"

"Don't have a jukebox." He mumbled.

"No? Well, perhaps that element of the tapestry is the result of my overactive imagination. Forgive me." Patterson smiled magnanimously at the jury. "But I put it to you, Mr Hawthorne, that the picture you have painted is far from accurate. Isn't it closer to the truth to say that it was a packed pub, heaving with dozens of large burly men - many of them drunk, supporters from both sides -

and that you were a lone figure in this crowd. A fine figure of a man, to be sure, able to deal with two or perhaps three disorderly rugby fans, but dozens? And across this crowded, noisy room, you can hear and see a scuffle break out. Albeit ten yards away. Your priority is to stifle it, with the minimum of violence - not least to yourself. So you scoot over there as fast as you can, mindless of who did what and who said what to whom - details that can be corroborated or invented later-"

"Mr Patterson!" The Sheriff warned.

"Sorry, my Lord. Details which could be… secured later. Right now, eject someone - anyone - who seems to be prominent in the melee. Put a stake in the ground and show that no trouble will be had here, you're in charge, and that any difficulty will be stamped out as quickly as it starts. You didn't care who's neck you grabbed, which heads you knocked together. Pick someone, anyone, out and eject them as an example to the others. And do it quickly and smoothly before it all *kicks off*. Because, if it really were to all *kick off*, the whole pub would turn into a battleground and the impact one man like yourself could have, would be minimal. Negligible. Pointless."

Patterson watched as Hawthorne stood and glowered, and pushed on - every inch he gained was another inch less the jury needed to be nudged.

"So you ejected someone. Anyone. Show them who's boss, hmm?"

"No"

"Perhaps not even my client? Someone else?"

"No." Hawthorne managed, clearly feeling under attack now.

"Really, Mr Hawthorne? When did you actually find out about the pailmerk insult? That was afterwards wasn't it? Long afterwards, when the place was emptier and quieter and you had time to ask around? Isn't that the case?"

"No."

"I put it to you that it was, Mr Hawthorne." Patterson tightened his smile and gave a nod to the jury at his side. "That, in doing your job, which was keeping order, you jettisoned someone from the pub, thus managing to keep order. And were able to construct a justification for your actions, after the fact, so that everyone was happy. You were happy. Your boss, the landlord, was happy. The other customers were happy. And the only person who wasn't happy, was the person who no longer mattered because he was no longer a patron of your establishment. And that person was not my client."

"That's not what happened." Hawthorne said, his jaw set.

"Isn't it? Are you sure, Mr Hawthorne? Isn't it possible that that is what actually happened? Is it so preposterous a possibility?" Hawthorne didn't answer but Patterson no longer cared. He smiled over at the jury and let his gaze linger as he scanned each row. "I'll leave the ladies and gentlemen of the jury to make their own minds up."

"Mr Patterson! I trust this is the end of your showboating for today?" The Sheriff said, but Patterson had closed his large notebook with a thud and was striding from the lectern, his gown floating on air, an easy grin on his face.

"No further questions, my Lord."

Behind the rail, Wingnut leant back in his seat and smiled broadly at the jury.

BOXING DAY: PART II

The Greenyards ground, and the whole of Melrose it seemed, was quiet and dark by the time Sam and Sean had walked there. They came in over the footbridge from Gattonside and along the lane, skulking past a row of large detached houses sitting behind high stone walls and neatly trimmed beech hedges.

Standing at the back of the ground, the main (and only) stand stood on their left and the pitch stretched before them, out towards the low wall at the far end and the main road into town. Their breath rose steamily in the night air as they trod up the back of the frosty bank which led them down onto the marked-out turf. Sam was shivering without his coat, despite the brisk pace he'd led them on from Galashiels.

"We need to get these goalposts down first." Sam looked up at the white metal construction towering above them.

"We should go." Sean said, looking nervously around. "This is a bad idea."

"Is it fuck" Sam shot in a loud whisper. "They've got this coming to them. Had this coming for a long time. Over a hundred years actually."

"What are you on about?"

"You should know your history better, Tiny Tim. In the 1880's Melrose literally stole the goalposts from Gala's ground and brought them here to set up their own rugby pitch they could play on. We never got 'em back and these are those very posts."

Sean looked dubiously up at the towering poles. "I don't think so, Sam. These look almost brand-new." He rapped one with his knuckle and the icy echo rang out around the ground. Sean looked warily around, afraid.

"Well, alright. Those old ones probably rotted away or something. That's irrelevant. Detail. What's important is that we get them back for the damage they done all those years ago. Bastards not only stole the goalposts, they ran off with our fucking strips. Did you know that? We used to play in black and gold and they took the strip and made it their own. That's why we wear maroon. And that is why, tonight, Gala will be avenged!" Sam raised one fist in salute into the air.

"Ssshhhh!" Sean hissed. "Someone'll hear us!"

"Who the fuck's gonna hear us? It's gone midnight. In Melrose! The posh twats round here all turn in before ten, Boxing Day or no. Cocoa and slippers and the fucking Telegraph crossword in their pyjamas. Or summat. Detail. Irrelevant." Sam glared at his brother, daring him to disobey. "Come on, let's start a fire!" The light in his eyes shone brightly at the mere mention of the word and Sean could imagine his whole face flickering and grinning in the reflected light of a furious blaze.

"You're going to set light to goalposts?"

"No. *We're* gonna set light to goalposts."

"Well, I'm not."

"Oh yeah?" Sam thrust his face up into his brother's, his beery breath punching him in the cold air. "Why not?"

"Well, firstly, I don't want to. And secondly, I don't think you can actually set fire to metal."

Sam swivelled his eyes in thought, looking as if this aspect of their endeavour had only just occurred to him.

"Can't you?"

"Not without a blowtorch or something. And then I think it would just melt. I don't think metal is flammable." He looked at his brother, suddenly crestfallen. "Do you have a blowtorch?"

"No!" Sam crumpled up his face. "But maybe there's one in the groundsman's hut. Or summat." He strode off towards the stands and Sean stood watching him go, torn. After a few moments he thrust his hands in his pockets and scampered after his brother.

"Right." The sweat was dripping off Sam's brow but he had beaten the bloody posts. They had heaved and pulled and swayed like two mighty highlanders tossing enormous white cabers. But they had managed to pluck the posts from the turf and watch them collapse onto the frosty ground, reverberating with an icy wha-a-a-a-ng. With them down and laid out on the ground, Sam now stood proudly, arms on hips like some rugby superhero as he surveyed the damage done to both turf and posts. "Ok. Now, phase two."

Sean looked on, dismayed. "Can't we just leave it like this, Sammy?"

"No, we fucking can't. This job is getting done. Tonight."

"But it's really late. And we've made a hell of a noise. And someone is going to see us and we'll get done for this and-"

"Will you shut your snivelling and give me a fucking hand here?" Sam snarled at his brother. Sean took his hands out of his pockets and skulked over. They each lifted up one end of the goalposts, like dragging a pair of gigantic pole vaults, albeit joined together by a crossbar several metres away. Their weight was considerable and it took all their heft and muscle to wrangle them into anything approaching a grip.

"Right. Drag 'em over this way." Sam nodded towards the centre of the pitch.

"What for?" Sean hissed.

"It's called making a statement, Thumbelina. On three."

The pair dragged the posts slowly across the pitch, their trailing ends kicking up frost and gouging two furrows through the turf. Struggling to get a firm grip on the slippery metal, the brothers inched their way, huffing and puffing. Like Egyptian slaves hauling stones up the side of the Great Pyramid, the boys dragged the posts to the halfway line. Waiting for them, were two stuffed and heavy bin bags that Sam had retrieved from the groundsman's storage shelter beneath the stands.

When Sam gave the word, they dropped the weighty posts onto the ground, again with a dull echoing clang. Sean wiped his brow with a sleeve and looked anxiously around once more. "Right, can we go now? Please?"

"Not so fast, matey boy. One last job to do." Sam bent down to open the neck of a bin bag and started pulling out rugby shirts, shorts and socks. Melrose RFC kit, the yellow vivid even in the moonlight.

"Now what?" Sean was freezing cold and bemused. Clammy from sweating made him feel even colder.

"Stuff a shirt into the ends here-" Sam illustrated that Sean should copy him. "And then… swaddle… the posts… with whatever… will stay… wrapped… around… 'em." Sam was mummifying his piece of the goalposts, wrapping it in rugby kit, winding each garment clumsily down his post like a badly applied bandage. He looked up to see Sean staring blankly at him. "They took our strip and they stole our posts. Now they shall reap the whirlwind. Come on! Don't just stand there."

Sean numbly picked a couple of items randomly from his bin bag and started wrapping them around the post, resting its full weight on one knee as he worked his way down its length, pausing to retrieve more kit from the bag as needed and then shifting his knee down the post to apply this new swaddling. It was slow and heavy work but when both bin bags were empty, the goalposts were two-thirds covered in yellow-striped cotton, lying on the icy turf like a enormous, badly-bandaged TV aerial.

Sam half-stood, panting, hands on his knees; his lungfuls clouding the air, wreathing him in his own breath. Sean waited uncertainly for his brother to get his breath back, ears pricked for the faintest dog bark or slightest indication of movement. All was still.

Eventually, Sam stood erect and composed.

"Right. Hand me the lighter, Seanie."

Sean looked at his brother, horrified. "What? No."

"What do you mean, No? What do you think we've just done all this for? Give me the fucking lighter."

Sean unconsciously handled the Zippo in his trouser pocket. It may have been a belated birthday gift from his father, but he knew by rights it was really Sam's. And that was one key difference between the brothers - although, in truth, there were many. Sam treasured this lighter, and the memories of his father that it embodied; Sean held dear the spinning necklace his mother had given them both, as a much more emotional and meaningful representation of parental love than a shiny fire-starter. That was an enlightening illustration of what separated their mother and father right there - symbolically: one represented by a brash, flashy piece of technology designed with the express purpose of destruction; the other by a small, delicate, precious object of beauty that could be worn next to the skin and need never be taken off. Sean knew which one he preferred.

"No. I'm not doing this." Sean heard a voice say; quiet but calm and sure. It was his own.

"Fuck you are."

"No, I'm not."

Sam stood and squared up angrily at his brother, muscling his face right into Sean's own, his breath ragged between them. "Give me the fucking Zippo."

"No."

"Sean. It's mine."

"Was. Was yours. Dad has now passed it to me. So it's mine. And you're not having it. And certainly not using it to do.... this!"

"Sean. If you don't want to do this, then don't." Sam backed off a little, as if adjusting his strategy. "But I'm doing it. And you're not going to stop me."

Sean stared lazily at his brother and said nothing. Sam waited briefly and then resumed his verbal attack.

"Give me the lighter and then leave me to get this done."

"No." Sean shoved his hands deeper into his pockets, as if protecting the lighter from being reached.

Sam pounced. He launched himself at his brother who, hands still in pockets, was less stably planted on the ground. Sam's ferocity and weight felled them both but, by the time they hit the turf, Sean had freed his hands and was wrestling with his brother as he tried to reach into his pocket for the lighter. They rolled back and forth in the frost, each grappling for dominance, until Sam managed to use his momentum to end a roll on top of Sean. He momentarily abandoned his raid on his brother's pocket, pulled himself up so that he was sitting on Sean's chest, and then slammed his right fist into his brother's face.

Sean's head rocked to the side and his face was plunged into the icy ground. He spotted the Zippo shining on the frosty ground a few feet away and Sam followed his gaze, scrambled off his brother and lunged for the lighter. Sean struggled up onto his elbows and watched, defeated, as Sam brandished the Zippo with a leer and then stomped off back to the goalposts.

Sam liberally squirted lighter fluid on the shirt swathing one goalpost end and watched the flame catch. As it flared and snacked its way along the pole, he moved over to the other post and did the same. Within thirty seconds the entire upper-half of both goalposts was alive with flame.

The pair watched as the smell of burning cotton rose into the night sky. Sean stood, shoulders sagging, deflated by his failure to stop his brother. He looked across at him, the bright fire flickering in Sam's crazy eyes.

Sam smiled "Phase Three!"

"What?"

But Sam didn't answer. He just turned and ran towards the stand.

Winding the window down, Wingnut had hoped that when the icy air hit him like a fully loaded chest freezer, he would feel himself sober up. Nope.

Well fuck it. His blood was up and he had a plan. Duffy had told him to have a fucking plan, and now he had one. Let's see how the fucker liked it.

The track to Duffy's house was rutted and icy. The van bumped and jostled as Wingnut tried to wrestle the vehicle into keeping away from the ditch on one side and the electrified fence on the other. As the house came into view, at the top of the steepest section of the incline, Wingnut felt the van starting to backslide. He revved harder and begged for the wheels to bite.

In hindsight, it was probably unfortunate that they did. One minute he was sliding inexorably backwards, the next he was shooting forwards, skeetering left and right and finding that the brakes weren't hugely effective on this rutted surface. The rickety fence in front of Duffy's property was insufficiently robust to stop a two tonne Transit in full flight.

Neither was the front of the house.

Wingnut released his grip on the wheel at the last minute and held both arms in front of his face to protect himself from the collision. It was only when the van came to a stop and all around him was a sudden, fresh silence, that he realised four things:

1. He had crashed the van into Duffy's house and he was still alive.

2. He was clearly drunk and couldn't for the life of him understand why this had not occurred to him earlier.

3. No-one had seen him.

4. He no longer had an erection

With the quiet conviction of a zealot, shocked into sobriety by the invasive cold, Wingnut fell out of the driver's seat and staggered out into the snow. His hands were shaking and his right knee hurt but he could put one foot in front of the other. Bent into the wind, he headed back down towards the road. When he reached the crest of the hill, he stopped briefly to look back at the carnage he had left behind. Half the van was embedded in the side of the caravan-style bay, the windows amazingly intact. The impact had thrown back some of the roofing sheets and pieces of timber, a few had been propelled forwards somehow and dropped to the ground. The overall impression was that the roof structure was now more solidly aligned and the coverage had actually increased. One of the two-by-four gable ends had been pushed inward and now stood more upright than before.

Wingnut wondered if the crash hadn't actually added to the overall stability of Duffy's makeshift construction.

In the still night air, Duffy angled his face this way and that, letting the icy breeze cool his cheeks and ruffle his hair. This hill - this precise spot on the hill - was where he had watched and waited over the years. Heather had come here with him once. Back in the early days when he was still formulating his theories and pondering the universe. She had loved him, he knew; it hadn't been her just humouring him like so many of his erstwhile, so-called friends. Her sisterly support and love had been genuine and he truly missed it. They had sat on this spot and chatted, shared some Bovril and watched the stars. She had listened to him babble and theorise, resting her head on his shoulder, content to let him speak and have his voice wash over her. She could have been asleep, so quiet and comfortable and reassuring had been her presence. He remembered it clearly. Remembered it every time he came back up here.

As he shifted his face this way and that, he heard a faint shout carried on the breeze. Then another. He couldn't establish the direction and the night was now too dark for his binoculars to be trained on anything. He cast his gaze over the sleeping town from his southerly vantage point: the ruined abbey, gently spotlit in the East; the Tweed meandering to the North, a thick, black band edging the ribbon of street lights which marked out the Gattonside road; the rugby ground to the West, a black hole in amongst the scattered lights of the large houses that surrounded it.

And there, from nowhere - shimmering in this dark void out West - was his sign. Goose-pimples rose on his skin, the hair crackled and rose on the back of his neck. He scrambled to his feet, staring and blinking hard as if to force himself to make sure that what he was seeing was real. His fluttering hands stilled and his notebook fell to the ground, unheeded. Standing now with fists clenched, he looked up to the stars for any indication of movement and found none. Dropping his eyes back again to the sign, he blinked deliberately once more to check that this was not a mirage. The sign remained. If anything, it had grown bigger and brighter and continued to do so as he looked at it.

This was it. He had no doubt. Eight years of waiting was at an end. Duffy started to cry. Couldn't help himself. Below him, displayed - he was confident - only for him, was a flaming, blazing, upper case H.

H for Heather.

Sandra, Des's ex-wife, used to describe him as a slimy, oleaginous scumbag who thought he was God's gift to women. On a good day.

That was why she was his ex. That, and the fact that he had been about as faithful as a whippet at a lamp-post. Des wasn't picky because Des wasn't God's gift - not unless the God you're talking about was a particularly unimaginative and unfussy God with questionable standards. Des was a ladies man who was a little too jowly, a little too paunchy and a little too stupid to be what he aspired to be: the Melrose George Clooney. He was more like the Culross George Melly.

Desmond Arthur Halliwell was the Honourable President and the Honourable Treasurer of the Melrose Rugby Club. As Big Swinging Dicks went, he was, well, a Dick.

Post-divorce he had become a denizen of Gala's tanning salon - Melrose wouldn't be caught dead with a tanning salon within its boundaries - and a frequent patron of a new Turkish Barbers, Face/Off, which had opened up on Dingleton Road. In his heyday he had possessed a full head of brown hair but, as his waist had thickened his thatch had thinned, and he had resorted to comb-overs and comb-backs to hide an ever-increasing bald patch. Reluctant to go the full Trump, he had reluctantly had it shorn down to a buzzcut and dyed so that he now resembled an out-of-condition, platinum-blonde action man with alopecia.

He was wearing a pale blue linen jacket with the sleeves rolled up to better reveal his tan and, one of his best features (he thought), his thick and hairy forearms. Underneath this he wore a bright white polo shirt, fully buttoned for maximum smartness, and a pair of black trousers which nestled perfectly atop his black tassled loafers. If this had been Miami sunshine, in the nineties, he would have looked right at home. In Melrose's wintry greyness he looked like an aged nightclub-singer throwback trying to squeeze into clothes that were a size too small.

Des, however, thought he looked the business.

And, tonight, being Boxing Day when standards dropped and blood-alchohol content rose, so too did Audrey. It was safe to say that, for the past month or so, Audrey had had the hots for Des and she had decided, after a couple of Bacardi's and a nudge from her pals, that she was going to get him. He was going to be the Christmas cracker she intended to pull.

Audrey hadn't had her share of men since her husband had passed on. He hadn't died, he had just passed on… to a younger model who had stolen his heart, his energy and finally his money. Last Audrey had heard, he was looking for his future in the bottom of a pint glass over in Lauder while his blonde bimbette was shagging her way through the Cricket team second XI. She raised a glass to him: serve him bloody well right.

She had kept her powder dry, looking for Mister Right and as far as she was concerned, if Des wasn't Mister Right, he was top candidate for Mister Right Now.

The aftermath of Melrose's win over Gala at the Rugby Club had been raucous. When the last of the regulars had rolled home, Des had given a wink to Terry behind the bar and told him that he would lock up, nodding his head over to Audrey who was slumped unconscious on the banquette next to him. Terry had draped his tea-towel over the beer pumps and shucked his jacket on, leaving Des with a thumbs up and a knowing grin.

Des turned to what he now considered unambiguously to be his promise for the night and tried to loosen Audrey's blouse. She woke with a start and sat up, accidentally headbutting him in the process.

"Oof! Fucking hell!" Des put a hand to his nose and it

came away bright red. He looked down through unfocussed eyes and saw a spreading scarlet stain on his pristine shirt.

"Sorry, lover! Sorry, sorry." Audrey waggled her head to and fro, shaking off what may have been a headbutt to him but had actually cleared her own wooziness. She put her hand on the back of his fuzzy-felt head and pulled him down onto her bosom - currently enhanced by a cup-size-too-small Ultimo. The gush from his nose bled freshly onto her own sparkly top and she recoiled, annoyed. "Ooh, now look! I'm going to have to take this off."

Des sobered up rapidly and pulled his head out of Audrey's ample bosom, admiring the way the bloodstain contoured her curves. He pulled off his jacket and used it to stem the flood from his nose. "Good idea." He muffled through the linen. "It's easy to get blood out of linen, is it?"

"No idea." Audrey replied, through the polyester as she pulled her top over her head. "You bothered?"

Des looked at the mottled cleavage and shimmering tattoo of a leaping tiger over her left shoulder and felt a familiar surge in his pants. "Not really, no. Is that a Sumatran tiger?"

"Hmm?" Audrey was busy looking for her drink which she was sure she had left somewhere to hand. There was currently no sign of a glass anywhere. "Sure, why not? Any chance of another drinkie-doo, lover?"

"Sure." Des stood up making every attempt to draw her attention to the erection in his trousers. "It's just that I was in Sumatra, back in the nineties, and I remember-"

"You've been to Sumatra?"

"Uh-huh. Was on a month-long business trip out in the Far East. Stopped off at Singapore, Hong Kong, Kuala

Lumpur-" He purred. "See these? I brought these back. Had 'em framed." Des pointed to a few signed rugby shirts up on the walls.

"Wow!" Audrey stood unsteadily and tottered over to get a closer look. Halfway, she stooped and removed her heels, which took four inches off her height. She padded over to the frames.

"Yeah, well. Done a lot of travelling in my time. Mainly business, you know. Champagne?"

"Lovely." She said as she traced the shirt outlines wonderingly in their frames. "I've never been out of Scotland." She sighed. "Although been to Gretna, that counts as England doesn't it?"

Des preened as he dived into the mini-fridge behind the bar and plucked out a bottle of Prosecco, his nosebleed forgotten. "I'll allow it." He came back to the table with two flutes and opened the bottle with a quiet pop.

"Where else have you been?" She asked as she traced her way along the wall, frame by frame.

"America, Australia… er, Albufeira." He managed. "That's just the A's."

"Wow." She reached the end of the frames and stood in front of the display cabinet, eyes lingering on the silverware. "Here! Never mind drinking out of those." She turned and nodded to the flutes. "Let's drink out of these!" She pointed back to the trophies, eyes wide with naughtiness.

"Well, er. Not such a good idea, really. They're rather-"

"I'll give you a champagne blowjob!"

Des dived into his pocket for the key and unlocked the cabinet.

Sam reached the relative safety of the darkness beneath the stand and started trying every door handle he came across. He was so surprised when one actually moved that he tried it twice to make sure it wasn't a dream. The hinges didn't even creak and he slid smoothly into the corridor and cocked his head left and right to catch any sounds. Nothing.

He trod warily along the dark corridor towards a bright yellow light at the end, stopping every so often to hold his breath and listen. He thought he could make out faint voices but he only caught snatches here and there so wasn't sure.

Until he rounded the corner and looked through the door of the trophy room.

The man wore a plain white polo shirt and nothing else. His trousers were down around his ankles, showing a pale hairy arse, tanned legs and the merest hint of white ankle sock. The woman - Sam assumed it was a woman but she was largely hidden from view - was bent over the table as the man thrust into her from behind. Each thrust was accompanied by a muffled *oof* and the occasional female moan. He could make out some bright red nail varnish on hands gripping the front of the table furthest away from him, presumably for purchase.

Between him and the coupling couple was a small side table on which sat a small silver chalice atop a blue crumpled jacket, covered in what looked like blood. Sam watched mesmerised for about twenty seconds and then, as the man's tempo quickened and the noises became more urgent, he made an executive decision. He took three steps forward and snatched the chalice off the table.

It released a large splurge of liquid over the jacket and splattered on the floor. Without looking back, Sam bolted back down the corridor and out into the night, holding the silverware aloft as if he had just crossed the finishing line with it.

He ran headlong into Sean who was striding around the corner of the stand.

"What's that?" Sean asked, partially winded.

"Memento." Sam grinned and slurped the last of the liquid from the cup. "Mmm. Tastes like success to me!"

"Where'd you get it?"

"Never mind. Come on, our work here is done." He broke into a jog and headed back along the stands towards the rear entrance through which they'd come.

"Hey! Wait." Sean half-heartedly followed after. "Did anyone see you?"

"Oi! You, there! Stop!" A bold shout echoed across the pitch.

"Looks like it!" Shouted Sam over his shoulder. "Last one home's an arsewipe!"

The pair accelerated up over the bank and out through the gap in the wall, running along the road and away into the night.

Sergeant Walker fucking hated nights. But he also hated Christmas, so it was swings and roundabouts wasn't it? On the night shift, bad. On his todd, good. Over Christmas and Boxing Day night, bloody excellent. Triple time, nothing to do except watch the telly and eat pork pies he'd got on the knock-off late on Christmas Eve when the Co-op was about to shut down for the duration. Bloody marvellous.

What could possibly go wrong?

Well, the winking red light on the alarm control panel is what. It took him a while to twig and then he had to check the manual to find out which system had been triggered. But when he saw it was the trophy cabinet at the Greenyards he heaved a sigh, thought *Ah, well, could be worse. It's only over the road* and shrugged on his overcoat.

When he opened the front door, smelt burning cotton and saw flames and smoke rising from the pitch, he grabbed his radio, hat and truncheon and bolted across the road.

There was never any risk of him giving chase to the two shadowy figures running off in the direction of St Mary's Road. Not at his age, or weight. He gave his best menacing shout and called for backup on the radio. Seeing a door swinging open and a light on inside he looked around in case any other figures should be lurking in the shadows, and trod warily over to the main stand, truncheon firmly in his grasp.

When he entered the trophy room, truncheon extended, he saw a half-naked, bleeding man with his head in his hands. A woman with her back to him was fastening her bra and hastily shuffling a skirt up from around her hips.

"Hello, Audrey." Walker said.

The woman looked up, shocked, and smiled thinly, not a little embarrassed. "Oh. Hello Frank."

"What's with the alarm then?" He addressed the man who was still holding his head, moaning. "I can see pitch is on fire 'n' that, but …" Walker scanned the open trophy cabinet to his left. "The alarm's for the cabinet."

The man raised his head and looked at Walker like a puppy caught with a pet tortoise in its mouth. Walker looked him up and down.

"And you are?"

"Des Halliwell. Club President." He rolled his eyes and nodded his head back to indicate he meant *this* club. "I am authorised to be here."

"I bet." Walker threw a look at Audrey again as she finished dressing and then turned back to Des. "And are you authorised to set the alarm off?"

"I didn't mean to."

"There's keys in the door."

"Well, I opened the cabinet." Des winced. "Obviously."

"And took out a trophy."

"Yes." Quieter now.

"To do what with it, exactly?" The silence was palpable. Walker looked over at Audrey as Des hung his head. "Hmm?"

Audrey was brushing her hair as if Walker had just walked into her bedroom while she was getting ready. "Just wanted a little drinkie-doo from it. That's all, Frank. Really."

"Uh-huh." Walker cast his eyes around the carnage in the room. "Just the pair of you?"

"That's right." Des glared up at Walker. "Just the two of us."

"So… where's the cup then?"

"What?"

"The Ladies' Cup."

Des followed Walker's eyes to the empty space in the wall cabinet. "Oh."

"Aye."

"Oh, bollocks." Des scanned the room wildly, standing up and casting clothes and bottles around hoping to find something hidden. "Where's the fucking Cup?"

"Is that we're calling it now, then?" Walker couldn't help stifle an amused chortle.

"Hey! This isn't fucking funny. Oh shit. Shit shit shit shit." Des slumped back into his chair and put his head back in his hands. His shame was as palpable as the dried blood caking his nose and mouth. "I'm fucked."

"Aye. Looks like you have been." Said Walker.

IN COURT: KATE

"Latest thing? He's only gone and bought a motorcycle sidecar!" This was Lorraine. "In Orkney, I ask you! Orkney!"

Val desperately wanted to finish the quick crossword in her *Chat!* magazine - clue: useless cretin who judges on X Factor (5,6) - but this woman's incessant chatter was worming into her brain and restricting the blood supply to her treasure chest of TV and showbiz knowledge. She gave a stilted smile with her mouth but not her eyes, and hoped her silence and the non-committal set of her remaining facial features would communicate the lack of interest necessary for this jabbering woman to give up the ghost.

It didn't.

"Doesn't even own a motorbike!" Lorraine continued. "God alone knows how he's going to get it home from there! And then, what's he going to do with it when he gets it? If he thinks he's going to get a motorbike at his age he's got another think coming! It's like I was telling that lady." Lorraine pointed to Moira.

Moira nodded, sagely, but kept her counsel. She already knew the only way to let Hurricane Lorraine blow herself out was let her monologue herself into silence. It was Jerry, not even bothering to look up from the form guide for the 2.15 at Haydock Park, who stopped her - and everyone else - in their tracks.

"Well, just because he did it, doesn't mean he's guilty."

"What?" Lorraine looked at Jerry in astonishment. "You do know you just said that out loud?"

"So?" Jerry shrugged, sucking his pen. "It's true."

"How can it be true? Listen to yourself. If he did it, he did it. Therefore he's guilty. Jesus!"

"Not if it was self-defence."

The businessman at the other end of the table, shook his head wearily and wagged his pen in Jerry's direction. "You can't drive a car into someone else's house in self-defence!"

"Van." Corrected Lorraine.

"Car, van, same difference." The businessman waved a hand dismissively. "And it's irrelevant right now. We don't know he did it. Way too early to be jumping to conclusions."

"Yes." Added Lorraine. "And the fact is-"

"Yeah, that's all we need - bloody facts!" Interrupted Frank. "We're supposed to be listening to wossname. Evidence. If I want facts I can watch thing. David Attenborough."

"I really do hope you're joking" Swatted Lorraine, not in the least amused.

"My daughter had a car drive into the back of her at the lights over Christmas." Val spoke up. "I bet he did it."

The businessman glared at her.

"And his eyes are close together. That's a dead giveaway." She added.

"Give me strength." sighed the businessman, still completing his slow series of headshakes.

The room fell into an awkward silence until Marjorie chimed in.

"I'm eighty-two, you know?"

"We know." The businessman placed his pen precisely

on his pad and clasped his hands, as if in prayer.

"I thought she said she was eighty-five?" whispered Jean, next to him.

"Whatever." He said. "Twelve good men and true. What a joke."

"Fifteen in Scotland." Said Marjorie.

Kate sat outside the courtroom waiting to be recalled, skimming through email on her phone. The lack of imagination or initiative of some of her colleagues baffled her. The police, she felt, had managed to take the democratic ideal to its logical extremes: not only did they no longer discriminate on the grounds of race, creed or colour, but also now on the grounds of ability. She stabbed a response to the most recent email, only to hear the courtroom door open and her name called.

She dropped the phone into her laptop bag, stood up, strode into the courtroom and climbed up into the witness box. She put her bag down on the floor and stood erect, both hands on the lectern edging, waiting to take the oath.

"Please take the book in your left hand. Do you swear by Almighty God, to tell the truth, the whole truth and nothing but the truth?"

Kate looked sadly at the bible she'd been handed. What was she doing? This was all wrong - the whole system was wrong. Wrong enough already, without this need to drag religion into it. To her mind, religion was like a penis: it's ok to have one, it's ok to be proud of it. It's not ok to force it on your children, ram it down people's throats, or base your laws on it.

"I do." She raised her eyes to the ceiling as she finished speaking.

"You are Detective Superintendent Lorimer, Borders Police. Is that correct?"

"Um, yes." She blinked hard and turned her attention to the barrister. "Yes. I am." She added, more focussed and forceful.

"And in what capacity were you involved in the incident on the night of Boxing Day last year?"

"I was called to attend the site of an incident involving a van having been driven into a building."

"The building in question being the residence of Macduff and Gloria Ingoglia?"

"Correct."

"Was it usual for you to be on duty on Boxing Day?"

"Not at all." Kate set her jaw. "I wasn't actually on duty at the time."

"Really?" Said Whittaker. "So why did you attend the scene?"

"Well, I had been called by the station because of an unrelated incident at The Greenyards earlier that night."

"The Greenyards. That's Melrose rugby ground, is that right?"

"Yes. There'd been an... incident. And since I live locally *and* I'm on the committee the Duty Sergeant called me and suggested I came and had a look. While I was wrapping that up, the call about the van came in so I went along. Strike while the iron is hot so to speak." Kate smiled thinly.

"Sorry, I don't follow."

"Well, if there's any evidence at the scene, your best chance is to get there early. Reduce the possibility of tampering or contamination because someone's been careless or forgotten to make sure everyone is aware not to touch anything."

"And did you find any evidence?"

"The vehicle had been abandoned when I got there. But the sole witness, Gloria Ingoglia, said she recognised the driver. And Forensics found Derek Marshall's fingerprints on the vehicle and fibres from his clothing on the driver's seat."

"I see. So you were in no doubt that Mr Marshall had been the driver at the time of the incident?"

"Correct."

"So you arrested Mr Marshall?"

"Yes. I went around to his house first thing in the morning and arrested him."

"Thank you, Superintendent. Would you remain there please in case my colleague has any questions for you."

Patterson gathered up his paperwork and passed Whittaker on her way back to her desk.

"Superintendent." He began. "Who is the owner of the vehicle?"

"It is a company vehicle, registered to Fine Motor Skills Limited. The company where Sam Marshall works. The vehicle is one assigned regularly to him."

"Sam is Derek's son, correct?"

"Correct."

"So this vehicle was used by Sam a lot, would you say?"

"Depends what you mean by a lot."

"Well, regularly then? More often than not, perhaps?"

"Regularly yes."

"And would it be unusual, then, to find his father's prints in the vehicle?"

"Not just in the vehicle, on the steering wheel."

"Could his prints not have found their way onto the steering wheel without him sitting at the wheel?"

"No."

"Have you never been a passenger in a car and had cause to touch the steering wheel? Perhaps when the vehicle was stationary? Or when reaching into a cubby or for a door handle?"

"No."

"I put it to you, Superintendent, that it is entirely possible - if not likely - that this could be innocently done."

Patterson waited for Kate to respond but she didn't.

"Superintendent?"

"You didn't ask a question."

"Ah. Quite so. My mistake." Patterson said through gritted teeth. "Isn't it the case, that my client could have actually driven this vehicle before the incident and left his fingerprints on the wheel then?"

"It is possible, although the prints were fresh and some were very distinct. You would expect some partials or unclear prints whenever someone drove the van. But to have clear prints on the wheel would imply they were from the last driver. And that no-one had driven it since."

"But it is possible?"

"It is unlikely."

"But possible?"

"Theoretically possible, yes. Practically possible, no."

"Or that anyone could have driven the vehicle after my client left prints on the wheel if they had been wearing driving gloves?"

Kate snorted. "Nobody wears driving gloves anymore."

"Really, Superintendent?"

Kate gave Patterson a look which clearly said *give me a break*.

"Would you be interested in the sales figures for

driving gloves in the UK last year? I have them here." He brandished a sheaf of papers in his right hand. "Or that there is a company which has been trading since the eighteenth century - before cars were even invented - who have been making and selling leather gloves since then and have a particular style of driving glove, which is one of their bestsellers?"

Kate stood her ground and remained silent. Patterson pressed on.

"I put it to you, Superintendent, that you cannot guarantee that my client was the driver of the van at the time of the incident. That there are other ways in which his prints could have got on the steering wheel and that there are other possible circumstances which could have caused his prints to remain on the wheel until the time you brushed it for fingerprints."

Patterson was so pleased with himself that he only realised he had again forgotten to ask a question when he paused for effect. He quickly recovered. "Isn't that the truth, Superintendent?"

"Give me strength." Kate said under her breath.

"I'm sorry?" Patterson asked innocently.

"Superintendent, could you speak up please so that the court may hear you?" The Sheriff encouraged.

"Sorry, my Lord." Kate set her jaw. "It is highly likely, in my view - and very probable - that the prints we found were those of the driver of the vehicle at the time of the incident."

"But can you guarantee it?" Patterson insisted.

"If you want a guarantee, buy a toaster." Kate snarked.

Patterson broke into a smile. "Thank you, Superintendent. That will be all."

Kate stooped to pick up her handbag and when she

raised her head she saw Cullen staring at her from the jury box. Her mouth involuntarily fell open and she felt the world wheel silently around her, the jury box the only stationary image.

THE POLICE

"Sarah, do we have to have a debate? It's Christmas!." Kate raised another biscuit to her mouth. "Hmm, these are nice." She managed through a mouthful of chewy moistness.

"Well, you were the one provoking an argument." Sarah pouted. "I'll happily put a lid on it, if you'll stop talking about toilets full of shit!"

"I said: *these are nice*." Kate said, trying to change the subject and make peace.

"Yes, I heard you. Thank you."

Kate sighed. She knew she had better things to do with her evening than rile her sister, but she couldn't stop her brain from worrying at the seams of her existence, and picking them out loud.

"It was a metaphor."

"I get that. It's just a very provocative metaphor."

"It's meant to be, Sis. The system is clogged. All the foulness and human detritus that litters the streets, living lives behind your back, it never goes away. Just 'cos you don't see it. I see it, or the results of it, every day. And the effects to clear it? They're just not working. Haven't been for years! Why can't anyone see that? Why won't anyone do something about it?"

"You mean, why won't anyone listen to you? Or let *you* do something about it?"

"Exactly!"

Sarah rested her chin on one fist and looked at her

sister as kindly as she could. "You are referring, no doubt, to your superiors?"

"Yes. And I've had conversations like this with my *superiors* a thousand times."

"And what, do you suppose, is the reason they don't listen?"

"Because they're morons, Sarah. Lifers. Clock-watchers. Perfect examples of the Peter Principle in action - promoted above their competence. Afraid to step out of line in case it affects their next promotion - which isn't going to happen - and without the wit or intelligence to think for themselves and initiate anything that might be considered an effective response."

"Don't sit on the fence, Sis. Say what you mean."

"You think I'm exaggerating?"

"I think you are prone to using emotive language, generating evocative images in people's minds which ironically make the problems and issues at hand seem more intractable or insurmountable, such that the very urgency of your description of the problem discourages anyone from addressing it to your satisfaction."

Kate looked at her sister in astonishment. "Fuck me."

"Psychology degree talking here, don't you know." Sarah buffed her nails on her jumper and regarded them proudly. "Just tellin' it like it is. Which is what you do. So perhaps you can see why *they don't listen.*"

"But I'm annoyed!" Kate protested.

"Clearly. And how does that help you?"

"Look." Kate put down her cup on the kitchen worktop and started counting off the fingers of her left hand. "The system is clogged. What is the system clogged with? Crap. Human crap. Bad men, Sarah - usually men, anyway. Bad men who do bad things to good people like you and me. People who don't deserve to have bad things done to them. So what systems get clogged up with shit? Toilets, sewers - things like that. Everyone can relate to a blocked toilet, full of shit. The analogy is clear here, isn't it? Maybe it's too evocative but that's not my fault. It's the most accurate analogy in this case, isn't it?"

"Metaphor."

"Whatever." Kate stopped counting her fingers and waved away her sisters nitpicking. "So, when your toilet is blocked. Full of shit. What do you do?"

"You call a plumber."

Kate sighed. "Before that."

"Turn the water off?"

"No!"

"Well, I don't know!" Sarah gave a mock-sneer. "What *do* you do? Tell me, oh wise one."

"You stop putting more shit in the toilet! You put more shit in it, it overflows and shit goes everywhere. You no longer have just a blocked toilet to worry about, you've got a… shitty bathroom."

"Yes, well I think I've spotted the point where this particular metaphor breaks down."

"You take my point." Kate concluded.

"Yes." Sarah replied, tartly. "Do you?"

Kate had been a regular visitor to Sarah's for the past twelve months, since her heart murmur. No-one on the force knew about it and Kate was intent on keeping it that way. It had come out of the blue but, with hindsight, had been on the cards for a long time. Her job, her mood and her philosophy all bore deep imprints of the same personality trait: intensity. She gave 110% to everything she did, and she committed to everything she did as if it was the only thing in her life. Which, apart from her sister, it usually was.

The heart defect was genetic. Kate had known she had it when her mother had died, aged 59, and her father had told her about it. Kate had been in her twenties, Sarah still a teenager. Both of them had the same defect and both of them knew what things to avoid to try and manage it - since managing it was all they could do.

Kate was just way, way worse at it than her sister.

Sarah had had the advantage of knowing about the health condition before she chose a career and had decided to take a laid-back, lifestyle business choice, get lots of fresh air, exercise and live where the air was clean and stress was low. Over the years she had built up a kennel business in St Boswells and branched out into dog-breeding: Jack Russell terriers to be exact. She bitched and moaned about it - the food and heating bills for the sprawling property, the planning obligations when she wanted to build new out-buildings but Kate knew her sister's life was good and the only thing she felt missing was a man she could share it with.

Kate wanted to retire. But she also wanted to sort out the police force and make it a functioning and efficient organisation. An obsession on which she worked tirelessly. Unfortunately, no-one else (in her view) did. She waged a lone war on what she saw as inefficiency, waste and bureaucracy, using her every spare hour on proposing, promoting and affecting improvements in police processes. And she was no stranger to the word *No* and no fan of fence-sitting. Her style was vocal and combative: one of her colleagues, when querying her about her self-confessed brutal honesty, had wondered whether she didn't enjoy the brutality somewhat more than the honesty. The truth was, Kate didn't herself know. Nor care. All she cared about was making things better - for everyone. And if a few desk-jockeys felt uncomfortable or challenged by her attitude then, she reckoned, she was on the right lines.

But fifty was, well, fifty. And the heart condition meant she had to be more measured than she would like to be. Another issue which really just elevated her frustrations with life and, consequently, her stress levels. Her choice was either to keep her condition hidden so that she could concentrate on the thing which meant most to her and got her out of bed every morning, or come clean about it - which would guarantee an earlier retirement on health grounds thus removing her sole *raison-d'etre.*

At a stroke, you might say.

More than anything else, she wanted a crack at the Detective Chief Superintendent position. That would really give her some clout with which to initiate changes and make a difference. A few years at that and she could happily retire after her full thirty years on the force with good grace. Then, and perhaps only then, would she be able to look in the mirror and tell herself she'd done all she could. Her future would then look much like her sister's, who she would help out in the kennels and breeding centre.

But this morning she had woken up and felt every single one of her fifty years. Every day, she would look at herself in the mirror and see only lines, crow's feet and bags under her eyes. Her dyed silver-blonde hair, cut short, was the most youthful-looking thing about her, by far. Elsewhere she saw just a collection of distressed features: pale tired eyes; lips too thin on a mouth too wide; skin grey and worn from years behind a desk, reviewing cases and files, signing forms and authorising slips, chairing meetings and writing reports. She lay in her sister's guest bedroom, gazed blankly at the ceiling, did a mental assay of her life's accomplishments and came up short.

Sarah had breezed in without knocking, the tray in her hands bedecked with flowers, gaily-wrapped gifts and a mound of freshly made pancakes.

"Merry Christmas!" she trilled, beaming as she put down the tray and drew the curtains. Sunlight streamed in. "On this day of days I have allowed you one, whole, unblemished lie-in. My gift, to you."

"Bollocks." Kate buried her head under the covers and waited for tomorrow.

"Now, now." Her sister admonished her mock-sternly, not in the least put out by this display of petulance. "Big sisters are not allowed to be grumpy-chumps on the birthday of Our Lord."

"What time is it?" Kate grumbled from beneath the quilt.

"Eight of the clock. The sun will be shining, once it's up, the birds are singing-" There was a sudden cacophony from outside the window which Sarah winced at. "The dogs are barking - sorry about that - dogs will be dogs. And all's right with the world."

"Do fuck off Sis. What's with the Anne-of-Green-Gables, Pippy-Longstocking act? It really doesn't suit you, you know."

"Well being a miserable bastard first thing doesn't suit you!" Sarah sneered sarcastically. "Although, most days, actually, it rather does. But today *es ist verboten, Ja? Du bist nicht ein grumpy-chump ver-beben, dumbkopf!*"

"Oh, so now I have to translate from German do I?"

"Nein! I vill ask ze qvestions!"

"Yes, well that's quite appropriate isn't it? Germans - known and widely-revered for their sense of humour and fun-loving ways."

"Oh for Chrissakes, Sis. Cheer up! It's Christmas! Look, brekkie! And pressies! Come on, budge up, open 'em. Let's see what you got?" Sarah plonked the tray down on top of Kate's submerged torso and wedged herself onto the bed, squashing herself between Kate and the bedside table. Kate was forced to move and reluctantly she appeared from beneath the covers and sat up in bed. She trained a weary eye on the small pile of presents on the tray.

"These are all from you I take it?"

"Natch."

"So, you know what I'm getting don't you? You got me them."

"Oh, blooming hell, Sis. Open the fecking pressie's won't you? And cheer the F up before I set the hounds on you."

Kate took the top gift from the pile and carefully unwrapped it. "A Thai phrase book?"

"Thought it might come in useful when you have your Rugby Sevens visitors staying."

"Oh great! I'd forgotten about them. Until now."

"Unlucky Sis." Sarah stuck her tongue out at her sister. "But anyway, you offered! Not regretting this fit of generosity now are we?"

The honest answer, Kate knew, was *yes*. What the hell was she playing at? It was as if she had taken leave of her senses since her scare. First she had agreed to serve on the board of the Rugby Club, then she had volunteered to chair the funding sub-committee for the Legacy 1883 project. This was a massive effort to rebuild the entire Greenyards ground - pitch, stands and all - named in honour of the year in which Melrose Rugby Club had been founded. It was true that the place looked a bit tired and jaded after all this time, but finding the millions that would be needed to demolish and resurrect a shiny new vision of Rugby's future? And through crowd-funding as well? It was exactly the sort of futile project Kate could use to dash her forehead into a bloody pulp during the spare time when she wasn't doing the same thing in the police force.

Then, to cap it all off, she had filled a gap in the residency roster when it turned out that there were going to be two fewer berths available for the touring teams participating in the Sevens tournament next April. Local families always stood ready to act as free B&B's for foreign teams. She had now put her head above the parapet as a fine, up-standing and willing member of the Melrose establishment. It was the logical next step. She was on the board, lived locally - alone - and had room to spare. What was the problem.

"The problem is..." Kate said aloud, not realising that her sister had not been privy to her inner thoughts. "I'm not at all used to the idea of someone else being in my home. Using my stuff. Being in my way."

"It'll only be for a few days. Be some company."

"I don't want company." Kate griped.

"Yes, I can see that." Sneered Sarah. "So why *are* you on the committee? Why *have* you thrown yourself right into the beating heart of Melrose life, if you're such a miserable sod?"

Kate smiled beatifically. "I am a giver, Sis. As well you know. And when I give, I give my all. And on this day of days, perhaps we can all learn a little something from those of us who give, can we not?"

"In the words of a noted philosopher: *Do fuck off, Sis.* Come on! Open the next one."

Kate picked up the next present from the tray and tore it open. It was an enormous elaborate vibrator.

"Really?"

Sean woke up with a sore head and a mouth like the inside of a Turkish wrestler's jockstrap. The ceiling above him was refusing to sit still, the swirls of artex merging and dancing a Scottish reel at some ungodly miles per hour. He leant over the side of the bed and was promptly sick into the Ladies Cup sitting proudly on the floor.

Cigars didn't agree with him, he knew that. And beer didn't help. Sean realised he had some genetic abnormality - that was Sam's opinion anyway. Some defect which meant he couldn't hold his drink. Well, actually, he could hold it - just not for very long. He didn't so much buy a beer as rent it. Rent it until his stomach rebelled and called in the bailiffs, who then chucked all his stuff out on the pavement where everyone could laugh at it.

The events of a few hours earlier were slowly coming back into focus and, whilst he was sketchy on some of the detail, the circumstantial evidence was confirming what his impaired memory was digging him in the ribs to tell him. His hair stank of smoke, his mouth reeked of stale beer, his forehead was throbbing like the Tardis console, one side of his face was tender and stinging, the heavy stench of tobacco wafted up from his fingers, and he'd just chucked up into a stolen trophy. Check check check. He felt sure he was pretty much up to speed on the evening's events.

Sean looked down at the puke-splattered trophy and then struggled to his feet, catching his reflection in the strip of mirror running down the wardrobe door. There were deep grazes down the right side of his face and a large gash on his chin. He looked like a badly mugged pensioner. His bedroom door opened and his father's head poked round the door.

"Good mor-. Ey up! What does the other guy look like?" His father came into the room wearing only pyjama bottoms, his torso and arms covered in many and assorted badly-applied tattoos.

"The other guy..." Sean's speech was slow and he found it difficult to form words properly without feeling sick. "Was Sam."

"Sam did that?" Wingnut didn't know whether to be furious or proud - his two grown sons fighting.

Sean nodded his head, slowly and sadly.

"Is that because you won first prize and he didn't?" Wingnut nodded down to the trophy on the floor.

Sean shook his head warily.

"What was the prize for?"

Sean thought for a moment. "Dishonesty."

"Initiative!" Sam proclaimed, marching into the room.

Wingnut looked from one son to the other and then again at the chalice on the carpet containing, and splattered with, vomit. "Isn't that the Ladies Cup?"

"Sure is." Sam beamed.

"Huh? Isn't it… valuable?" Wingnut's eyes widened.

"I guess." Sam shrugged.

"No, no, no." Sean said, staggering to his feet.

"Steady, Seanie. Let's not be hasty. We could be rich."

"You's are the ones being hasty." Sean slurred. "This was a stupid prank. His idea!" he pointed an accusing finger at Sam. "And the cops will know we've got it so we have to get rid of it before they find us."

"What do you mean, the cops know?" Wingnut was suddenly all ears pricked and up on the balls of his feet. Sean had never seen him so flighty or potentially agile. "Sam? Is this true?"

Sam reflected upon his own recollection of the evening's activities. "Well. A copper turned up. Didn't really see us, mind." He shrugged again. "I reckon we're good."

"Good? How're we good? Look at my fucking face for starters. Does this look like the visage of an innocent man?"

"Visage?"

"Face! Ok, face. Fuck sake, Dad. He made me go through with this and we got away by inches. Everyone'll know it's been stolen. How can we be rich unless we get shot of it? And who's going to want it when it's hot?"

"Someone always wants something. There's always a market - you just got to strike the right price. It's that simple."

"No, it's not that simple." The sobering effect of the pain from his face was bringing him to his senses and Sean's senses were telling him that he'd had just about enough of this and wanted out. "We're getting rid of it. Today."

"Oh yeah? Well, first you're gonna have to convince me." His father muscled up to him, his morning breath joining the ugly chorus of odours adorning the air in the room.

"And me." Sam sidled up to his father and the pair stood side-by-side, glaring at Sean.

Sean looked to one and then the other, his newly-found

determination already fading in the face of this combined defence. He sighed heavily, consulted with the pain on the inside of his head and, coming to a decision, he sat sullenly down on the bed again.

"Now you're getting it." His father turned to smile at Sam. When he turned back to Sean, Wingnut and Sam both got half a chalice of cold sick, full in the face.

Sean had not long departed when the bizzies turned up at Wingnut's front door. They hadn't even bothered to ask him any questions or listen to his side of the story - simply bundled him into the back of a car and then left him to stew in an interview room for an hour before anyone had even bothered to get him a cuppa. Presumably this was in honour of his ex-lag status.

If he was honest with himself - which he seldom was - prison had been a nightmare. He might have tried affecting the gait of a prize-fighting heavyweight but inside he'd been a snivelling ball of drool, forever twitching that someone would cut him, bugger him or both.

His early release - a standard procedure which was triggered at the two-thirds stage of his sentence - came with strings attached. He wasn't exactly sure what they were - some social worker had told him what they were but he hadn't really listened, just focussed on the "release" bit - but he was prepared to bet that being convicted would be a breach of them. Get found guilty, regardless of the charges, and he'd been staring at another four years. It was that simple.

"Well, it's about fucking time." Wingnut thrust his jaw out when the interview door eventually opened and tried to appear as menacing as he could, despite the fact that he was slouched in a chair with his hands in his pockets. The overall appearance was truculent man-child rather than hard-hitting hard man.

"You late for something, then?" The blonde lady detective looked bored and tired and not in the least impressed, worried or bothered by Wingnut's defiance. Presumably, she'd seen the likes of this before and nothing moved her.

"Late for tea. Any chance?"

"Of getting home in time? None whatsoever." She slapped a manila folder down on the table, pulled up a chair and then browsed the first page within it.

"I meant, of a cuppa."

"Oh, you're funny." The detective deadpanned. "I like you."

"Doesn't look like it." Wingnut attempted a sneer, it came out more like a whine.

"Mumumumumumum." The detective babbled, sticking out her lower lip and looking sad.

Wingnut folded his arms and sighed. This was going to be a drag.

"So, Mr Marshall." The detective, closed the folder and leant back in her chair, folding her arms. "Let's have your version of events shall we? What little jackanory tale have you got cooked up for me?"

Wingnut was immediately indignant. "Why you assuming I'm gonna lie? I'm a law-abiding citizen, me." He poked himself in the chest "I've done my time and you've got no right to assume-"

"Ha! Done your time? One third left to go, pal."

"I'm not your pal."

"You're on your way back to the slammer. Better get

used to the idea of slopping out again."

"I'm an innocent man."

"Yeah. And I'm Hillary Rodham Clinton."

"What's the charge?"

"Didn't they tell you?"

"Wasn't really listenin', I'll be honest."

"You do understand the principle of early release, don't you?"

"Yeah." Wingnut said, in an uncertain tone meaning No.

"Then you'll know that, should you be found guilty. Sorry. When you're found guilty." She smiled at her own little witticism. "You'll be back in Hamilton serving the rest of your sentence. Which is another…" She flicked through the folder again. "Four years. That'll be nice, won't it?"

Wingnut glared at her and kept shtum.

"So, come on then. Once upon a time. Let's be having it."

"I didn't do it."

"Do what?"

"Anything."

"When?"

"Ever."

"You've never done anything?"

"Nope." Wingnut grinned madly and raised his eyebrows.

The detective leant forward, arms still crossed and put her elbows on the table, earnestly. "Look, let me explain. Maybe you didn't get the memo. You have been arrested. You're not here helping us with our enquiries. You're not free to go. Vague airy statements amounting to "I done nuffink" will not wash. You are nicked. You are going to court, you will be found guilty and you will go back to prison to finish your original sentence as you will have breached the terms of your early release. In short: you. Are. Fucked. So… still want that cup of tea?"

Wingnut did his best to keep his expression blank. He looked into the eyes of this detective and searched for something, anything, which might be mistaken for humanity, falsehood or charity - and found nothing. "Yes. Please."

The detective sighed, disappointed, stood and shambled out of the room. Wingnut breathed out loudly and took a few mental laps round his brain. By the time Plod returned with a styrofoam cup of tea, he had decided upon a strategy: dumb insolence. It wasn't like he had much option since this was the only strategy he'd ever adopted and no amount of laps would unearth another.

"So. Where were you on the night in question?"

"Which night was that?"

"Oh, do fuck off. You have to make a statement. I have to write it down. Fucking pain, but there it is. So can we just do this? I can go home, you can go back to your cell. Life can return to normal."

"Can't I go home?"

"No. Not yet any road. Sheriff may grant bail. Tomorrow. 'Til then, your home is here. *Mi casa su casa.*"

"What?"

"No. You can't go home." She parroted. "You're in the cell until - unless - you get bail. Won't be until tomorrow now - so tonight, you're staying here. How many more ways do you want me to say it?"

"Fine."

"Fine. So, where were you on the night in question?"

"What night was that?"

"Fuck."

Kate was only half-listening to Des explaining exactly how the Ladies' Cup had come to be out of its locked cabinet after the Gala-Melrose Boxing Day fixture. She looked at this perma-tanned middle-age lothario as he tried to stutter his way through his story to her and the clutch of elderly gentlemen sitting around the committee table and decided she'd half-heard enough.

"Long story short, Des. You fucked up."

Des cast his eyes down into his lap and abandoned his poor attempt at a *mea culpa*. No-one else would have dared speak to the Club President like that, but he sat and meekly took it from Kate.

"I'll say." Roger interjected, feeling brave. "Although, it sort of doesn't make any difference right now, though, does it? The Cup's missing and we need to find it before April."

Roger was a spry widower with a thick shock of white hair, deep blue eyes and an another man who was a fan of the tan. Rumour had it that it was from a sun-lamp rather than his claimed weekend Saga breaks around various Mediterranean hot-spots. But if the rumours were true, he made sure he was invisible every other Friday-to-Monday, so either he was sunning himself around a Spanish pool with a bevy of octogenarian groupies while the rain fell here in Melrose, or he was cocooned in his bungalow behind blackout blinds with a boxset of Game Of Thrones and a stack of microwave ready meals. Whatever the truth, he had overdone it so that his current pallor was somewhere around medium-rare.

"Yes, you're right." Agreed Kate. "Much as it doesn't

make any fucking difference to the freezing temperature." She rubbed her hands vigorously together and jiggled her knees up and down beneath the table. "Why is it always so fucking cold in here? Can we not afford fifty pee for the meter?"

They were meeting today in the Eildon Suite - although it would, she knew, be just as cold in their usual venue, the Centenary Suite. Saving money was one thing, but some of these old codgers wouldn't last the winter if they didn't turn the fucking radiators on.

"More grist to the 1883 Legacy Project mill." Roger grinned. "This place was never intended to last this long, never designed with twenty-first century needs in mind. Costs a fortune to heat and maintain."

"And insure." Des chimed in. "Premiums going up all the time. Not fit for purpose, Ma'am."

At the outset of being drafted in to lead this 1883 Legacy crowd-funding campaign, Kate had introduced herself to her fellow sub-committee members and carefully instructed them that she should be addressed as *ma'am*, in her capacity as Detective Superintendent Lorimer (much as most of her colleagues addressed her, at work). She would let them know when she was comfortable with them calling her *Kate*. That would be when large drifts were accumulating at the gates to Hades. Or Galashiels, whichever could be considered most unappealing.

"Yes, that may be true. But until we have raised the money, we are in no position to knock down the Greenyards and rebuild it. In the meantime if we could just ring-fence a tiny bit of the money we have raised so far and *turn the fucking radiators on.*"

Des rose from his feet and obediently toured the room,

turning up the thermostats on each of the radiators.

"So this is what happens every Christmas round here is it? We have a Melrose crime wave caused by some Gala fuckwits cheesed off that they got their arses kicked while trying to chuck a pigs bladder round a field?"

"With respect, Ma'am. We are in the hallowed halls of rugby history here as we speak. Perhaps a little more respect for the game would be appropriate?" Des piped up.

"And a little more respect for the fact that I am not the police-officer-on-call for this fucking rugby club." Kate snarled. "I have a day job and, in my day-job capacity, I am now dealing with a mass brawl in The Ship, a stolen trophy, pitch vandalism, petty arson and some wanker who thinks it's a good idea to try and demolish a house with a van. I am tired and I am cold and I-"

There was a bustling knock at the door and it opened before anyone, Kate included, could respond to it. A muddy workman entered, wringing his hands in embarrassment as the Club Secretary stood behind him.

"Does the sign on that bloody door mean nothing to anyone?"

The workman was now shaking, his muddy boots had left a trail on the boardroom carpet.

"Sorry, Ma'am." The Club Secretary, Colin, spoke up from behind the workman. "There's been a, er, new development."

"Well, it better be a bloody good one!"

"Actually, it's a bloody dead one."

"What?" Kate screwed up her face, her expression transforming from annoyance to confusion.

"A body." The secretary nudged the workman into life. "Tell her, Trevor."

The workman was getting on in years and not the most confident of individuals. "It's an arm. Well, two. I think. I stopped the digger the minute I saw it but I couldn't have seen it earlier. It was buried."

"Where?" Kate was looking from the workman to the secretary and back, wanting only information now.

"By the Club Shop. The portakabin? The wall's bellying out, threatening to collapse on it. They've just started digging." Colin said.

"Have you called the police?"

"Well, I thought…"

"I am the police?"

"Well, yes."

She stood up and pulled her coat from the back of the chair. "Has anyone touched anything?"

"No. No-one. Trevor came to me and I have come straight to you."

"Anyone?" She trained her eyes on the workman once more. "Anything? Anything at all?"

Trevor shook his head mutely, keeping his eyes on the muddy carpet in the hope that only he could see the mess his footprints had made.

"Right. Come on. I'll take a look and then I'll call the station. In the meantime I want everyone on site taken to reception immediately. No-one is to enter or leave the grounds until I have said so, is that clear?"

"Yes, ma'am."

Kate shucked her coat on as she strode from the room. "One of these days I swear I'll get to the end of one of these fucking meetings."

"You've got to give it back." Janine pronounced, hands

on her gorgeously extravagant hips.

"Hmm?" Sean couldn't quite focus on what she was saying to him.

"You've got to! They'll put you in jail if you don't."

"I can't just give it back. They'll arrest me."

"Tell 'em you found it."

"But I didn't!"

"I know." She patted his hand. "But tell them you did."

"I can't"

"Why not?"

"They'll know!" Sean was feeling stressed and embarrassed. He had worried and fretted about whether to tell Janine at all. Now he was being bombarded with unacceptable solutions to his problem when all he wanted was for this problem to go away.

"How will they know?"

"They just will. I can't lie. They'll be able to tell. I'll sweat or go red or look in the wrong place. Or they'll connect me up to a lie detector and worm it out of me" Sean was struggling to hold back the tears.

"Oh, babe. They won't do that. Look at you! You're an innocent young lamb. They'll just thank you and send you on your way. They might even give you a reward!"

"Where will I say I found it?"

"Anywhere!"

"But they'll look where I told them and see no evidence that it was ever there!"

"Well, then, choose somewhere and leave it there for a day or two. Bury it or something. Then, go back and get it and hand it in. Voila! Local hero."

Sean looked at her in amazement. "That simple, huh?" He smiled at her, despite himself.

"That simple." She smiled back and wiggled her hips

coyly at him.

"Hmm." Sean looked at Janine, looked at the now-clean trophy sitting on the coffee table, and then back at Janine's curves. "Come here."

IN COURT: CULLEN

"I'm getting really quite cheesed off with all this in-and-out business." Carol complained. "I was hoping for some meaty drama, you know, that you can settle down in front of - like Corrie? This is just too bitty. Why can't they organise themselves properly? It's not asking too much is it?"

"Things come up." Said Lorraine. "Things change. Got to respond to change haven't you? I mean, take my Harry. Got an email yesterday saying the shed he's bidding on has been withdrawn from sale. He was really looking forward to that. Although God knows where he was going to put it - on the balcony? Now he's bidding on a pigeon coop instead. It's Newtonian isn't it?"

"The coop?" Carol said.

"No! Changing in response to circumstances. Every action has an equal and opposite… thing. Isaac Newton."

"Oh. Well, all I know is we're in one minute and out the next. I've got arthritis in my hip. Can't keep getting up, shuffling in, sitting down, then getting up again and shuffling out. I need to get settled."

"At least you get the chance for a cuppa tea." Lorraine reminded her. Carol seemed to drink *a lot* of tea.

"True. But we're the bloomin' jury aren't we? How're we supposed to form an opinion if we don't get to see and hear everything that's going on?"

"They only do this sort of thing when it is legal technical discussions. What is and isn't admissible.

Procedural stuff, like that." The businessman assured them, in soothing tones. "If we were listening in on it, we'd either be bored witless or completely lost by all the impenetrable jargon."

"Or Latin." Added Moira, nodding knowledgeably. "They use a lot of Latin in court. My Cyril told me."

"Just like up on that shield behind the Sheriff." Said Lorraine. "*Dulce et decorum est.*"

"I thought that was French?" Sniffed Moira.

"It's called sitting *in camera.*" Added Marjorie.

"No, I don't think so." Argued the businessman. "When the court sits *in camera*, that includes the jury. Just excludes the public."

"Not in Scotland." Marjorie shook her head, doubtfully.

"I know a joke about that." This was Jerry, looking up for the first time from his Racing Post like some kind of bearded marmot emerging from hibernation.

"Go on then" the businessman said with a weary sigh, rolling his eyes to Jean sitting next to him.

"Ok. Well there's this man from Liverpool on trial and he's in the witness box giving evidence and the lawyer says: "So, you were in the park with your girlfriend and feeling… frisky, I believe was your word?" "Yeah, s'right." The witness says with a lascivious grin. The lawyer turns to the judge and says: "Your honour, I believe my client's testimony contains some details of a sensitive nature. Perhaps I can request holding the court *in camera* for the rest of his testimony?" "Very well." Says the judge. "'Ere, hang on!" Says the witness. "What's this *in camera* lark?" The judge looks wearily down over his glasses at the witness and says: "Mr Wilkins. I know what *in camera* means, the Defence knows what *in camera* means, the

Prosecution knows what *in camera* means and the jury knows what *in camera* means… so we'll hold this court *in camera*." So the press and public are dismissed from the public gallery and they hold the court in camera. The lawyer resumes with the witness: "So, Mr Wilkins, you were in the park with your girlfriend. Perhaps you can tell us what happened next?" And the witness says:" Yeah, well, I was in the park with me Judy and I was feelin' frisky, you know, so we went into the bushes for a bit of dibbery-doo-dah." The judge interrupts: "Mr Wilkins, what exactly is, erm…. Dibbery-doo-dah?" And the witness says: "Your honour, I know what a bit of dibbery doo-dah is, the defence knows what a bit of dibbery-doo-dah is, the prosecution knows what a bit of dibbery doo-dah is, and the jury knows what a bit of dibbery-doo-dah is…. and if you'd had your fucking camera in those bushes, you'd know what a bit of dibbery-doo-dah was 'n' all!"

Jerry burst into laughter at his own joke. Nobody joined him.

"Ooh, language!" squawked Marjorie. "I'm eighty-four, you know."

"Need a lift, stranger?" Kate wound down the passenger window and leaned over so she could look up at Cullen walking by the side of the road. He was wearing a stained green waterproof with a small tear in the hood, a pair of black waterproof trousers and brown battered walking boots. "What happened to your hat?"

"Can't wear it in court." He muttered, his voice deep and steady. "Didn't see the point in bringing it to not wear it."

"You need a haircut." She ran her eyes over his greying

curls, wiry and thick, an unruly shock which fell this way and that over his forehead and ears. "And a shave." He had uneven stubble on his chin and throat, bare patches at his jawline.

"I had a shave." He protested, ran his fingers over his face.

"What with? A spoon?"

"Access to the amenities required for a good shave is currently… limited." He monotoned.

"Access to…? You haven't changed." She smiled ruefully and motioned for him to get in. He looked anxiously up and down the road and then at the door handle.

"You shouldn't be doing this."

"Yeah, I know. That's why I waited until we were well clear of the courthouse and any witnesses."

"I'm a juror on a case that you are giving evidence on."

"Like I said, I know."

He continued to scan up and down the empty road. "I'm… out of your way."

"No you're not. You're not far at all."

Cullen looked down at her and frowned. "How do you know that?"

"I'm a detective, remember?"

"I remember." He smiled and she caught a small glimpse of his old self.

"And so were you. Look, you're on jury duty. Need to be here every day. You don't drive or own a car so you need to be close by - walking distance."

His eyes twinkled at her. "I could be getting the bus."

She grinned and shook her head. "I don't see you as the public transport type."

"I have my moments."

"I recall." She ran her eyes over his face as he stared ahead. "You look well. Perhaps a little careworn."

He looked down at his hands, turning them over, examining them. "It's not the years, it's the mileage."

Kate smiled briefly. "You still… off the grid?"

"Uh-uh."

"So, how the hell did they get you on jury duty?"

"Long story."

"I've got time." She smiled and wanted him to look at her. He didn't.

"I don't."

"Cullen. Look at me. Please?" She waited until he slowly turned to face her. She remembered that fierce intelligence behind those grey eyes, the lines in his face etched from worry and caring too much. "Are you ok?"

"Mostly." The corners of his mouth turned up ever so slightly. "Sometimes I get in this weird mood where I don't want to be around people or talk to anyone."

"Me too."

"I call this mood *awake*."

She watched him and waited in silence. After what seemed like a long time, Cullen grabbed the handle and swung himself into the car.

"What are you up to, these days?" Kate asked.

"Same old, same old."

She realised she'd forgotten how to traverse conversations with him, his rhythm and cadence. He confronted talking as if tacking into the wind.

"You've been…" She searched for the right words. "… out there. Alone, too long."

"It suits me."

"Does it? I'm not so sure." She looked through the windscreen at the clouds threatening rain. "Where to?"

"It's a mile or so up here."

"Cool beans."

Cullen gave a quizzical look but said nothing.

A few minutes later Kate swung her car onto the sunken gravel drive in front of a detached monstrosity of a house. The frontage was a collage of green mould, grey damp and black decay. "Nice place you got here. The Seventies called, they want their architecture back."

"This was the future once." Cullen said, almost dreamily.

"Yeah. Now look at it." She switched off the engine and sat gazing at the dismal sight through her windscreen. "Age. Terribly sad thing sometimes." She looked across at him, watching his eyes wander over the decrepit glass and concrete edifice. They sat in contemplative silence for what seemed like a long, long time. Then Kate blurted out: "I'll be fifty-one soon."

"Spring chicken." Cullen actually turned to her and smiled. A warm smile that took years off him and she saw again that younger man she had known and looked up to.

"I need to get out. Off the force."

"Retire? You?" He was genuinely surprised.

"You did." She said and then instantly regretted it.

"Yeah." He turned back to look at the house again. "I did. Well, they did. You don't have to."

"I'm sorry, Cullen. I didn't mean to-"

"It's ok. Never took you for the retiring type."

"Yeah, well I didn't know Melrose was going to be the crime capital of Scotland when I moved here."

"Really?"

"No, just seems like it sometimes." Kate frowned and

looked at her lines in the rear view mirror. "Even found a dead body this winter."

Cullen raised one eyebrow. "Murder?"

"Can't tell. Blunt force trauma to the back of the head." Kate continued pulling and stretching at her face in the mirror as she spoke, testing her skin elasticity. "Been buried years, mind. Not much left. No DNA match. Only ID was some necklace with SHS on it."

"What does that mean?"

"Dunno. Initials maybe."

"Missing persons?"

"Nothing. Not in Scotland. Checked all the other UK forces too. No-one with the initials SS or SHS reported missing. Dead end. Ha!" She abandoned the mirror and looked at him, sadly. "I have a health problem." She made her mouth smile while her eyes were wet and cold. "Heart. Genetic - my sister has it too."

"Sarah? How is she?"

"She's… fine." Kate narrowed her eyes. "It's not like you to ask after someone."

"Maybe you were right. Maybe I have been out here on my own too long." He turned back to her and wrinkled up his nose, making her smile. "So, retire then. Take it easy. You must have put your years in by now?"

"But there's so much to do! So much that's broken." The familiar surge of frustration and anger grew hot inside her. "It needs fixing!"

"It always has. It always will."

"Are you saying I should just give up then? That a shitty system is inevitable and I should just accept it?" She glared at him, suddenly alive with frustration.

"No." Cullen said, calmly. "It's incredible that you care. Still care, after all this time. Many don't - either they didn't in the first place or the system wears them down. You know that."

"World's fucking full of them." Kate spat, the resentment vivid in her eyes.

"Yes, it is. So your passion is a strength. How you find the energy to keep caring is beyond me."

"And me."

"And that is my point."

"It is?" Kate cocked her head to one side. "Care to spell it out for me?"

Cullen sighed. "I have a friend who-"

"You have a friend?"

"Yes."

"When did this happen? Anyone phone Reuters?"

Cullen ignored the sarcasm. "It happened while your back was turned. While you were focussing on fixing a system that is broken."

"Yeah, well it's still broken. And I'm still trying to fix it." Kate sulked. "And I'm still struggling to understand your point."

"My point is that you can only do so much. One person can only do so much. Seems to me, you've done enough. You may not think it is enough but, if you do more, it won't be the system that gets fixed, it will be you that gets broken."

"So you're saying: if I can't save the system, I should at least save myself?"

"If I may quote my friend - and I can't believe I'm actually doing this - anyway, he once said: *all that is not saved will be lost*."

"Huh. Deep. Is that Confucius?"

Cullen shook his head. "Nintendo, apparently."

THE TROPHY

Big Paul had been sweating like a gypsy with a mortgage. He was walking his dogs out over Minch Moor and the spring sunshine was unseasonably warm. As he walked, he was unconsciously playing fetch with them. Ant would retrieve the scabby old tennis ball from the undergrowth and trot back to Paul with it; Paul would extract the slobbering article from the dog's soiled mouth and mindlessly throw it overarm, whereupon Dec would take up the chase, find the ball and bring it back. The three participants all knew their roles and played them on auto-pilot - the only difference being that the dogs were having a rare old time of it; Paul was otherwise occupied. Whilst they happily snuffled and frolicked in the heather, weeing up against the small conifers, Paul had other things on his mind.

Well, one other thing.

Shirley.

Paul and Shirley had been a thing for over a year now and whilst all was lovey and, indeed, dovey on the surface, even Paul's atrociously underdeveloped senses were picking up signs that Shirley was dissatisfied at the moment. What the problem was, and what he could or should do about it, however, were issues which completely evaded him.

He ran his mental slide rule over the problem at hand. First off, he obviously couldn't ask her what the problem was. Noooo. Schoolboy error. Asking a woman what the matter was merely opened you up to an accusation that you were insensitive, unfeeling or insufficiently engaged in the relationship. A man should know what the problem was - since, usually, it was the man that was the problem.

On the other hand, maybe he could resolve the situation by buying her some flowers. Didn't even matter, then, if the problem was real or all in his imagination. If it was real, flowers would fix it; if it wasn't, she would love them anyway. What woman doesn't love flowers?

That'd sort it. If he had money.

Flowers were expensive and right now Paul had a minor cashflow problem. Again. Buying flowers was a ten pound solution to a five pound problem. He tried to recall when he'd last bought Shirley flowers. Her birthday, was it? Shit! Had he missed her birthday? No, that was September the *somethingth*. He made a mental note to see if he could somehow pry free the actual date from her later.

Anniversary then? How long had they been together now? He couldn't recall buying her anything for an anniversary, or celebrating one with her. And he'd have remembered if Shirley had proudly presented him with a card and a gift one day only to discover that he had no clue what was going on. He'd not forget a real dignity-stripper event like that.

So there was still time. Cool! He didn't know how much time, right enough, but he wasn't too late. That in itself was a novelty he was prepared to relish while it lasted. Pleased with this mental exertion, he corralled his dogs off the moor and onto the track heading down to the car park. So, if their anniversary was coming up. And he had no money. What exactly was he going to do?

"No." Cullen had said.

"Why not?"

"Neither a borrower nor a lender be."

"But it's only a few quid! I'll pay you back."

"That is not the point."

"Well, what is the point?"

"I've just told you."

"Aw, fuck." Paul's huge shoulders heaved beneath his black T-shirt. "You realise this'll ruin me and Shirl?" Cullen remained impassive while Paul rumbled around the sink and poured boiling water from the kettle. "It's alright for you. You don't have a partner. You don't have to consider anyone 'cept yourself. Me and Shirl - we've got a good thing going here. Don't want to fuck it up."

"In that case you should have thought about buying her an anniversary gift."

"I have! That's why I need the money."

"Beforehand." Cullen emphasised. "It's called budgeting. Planning. Thinking ahead."

"I am thinking ahead." Paul slopped a mug down in front of Cullen. "I'm thinking of what it's like trying to find a potential partner once you're past forty."

"By a considerable margin."

"Alright, Methuselah. I'm still younger than you."

Cullen regarded the muddy liquid in the mug in front of him. "I didn't want tea."

"Well I've made it now so get it down you."

Cullen took a sip and grimaced. "What is this?"

"I've told you. It's a nice hot cup of tea. Get it down you."

"Hmm. Let's not be so free and easy with the noun tea here, shall we?" Cullen put the mug down. "I think what we have here is… a cup of hot. Let's just leave it at that, hmm?"

"Everyone's a critic." Paul snarked. "Look. My point is, once you get past forty, finding a potential partner... it's like trying to find a parking space in Sainsbury's. They're either taken, handicapped, or wa-a-a-a-y out there."

"Like I said. Thinking ahead. You should try it sometime."

"Thanks, pal. Thanks a fucking lot."

Cullen sighed and looked at his friend thoughtfully. "You know what you should do?"

"No." Said Paul. "What?"

"Trust the soup."

Trust the soup was Paul's unofficial motto. His official motto was: *Ah, That'll do.*

What *trust the soup* boiled down to was: don't worry, be happy, something will turn up, the universe will provide and everything will be alright, you'll see. Paul had, it was true, come to rely upon this to the extent that he repeatedly pushed the very fabric of the universe to its limits, in attempting to fulfil its duty to provide. But it usually came through, so Paul continued to push, while the universe continued to heave and sweat and toil and still, somehow, deliver. If Paul had been a reader of management theory (or, come to that, a reader), he would have realised that what he had managed to do - very successfully - was outsource the need to worry. To the point where the outside observer might even replace the term *outsource* with the verb *abdicate.*

He unlocked his van and slid the door open for his dogs to leap in but only Dec obliged. He sat obediently on the dirty towel, draped over a couple of bags of finishing plaster, while Paul did his best to wipe most of the mud off his legs and belly.

"Ant, mate?" Paul looked round. "Here boy!"

When the dog didn't materialise, Paul gave a loud whistle and looked back up the hill to see if he had absently left him stranded somewhere on the trail. He heard a series of barks behind him and turned to spot a tail stump wagging excitedly in the bushes at the edge of the hard scrabble area.

"Mate!" Paul shouted, but Ant resolutely stayed put. Paul let out a deep breath, pointed at Dec to stay, and strode over to the bushes.

Ant was scratching around in the dirt and when Paul pulled him away he saw a glint of gold shining up through the soil and brambles. He reached down and picked up a dirty sack with a torn neck and peeled back the sacking to reveal a slender silver trophy on a mahogany base. It was inscribed The Ladies Cup, Melrose Rugby Club and some smaller cursive writing that Paul's eyesight couldn't make out.

Ant returned his nose to the shallow hole and continued scrabbling and scooping earth back between his hind legs.

"Mate! Come away. I think you've found the treasure." He reached down and grabbed Ant by the collar, dragging him out of the bushes while the dog continued to resist. When Paul had wrestled the determined creature back into full daylight he saw more gold glinting in the dog's mouth. He held Ant's snout and put his fingers into the dog's mouth to prise its teeth apart. What dropped into his grimy hand was a necklace on a gold chain. The pendant on the necklace was a gold disc with S S on one side and a centred H on the other. Paul flicked it with a finger and the small disc spun quickly round, creating the appearance of a single side bearing the initials SHS.

Well, bugger me, thought Paul. SHS. Shirley Harriet Stevenson.

The soup had truly outdone itself this time.

With only a few days before the trial, Cullen had found the house. It stood back from the road, almost hidden amongst thick conifers which stretched back down the hillside towards the river.

Not many people came this close to the house, really only the occupants of the cottages close by which shared part of a untarmacc'ed driveway which led from the main road. Most people either missed the house completely as they whizzed past round the bend heading away from Selkirk, or caught a glimpse of it between trees, did a double-take at the incongruity of its appearance in this setting and then turned their eyes back to the road as the S-bend required them to slam their brakes on or end up embedded in a tree.

And incongruous it was. A modern architect's wet-dream - if the modern architect had been designing a house in the Seventies (which, in this case, he had). Spaciousness, straight lines, concrete, smoked glass. That was how it was conceived and constructed. Now it looked like it had captured only brutalism, mould, impracticality and energy inefficiency. Any such extensive use of glass for wall and windows construction was always going to end up badly in a climate this cold and damp. If you wanted chilblains and mildew, this architect was your man. If you wanted swimming pools and 21st century living you would have needed to demolish the house, piece by piece, carefully numbering each and transporting it halfway round the world to a dry, blue-sky climate whereupon you would look at the hillside plot you had bought, look again at the plans for this house and the lorries full of pieces, and then throw the whole lot away and build something completely different.

The designer had been an award-winning architect but what he had done here was a shame. An award-winning shame. The boat for this sort of design had not only been missed, it had departed, done a five-day cruise of the Outer Hebrides, returned, had all its passenger disembark, been dry-docked so its hull could be anti-fouled, and then made ready for its next trip while public opinion stood on the jetty, took a long hard look at itself and then changed its mind. This was not the sort of thing they were looking for - then or now.

So, here it mouldered, as cold as a Scotman's doorstep. Alone, unloved and unserviced by any utilities, untaxed by any council, and uninhabited for almost two decades. An unwanted, unappealing and mostly unnoticed memorial to a decade the snowflake generation would regard as pre-history.

Just the sort of place Cullen had been looking for.

The door lock gave with a snick - third time of asking.

The floor layout was like more a modern office than a home. Almost a perfect square, there was an inner core which housed the utilities, pipework, and ducting. Then the entire floorspace around this core was open plan, bounded on all sides by dirty glass. One side of the inner core was lined with kitchen units and a sink. Between this and the front glass wall of the house was a large kitchen island containing a hob and various other units. An extractor hood hovered unwelcomingly over it.

This kitchen hadn't seen any action in a long time.

Neither had the rest of the house. The floor was littered with bits of piping, cardboard boxes and packing crates, some discarded newspaper and fast food cartons. Signs that someone at some time had also gatecrashed what used to be a luxury home.

An unlit, concrete slabbed staircase led upstairs. Menacing and monstrous, each step was a foot thick and five feet wide - a sepulchral stairway to a freezing cathedral. On the first floor, condensation and ice build-up was evident on most of the windows and the entire rear-facing side - Cullen hesitated to call it a wall since it was almost entirely glass - was smeared with mould, mildew, condensation and dust such that there was no way anyone could see either out or in.

Perfect.

On the top floor, the north-east corner of the building was effectively hidden by trees from both the road and the cottages behind. Cullen dragged out a one-man tent from his backpack and set to work erecting it. When he was done he lit a small portable stove, filled a small pan with water from a bottle in his pack and made himself a cup of tea, black, and went to sleep.

"You do realise the station's just over the road, Colin?" Kate had asked as they strode along the main corridor of the Greenyards stand.

"Yes, Ma'am. But - as you're here. You know?"

"Yes, I know I'm here but that doesn't alter the fact that the station is *just over the road*." She pulled a snarky face whilst talking to his back.

The main room on the ground floor of the stand was a large rectangular affair with a shuttered bar at one end and paintings, photos, jerseys and other memorabilia arranged around the walls in assorted frames. All the tables were pushed up against the left-hand wall and, at the far end, was a large booth with banquettes around three sides and a few loose chairs in front of it. The seats were covered in a faded red velour and the polished wooden floor smelt of wax and wet leather.

A massive man sat hunched, testing the strength of his chair to the limit, cracking his knuckles loudly. At the sound of her heels on the floor he looked up. Kate couldn't determine whether he looked sheepish or proud. He stood up as she approached and grabbed hold of a grubby sack on the table behind him.

"Please, don't touch it." She raised a hand towards him. "I appreciate you brought it here and have probably touched it a lot already, but the less contamination we have on it the happier the forensic boys will be."

"This is Detective Superintendent Lorimer." Colin gestured towards Kate and she gave a quick formal smile. The man slowly placed the sack back on the table as if it any sudden movement would make it go off, like a criminal being asked to lay his gun on the ground.

"And you are?" Kate looked at him over her reading glasses and then, realising she had no need for them right now, removed them and folded them into her coat pocket.

"Paul. McInnes."

He was very tall and very broad, with hands that looked like vulcanised gloves. His head was smooth with black, shiny hair at the sides and a matching goatee. He had olive skin and dark eyes, which glistened in the reflected lights from the framed paraphernalia around the room, and wore an old navy blue fleece, a pair of paint-splattered overalls and steel toe-capped boots.

"Thank you, Mr McInnes for returning the trophy." She turned to Colin. "I assume it is our trophy?"

Colin was taken aback. "Erm, well, erm, yes. I think so. I mean, I've haven't really…"

"It says Ladies Cup, Melrose Rugby Club on it." Paul offered. "That's why I brought it here."

"Yes, well I suppose there can't be two Ladies' Cups now, can there?" She admitted.

"Well, actually Ma'am…" This was Colin.

"What?"

"Well, you see there are actually two. More in fact, if you count the copies." Colin looked like he was trying to solve a tricky long-division problem in his head, so Kate stepped quickly in.

"Explain."

"Well, the original Ladies Cup - that was made back in the 1880's for the very first Sevens tournament. It was funded by contributions from the ladies of Melrose and was given to the winners and never presented to anyone after that. So they made a new one. Doesn't look like the original at all, really. But it's also called the Ladies Cup and that is the one that gets presented to the winner every year."

"I see."

"And then there are the copies that get given to the winner each year for them to keep."

"Copies of the original Ladies' Cup?"

"No, this new one. Although it's not new at all, you see."

"So, this one…?" Kate nodded to the sack still sitting on the table.

"Well, I don't know-" Colin reached for it and Kate grabbed him by the arm.

"Don't. Let's wait for forensics." She turned to Paul. "Can you describe the trophy for me?"

Paul scrunched up his eyes and scratched an ear. "Well. It's silver. There's two handles on it and a mahogany wooden base-"

"How do you know it's mahogany?"

"I'm a joiner." Paul said blankly.

"Right. Ok. Anything else?"

"There's inscriptions on it an' that." He shrugged. "About it."

"Well?" She addressed this to Colin.

"Well, it's got to be ours. No-one else has reported any trophies stolen… have they?"

"Not to my knowledge." Kate sniffed. "Although the rate we're going I wouldn't be at all surprised. Well I guess we can wait for a formal ID." She turned back to Paul. "Where did you find it?"

"Traquair Village Hall. Car park."

"Right. Just this, on its own. Nothing else?"

"Yeah." Paul shook his head, then quickly changed it to a nod. "No. I mean, yeah. Just this."

Kate scrutinised his features, an expert eye doing a quick reconnaissance. Something felt slightly off but she couldn't put her finger on it.

"How long ago was this?"

"Well, yesterday." Paul seemed surprised by the question.

"What time?"

"Erm…" The big man looked confused. "Late?"

"Could you be a little more specific?"

"No, not really." He grinned sheepishly. "Don't have a

watch."

"Yes, but late as in midnight, early evening, late afternoon? What?"

"Oh, right. Evening, was goin' dark."

"O… k..." Kate said, but a small itch in her brain said this wasn't the entire story. Still, a trophy had been returned and hopefully there'd be some prints or fibres of something which would give them a lead. "Colin, call Frank at the station and have him get the lab boys on this. No-one else is to touch it until they get here, you understand?"

"Yes, Ma'am."

"And then have him check out the place where Mr McInnes found it. He can take them there." Kate suddenly picked up an anxious vibe from Paul and turned back to him. "Is something wrong, Mr McInnes? Are you unable to recall exactly where you found it?"

"No." Paul said, shifting his weight from one foot to the other. "Just got a job on, is all. Need to get back to it an' that." Kate thought he looked like a very large, guilty schoolboy. "Thought I could just drop it here and leave it all with you."

"Well, with my Rugby Club hat on, we are very grateful for your honesty and for returning it to us. But, with my police hat on, I'm afraid you will be required to give a statement. At the station." She was pretty sure Paul had blanched at that, so she chose her words carefully and watched his features as she enunciated each word. "And if you could accompany an officer… to the site where you found it… whilst that is not an obligation on your part… it would greatly speed up our investigation if you could… since I can clearly see an honest man like yourself would have no reason not to help the police with their enquiries."

Paul had kept a stony countenance throughout her little speech but there was definitely something wrong here. He seemed shifty and was clearly withholding… something.

"Ah, there you are! Thank you, thank you, thank you!" From out of the door next to the shuttered bar the perma-tanned figure of Des flew out and extended his hand towards Paul. "Thank you so much, you are a life-saver! I have been worried sick, honestly." He pumped Paul's hand enthusiastically. "And just talking with the insurance people - nightmare! Glad I can knock that on the head, I can tell you. So, is this it then?"

Des pulled his hand away and reached for the sack, pulling the trophy out into view before anyone could move.

"Des, no!" Kate protested, too late.

"What?" He looked puzzled and brandished the trophy towards them all as if he'd just been awarded it personally. "Hurrah! Look, we have it back."

"Don't we just?" Kate gritted her teeth. "I guess that counts as a formal ID. Now, can you please put it back in the sack. Carefully. And leave it there until the police get here? That is evidence and nobody should be tampering with it."

"Right-o" Des said, completely unabashed. Putting the cup back in the sack he then reached for Paul's hand again. "And you, my friend, shall be suitably rewarded. I will make sure you receive two VIP tickets. To the Sevens next weekend. Everything on the house, no expense spared. You and a friend will be wined and dined in splendour. Least we could do!"

Paul's eyes lit up. "Cool."

"You're welcome! Anything you want, just ask."

"Anything?"

"Anything."

"Can I bring my dogs?"

"No."

Kate glared. "I'm very happy for you all. Ah, Frank. Finally. I was beginning to think you'd got lost."

Sergeant Walker skulked into the clubroom, wincing at his superior's greeting.

"Sorry, Ma'am."

"It's, what? A hundred yards to the station. How'd you get here - canal?"

"Sorry, again. Ma'am. I was in the middle of-"

"Never mind. I want forensics down here asap and a witness statement taken from Mr McInnes here."

"Yes, Ma'am."

She saw an odd expression shoot across Paul's face then vanish. "Oh, and we'll need prints." Kate glared at Des and Paul. "From all of you."

"What do you reckon?" Paul asked, dangling the slender necklace from his meaty fingers.

Cullen, half-asleep, settled for: "Very nice, yes."

"Think she'll like it?"

"Shirley?"

"No, the Marquess of Queensberry. Of course Shirley!"

"The Marquess of Queensberry was a man."

"Really? Sounds feminine." Paul filed this information away under F for *future pub quiz material.* "Any road. That's what she's getting."

"Right." Cullen. He had crept out from his tent and was half-lying, half-sitting on the floor still in his sleeping bag while Paul towered over him. He rubbed some sleep from his eyes. "Is this why you stole into my house and woke me up?"

"Whoa, hello Mr All-property-is-theft. I'm Mr Only-friend-you-have, nice to meet you."

Cullen raised one eyebrow but thought better of responding. For the moment.

"Any way. One: this isn't your house. Two: I didn't break in, door was open. Three: You're the one who actually broke in."

Cullen looked at his friend for a moment. "Four: you did wake me up."

Paul looked around the stuffy sun-room and out through the sparkling trees. "So, how did you get in here anyway, then?" Paul was genuinely interested. Whilst he knew Cullen moved in mysterious ways, the man wasn't a superhero or a ghost. There had to be some practical tips and tricks he could learn from his friend.

"Tools of the trade. Number Six: Set of lock picks." Cullen removed a small leather pouch from his pocket and launched them at Paul. Paul caught the pouch and opened it, easing one of the slender strands of metal out from its sheath and flexing it between his thumb and forefinger. "Fool-proof."

The pick snapped in Paul's gigantic hand and Cullen sighed. "Fool-resistant, then."

"Soz." Paul muttered, putting the broken pieces back into the pouch and throwing it back to Cullen. "Got anything to eat?"

Cullen's eyes narrowed. "Thought you were on a diet?"

"Ahm. Well, Shirley's idea. Not mine."

"Aye, well. Regardless of who's idea it was. You on a diet or not?"

"Yes, if she's around; no, when she's not." Paul

grinned. "What've you got?"

"Chocolate biscuits is all." Cullen rummaged in his tent and threw him the pack. "But I'm with Shirley. There's plenty of you to go around. You could give loads away and not miss it."

"Gee, thanks. You're a real diplomat you know?" Paul sulked, biting a biscuit hungrily in half. They sat in silence for a while, the spring sunshine streaming in through the dirty glass while they both munched on the biscuits.

"You found me alright, then?" Cullen asked.

"Third Wanksy on the left, just like you said." Paul shucked himself down onto his haunches to meet Cullen at something approximating eye-level and dangled the necklace again, this time right in his friend's face. "So, do you really think she'll like it?"

"Yes." Cullen sighed and sat up properly. "Where did you get it?"

"Found it!" Paul could not have been happier unless he'd just received the Nobel prize for beer-drinking.

Cullen's eyes narrowed. "Uh-huh?"

"Straight up! It was with the Ladies Cup."

"Of course it was. And the Ladies Cup is…?"

"Oh, thought I'd told you this." Paul knelt down, immediately taking up much of the floor area. "Well, I found it and there was this necklace with it. So I gave the cup back and kept the necklace."

"Nice one, Tolstoy. Hope you haven't given away the film rights."

"Look, ok. I was out with the dogs, near the burnt-down bothy, and Ant found this sack in the undergrowth containing the Ladies Cup-"

"Which is?"

"The Ladies Cup? It's the trophy you get if you win the

Melrose Rugby Sevens tournament. Nice little thing. Gold apparently, although it looks silver. Worth a few bob I reckon."

"And you gave it back?"

"Yep!" Paul looked well pleased with himself.

"Just like that?"

"Just like that."

Cullen mulled this over for a moment. "This you turning over a new leaf then, hmm?"

"Aye!" Paul brightened still further, appreciating the recognition of his good dead. "Reckon it is."

"But you kept the necklace."

"Well, aye." Paul scrunched his nose up. "Baby steps, eh?"

"Kind of like a finder's fee, maybe?"

"That's right!" Paul grinned. "It is. Finders keepers and all that. If it hadn't been for me, they'd have no trophy to hand out next weekend."

"Let's have a closer look." Paul dropped the trinket into Cullen's outstretched palm and watched as his friend held it up to the light and brushed it carefully with a finger and thumb before spinning the disc. "Who's SHS?"

"Shirley!" Paul beamed. "That's her initials."

"But not her necklace?"

"Well, it is now. Bit o' bloody luck, eh?"

"Aye." Cullen said, absently. "And you found this with the trophy?"

"Yup. Wasn't in the sack, like." Paul looked up and to the left, trying to recall the scene. "I don't think. Dog found it in the same place though, so…"

"What did they say when you handed the trophy back?"

"Well they took my bloody fingerprints! Shit. I was sweating like Susan Boyle in a cake shop, let me tell you."

"Why? Are your fingerprints on file?"

"Who knows? Could be. Might be getting fitted up for something I did yonks ago, right at this very minute."

Cullen looked sternly at his friend. "If your prints were on file you would know, since you would need to have had your prints taken previously. And they can't take your prints without your knowledge - or permission, come to that."

"Well, they're on bloody file now. Bollocks!"

"Plus..." Cullen ignored Paul's interjection. "... you can't be *fitted up* for a crime you committed. If you actually did it - and they catch you - that's called being caught."

"Yeah, well. You know what I mean. I was..." Paul searched for a suitable euphemism. "Understandably nervous."

"I can imagine."

"Still." Paul brightened. "Got myself two VIP tickets for the Sevens out of it!"

"Really?"

"Aye. The Club President himself gave them to me - all-expenses paid, corporate hostility tent, backstage pass, free bar, the works."

"Hospitality."

"Same difference. Listen, can you keep a secret?" Paul looked over his shoulder - in the empty room in this abandoned house - put his head down low and whispered. "Thinking of using the opportunity to pop the question to Shirl."

Cullen's eyes widened.

"I know right?" Paul nodded.

"You're going to propose marriage to her? At a rugby match? Using a stolen necklace?"

"Ha! I know what you're thinking." Paul was ebullient.

"You're thinking: there's no way she can refuse!"

Cullen looked at his friend, sadly. "That is not what I was thinking."

IN COURT: DUFFY

"Please state your name clearly for the record." The Procurator Fiscal was standing at the lectern, riffling through a sheaf of papers.

"MacDuff Angel Ingoglia."

"Thank you, Mr Ingoglia. Could you please tell the court what you do for a living?"

"I'm an electrician." He nodded repeatedly at the wood panelling, as if to reassure himself that he had the right answer. "Electrician, yes."

"And you reside at the property in question - Ramsdale Cottage in Housebyres?"

"Yes."

"With your wife."

"Yes. Gloria. Yes. Gloria is my wife. She lives with me. We live together, yes."

"Thank you. Mr Ingoglia, why was your wife having sex with your brother-in-law?" The Fiscal stole a glance at the jury while she waited for his answer.

"She wanted a baby. Wants. Wants a baby. She wants a baby." Duffy's fingers flew as he spoke, head down and shaking slowly left and right.

"Mr Ingoglia?" The Sheriff said. "Could you please look up and speak out into the courtroom so that the jury can hear you clearly?"

Duffy brought his head slowly up, dragging it heavily against the pull of gravity even while still waggling it from side to side. His eyes darted everywhere.

"And this was your idea? Her having sex with Mr Marshall?"

"Yes." Duffy hung his head again and nodded shakily.

"Mr Ingoglia?" The Sheriff reminded him and Duffy dragged his head back up.

"Because you couldn't have children?"

"No. Had tests. Lot of tests. Many many tests."

"And this means you are unable to have children?"

"Yes. Motility is low. 5%. Less than 5%. Very low. Very very low."

"I see. What made you decide to… proceed with this arrangement? With Mr Marshall?"

"He has two sons. Big sons. Good boys. Strong boys."

"Sam and Sean?" The prosecutor consulted her notes.

"Yes. Big boys. Both big, big boys." Duffy nodded to himself and riffled imaginary playing cards with his fingers.

"And Mr Marshall was happy with this arrangement?"

"Yes. Everybody was happy. Everybody."

"Even your wife?"

Duffy hesitated, tossing his head left and right as if arguing with himself. "Yes. Gloria was happy. She wants a baby and this is how she can have a baby."

"So why did you put a stop to it all? If everyone was happy?"

"Because it wasn't working." There was a catch in Duffy's voice. A plaintive cry. "Months and months and months and no pregnancy. No baby. After months and months."

"You weren't happy?"

"No." Duffy started to sob quietly, his shoulders silently shaking.

"Mr Ingoglia?" The concerned prosecutor asked

gently.

Duffy sniffed. "I couldn't take it anymore. It was hard. Very hard. For me. Gloria wants a baby. I can't give her a baby. And I can't even bear the alternative, imagining her… I failed. I failed her. Couldn't bear it."

"What did you do?"

"I told him…" Duffy tried to lift his head to look at Wingnut but couldn't do it, managing only to nod the top of his head in the general direction of the dock. "Told him to stop. It was over."

"When was that?"

"Boxing Day."

"You told him on Boxing Day itself?"

"Yes. Told him, yes."

"What time would you say?"

"Evening. Late. I was up on the hill. Texted him."

"You texted him late on Boxing Day evening. Could you say approximately what time that might have been?"

"10:26. Pm. 10:26pm."

"10:26? That seems very specific. Are you sure about the time?"

"Yes." Duffy stopped agitating briefly and bunched his fists over and over, flexing them by his side. "In my logbook. Detailed record. Recorded the time. Also, have the texts. On my phone. 10:26. PM. Last message 10:54. Boxing Day."

"How did Mr Marshall take the news?"

"Objection, my Lord. The witness can't speak as to my client's state of mind. Now or then." Patterson said wearily.

"My Lord." The Procurator Fiscal smiled at the Sheriff. "The witness can account for a text conversation which took place between himself and Mr Marshall which tells its own story."

"Very well. I'll allow it. As long as it is the record of what was said."

"I'm obliged, my Lord." Whittaker turned back to Duffy. "Mr Ingoglia, how did Mr Marshall reply when you told him to stop seeing your wife?"

"He said *No*."

"My Lord, Exhibit 35 is a transcript of the text conversation which occurred between Mr Ingoglia and Mr Marshall on the evening of December 26th last year." Whittaker waved a stapled pair of A4 pages lazily, while the clerk handed a copy to the Sheriff and then passed them round the jurors. "What else did he say, Mr Ingoglia?"

"He said he wanted to see what my wife had to say about it."

"Anything else."

"He said we had a deal and he didn't renege on deals. That we were nearly there. I told him to stop and he said '*Maybe. Maybe not.*' When I said '*stop please stop*' he said '*We'll see about that*'.

"Thank you, Mr Ingoglia. Would you please wait there in case my colleague has any questions for you."

Patterson was up on his feet before she had finished speaking and crossed paths with the Procurator Fiscal as she swept back to her seat. "Oh yes, I have some questions for the witness. Mr Ingoglia."

Duffy looked at the foot of the jury box, eyes scanning the woodwork left and right, his fingers on his left hand - hidden out of sight behind the panelling of the witness box - waggling furiously. He was trying to remember what the Procurator Fiscal had told him about any possible cross-examination: that any defence barrister worth his salt would have a field day with his mannerisms, behaviour and belief systems.

She was not wrong. Mr Patterson was doing his best to hide a massive grin. As far as he could see, all he had to do was wind Duffy up and let him go. He felt sure that Duffy's manic attitude would do the rest.

He was not wrong either.

The reporter from the Southern Scotland Gazette would later describe it to his colleagues as quote *a car crash,* end quote.

Sitting in the front row of the public gallery, looking around at the courtroom while Duffy gave evidence, Robert was having his own epiphany. Wedged into the bench seating beside the giant Mongkut he had been absorbing as much of the detail as he could.

The white walls were peeling in places, the wooden benches and dividers were smoothed and scarred and splintered here and there, but the sunlight streaming through the enormous windows gave the place a brightness and freshness that it's decor badly needed. He sat entranced as the sluggish movement of the court had wound slowly into life.

There were a handful of other people scattered behind him in the gallery. A uniformed officer stood by the main door. Black trousers below a short-sleeved white shirt bearing insignia, epaulets; handcuffs at his waist. He stood feet apart with his hands clasped behind his back, the practised stance of someone used to having to remain stationary and on their feet for long periods of time.

In front of the judge's bench was a cluster of desks, at one of which sat a short woman all in black with a blonde bob and a deskful of paper. She was flipping through an in-tray, scribbling on some pages and not others. To her left was a large black metal cabinet with a glass door, containing a bank of black metal electronics, a single monitor on top. On each desk was a computer screen and, on the Sheriff's bench, three all told.

A tall woman in heels, all in black, with a black gown and long black hair pulled into a pony tail, sat at one of the desks. She was wading through a heavy pile of thick manila folders stuffed with paper. Across from her was a young smart fellow, all smooth-shaven and slicked-down hair, who had bounced into the courtroom light as air and placed his own slender briefcase on the remaining desk and extravagantly sat down, flipping his gown from under him so that he didn't sit on it.

Behind the judge's chair was a coat of arms bearing a lion and a unicorn and some words scrolled beneath. To the far left was another door and out of this had come a slow procession of people led by a smart grey-haired man in a white shirt and tie. The grey-haired man had moved over to the door next to the standing guard and sat in a chair beside the door. The people behind him had filed into the jury box, pulled down the seat of their allotted chairs and sat quietly, some holding clipboards and a pen, others not.

Everyone had risen to their feet when the Sheriff had marched in. He entered from a private doorway to the right and up some steps onto a raised platform walled off by a shoulder-height section of oak panelling. As he sat in his splendid throne, the clerk stood on tiptoe to pass a piece of paper up to him for his perusal. He was a smart middle-aged man with short grey hair showing beneath a tiny legal wig, and a pair of black spectacles perched halfway down his nose, who occasionally scanned the courtroom as if about to take the register.

Just as Duffy began to give his evidence, the main door to the courtroom opened and a latecomer entered. That was when Robert's jaw hit the floor.

There was absolutely no doubt in his mind that the woman apologetically tiptoeing up the side steps of the gallery, head ducking apologetically, was Gloria. His Gloria. She had barely aged, despite the years, and carried herself with the same easy elegance and fluidity that he had seem a thousand times in his dreams and would have recognised anywhere.

He turned and watched her as she found a seat a few rows behind them and elbowed Mongkut in the ribs. The giant blinked heavily and glared at him.

"It's Gloria" Robert hissed.

Mongkut frowned, peering down onto the court. "Where?"

"There!"

Mongkut twisted awkwardly to watch the back of the woman's head as she climbed the steps and then looked back at his friend with a doubtful expression.

"It is!" Robert insisted. "Look at her."

Mongkut contemplated her appearance again, putting his head to one side and then the other, before turning back to his friend and simply raising his eyebrows as if to say *How about that?*

But Robert sat entranced and felt his heart explode. The rest of the courtroom drama had melted away and all that was left, haloed, was Gloria. She was here, and he was here. Fate had magically, finally, brought them together - as he'd hoped and prayed all these years. He shifted in his seat, half-turning, the courtroom procedure abandoned, willing her to look up and catch his eyes.

Gloria had walked into the courtroom, nervous as anything, and kept her eyes glued to the floor. That she was here at all was bad enough. But she had made herself come and be seen, again, by the people who had already heard her and judged her. It didn't matter that it wasn't her on trial, it was Derek. And that was another reason she kept her eyes cast down: she couldn't bring herself to look at him. Whatever he'd done, it had all been Duffy's idea. Derek might have enjoyed himself a little too much but ultimately, as far as she was concerned, he was the innocent party. Duffy was guilty for coming up with the plan and persuading them all to go along with it; she was most guilty for allowing her own selfishness to take her pride, fidelity and moral compass and throw them all out of the window.

She had wrestled with the morality of her situation many times: prayed for insight and sometimes for forgiveness. By obeying her husband she was being a dutiful wife; by seeking to have a baby they would raise together she was helping create new life and build a happy marriage; but by engaging in sex with Derek she was being unfaithful and disrespectful to her husband and the very institution of marriage itself. Shame on her.

The row this morning with Duffy hadn't helped her mood. He didn't understand and she had failed to make him. They had travelled to the courthouse together in silence, and she had sat down in the hallway while he went to the witness room. Her heart had been hammering in her chest and her face blazing red but she forced herself to sit down and breathe.

"You're obsessed!" Gloria had cried, throwing her bag on the scuffed table and grabbing a sheet of kitchen towel to blow her nose on. "This whole fucking thing was your idea. Your fault."

"I did it for you. You wanted a baby. A baby, remember. I did this for you."

"I didn't want this! I don't want a baby like this! With him! It's a cwazy fucking scheme and I'm glad it's over."

"Not crazy. I'm not. Not crazy." Duffy had looked down at the floor and started threading his fingers together, his head pinballing from side to side.

"I didn't say you were cwazy, I said the scheme was cwazy."

"Not crazy, no." Duffy flapped his fingers against the heel of his palms, making a clapping noise, rhythmic and strong. Gloria watched him apprehensively. It wasn't a good sign.

"You're not fucking cwazy! Not, I said." She wiped her nose and turned towards the fridge.

"I am not CRAZY!" Duffy slapped his hands violently against both sides of head, a man-toddler hitting himself painfully hard.

"Stop it!" Gloria turned back and rushed towards him, trying to wrestle his arms down by his side. "Stop, Duffy. Stop!"

"NOT CRAZY! NOT!" Duffy's strength was too much for her and Gloria found herself being swung left and right, jostled helplessly like keys on a chain as he pounded his head. The thumping sound made her frightened.

"Stop, Duffy. Please!"

Duffy wheeled sharply and she was thrown backwards and smacked herself painfully against a kitchen cupboard.

Sitting awkwardly, cold on the flagstone floor, Gloria started to cry.

"Why did you make me tell everyone?" She was heaving out her words between sobs, sniffing and swallowing. She wasn't looking at him and he was no longer looking at her. "A woom full of strangers. I had to tell them… everything."

"It's called giving evidence. Giving evidence. Have to do it if you want to find someone guilty. Find *him* guilty. Have to." Duffy flashed back at her and she saw hatred in his eyes.

"But he's not guilty!"

"Yes he is." Duffy rounded on her, snarling. "He. Is. Guilty. Look at our home!" He spread his arms and scanned their living room, still unrepaired, still devastation apart from the lack of dust and rubble. He had no insurance and all they had been able to do was make the destruction look tidy, an intentional interior design disaster.

Gloria followed his gaze and shook her head sadly. "And is it worth it? Is putting Dewek in jail worth it?"

"Is what worth it, hmm? What? Your humiliation, do you mean?"

"Yes!" Gloria sobbed. "That man asking me nasty questions I had to answer."

"Nasty? Nasty? He's just doing his job, defending Derek." Duffy was shaking his head slowly now, his hands back down by his sides, his anger subsiding. Rationality was returning as he pieced together his argument. "Seems to me like he did a pretty good job too. Excellent job. Defending Derek. Yes, excellent job."

"Well, maybe he'll go fwee. Maybe that is justice." Gloria sobbed.

"Justice! How is that justice? No, we will have justice when I have given my evidence. Then the jury will decide. They will decide."

He had left her disconsolately on the floor, drying her eyes. She had felt humiliated giving evidence, Duffy had been right about that. And she just wanted this whole wretched affair to vanish. Why had she agreed to it? Why? She couldn't have been more unhappy if she tried. And now Duffy disagreed with her. What was the point of all this? Why was she here with a madman who couldn't give her a baby, pushed her into a crazy scheme - yes, it was crazy - which reminded her of a past life she hoped she'd left behind, and who could barely afford to put a roof over their heads? A roof which Derek had almost managed to demolish.

Here in the hushed courtroom, she closed her eyes and tuned out the narrative. Instantly she saw Worrawut how he had appeared in her dream. Though she hadn't seen him for years, he was completely familiar, despite being no longer the youth she had last known. His bearing and stance were instantly recognisable. He had appeared regal, yet other-worldly. Noble and serene, but unperturbed by what he had witnessed. This was his home and he was relaxed and supple - the two Scotsmen alien and uncomfortable, despite their semi-nakedness. Worrawut had looked like a god.

She had been sixteen when she had said goodbye and there had been tears in his eyes. He was a little younger than her and had yet to feel the burden of family duties. He had almond eyes and chubby cheeks, which shook when he grinned - which he did often - and eyes which flickered like orange flames on a windy day. There had been love in his eyes when they had parted, and she had known he had loved her (or thought he did) but she was a woman now and above such things. Love and romance were for storybooks and fairy tales; cold hard reality must eventually reach them all - even here in the jungle-clad hills of north-east Thailand.

She had kissed him and hugged him and looked deep into his eyes and told him everything would be alright. They would meet again, she had lied, and live a long and happy life in the shadows of their family homes. He had smiled through his tears and told her he would wait for her. Would make a home fit for her when she returned. A dutiful husband is what he would be and he would craft a sustainable livelihood for them both to share. Gloria had cried at the glory of his innocence as much as the beauty of the thought and wondered what had become of him. Whether he still waited for her, tilling fields, harvesting crops and treading through muddy rice paddies. Still drove swaying oxen with the sun on his back and children shrieking in the shining streams emerging from the water pump. She could see the heat from the day rising from the rain-soaked ground, steaming forests reaching high to the white-blue sky, the grizzle and whine of two-stroke motors from mopeds and tuk-tuks flashing by on the dirt track that passed for the main artery in and out of this jungle realm.

Gently crying now from this memory, she opened her wet eyes here in the courtroom, and looked into the face of an enraptured Worrawut.

WORRAWUT & MONGKUT

The journey from the airport had been a revelation. Exiting the aeroplane, Robert had seen the grey sunlight and felt the chill air of Scotland and wondered whether he would ever be warm again. He hadn't been this cold since he'd had an icebath for his injured muscles after the final of the Bangkok Sevens last year. This was colder. For the past two hours, they had driven through rain and mist, the landscape a grey blur around them. He had pressed his nose to the window and tried to inhale the very scenery, it was so intoxicating and alien. But there was no denying that the predominant colours were drab. He saw no temples, no gold, no fluttering flags or tuk-tuks. Just mile after mile of concrete and steel, tarmac and traffic.

The man from the rugby club who had accompanied the driver, had kept up an informative and entertaining narrative as they had sped along, dropping all sorts of new words into Robert's lexicon: motorway, underpass, flyover, contraflow, retail park. In this country even the words were grey.

It wasn't until the second hour that the sky brightened slightly, even as the sun lowered, and the scenery around them changed from urban to rural. There were fields and cattle - albeit no oxen - and hills and trees; all in deep and dark hues of grey and brown and green. The cityscape had been slashed and burnt and replaced with a rolling carpet of muddy watercolours.

The flight had been long but enjoyable, although he

couldn't say the same for Mongkut whose giant frame squeezed between the row of seats had threatened to tear the fuselage apart. The stewardess had told them they must have the seat arm between them down for take-off and landing but it wasn't physically possible and she had muttered something inaudible before handing them a packet of peanuts each and telling them not to tell anyone.

The couple sitting in front of them, though, had got on Robert's nerves. Maybe they were on honeymoon or something - perhaps just loved-up - but they were certainly tanked up (on Bacardi breezers) and pent up (with lust). He was just fed up, listening to them flirt in stage whispers the whole cabin could hear. It had been a very long flight and they had been drinking and giggling the entire time.

"Ooh. What on earth are you trying to do, Phil?"

The man had one hand jammed in her short dress.

"Just need to secure your belongings, madam." He wrestled with her faux reluctance as the pair squirmed in their seats. Robert had looked forlornly down the aisle. The route map on the TV showed them in sight of Glasgow. This would all soon be over.

"Might be in for some turbulence, if the flight goes to plan."

Robert reached into his seat pocket and took out his information folder emblazoned with their team logo. He skimmed through the sheets of paper for the umpteenth time, making sure he had their itinerary and key dates clear in his head.

They were arriving today, the 9th, and staying in Scotland for the rest of the week. The Sevens tournament was on Saturday 14th and the days between now and then were to be training days alternated with days of rest. Once the tournament was over, almost immediately afterwards in fact, they had to rush to the airport and a return flight to Heathrow where they would have a one-day stopover to visit London before heading home.

He checked the weather information sheet which described overall climate conditions in Scotland for April and also a long-range forecast for the week ahead. It all made grim reading when you were used to tropical temperatures throughout the year.

"Hmmm, would I be allowed access to the cockpit, do you think?" The woman piped up again.

"I think you already are, madam." The man shifted awkwardly, now shielding the woman from view as she wriggled next to the window. "Now, is this the, er, landing strip?"

"Uh, yes." She giggled and the distinct aroma of sex filtered up from their seats. "Do you mind if I just check, um…."

"Sorry, madam. Just adjusting the flaps."

"Uh… mmmm. Feel free to… roam about the cabin."

"Roger that. Doors to manual." He chuckled involuntarily. "Oops, I think have hit an air pocket."

"Hey, stop that! That's the emergency exit."

"Sorry. Think something might have shifted in transit."

"Well, let me check the nuts for tightness." Robert got a bang on his right knee as the man's seat jerked backwards. "Ah, yes.

The stewardess came on the intercom: "Ladies and gentleman, we are making our final approach."

The pair elbowed each other frantically and tried to contain their giggling.

But they both completely lost it, when she added: "Please make sure your tray table is in the upright position."

When the team coach pulled into the car park. Mongkut and Robert both clutched the seatbacks in front of them, pulling themselves up for a better view of the pitch. Here, finally, was their destination. The hallowed turf of The Greenyards. Robert hustled his bag down from the overhead shelf and shuffled along the aisle and down the steps into the car park. A small crowd of people were standing at a distance, watching. Some filming on their cameras. He inhaled a lungful of cold, damp air and felt an unfamiliar chill and a rush of freshness and purity. He stood weary and blinking, his tiredness from the long flight finally hitting him and then he heard his name called.

"Mongkut? Robert? This is Ms Lorimer."

"Kate, please." A tall, serious-looking woman with silver-blonde hair pulled up in an untidy bun held out her hand. She smiled politely and saw it vanish in the huge paw Mongkut extended to her. He beamed a megawatt smile, all teeth and gold; Robert waited his turn to shake the lady's hand and then scrutinised her face. She had sad eyes and a mole to the right of one nostril which made her look a little off-centre.

"This way. I'm parked over here. But don't worry, I'm only a few minutes away."

The pair gathered their cases from the coach hold and dragged them across to the boot of a large grey 4x4. They both sat mutely in the back while Kate fastened her belt and then indicated that they did the same. Obedient, like two boys on the first day of term, they followed, and then the car chimed as she reversed out of the space and pulled out onto the main road.

"Welcome to Melrose." Kate said, smiling again, this time looking at them through the rear-view mirror. "I see you didn't bother bringing the weather with you? Is that because it would have taken you over your baggage allowance?"

Robert didn't understand the reference but returned her smile politely and then turned to stare out of the window at the cold grey mist. It was like looking through a dirty window. He hoped that things would look a lot better after a meal and a good night's sleep.

"So, how do I pronounce your names?" Kate asked over breakfast the next morning. Now this was more like it. Kate had made bacon and scrambled eggs, toast and mushrooms and something she called sausages. Robert liked them very much and was now on his eighth. "Gosh, you two can put it away can't you?"

"Mongkut." Mongkut said. "Mong. Kut."

"Monkhut?"

He nodded - that was close enough. She looked at Robert. "And you?"

Robert struggled to swallow the last mouthful of sausages only managing: "Wowwert."

"Robert?"

Robert nodded and carried on emptying his plate.

"Well, I'm imagining you'd like to do something today would you? Stretch your legs after being cooped up on the plane all day yesterday? Or do you have any training planned?"

"Training today and Thursday." Mongkut said. "Tomorrow…" He shrugged.

"Oh. Ok." Kate twisted her mouth into a knot. "Well,

I'm working today - and tomorrow too, actually, although I'm in court so don't imagine I'll get much done. They mess you about with times and so forth, can't guarantee how long you'll be there or whether they'll even need you that day." She looked from one to the other and realised she was gabbling. "This is the first time I've done this, you see. Putting up visiting players. This happens all the time, I'm told - foreign players staying with local families the week before the tournament. And I've got the room - plenty of space, when there's only me here. But I can't do anything about my availability, you see. Duty calls. I'm a police officer." She said by way of an explanation, realising she was having a one-way conversation with the pair of them. "Look, there's house keys on the hook there and I've left a map and some leaflets on the hallway table - about Melrose and the local area. You can have a mooch, climb up the Eildons, visit the abbey, wander down by the river. Take a closer look at the rugby ground?"

They both brightened considerably when she said that, so she pressed on. "Actually, look. I'll be done by half-five. Maybe earlier. How about I give you both a guided tour of the Greenyards when I get back?"

"You can do that?"

"I'm on the committee! And I'm a Police Superintendent! I can do anything!" She smiled cheerily, grabbed her handbag and waved them goodbye.

Mongkut sat silently watching while Robert finished scooping up his sausage and eggs into his expressionless face.

Robert was not his given name, that was Worrawut. But back home in Thailand, Worrawuts were two a penny and his surname, Pornpitpatpong, did not exactly trip off the tongue. In the English speaking world - which is what most of the international rugby community was - both names were easy to ridicule and difficult to pronounce.

So Robert Patpong was his adopted rugby name and he quite liked it.

Robert had grown up in a dirt-poor area of North-eastern Thailand and shown no talent for anything whatsoever. Until someone gave him a ball. His first ball was a football and he loved it so much he would sleep with it and take it everywhere he went. He was a gifted player with natural speed and fast feet but he was also far too strongly built. As he grew he became bulkier, and it wasn't long before he found his ball skills compromised by his ungainliness. He had vision and a good footballing brain, but he was just too damn immobile for the beautiful game. Even a stint in goal had not helped him fit into the team.

But he was disciplined and committed, stubborn and tenacious. He persisted, but while ball games remained his second love, his first love had always been Gloria. The pair had known each other since before they could remember and been boyfriend and girlfriend before those terms really meant anything. Naive innocent days of holding hands and stealing kisses in the tropical hills, looking down on the sleepy river that chugged down the valley between jungle-clad slopes.

And when she had left the village to seek a life in the city he had wept and turned his back, watching from afar as she bid farewell to her family and rode the back of an oxcart, unsteadily, until it disappeared from view. He wrestled with his emotions, unfamiliar with the wrenching guts and a sudden tearfulness that would steal up unannounced and floor him. Calling on his inner discipline he adopted a plan for dealing with this turmoil: he would give it six months. If the pain and sadness had subsided by then - his mother had gently told him that time was a great healer - that would be the end of the matter. He could endure a six month wait. But if, after all that time, he was still pining and whining like a runt boar abandoned by a sow, then he would steal away and go and find Gloria.

He was resourceful, resilient, strong, dogged. How hard could it be?

He had made it as far as Bangkok before he realised the enormity of his task. He had no money, no friends, no local knowledge, no home, no shelter, help or guidance. He didn't even know where Gloria had gone. And he was only fourteen years old.

But he survived. Long enough to be saved, anyway. And his saviour, the man to whom he owed his love of rugby, and his new name, was an Australian English teacher called Max.

Max had come to Thailand on a one year assignment, fell in love with the country, met and married a Thai girl and never left. He was rugby mad and an avid Wallabies supporter. Having grown up in Perth, he was a strong, athletic player good enough to be semi-professional but a knee injury had seen an early end to his playing career and he had had to settle for coaching and watching from the sidelines. He started volunteering at one of the Bangkok YWAM missions and graduated to setting up a rugby school which would one day grow into the Nak Suu Tigers Rugby Academy - a charity devoted to helping slum kids to develop life skills, social skills, English language skills and teamwork through learning, playing and competing in rugby. Run by volunteers and managed with energy and drive by Max, it saved many kids from a helpless future.

And Robert was one of them.

One night, out scavenging on the streets, as he had become accustomed to doing - begging, stealing food from handcarts or leftovers from market stalls - he fell in with a small gang of street orphans. Robert was bigger and stronger, but they were nimbler and faster. Together they made a great team and soon this group of seven boys became a family unit, looking out for each other, helping and finding food for each other. And this was how Max had found him - with his new family unit, sleeping in a cardboard shelter, lined up like chess pieces in a box.

Max saw in Robert a raw talent and strength that was no loss to football but was of immense value to rugby. He threw him into training sessions every Thursday and Saturday and gave him individual coaching on Mondays and Fridays. The academy funded its work with the profits from an annual Rugby Ten's tournament which attracted many famous former rugby players: *The Rugby Legends*. And it was on this stage that Robert was able to grow, meet rugby greats, learn skills and the English language, and begin to build a dream of a future as a professional rugby player.

At fourteen, he'd never seen a rugby match before, nor a stadium crammed with 8,000 people cheering. By eighteen he was competing in an international rugby 10's tournament in Bangkok and on the verge of selection to the Thai national Under-21's squad. And every night he would return to sleep in his cardboard shelter, clutching a rugby ball to his chest, and dreaming of Gloria.

Robert's intensive induction into rugby via Max had been accompanied by a similarly persistent programme of missionary zealotry - all part of the YWAM regime. In a country so defined and enmeshed in Buddhism, Robert's indoctrination into Antipodean Christianity had inevitably led to him having a peculiarly wonky world view.

At the heart of his confusion - which his missionary advocates had done almost nothing to reconcile - was that surely there must either be a God or not. Christianity represented a single, all-powerful creator and all other Gods were false; Buddhism rejected all Gods and the very idea of a creator. It was a binary choice and one he found unable to make. His missionary friends would go to great lengths to explain - for explain, read *obfuscate* - that the one Christian God was in fact three separate manifestations of the same Godhead: the father, the son and the Holy Spirit.

None of this helped.

So Robert took a very pragmatic approach: rugby was why he was here and rugby was what he would focus on. All of this religious stuff was necessary, it seemed, to give him access to the rugby - a tax, if you will, to be paid so that he could reap the benefits of the game he loved - so Robert went along with it, sang hymns, prayed and generally went through the motions so that the brothers and volunteers of the Academy would consider him devout and enlightened enough. At least to be selected for the first team.

And as his young brain wrestled with these thoughts, much as his young body fought and struggled with the increasingly testing physical regime, he slowly incorporated all these concepts into a single belief system which synthesised and integrated these disparate ideas, in a way that he could use to guide him and provide him with a moral compass.

He called this belief system: *Ruggism*.

Rugby was the eternal constant. A game which, when

played to its limit, produced beauty and life and passion and pleasure. At that perfect moment when hand and eye and ball combined to complete a pass, score a try, or commit a tackle: that was where a universal spirit alighted on him, briefly, and blessed him with insight and acceptance. He lived only to worship the game, its streamlined compact rule set, its formulation and its grandeur.

Worshippers would gather together in stadia to pay homage to the game; the World Cup trophy was The Holy Grail; he himself was The Chosen One; the codification of Rugby Union rules was the Creed.

And the supreme Goddess of Ruggism, was Gloria.

He had never lost his hope of finding Gloria, just changed his strategy. The naivety of a penniless fourteen-year-old teenager in believing he could scour an entire country and find her, had been replaced by a genuine (if a little self-serving) vision of an ambitious and determined eighteen-year old young man: if he could one day become a famous rugby player - his face on posters and hoardings, cereal packets and TV screens - then maybe, just maybe, she could find him.

Max had one other protégé at the Academy, and that was Mongkut. Americans would call him an *absolute unit.*

Mongkut was two inches short of seven feet tall and larger than anyone Robert had ever seen in his life. Every single inch of him looked like it had been hand-made by skilled craftsmen with the express purpose of dominating on the football field. His fingers were thick and smooth, and powerful muscles bulged and rippled across the backs of his hands like rope.

He was a powerhouse of strength and sinew, able to stampede through any line, past any back, and carry any number of hangers-on with him as he went. Literally. He was a bipedal rhino who could lift any weight, stop any attacker, and charge through any obstacle as if it was a net curtain. Defenders clung to him, briefly, until they were jostled loose by the horsepower of his steaming pace.

Overall he represented a human figure almost too large to be true - less a human, more a demi-god. A hero of biblical proportions whose physical form couldn't all be taken in in one go. You had to kind of traverse him, a piece at a time, like scaling an impossible cliff-face. Catching him out of the corner of your eye was the only way of seeing him properly but, when you moved your head to regard him full-on, he had already moved and you were left contemplating empty air, the only vestige of his presence that remained was more a sense of his gargantuan absence.

His mighty head was shaven and shone like the golden Dome of the Rock. His feet were broad and wide and could have supported the Colossus of Rhodes. He had the arms and shoulders of Atlas, the chest of Hercules, the back of Sisyphus, the speed of Mercury.

And the heel of Achilles.

Because what he couldn't do, was throw a ball. Mongkut was the man you gave the ball to. From that point on, the only practical thing that could prevent him scoring a try was a natural disaster. But you had to give him the ball. Physically. Place it right into his hands and make sure his grip was firm before you let go. Maybe it was the bulk in his chest and shoulders, or maybe it was some kind of oxygen deficiency up at the altitude he normally breathed in. The fact was that Mongkut was a point-and-shoot missile that had to be locked and loaded before you pulled the trigger. He couldn't pass, he couldn't catch, but he could make it to the try line except in the event of nuclear war.

His footballing brain was tiny, but no matter. Give him the ball, show him the line, put the points on the board.

And he loved Robert and doted on him like some educationally subnormal genie. Robert, in turn, saw him as a physical manifestation of Ruggism, brought to earth to show the way. Not so much the Jesus Christ of Ruggism, more a kind of John the Baptist. He was Robert's rock - for the past ten years Mongkut had kept him safe, made him comfortable, given him companionship, shown him devotion.

And now they were at the home of Rugby Sevens together.

"And this is the trophy room." Kate led them left into the smaller room bearing the glass wall cabinet and the collection of silverware. "The Ladies Cup - the Centenary cup. The one awarded to the Sevens winners. Only recently recovered actually."

"In silver?" asked Mongkut.

"Sorry?"

"Re-covered? In silver?"

"Oh, no. I don't mean restored, I mean... Never mind. And this is the original, historic trophy. Very valuable."

Robert wandered around the room, scrutinising the various photos and pictures on the walls. He stared in fascination at the trophies, nose almost pressed up to the glass. Kate stood in silence observing the pair for a short while. Robert was shorter and stockier than the giant

Mongkut. There was something about this leviathan that made her think of the sea, for some reason. He was like an aircraft carrier perhaps, or a whaling ship: prow first, towering presence, projecting the ability to withstand any waves and any force. Robert was more of a tugboat: squat and strong, she could envisage him head-down using all his strength to wrangle a scrum this way and that.

"What do you do, Robert?" She asked.

"Hmm?"

"Back home? In Thailand? When you go home next week what will you be returning to?"

"I am student. Bangkok University."

"Oh, right. Studying… what? Sports Science?"

"Law."

"Oh, wow." Kate was taken by surprise and then wondered why that was.

"Third year. Of four."

"Ok. And what do you want to do when you graduate?"

"I want be lawyer. Barrister at court."

"Well, good for you. The law needs all the help it can get - in this country at least." She smiled wistfully and wondered what the legal system might be like in Thailand and whether it would compare favourably to her native one. "Listen, would you like to attend a Scottish court? See the law in action?"

Robert's eyes widened. "Is that.. Can you do that?"

"Well, yes. I mean anyone can attend court, sit in the public gallery and watch. There's a trial on this week, actually. I could take you with me and you can sit and watch. Might be interesting. Might be boring as hell. Up to you." A thought occurred to her. "Does Monkhut study law too?"

Robert grinned. "No. Sports Science."

"Oh."

"But he will come too." Robert broke into Thai and hailed his friend across the room. A very brief conversation ended with Mongkut saying a clear "uh-huh" with a curt nod.

"Right, then." Kate concluded. "We're sorted for tomorrow."

IN COURT: DUFFY AGAIN

Patterson took a deep breath. He wanted to take maximum benefit of the rapid-fire nature of Duffy's statements versus the slow, deliberate, unflashy questions he was posing. He wanted there to be no accusations of provocation raised once Duffy reached escape velocity.

"Mr Ingoglia. You were on the premises, at home, the evening of Boxing Day last year? When the alleged events occurred?"

"Yes. Yes I was."

"But not at the time of the incident?"

"No."

"You were only aware of the incident when you later arrived home?"

"Yes."

"Mr Ingoglia, could you describe your movements on the night in question please?"

"My movements?"

"Yes. You say you were at home and then you were…" Patterson consulted his notes. "*Up on the hill.* Your words. So could you tell the court what time you left home, where you went, what time you returned home."

"I was at home until… until…" Duffy's brow creased as he started to panic.

"Mr Ingoglia?" Patterson prompted.

"Yes. I… I… don't know exactly. We had an argument. Minor argument. Very very small argument. I went out. Walked to Melrose. It was dark. Dark, yes. Very,

very dark."

"But could you give an estimate perhaps?"

"An estimate?"

"Yes. You know. An approximation. What time *approximately* did you leave home, would you say?" Patterson rolled his eyes at the jury, sharing his exasperation at such a simple request.

"Can't be approximate. Have to be exact. Have to be. Yes. 100%. Exact. Yes."

"Ah." Patterson, was magnanimous in accepting the witnesses inability to answer. "Well, perhaps you made some record of the event? Something which could help us work out what time you left home?"

"Yes. I did. Yes." The witness, jerked his head up and looked at directly at Patterson. "Made a record. Yes. Always make a record. In my notebook. Always. Write it down. Future reference. Analyse the data. Look for patterns. It's what they'd do."

"You have a record?"

"Yes. Yes. Always. Always make a record. In my notebook. Yes." He reached into his pocket and produced an A6 notebook, thick and made thicker by additional scraps of paper wedged into its pages. The book was held together by a thick green elastic band and the pages were curled, deformed perhaps through usage, water damage or both.

When he started removing the rubber band, Patterson interjected. "My Lord? Perhaps we could have this notebook recorded as evidence and adjourn while we have opportunity to study it before proceeding with the witness's testimony."

"Take the book into evidence please." The Sheriff nodded down to the Clerk of the Court who stood and walked over to the witness box to take the notebook from Duffy. "Exhibit F, I think? But, let's have the witness continue with their testimony just now, shall we?" The Sheriff looked at his watch. "Only a couple of minutes or so until we break for lunch, anyway."

"As your honour wishes." Patterson bowed. "Mr Ingoglia, what does your notebook say about the events of Boxing Day?"

Duffy waited for the Clerk to return the book to him, then he opened it and quickly found the relevant page.

"Nine thirty-eight. I left home at 9:38. PM. Walked to Melrose, arrived 10:17."

"Arrived where?"

"Melrose. 10:17." Duffy repeated.

"But where, Mr Ingoglia? Where in Melrose were you, when you *arrived*?"

"Eildon hill." Duffy was massaging the book between his fingers and thumbs as he spoke. "Definitely Eildon hill. Eildon North." He looked again at the page. "10:17 arrived. First notes taken, 10:19."

"Eildon hill? What were you doing up there?"

The Procurator Fiscal shifted in her seat and looked anxiously towards Duffy but Duffy was busy staring down at the book in his hands, running his fingers over the fine green writing on its pages. Lost in his own thoughts he failed to see his counsel's concern. But Patterson detected it and pressed on.

"Mr Ingoglia? What was so important that you had to climb Eildon Hill, for? On Boxing Day night. In the dark."

It seemed to Patterson that, in every trial, there were moments in a courtroom when everyone assembled collectively held their breath. Some unreasoned and sixth sense pricked everyone's awareness and they instinctively stopped what they were doing and listened as the words rang out across the empty air. Portentous. A vital answer was about to yield up significant information and everyone could somehow tell.

Everyone except Duffy.

"Waiting for aliens."

"Well, I would have to say that - all things considered - either that man is suffering from serious brain damage, or his mother was a vacuum cleaner." Jerry sniffed over lunch. "I mean, come on! Bloke's an effin' nutter. Aliens is it?"

"We're not here to judge the witnesses. We're here to judge the accused." Intoned the businessman,

"Defendant." Interjected Jean, ever watchful at his side, for any minor misdemeanour.

"Sorry, yes. Defendant."

"Yeah, but, if the witnesses are effin' mental you can't rely on their evidence can you? I mean, what are you supposed to believe? The word of a nutter who spends his nights sitting on a hill waiting for aliens? Or his missus who can't barely manage a word of English? It's a ruddy joke innit?"

"That's quite a good point though, isn't it?" Moira said, all bristle and bustle today in a nice blue jumper with imitation pearls knitted into it around the neck. "We are supposed to make up our minds about all this, aren't we? And the Sheriff did say *reasonable doubt.* So, my question is: does what Mr Imbroglio say sound reasonable?"

"You know the slimy lawyer's doing this to make him sound unreasonable, don't you? He's not focussing on any actual relevant evidence. He's just poking this bloke with a stick to see how high he jumps."

"That is, I believe, the whole point."

"No, it's not. Their job is to extract the evidence from the witnesses, and show both sides of their stories so we can determine where the truth lies. It's not meant to be an exercise in character assassination. This is the criminal justice system, not Twitter."

"Ooh, yeah. It's a bit like trial by telly, innit?"

"Well, I don't approve of the way that young man asks his questions and swaggers about like he's some kind of movie star, but surely if he was doing the wrong thing wouldn't the Sheriff step in and put an end to it?"

"He has stepped in. Several times."

"Yes, but he hasn't put an end to it though."

"Ach, they're all in this together aren't they? It's all a game to them, just their day job. They don't care that lives hang in the balance or that decisions here might ruin someone's life. They just go through the motions, play their little legal games, chalk up a win or a defeat and then go onto the next one. End of the day, they all go home to their cosy middle-class lives, kiss the wife, have a gin and tonic and watch University Challenge."

"That's a bit sexist isn't it? The Procurator Fiscal's a woman. She won't have a wife."

"She might. Could be a lezzer." Injected Jerry from behind his Racing Post.

"The word is lesbian." Snapped Moira. "And there is nothing wrong with being a lesbian."

"Oh aye. Are you one then?" Asked Jerry.

"Certainly not!" Moira retorted.

"Ooh, did he say lesbian!" Marjorie asked Lorraine next to her, dropping her voice to a whisper at the final word. "I didn't get to my age listening to talk about lesbians. We didn't have lesbians in my day. I'm eighty-eight you know?"

"Can we get back to talking about the evidence? All this… other stuff… is just a distraction." Complained the businessman.

"Well, I think it's really entertaining, but I'm not sure I can remember any actual evidence."

"There was the fight in the pub."

"Well, there's some doubt about that."

"Hmm. But he must have been drunk when he smashed the van into their house."

"But we don't know if he was driving!"

"Oh come on! His prints were all over the steering wheel."

"Doesn't mean he was driving."

"Well, no. But it might. Is it reasonable to suppose that he was driving? Or is it really more likely that the prints were put on earlier and never smudged or wiped?" The businessman seemed relieved that they were finally talking about issues of substance.

"Dunno. That police lady seemed quite convinced he must have been driving."

"Yeah but she's the filth, ain't she? Course she's gonna say that. That's her job." Jerry didn't even bother looking up this time, eyes busy scanning the runners in the 4.30 at Worcester.

The businessman looked at Jerry disapprovingly, then addressed himself to the whole group. "It's a case of Occam's razor."

"Oxo's raisin?" Marjorie screwed up her face.

"Occam's razor. It's a problem-solving tool."

"Like an Allen key?"

"No. It is a principle which basically says: if you have

any two possibilities - two different explanations for something - the simplest one is usually the correct one."

"You mean like KISS: Keep It Simple Stupid?"

"Sort of, yes. So if one explanation is that he drove the car that night, and the other that he didn't and his prints got there some other way, at a previous time when he was in the car, but that they had not been wiped in the meantime. Well, Occam's razor says you accept the simplest of those two explanations."

"Which is?" Marjorie asked, still confused.

"You say Occam's razor, I say Market Rasen." Jerry quipped to no-one in particular.

Patterson started mentally rubbing his hands with glee. This was too easy. Ingoglia was jittery, sweating, alternately wringing his hands and then allowing them to flutter wildly at his sides. The entire time he had been in the witness box he'd been bending his head this way and that, as if trying to decipher a pattern on the floor. With everyone now fed and watered after lunch, Patterson had the rest of the afternoon to tear this witness apart.

He smiled at Duffy. "So, Mr Ingoglia. You were up on top of Eildon Hill. In the dark. Late at night. On Boxing Day. Looking for aliens." Patterson swung his gaze slowly along the row of jurors. "Was this a… normal event?" Patterson had deliberately swapped *traditional* for *normal* at the last minute, lest any jury members fail to get the message. The Procurator Fiscal spotted it.

"Objection!" Whittaker was up on her feet.

"Yes, Ms Whittaker?" The Sheriff peered amusedly at the Fiscal over his glasses.

"My Lord, this is not germane to the case or to the

incidents in question. How the witness spends his free time is of no concern of this court."

"My Lord." Patterson replied. "It has a bearing on the credibility of the witness and any other evidence he may be asked to give in this case."

"Does it, though?" The Sheriff asked.

"Yes, my Lord." Patterson briefly tried to imagine what other questions he might want to ask this witness in case the Sheriff pressed him as to what shape this *any other evidence* might take. To his relief, the Sheriff didn't. He raised his eyebrows curiously at Duffy and glanced at the clock at the back of the court.

"Yes, well. You have my indulgence, Mr Ingoglia. And that, I'm sure, of the ladies and gentlemen of the jury. For the moment."

Duffy frowned at the Sheriff, uncertainly. Then looked at Patterson, who was standing there expectantly, waving his spectacles in his hand. Finally, he looked over at the Procurator Fiscal who met his eyes and then sadly nodded her head.

"Was it a normal event?" Patterson repeated

"Yes. Since 2010."

"Every Boxing Day?" Patterson puzzled.

"Yes. But also every day. Every day."

Patterson theatrically shook water from his ears. "Every *single* day?"

"Yes. Every day. Every day, yes, every day."

"*Every* day?"

"Mr Patterson." Interrupted the Sheriff. "Perhaps we can dispense with the dumb show? I believe everyone in court understands fully the normal usage of the term *every day*."

"I am obliged, my Lord." Patterson smarmed. Bastard.

Still, he had struck gold. This was going to be a home run and an early bath for all involved. "So, Mr. Ingoglia. You are telling the court that you climb Eildon Hill, every day, to look for aliens?"

"Yes. Yes." Duffy nodded enthusiastically, finally pleased that his message had been fully grasped.

"And that, furthermore, this is something you have done every day. Every single day, since 2010?"

"September 9, 2010. Yes. September 9."

"And it is for this reason - looking for aliens - that you were absent from your property at the time of the alleged incidents on Boxing Day last year?"

"Yes. Gloria was there. I was out. Looking for them. On the hill."

"And it was during this time on the hill that the text conversation with my client occurred?"

"Yes."

"So what happened then?"

"I saw a sign." Duffy smiled to himself and shook his head in self-satisfaction.

"A sign?" Patterson nodded as if impressed. "What sort of sign?"

"An aitch. On fire. A fiery aitch. Huge, in flames. Fiery orange aitch."

"An aitch?"

"Letter H. Aitch. Letter H."

"You saw a huge letter H on fire?"

"Yes. On fire. Yes."

"And this was a sign?"

"Yes. Yes. Oh yes. Clear sign. Waited years. There it was. Years." Duffy was really excited now, his whole upper body twitching and on the move. Fingers like a shuttle threading the weft through the warp.

"Mr Ingoglia, if I may drag you away from aliens and signs for just a moment. Focus on the matter of the text conversation?" Patterson fawned. "The conversation with my client when you told him that the arrangement of having sex with your wife was to come to an end."

"We had the text conversation. Yes. In the notes. Exhibit 35."

"Yes, yes. And then?"

"Then I saw the sign." Duffy cocked his head, this way and that. A confused bird in a cage.

"Yes." Patterson rapped impatiently. "And then?"

Duffy raised his face at his interrogator, albeit focussing his eyes on a point in the middle distance over one shoulder.

"Then I went home."

"You went home?"

"Yes. Home. Straight home."

"But it wasn't straight home, though, was it?" Patterson raised his eyebrows, Duffy lowered his.

"Yes." Duffy consulted his notebook again. "Left the hill 12:28. Arrived home 12:56."

"Yes, but the last text message of the conversation with my client was 10:54. You didn't go *straight* home, did you?"

"Because I saw the sign." Duffy smiled at the simplicity of the explanation.

"The sign." Patterson sighed, gratefully. "Which you recorded sighting at 12:11. Over an hour later."

Duffy said nothing but looked uncertain.

"My point, Mr Ingoglia, is that there was nothing in the conversation with my client which led you to believe that anything precipitous was about to occur. Was there? Because if there had been - if there had been any intimation that something was about to happen, such as a van crashing into your house - you would have rushed down off that hill the minute the conversation ended. Not remained there continuing your search for aliens."

Duffy didn't know what to say.

"The conversation, Mr Ingoglia, gave you no reason to suspect that my client was about to commit any crime, isn't that right?" Duffy looked lost while Patterson pressed on. "You had no reason to believe, arriving home, that it was my client who had driven a van into your house. No reason to believe that this incident was connected to the text conversation you had just had."

"I…"

"Because any connection between the conversation and the incident exists only in your mind, doesn't it? You have invented a connection, seen some conspiracy to get revenge on you that really isn't there at all. Isn't that right?"

The Fiscal started to get to her feet, thought better of it halfway up, and sat down again. Patterson let Duffy's hesitation hang in the air for a moment as he slid his eyes down the row of jurors off his shoulder. Then he abruptly changed tack

"Did you find any?"

"Any…?" Duffy was thoroughly lost now.

"Aliens. Did you find any?"

An excitable titter ran through the courtroom and the Sheriff glanced up frowning disapproval.

"I… I saw the sign."

"Oh yes." Patterson nodded as if he had completely forgotten. "The sign. This flaming letter H"

"Yes." Duffy breathed out, relieved to be back on more solid ground

"And what did the sign mean?"

"It means she's alive. Safe. Coming home."

"Who is… she?"

"Heather. H for Heather. My sister, Heather. H for Heather."

"Heather Marshall? My client's estranged wife?"

"Yes. My sister, his wife. Yes. Heather."

"And she's coming home?"

"Home. Coming home."

"From where, Mr Ingoglia? Where has she been for, what, these past eight years?"

"With them." Duffy looked up, triumphant, a beatific smile splitting his face.

"The aliens? Who made the sign of the H?"

"Yes. Fiery H. H for Heather."

"Your sister has been with the aliens for eight years?"

"Yes." Duffy looked at Patterson as if was an imbecile. The Procurator Fiscal bowed her head, put one hand to her eyes, lifted up her glasses and pinched the bridge of her nose. "The aliens abducted my sister."

"My Lord?" Whittaker was on her feet. "Could I request a short comfort break. Ten minutes perhaps?"

The Sheriff looked down at her and sighed. "Very well."

"Court!" pronounced the Clerk, and everyone stood while the Sheriff sailed through to his chambers.

"You need to deny it, Mr Ingoglia." The Procurator Fiscal was anxiously looking at her watch, realising they were up against it.

"Can't deny it. Can't. It is true. I have evidence. Lots of evidence. Lots and lots."

"You must. Don't you see. This will strike at the very

heart of the way the jury see you. If they believe you to be some kind of-"

"I am not a crackpot."

If Thomas Hobbes had been in the courthouse, he would have taken one look at Duffy and thought the witness came close to matching his description of life: solitary, poor, nasty, brutish and short. It wasn't that Duffy hadn't tried to dress up, it was just that he lacked the means of assessing how smart he looked. Whether items of clothing matched or clashed was a matter of supreme indifference to him. In fact, he was barely aware that such definitions existed. Clothes merely clothed you. Kept you warm or dry. The end.

Today he was wearing a herringbone jacket over a white shirt and a dark blue tie. All acquired from the Marie Curie shop in the High Street the previous day. The shirt was hardly ironed and the jacket sleeves were fraying, if you looked closely. The tie, rather than disguise all this, merely served to emphasise it. It's brightness, sheen and starched clean lines said: take a good look at what I'm attached to - a harassed elderly relative at a hurriedly-arranged funeral.

His indifference to clothes matched his attitude to personal hygiene. Duffy wasn't dirty or smelly, he just looked it - mostly due to excessive and unruly hair. A full head of unkempt grey curls, semi-permanent stubble, hairy knuckles and arms. Eyes deep set in a worryingly Neanderthalesque brow, a compact barrel of a man who resembled a drunk Maradona after a rough flight.

"I never said you were a crackpot, Mr Ingoglia." Whittaker was straining every sinew right at this moment not to run screaming from this room, this court, this life. "I understand. But the members of the jury may not. It is vital that you show them you are an intelligent, rational man. Keep your answers short. You need to appear decisive, clear, concise." She resisted the urge to use the word *credible*.

"I have evidence. Lots of evidence." Duffy repeated.

"Mr Ingoglia. You have … different beliefs than theirs. Not better or worse, just different. They, however, may not see-"

"My beliefs are justified. Justified. The truth is the truth. That is a fact. Fact, truth. Same thing. Always the same thing. Always."

"Mr Ingoglia, perhaps you can leave matters of truth and fact to me and we can focus on the evidence we need to convince the jury that Mr Marshall committed the crime you say he did."

"He did! It's the truth. And it's a fact. "

"I know it is. But we need to persuade the jury. Can you see that?"

"No. Yes. But-"

"But nothing. Nothing else matters, does it?"

"The truth matters. Always matters. Always."

"The truth of the crime he committed, or the truth about your beliefs?"

Duffy stopped momentarily and waggled his head, thinking. "Both."

"But if you can only choose one?"

"I choose both." He blinked hard and muttered under his breath. "Both. Choose both. Choose both."

"Mr Ingoglia!" Whittaker pursed her lips and took a deep breath. "We are out of time. You do not get to choose. The choice of what the jury believes is not up to you. Or me. They will believe what they choose and then your choice - your only choice - will be to accept it. Right now, your choice is really whether you want to make it easy for them. Or impossible."

"Choose both. Both. I choose both." Duffy continued to mumble. Whittaker shook her head and swept back down the corridor and into the courtroom.

"Mr Ingoglia. Perhaps we may return to the subject of your purpose on Eildon Hill on the evening of Boxing Day last year?"

Wingnut leant forward, elbows on his knees. He had watched expectantly as his smarmy lawyer had smarmily smarmed this way and that, leaving a slick trail of smarm like some smarm-laden snail gorging on his favoured diet of naivety, trepidation and uncertainty amongst witnesses. Wingnut had no say in who had been appointed to defend him - legal aid had taken care of that - but this Patterson had told him that he was basically a freebie; a charity case that this self-proclaimed meteor intended to use to further his own career and enhance the glorious aura which had started to develop around him as he entered the legal atmosphere. Wingnut hadn't like to point out to Patterson that a meteor's journey must actually be a descent that would involve him crashing to earth at terminal velocity. He figured Patterson was too engrossed in his own splendour to stop for any minor impediment to his progress such as facts. To extend the meteor metaphor, he was burning his way through the sky and trivial motes of fact or tiny atoms of protest would be either swept aside by his grand profile buffeting through the air, or ignited by the brilliance of his flame and float like ashes to the barren ground.

Patterson stood now at the lectern, a sheaf of papers in

his left hand, his right hand gesturing openly ready to rifle through this fistful of notes to pluck out the killer line. He was up on the balls of his feet, balancing, shiny and sleek, ready to pounce like a Californian sea-lion on its handler's mackerel. "You say you saw a sign - from aliens."

Duffy's wild grey curls bobbed as he jiggled and jangled in the witness box. His eyes swept across the courtroom wildly, left and right, up and down, never settling, never focussing. He looked ready for fight-or-flight.

"Yes." He managed, chopping off his natural tendency to repeat and elaborate as per the Fiscal's advice. .

"By aliens you mean extra-terrestrials? Beings from another planet?"

"No."

The wind visibly dropped from Patterson's sails and he glared over at Wingnut upon Duffy's unexpected reply. Wingnut gave the merest *what-the-hell-do-I-know-you're-the-expert* expression to Patterson using only his eyebrows and then turned his gaze on Duffy to watch what happened next. The fact that Wingnut's own future was riding on this particular encounter between the slick smarm-merchant and the weird space-cadet didn't make this tussle any the less entertaining or thrilling. Despite himself, Wingnut wanted to know what the hell Duffy was playing at, denying his own belief system so bluntly before this battle of wits had even got going. Perhaps the sexy Procurator Fiscal - all fishnets, bustier and heels, at least in Wingnut's imagination - had a game plan of her own that she was leading Duffy through?

"But Mr Ingoglia, if I may quote your own earlier evidence back at you." Patterson, recovering some of his poise, flipped a few pages back in the papers he was holding and ran one finger expertly down the page. "I asked you who made the sign of the flaming H and you said, and I quote: *the aliens*."

"Yes. That's not what I meant"

"Not what you meant?" Patterson dripped sarcasm. "What you said, but not what you meant?"

"Yes." Said Duffy, already finding the brevity an uncomfortable restraint.

"Does that mean you have since changed your mind? Or perhaps, had your mind changed for you?" Patterson glared accusingly at the Procurator Fiscal sitting innocently at her desk, scribbling something down in an disinterested manner. She didn't return his look.

"Neither."

"So you don't believe in aliens, Mr Ingoglia?"

"No, I do."

"Oh you do?"

"Yes."

"And that they abducted your sister?"

"No."

"Mr Ingoglia." Patterson sighed heavily. "I am confused. I am sure the jury must be confused. Can we have a simple statement from you which explains-"

"They're not aliens." Duffy interrupted. "But other people consider them aliens so that is the term I use when discussing them with other people."

"These aliens?"

"Yes."

"So your sister was taken by someone - beings? - who most people would call aliens?"

"Yes. Beings, yes."

"But they're *not* aliens?" Patterson looked as if he had decided that he no longer wanted to be adorning this particular stage and that, perhaps, his view that this would represent the latest in a long line of forward steps along a glittering career path might be just the tiniest bit misguided.

"No. They're not. Not aliens. No."

"So, perhaps you could tell the court what they are then? These beings who took your sister and who are not aliens." Patterson was munificent in his search for the truth. There was no judgement here, no risk of ridicule. He was merely a vessel for good - the human form through which the heart of the matter might be revealed to the jury and the truth obtained. He swept his left arm towards the jury. "The ladies and gentlemen of the jury might consider them aliens, but you know that they are more precisely termed…?"

"Time-travellers." Duffy said, and smiled an honest smile.

"Time-travellers?" Patterson shook his head, not in disbelief so much as relief that his work here was done. He turned the wattage up on his smarm and beamed at the jury. "From the future?"

"Of course. Time travel hasn't been invented yet, so they can't come from the past." Duffy said matter-of-factly.

"Mr Ingoglia. Forgive me but may I just ask: are you serious?"

Duffy bristled and actually looked Patterson in the eye ever-so-briefly before returning to his previous over-the-shoulder focus. "Yes. I have evidence. Lots of evidence. Lots."

"Of time-travellers involvement in your sister's disappearance?"

"Mr Patterson." The Sheriff leaned forward, exasperated. "Does your incredulity serve any more purpose here than this line of questioning?"

"My Lord?" Patterson was thrown by this unexpected shaft of erudition.

The Sheriff removed his glasses and pinched the bridge of his nose. "Do we need to sit through any more of this? I fail to see the relevance in this case. Mr Ingoglia's beliefs are not on trial here today. We are here to establish whether - as you told me - there is a clear motive or not."

"My Lord, I intend to show that the witness's persistence with outlandish beliefs is an indication that he is delusional and that his opinion as to the guilt of my client, his intentions and even his involvement in the alleged incidents, are similarly deluded." Patterson smiled. "Even I did not expect us to be discussing time travel in the court today, my Lord."

"Very well. But keep it brief can you? I am not Stephen Hawking, and neither are the members of the jury. We can all get the gist without the need for diagrams."

"Very good, my Lord." Patterson gave a micro-bow and turned back to Duffy. "Mr Ingoglia. Are you sure time-travellers abducted your sister?"

"Yes."

"And do you think this belief is one which would be shared by the average man in the street?"

"If they had my evidence, yes. I have lots of evidence. Lots and lots."

"Really? Ok, let's have a brief - very brief-" Patterson nodded up to the Sheriff. "Look at your theory shall we?"

"Of course."

"I am a simple man, Mr Ingoglia. Not a scientist. But I am a legal professional so perhaps I could explore this from a legal standpoint. Starting with motive. Why did these time-travellers take your sister?"

"For observation. Experiments. And information."

"Information? What possible information would they need from your sister?"

"Information about what life is like in our time. Now. Others were taken. Hundreds, maybe more, are taken every year."

"Because our time, this time we're living through is so… what, important? Significant?"

"No, they take people from all different times. Lots of eras. They want a complete picture of human history. Complete."

"Can't they read books, these people from the future?" A titter ran around the court and Patterson waited, a shit-eating grin smeared across his shiny face.

"Yes, obviously." Duffy screwed his face up at his inquisitor's silliness.

"So why did they take her? Why can't they just read the Oxford History of Twentieth Century Britain like anyone else?"

"History is written by the victors."

"So people from the future do not wish to rely on biased versions of events when they can get it from the horse's mouth, is that what you mean?"

"Yes. Horse's mouth. Yes." Duffy nodded emphatically.

"But what about electronic media? TV, video recordings, photos, etc. In this day and age it is almost impossible to have an event go unrecorded or unanalysed. Why take notoriously unreliable eye-witnesses…" Patterson emphasised this phrase with a slow, sweep over the jury. "When you can peruse gigabytes of recorded information at your leisure?"

"Electronic media is unreliable. Can be erased,

corrupted. Formats change, compatibility gets lost. Lots of technical difficulties. Lots. They. They can see into the mind of a person-"

"They mind-meld do they?"

"I imagine."

"Mr Ingoglia. I imagine many things too. Some of them nutty." Patterson prodded, provoking more nervous laughter. "Are you seriously telling me, then, that aliens - sorry, time-travellers - came from the future, took your sister away in order to probe her mind and extract information about how we live today?"

"Yes."

"Why don't they just hang around? Disguise themselves as us and integrate themselves into society - then report back?"

"They do not want to cause a time-causality distortion." Duffy's eyes widened.

"A what? Mr Ingoglia, my Lord Sheriff has asked that we keep this strictly in layman's terms."

"If you go back in time and change something, you are risking a paradox which might adversely affect the future you wish to return to." Duffy smiled. "Like Back To The Future."

Procurator Fiscal Whittaker let her head slump to the table with an audible thud.

"But wouldn't abducting somebody cause such a paradox?" Patterson continued, enjoying himself now - even throwing himself into the argument. "After all, in the future where they invented time travel your sister hadn't been abducted, because time travel hadn't yet been invented?"

"Which is why they took her. She isn't important. Her absence is unlikely to cause any significant anomaly. They have technology. Model risk profiles, likely outcome scenarios. They are selective. Very selective."

"Or perhaps they could risk taking someone and then, if they find they have created a paradox, they just pop back and put that person back as if they had never been taken in the first place?" Patterson spread his hands like a magician requesting applause for his marvellous illusion.

"It doesn't work like that." Duffy shook his head, smiling.

"Why not?"

"Because it is too late. A new future will have been created where the abduction did occur. If you went back in time to before the point of the abduction and waited, you would then observe that very abduction occurring."

"I see." Mr Patterson obliged. "You are clearly something of an expert on the subject."

Duffy beamed with pride, victory in his eyes.

"So perhaps," Patterson concluded. "Perhaps, you could explain why your sister has been missing for eight years."

"What do you mean?" Duffy was stumped by this change of tack.

"Well, if they are time-travellers, Mr Ingoglia, surely they could take her for - ooh, I don't know, twenty years - but still bring her back to the point in time one minute after she was taken. That way, although twenty years would have passed for her, her loved ones here would not have to wait for her. In fact, they would probably not even have noticed that she'd ever been away!"

Patterson tucked both thumbs into his waistcoat and almost pirouetted at the lectern. Duffy looked into the middle distance, stunned.

"Mr Ingoglia?" Patterson persisted.

"Um..."

"No further questions, my Lord."

"But I saw a sign! They left a sign! It was-" Duffy blustered.

"Thank-you, Mr Ingoglia." The Sheriff interrupted. "You may step down."

THE TRIAL ENDS

"Well, what a bloomin' waste of time that was. I shan't be recommending jury service to any of my friends!" Jean was stuffing her pac-a-mac and gloves into her handbag and fussing to make sure she still had her phone.

"It doesn't work like that, Jean." The foreman said, stowing his pen into his jacket pocket. "You get cited, or you don't. Being cited is not up to the individual."

"Well, it's a bloomin' waste is what it is. I mean! That bloke Imbroglio - he's a nutter. Aliens and time-travellers. If I want all that I can watch Star Trek. I don't need to sit on a rock-hard seat for six hours a day when I can be on a comfy sofa in my own home!"

"Quite."

"I think the phrase I'm looking for rhymes with ducking lydiat" Jerry sniped, pulling his coat from the coatstand in the corner. "That stupid alien, time-traveller, wild-eyed, fidgetting uber-nutter! No wonder that Marshall bloke crashed his van into his house. I'd have bull-dozed it myself if he was my brother-in-law!"

"You mean you still think he did it?" Lorraine asked.

"Eh?"

"The accused? Marshall."

"Doesn't bloody matter now, does it? If I was the defence, I'd be rubbing my hands right now. Job done. His client's walking home, and rightly so. Far as I'm concerned it's a right royal clusterfuck. Time-travellers." He shook his head sadly. "I missed racing from Plumpton for this?"

"Well, I believe him."

"What?"

"I believe him." The quiet woman with the heart-shaped face had finally spoken up. Her hair was parted in the middle and framed her pretty features, the unargued highlights of which were round hazel eyes with soft, pale lashes. She was picking through a rucksack, looking for something, as she spoke.

Sitting stiffly in his chair, Cullen watched her, his interest piqued.

"It's Lois, isn't it?" Asked the foreman.

"Yes. And I believe him."

"About the aliens?"

"No, time-travellers." She confided. "We're not alone you know. What do you think spectral disturbances are? Ghosts?"

"Um… I don't know?"

"The echoes of us from the future. One day we will travel through time - and other dimensions. And when we do, we'll obviously come back here."

"Obviously…?"

"Yes." She stated, self-assured enough to leave her response at that.

"Well-" The foreman started.

"Well, it's irrelevant now isn't it?" Said Jerry, already at the door. "Game over. Right royal waste of time. I don't pay my bloody taxes to have them wasted on farrago's like this. What a carry on! I'm away for a pint in the hope I can rinse me brain of all this bloody bollocks. Time travel! Give me strength."

"It's not bollocks." Lois said, mostly now to herself, as one by one her fellow jurors filed past her and out into the courtroom. As Cullen stood and passed her chair, he popped a folded piece of paper into her coat pocket, unnoticed.

Cullen sat quietly waiting on the bench at the foot of the stairs and watched the Marshall family celebrate as Wingnut emerged from the courtroom. Two young men, one blonde, the other darker, both big and strong, embraced him and gave him beaming smiles. Cullen had seen them sitting in the public gallery and realised now that they were Wingnut's sons. Their father slapped them both on the back and hugged them enthusiastically in turn.

"Told you!" His voice rang through the hallowed space. "Best bloody brief in the country! What a star. I knew it the minute I set eyes on him. Smarm or no smarm."

"Aye, well he certainly looked like he knew it n' all." Said the darker one.

"Yeah, well. No harm in taking pride in your ability, is there? 'Swhat I always said, isn't it?" He gave them each a fatherly punch on the arm. "Touch and go there, for a minute, mind. Thought he'd let the cat out of the bag."

"What do you mean, dad?" Asked the blonde.

"Ah, nothing." Wingnut gave a dismissive shake of the head, briefly mindful of his location and that someone might be overhearing. "Doesn't matter, son. All's well that ends well."

"Is that it, then? It's all over?"

"Damn right. I am a free man. Free to go. Free to forget this fucking place." He raised his voice deliberately, looking around for someone to offend. "And the fucking cops." He looked slightly crestfallen when his words dissipated in the stillness. He lapsed into wistfulness.

"Wish I'd had him defending me all those years ago."

"Never mind that, Dad. All done now innit? Drinks on me!" The darker son rubbed his hands and then zipped up his jacket.

"Good lad! Plus, we can now get tickets for the Seven's on Saturday. Come on you Gala!"

The trio hustled down the stairs and out through the main door to the courthouse. As they passed him by, Cullen caught a brief but very clear view of a familiar gold disc on a chain around the dark-haired boy's neck.

Kate paced up and down the corridor looking for all the world like an expectant father in a maternity waiting room. When Whittaker appeared from the Ladies cloakroom, cape and court attire abandoned, Kate alighted on her and invaded her personal space.

"What was that? What was *that*!" Kate was venom personified.

"That, Superintendent, was the Sheriff pulling the plug on a waste-of-space case. A case that should never have been brought. You should be ashamed."

"I should be ashamed! What the-? There's perfectly good evidence and we haven't heard most of it!"

"And we're not going to. I have better cases to try than this. I don't know how this got through but I wish for all our sakes it hadn't."

"Oh, so your upset because it makes your prosecution success rate look bad?"

"No." Whittaker pursed her lips and held Kate's gaze. "You're upset because it makes your success rate look bad. I don't have time for this, Superintendent. Good day."

"Counsel." Kate spat as the Procurator Fiscal strode

out of the front door. Alone, Kate resumed her pacing and, by the window at the end of the corridor, swung her fist hard into the wood panelling. She heard a cough and turned to see Cullen standing, hands in his coat pockets.

"This fucking system. It stinks. It's rotten and I hate it."

"Can't hate it that much. You're Superintendent." He smirked.

"Fuck off." She looked at him earnestly. "You could have been a Superintendent if you'd stuck around. Deputy Chief Constable even, by now."

"No." Cullen shook his head and looked around the room. "Not my thing. You though - another story. I always knew you'd do well. Suits you."

"Oh, stop blowing smoke up my arse. Or I'll suspect you want something."

Cullen turned to face her. "Funny you should say that. Tell me about Derek Marshall."

"You mean the man you've just let walk free?" She sniped.

"Wasn't me."

"You were on the jury."

"And the Sheriff took it out of our hands. Witness discredited, case dismissed." Cullen sniffed. "Just as well, probably. I reckon that if you had asked most of the jurors to sort a big pile of arses and elbows into two, you would have ended up with two small piles of arses and elbows."

"Jurors." Kate spat. "Another shitty piece of a shitty system clogged up with shit."

"Well, it's succinct."

"And serious." She looked at Cullen and suddenly looked pale and worn. "I'm tired, Cullen. So tired of all this… this shit. It's all I can do, every day, to get out of bed and do whatever I can to make my targets. Because that's all anyone cares about, fucking targets. Get your numbers up so that you can show that you've done your job and who gives a fuck about the next bastard in line who takes your output as his input and fucks it up beyond belief. Not your problem, why should you care? No-one's looking at the system top-down. Everyone focusses, blinkered, on their own little piece and fuck the rest." Kate's shoulders sagged and she leant back against a table, grasping the edge of it with both hands. "I'm running out of energy. And hope."

"It's the hope that kills you." Cullen cast his eyes down at the carpet lost in some memory. "So, Marshall?"

"What!" She snorted. "You not been listening? That case is done. Closed. Cleared. Whatever. You can't bring it back."

"There's no need to bring it back. Doesn't have to be a case. It's just little old me making some enquiries."

"And you poke your nose in - how long before it becomes a case?"

Cullen looked at her intently. "I believe he did it."

"Of course he did it!" Kate tossed her head back and looked up at the ceiling. "The whole fucking world knows he did it! But that doesn't matter. The system has been fed, done its worst. Finito. The job is done."

"Justice has not been done."

"Fucking justice! The one up-side here? I am free to deal with the other stuff on my desk. Look, stop giving a shit when it's not your job to give a shit."

"But I do give a shit."

"Why?" Kate looked at him genuinely curious, a desire to know shining brightly in her eyes. "Why do you give a shit?"

Cullen blinked slowly, looking from one eye to another. "Because it's not right."

She gazed up at him and then gave a huge sigh.

"Do you want a bloody lift or not?"

"So, Derek Arthur Marshall - Wingnut to his friends - was arrested in 2010. By *moi*. Charged with GBH and sentenced to twelve years at Her Majesty's pleasure. Got out last June, early release."

Kate was driving down a leafy lane in the sunshine. Cullen sat in the passenger seat fiddling with an imaginary hat in his hands.

"What was the GBH about?"

"His missus had been having an affair. Wingnut came home one day, unexpected like, and found them at it. Beat seven bells out of the bloke - and pissed on him."

"Charming."

"Don't you remember him? Thug all his life, was around in your time, albeit minor offences involving being too handy with his fists. Teenage father - first at seventeen, then again at nineteen. Always getting into trouble. Hopping in and out of prison for short spells. Had one or two charges of assault as well before the GBH but they were always dropped."

Cullen shook his head. "Not ringing any bells."

"Probably below your pay grade, Inspector." She laced the title with sarcasm; Cullen ignored it.

"What happened to the wife and boy-friend?"

"Wife buggered off. Ran home to Mum, apparently. Had had enough anyway - so afraid of him that she left her two sons behind. Sam and Sean. They would have been around twelve or thirteen when it happened.

Wingnut goes to jail, wife buggers off, guess who steps in to look after the boys?"

"The boyfriend?"

"Nope." Kate smiles triumphantly. "MacDuff Angel Ingoglia."

"Duffy?"

"Yep."

"Fuck me."

"Not just now."

Cullen mulled this information over for a moment.

"And the boyfriend?"

"Archie Strachan."

"Oh aye?"

"You know him?"

"Knew of him." Cullen shrugged. "Fife lad."

"That's right. Well he fecked off back to Fife. Wingnut had threatened his life if he ever stepped back in Gala again, or had any contact with Heather. Archie didn't need to be told twice."

"So Duffy brought up the boys on his own?"

"Yep. While Wingnut was in jail. Wingnut gets out, Duffy asks him to shag his wife - which he does, tirelessly - they fall out, Wingnut drives a van through his house. Now you're all up to date."

"And the boys?"

"Sam and Sean? Sam's a bit of a chip off the old block, locals call him-"

"Fireman Sam." Cullen interjected.

"That's right." Kate scrutinised his face carefully. "He's linked with petty arson now and then - nothing proven. Sam never took to Duffy, apparently, kicked him out of the family home the minute he turned eighteen. Him and Sean been on their own ever since."

"And Sean?"

Kate sucked her teeth. "Don't know much about him. Maybe he's clean? Although I doubt it. But you never know."

"Is that it?"

"That's it. Unless you want his inside leg measurement."

"No."

Kate pulled up outside the house and turned the engine off. "You know you're squatting here, right?"

"I'll be gone tonight." He gave a weak smile. "It's been good to see you, Kate."

"You too, Mister." She watched him, wondering, as he climbed out of the car and strode away down the gravel path. She rolled the window down. "What're you going to do?"

But he didn't answer.

PART THREE

THE AFTERMATH

"Aren't you going to say anything then?" Duffy was clearly angry and sullen, throwing the words out at her like a spiteful challenge.

"What is there to say?" Gloria stared glumly out of the window as the first raindrops started hitting the dirty pane in front of her. She certainly wasn't going to tell him how she felt or how Derek had sidled up to her in the corridor, gleeful at his own release - and personal vindication as he no doubt saw it. He had appeared over her shoulder, out of nowhere, and mouthed breathily into her ear: *See you soon, sexy.* She had turned, horrified, as he sauntered away, looking back over his shoulder as he left through the courthouse door and actually winked at her. Terrified and disgusted she had hurried to the cloakroom so she could sit in a cubicle, alone, and seek an answer in the black and white floor tiles. No answer had come.

And she certainly wasn't going to tell him about Worrawut. That the pair of them had sneaked away from the courthouse earlier and billed and coo'ed like two young lovers who had never been apart. Her heart had trilled beneath her coat, her cheeks flushed and mind racing around a crazy golf course of twisted half-memories, cobbled together assemblages of fantasy and dream. A deeply-felt need to connect with someone from her own culture, her own past. She had felt the warmth of her home country seep into her veins just from the touch of his hand.

There was no doubting it was him. Leaving aside that he was the only brown face Melrose had likely seen since around this time last year, he stood erect and proud, youthful features gleaming in the pale straw Scottish light. He had squeezed her by both shoulders and kissed her, hard, on the lips. She closed her eyes and felt herself lifted up into the clouds and then violently shot out into space, like a rocket accelerating to light speed. The breath left her body and she felt an injection of heat and vitality which spread instantly through her - a long unfamiliar taste of lemongrass and chilli, galangal and lime.

She and Duffy had travelled home from the trial in silence, each unable or unwilling to speak, nursing their own thoughts and guilt. Gloria had made two mugs of tea on autopilot, placed his down in front of him as he sat at the kitchen table. Unable to bear the thought of sitting across from him and actually meeting his gaze - if he managed to look up, that was - she had sloped across to the window, plonked her mug down on the sill and stared out at the sage and heather hills.

"Say something. Anything. Just say something." Duffy repeated.

Gloria looked within herself, searching for an emotion, sensation or simple conclusion. Nestling in the dark, burrowed deep but shining hard, was a single message.

"It's over."

"Yes, well. You are right, there. Clearly. Clearly right. It is clearly over." Duffy played his hands over the mug on the table, tapping it, stroking it, tracing its outline. Never still, never at ease. A physical illustration of his state of mind. "And the time-travellers… the time-travellers. The shiny, smart-mouthed man is wrong. Has to be wrong. I will prove him wrong." He shot up from his chair and sped through into the living room to consult his messy whiteboard, his carefully compiled chaos of nonsense.

Gloria waited for a moment and then walked slowly after him, ghosting into the room, talking to his back.

"Not twial. Our mawwage." She spoke the words as a hollow mantra but the second they left her lips she knew they were real.

It took him some moments to respond, so busy was he scanning his notes, inspecting the connections. He wheeled around suddenly.

"What?"

When she looked up at him she saw he was actually staring at her, not hiding his gaze or looking away. His eyes were wet.

"It's over, Duffy. I don't want to do this anymore." Each word freed her from a straitjacket she hadn't seen or recognised, only felt.

"But we are married! Sickness and health, richer and poorer. 'Til death us do part. Married."

"This isn't what I want. I had a dweam; thought you could become it." She closed her eyes and looked at the floor. "You can't. It was just a dweam."

"Because of this?" He waved his hands at the board behind him. "Because of Heather and the sign? There was a sign! There was. Look! Look, I took a photo of it." He reached into a pocket for his phone and began skimming through screenshots, searching for the vital clue which he thought could convince her.

"It's not about Heather. It's about me and you."

"I am right. And you are right! Derek was in the wrong. You and me are in the right! It's all a mistake. The law's an ass. An ass. Right and wrong. Simple." He was pulling his hair now, tugging from both sides. "I could ask for a retrial!"

"No-one wants to go through that again. Me in particular. It's not about wight and wong. It's about me being wong for you and you not being wight for me."

"But we are right! For each other. And he… well, he doesn't matter anymore. That was my fault. My fault. Only my fault. I thought it up, I made you do it. I created this and now… still no baby. No baby. All my fault." Duffy sagged, shoulders slumped, as he sobbed into his chest.

"No! It's not all your fault."

"They didn't believe me. Me! With all my evidence!" He swept his hand vaguely at his whiteboard and piles of paperwork. "All my records. All my data. Lots of data. Lots and lots of data."

"It's not about that." She crept up to him and held him as he shook. "Forget the twial. Forget it. It doesn't matter anymore. I wanted a baby. You can't - *we* can't have one."

"Me! My fault! I can't give you a baby. Me! Not you. You can have babies. I can't. I am the problem. I have let you down. Failed. My fault."

"No." She tried to soothe him, stroking his ruffled hair. "I was selfish. I wanted baby. I wanted dweam life. In UK." She glanced at the decay and dereliction around her. "It was a dweam I loaded onto you. It's not your fault you can't live up to my dweam. It's mine."

"No! Let's talk about this! We could adopt - adoption's very popular. Over 5,000 children adopted in the UK every year. 2014 statistics. And 2015. 2014 and 2015. Could be more by now!"

"I don't want to adopt, Duffy. I don't want to stay."

"Stay? Here?"

"No." Gloria shook her head sadly. "Not here. Not anymore."

"But where? Where will you go? What about us? We're married! We can't just divorce. It's madness." Duffy started beating his head with the heels of his hands, violently trying to dislodge his thoughts.

"Home."

"Home? Thailand home?" Duffy perked up, his head on one side. "I could come with you! We could go back and live in Thailand!"

"No, Duffy."

"Glo! Let's talk about it, hmm? Talk? Talk is good, isn't it? Hmm?" Duffy had her by the shoulders now, searching earnestly in her eyes. After a lifetime of averting his gaze, it seemed he had now forgotten how to look away.

Kate sat at her desk, wading through the paper in her in-tray and looking at how few of the sheets she was able to field immediately into her out-tray. In fact, the only one she could hand off was the one she didn't want to: the dead body.

It wasn't just finding it at the Greenyards which had made it feel more personal - although being called down to see it freshly unearthed wasn't something she saw every day. Melrose was a quiet town and, even though Galashiels wasn't and was only four miles away, dead bodies were as rare as warm summer days. Maybe it was her age, and the fact that she was one of the few serving senior female officers on the force. Finding a woman's body - one that had been there a long time, undiscovered and - here was the key - probably unmissed. What must that be like? She herself was only too aware that as far as having a life and friends outside the force were concerned, she had neither. Police work, or her sister, or failing that industrial quantities of Pinot Grigio and Downton boxsets, was all she had. Who would miss *her* if she went missing? How long would her own absence go unreported?

She perused the two sheets in the folder one last time. Unidentified female, somewhere in her thirties at the time of death - which could have been anywhere between five and fifteen years ago. No matches with dental records, DNA, missing persons or the necklace. That was it. There was no point leaving this to sit for a few more months before it could be officially closed. But she couldn't bring herself to scrawl a signature at the bottom of the last page. She heaved the folder back onto her in-pile with a heavy sigh.

"Just off now, Ma'am." Walker had poked his head around her door.

"Right-o. Won't be long myself." She checked her watch. "Fuck sake. What am I still doing here?"

"G'night, then."

"Aye, goodnight."

She put her head in her hands and ran her fingers through her hair. It felt dirty and she suddenly wanted a hot bath. Last one and that's it. She pulled the next folder off the pile and opened it.

The mugshot of Derek Marshall showed a bleary, stubbled man with dark sunken eyes and an absence of the will to live. She ran a finger swiftly down the page and over onto the next one: burglary, assault, assault, possession, assault, assault. The sad predictability of a petty criminal's life laid bare in a handful of charges. If you were going to be a thug or a waster, at least try and excel at it. Make a name for yourself. Success in your field, or something. Some people had no ambition.

And the impression taken as a whole: the entire

sequence from the first youth charge and caution to the last violent offence and consequent lengthy imprisonment - a tediously inevitable end to a sorry tale. Had he expected champagne and life had poured him flat, non-alcoholic Liebfraumilch? Or did he have some twisted sense of entitlement brought on by having to stand up for himself when he was bullied as a child, and finding that violence and insolence got you some respect, gave you things? Work was for losers - the system pushed you into a recess and made you follow the rules, when anyone could see that the system and the rules were just to keep you in your place.

The system was fucking stupid.

Maybe Marshall and her weren't so different after all? They were both dissatisfied with the system. His solution was to say "fuck it" and do what he liked - because he kept getting away with it; her solution was to say "fuck it, the system's broken; let's fix it", but while it is still broken, we have to keep these bastards from taking advantage of a broken system by clogging it up. If they clogged it up enough, everyone in it would be too busy trying to unclog it to have the time or energy to fix it. It was bastards like Marshall who made the persistence of a fucked system an inevitability.

And now he was free to do what he liked again. What was the fucking point?

Kate rubbed her eyes and flipped another page. Photos of Archie, Heather's lover, covered in bruises and blood - barely recognisable as a human being. Wingnut had really let loose that time. His rage no doubt inflamed by catching them at it and being drunk as a lord and, possibly, high as a kite. She flipped to the last page to check his drug levels and blood readings and found the inevitable figures confirming her theory.

But it wasn't the last sheet in the folder. There was a pink slip attached to this sheet with a paperclip and she pulled it back to see it was Marshall's prison medical check-up and record - updated annually during his sentence.

About halfway down the sheet, above Sexual History but below Allergies and Chronic Conditions, was a single bald statement that stopped her in her tracks. Kate looked up from the folder and stared blankly at her office door for a long minute. She reached for the phone of her desk, then realised that she didn't know Cullen's number. Or whether he even had a phone. She looked again at her watch. If she was quick…

There was no point in knocking and Kate didn't want to risk flashing her lights or sounding her horn since, well, neither of them were supposed to be here. To her surprise the door was wide open and she wondered if she was too late. She froze and listened. Warily, in the faint moonlight, she looked around the empty ground floor before climbing the stairs, her flat shoes shuffling on the cold steps.

A large figure, far larger than the one she was expecting, was standing in the centre of the open space on the first floor. Looking very sheepish, even in silhouette.

"Do much of this, then, Mr McInnes?" Kate asked.

"Erm…" Big Paul had never felt quite so vulnerable as right at this moment.

Kate prodded. "Breaking in?"

"I, um… didn't."

"Who did?"

"Not me. Was already open."

"Really?"

He cast his arms around the damp and mouldy concrete and partially demolished kitchen units. "What do you think?"

Kate assessed the interior and the view of the grounds out of the window. "I think this property must have - once have had - a significant value. Must belong to someone."

"Doesn't look like it, though, does it?"

"No." She agreed.

"Do you have a warrant?" Paul asked.

"No!" She laughed. "I was expecting… an occupant."

"You missed him."

Kate hmm'ed. "Where is he?"

"Away in my van."

"Where to?"

Paul gave her a look she recognised. "Seems I don't need to know that."

"Huh. When's he back."

"Guess he feels I don't need to know that either."

Kate mulled this over for a moment. "So, what's your story?"

"I'm just… um… a friend."

"Oh, you're the friend? Mr Nintendo?"

"Er… no. I don't think so." Paul was confused.

"Hmm. How long have you known him? Cullen." The mention of his name rang strangely in the empty space.

"A while. Not sure." Paul tried to tot it up and realised he couldn't remember. "Yeah, a while."

"Don't give much away, do you? Working out this way are you?"

"Yeah. Gotta big job on." Paul brightened at this safe turn in the conversation. There was nothing he could trip himself up on here. Was there?

"Joiner, wasn't it?"

"Yeah. Big house in Melrose. Top of the hill. Converting into flats and they all need kitchens an' that."

"I see." She walked over to the far glass wall and scraped some of the white gunk on the window with a fingernail. "Bet you could make something of a place like this?"

"Aye." Paul looked around the cold shell and eyed it up, professionally, as if for the first time. "Gloomy mind. Not that spacey either when you look at it. Big on the outside, not much room on the inside. Dunno where I'd put a bedroom. Wouldn't want the world and his wife looking at me 24/7."

Kate nodded and paced along the length of the space, her heels clicking on the damp concrete.

"Easy to find mind. Third Wanksy and all that." Paul grinned sheepishly.

"I'm sorry?"

"Oh. Um. Doesn't matter." Paul said, changing the subject quickly. "Did you find out who stole it? The trophy?"

"Nope. Prints all over it, of course. Partials belonging to God knows who. Could've been anyone." She shrugged. "Doesn't matter now. Cup's back. Insurers are happy. And I can present it to the winners on Saturday."

"You're presenting it?"

"Aye." Kate gave a *who-knew* look. "Some bright spark on the committee suggested that, as the senior female board member…"

She trailed off and the two of them stood in silence for a moment. Paul summoned up some nerve.

"How do you know him?"

Kate paused before answering. "Used to work with him. For him, actually."

"You used to work for him?" Paul's eyes widened. "Aren't you a Superintendent?"

"Wasn't then. Just a lowly Detective Sergeant. He was my DI."

"How long ago was this?"

She did a quick calculation. "Ten, twelve years. Something like that."

"Wow."

Kate looked at Paul carefully, her face softening. "How is he?"

"Hmm?"

"How's he doing? How's he getting on?" She smiled apologetically. "It's… been a while since I've seen him."

"He's good, yeah." Paul said. "Well, I say good. You know. He's kinda… off sometimes."

"Off?"

"Yeah. Loses the plot for a while. Comes back, mind. Eventually."

Kate sighed and looked around at the dilapidated interior, and her presence here now with this giant. The pair of them sharing incomplete information about a poorly-understood absence.

"Does he still drink?"

"Drink?" Paul looked shocked. "Nah."

"Well, that's good."

"Did he used to then?"

"Once upon a time." She looked him over. "When it happened. And after. He didn't handle it well."

"When what happened?"

"His daughter?"

"He has a daughter?"

"Had. He never mention her to you?"

"No." Paul was confident he wouldn't have forgotten something like that.

"Maybe you're not as good a friend as you think you are."

"Never said I was a good friend." Paul grinned. "But, nah. We're mates. Don't hang out much or live in each other's pockets. You know. He's not like that."

"No. He's not." Kate nodded, understanding.

"One minute he's there, next minute-"

"What?"

Paul shrugged. "He's not."

"Well, ask him sometime. About his daughter. See if he'll… confide."

"You have met him, right? He's not exactly the confiding type."

"No." She admitted. "He's not. But it would do him good to share. Sometimes. And he doesn't have anyone else. Does he?"

"No. Well, not that I know of. I mean he doesn't really have me, if you put it like that." He paused and looked out the window, thoughtful for a moment. Kate gave him space, confident he would continue. "Kinda suits me, to be honest. Cos I'm not the most reliable of blokes. He is, but only when he's around, you know? Funny, really. I'm reliably unreliable and he's, kinda, unreliably reliable."

"Yes, well. All this reminiscing is nice and everything, but I have things to do, places to be." She looked at her watch and tapped one foot impatiently on the floor. "If he's not coming back soon, I can't hang around on the off-chance he puts in an appearance."

"Maybe I'll see you on Saturday? At the Greenyards?"

Kate frowned momentarily. "Of course. VIP tickets."

"Yep. I shall be there. Although my partner wants me all spruced up like." He grimaced, the prospect of a tie constricting his neck a real and genuine one. "Not really my thing. But, hell. I'm goin' anyway."

"You and the rest of the world." She rubbed the back of her neck. "Place is heaving. Construction people everywhere. Hospitality tent, temporary stand, walkways, TV gantries, giant screen. Can't get in the car park for love nor money. Supposed to have a reserved space. Bloody joke."

"TV screen?"

"Yeah." She sighed, the subject clearly boring her.

"I wonder…"

"What?" She looked up at him, interested.

"Ah, nothing." Paul clammed up.

"Ok, well. Nice to meet you. Again." She thought about extending a handshake and decided against it. "Give him this when you see him."

Paul accepted a large manila envelope and raised an eyebrow at her.

"Tell him *pink sheet, last page.* He'll know it when he sees it."

Paul watched her vanish into the stairwell and then moved over to the front window and waited until she reappeared by her car. It was only once she had pulled out onto the main road that he let out a huge breath and felt his shoulders relax. He hadn't realised how tense he'd been throughout that whole conversation.

"Very cosy."

Paul heard the words and spun like clay badly-centred on a potter's wheel. "Fuck! I thought you were away?"

"I was. I'm back."

"How long you been here?"

"Long enough." Said Cullen, leaning against a deconstructed kitchen unit.

"Why didn't you say nothing?"

"I have my reasons."

"Hmm." Paul was unmollified. "Well, now you're here. What's all this about a daughter?"

Cullen looked steadily at Paul and slowly shook his head. "That's one of my reasons."

Paul sighed and handed Cullen the envelope. "She left you this. She said-"

"I heard."

Cullen removed a thick folder from the envelope and opened it at the back. He ran his finger down the last page, stopped and then tapped it over and over.

"Well, I never."

The day beckoned and Wingnut could not have been less interested in getting up. After a while, the day abandoned beckoning and just left a passive-aggressive note on the windscreen along the lines of "It's your own time you're wasting."

Wingnut ignored it and slept on until the Spring sunshine began hitting his eyelids, around late morning. Wincing from the discomfort, but unable to hide from the light, he crawled out of bed and managed to drag himself downstairs, squinting, to make a coffee and grab some paracetamol. As the hangover slowly started to fade he contemplated his future.

It had been, thought Wingnut, a glorious trial - if such a thing were possible - spoilt only by the fact that he had not strictly been declared innocent. But an abandoned case meant that the jury hadn't found him guilty. He was free to go, so go he bloody well would. Wherever he could, and if anyone didn't like it they could suck his dick.

Which reminded him of Gloria, and the look of shock and fear when he had rolled his eyes at her in the courthouse and whispered into her ear. She'd be there for the taking now, and whenever he damned well pleased. No-one would ever believe Duffy, and Duffy certainly wouldn't stop him, and they probably wouldn't believe Gloria either. A woman who was prepared to have sex with her brother-in-law, protesting that she'd had to have sex with her brother-in-law? Pshaw! And anyway, wasn't there some law that said you couldn't be tried for the same crime twice? Well, even if there wasn't, it sounded like there should be. Wingnut certainly wasn't going to worry himself into researching for the truth of that little gem - let the intellectual legal beagles worry about that. *Carte blanche* they called it so, the day after the trial, he awoke with a stultifying hangover and a vicious intent to spend the next week - and who knew, perhaps the rest of his life - actually enjoying himself.

After all, he had eight years wasted in jail to catch up on.

So last night had been a slap-up meal in Chez Navarre's - a Spanish tapas restaurant (Sam's choice), which as far as Wingnut was concerned must have been run by someone's Nan who had dementia. They had served a burger the size of a small biscuit (called a *slider* or something) and six chips the size of fish fingers stacked on a roofing slate, and a dessert in a flowerpot containing something called *chocolate soil.* He had waited expectantly for a paella in a mini-fire bucket or a fragment of cheese served on a mousetrap but it seemed those would have over-taxed the imagination of the deluded gran.

This had been washed down with a pub crawl around Gala where Sam had encouraged him into a yard of ale competition - twice - due to the first one being considered null and void when one of the contestants puked up into his yard halfway through and then, failing to consume the replenished contents, had pulled the yard from his mouth mid-imbibe and drenched the other contestants with it.

Then they had all finished off a bottle of 18-year old Glenlivet which his sons had bought him as a freedom gift. Well, he and Sam had finished it off - Sean wasn't big on whisky. Or fun, Wingnut observed, replaying the few memory fragments from the night. Ah well, he was home now: Sean would soon pick it up under his expert tutelage.

And tomorrow was the Melrose Sevens. A bright spring day packed full of rugby and beer and nasty over-priced food. For a newly freed man, what could possibly go wrong?

Although his sons had done their best to dampen his enthusiasm when he had shown any excitement last night, he now recalled.

"What's up with the pair of ye?" Wingnut had demanded. "Be a laugh! Gala are in the same half of the draw as Melrose. We can watch 'em shove it up 'em!"

"I'd rather not, Dad." Sean hung his head and avoided meetings his father's glare.

"Why? Stopped supporting your local team have you?"

"No, it's not that."

"Well, what is it then."

"It's just… well… Janine's not a big fan of rugby."

"Well don't bring her along then! You a man or a mouse, hmm? What about you, Sammie?"

Sam had seemed to redden and fidget at the suggestion. "It's not going to be that great, Dad."

"What? Don't want to watch us give them a thumping?"

"I don't think it'll be us dishing out the thumping."

"Bollocks! We regularly hammer those bastards, home or away. Don't see why seven-a-side should make any difference."

"They're in a different league to us." Sam protested.

"What did I just say? Bollocks, is what I just said. Bollocks. We're as good as them any day!"

"No, I mean literally a different league. Melrose are in the Premiership. We're only in Division One."

"What? No way. We regularly hammered those bastards when I were young."

"Those days are gone, Dad." Sam's shoulders sagged. "They're just a much better team than us. I don't really want to spend a day there being humiliated by their supporters."

"Fuck 'em!" Wingnut spat. "Anyone humiliates us I'll have their fucking arse in a sling. I thought you-" he poked his finger at Sam. "You were made of sterner stuff than that. And you-" He rounded on Sean. "You better stop being pussy-whipped and show that girl who wears the trousers. We are all three going on Saturday and that's that. And if your bird wants to come along, under protest, she can buy her own fucking tickets."

"We're going to elope!" Robert announced, as he strutted through Kate's front door and dropped her keys on the hallway table. "Elope! Elope! Elope!"

A flurry of fluent rapid-fire Thai came streaming from the kitchen in Mongkut's *basso profundo*. It was all a bit sing-songy, given the urgent sentiment it conveyed: "She's back! She sitting here with me at the kitchen table. Switch to Thai if you want to say something!"

"Hi Robert!" Called Kate. "What was that, did you say?"

"Um, nothing." Robert poked his head around the kitchen door, red-faced. "Just letting you both know that I'm back."

"How was your walk?"

"Fine, yes. It is very pretty - Melrose."

"Isn't it?" She looked at him, askance. "Tea?"

Robert suddenly felt guilty beneath her gaze.

"Um, no thanks." Robert managed. "I need to talk to Mongkut. Urgently. About… training."

"Training?" Mongkut asked innocently. He was idly doodling on a photo in the newspaper using a black biro. The top of Mongkut's tongue was curling out of his mouth as he shaded in a Zapata moustache on Kim Kardashian: a giant child carefully holding a large black tool - Mongkut, not Kardashian.

"Yes." Robert hissed, trying to nod his head back over his shoulder. "I got a text from our coach. We need to get our stuff together and report for some last minute training." He nodded his head back again. "Get our stuff. From upstairs."

"Oh. Right." Mongkut said, finally twigging.

They trotted upstairs, Robert stuffed some random kit into two holdalls and then they skidaddled back down the stairs and out of the front door. "Be back later!" He called, closing the door.

"Why are we wandering the streets?" Mongkut asked as they passed from the main square down a lane towards the river.

"Because I don't want us to be overheard." They were

both speaking in Thai again.

"Overheard saying what?"

"Proclaiming to the whole world! That Gloria and I have found each other and are going to elope!" Robert stopped, put down his bag, threw his arms wide and raised his eyes to the cloudy evening sky.

"What does elope mean?"

"Elope? Means run away to get married. Me and Gloria are going to run away to get married! How about that?"

Mongkut pursed his lips and briefly crossed his eyes. "When?"

"After the tournament. We're going back to Thailand."

"Oh." After a pause he asked "Does her husband know?"

"Of course not! That's why we're eloping." Robert squinted at his friend. "That's why I said *run away* to get married? If her husband knew we wouldn't have to run away."

"Right."

"Oh, she's beautiful. Just like I remember her. She hasn't changed a bit." Robert picked his bag back up and resumed walking. "She has such amazing eyes. And she looked at me… like we'd never been apart." He drifted off into a reverie.

They walked in silence to the footbridge crossing the Tweed and Mongkut stopped on the bridge and watched the muddy river flow lazily beneath them. "Where will you live?"

"What?" Robert wrinkled his nose in irritation, his beautiful dream interrupted.

"Where will you live?"

"Um… don't know. She can stay with me in Bangkok. Then we can decide what we want to do."

"It's a very small flat."

"We'll be fine. It'll be… cosy."

"Hmm." Mongkut looked down at his feet as he idly kicked the metalwork on the bridge. "What about her husband?"

"Will you stop going on about her husband! This isn't about her husband, this is about Gloria and me."

"He won't be pleased."

"I'm sure he won't. What do I care?"

"He's her husband." Mongkut insisted.

"I said-"

"And she came all the way from Thailand to live with him. She probably has a career, maybe a family, a future. And you want to snatch her away?"

"Whoa! Where did all that empathy come from?"

"What's empathy?"

"Never mind. Who's side are you on here?"

"I'm not on anyone's side. I'm just trying to-"

"Why the hell not? Why aren't you on *my* side? You're *my* friend."

"Yes." Said Mongkut. "And as your friend, I'm suggesting that - before announcing to the whole world that you are going to rip a married woman away from her husband and take her halfway around the world to start a new life without having any idea how - that you give it a bit of thought."

"We want to be happy!"

Mongkut shrugged as if that was the stupidest thing he'd ever heard. "And then there's the law to consider."

"I'm the law student!"

"Then you should know that she can't be married to two different people. It's illegal. She'll have to get divorced."

"All in good time. We will be together and that is all that matters."

"The law matters."

"What is it with you and the law?"

Mongkut sulked. "What about your rugby career?"

"What about it." Snapped Robert, his patience expended.

"You want this tournament to help raise your profile? Want to go back and rise above the journeymen to become one of stars in the firmament of Asian rugby?" Robert gaped open-mouthed as his friend threw back at him the exact words he himself had used so many times to define his vision for success. "Want to be rich and famous and have High School sports halls named after you?"

"Yes, yes, yes."

"Well, how're you going to do that with a wife in tow?"

"I-"

"Think about it.

Robert leant sullenly on the bridge wondering why his brilliant vision for his future now lay trodden and sullied by his friend's flash of practicality.

"What's the plan, then?" Mongkut asked

"Hmm?"

"For the elope… ment?" Mongkut had tried on a few suffixes for size and settled on *ment*. He was rather pleased with himself for having done so.

"Well, I could smuggle her onto the team coach."

"When?"

"After the tournament."

"We're not going home the minute they blow the final whistle you know."

"As good as." Robert corrected. "Our flight's on

Saturday night, so we need to get to the airport for around 9pm. Coach told us to have our bags packed and at the ground for pickup after the final."

"Oh. Well, you'll need to hide her. How're you gonna do that?"

"Don't know."

"Does she have a passport?"

"She must have. She got here from Thailand."

"Could have expired."

"You're full of hope and optimism today aren't you? Is this you being helpful?"

"I'm just trying to test your plan, see if it holds water."

Robert pointed down at the muddy Tweed below them. "You're not careful, I'll throw you in there. See if you hold water."

Mongkut shrugged off his friend's empty threat and pondered the sluggish river. "It's no Chao Phraya is it?"

"No." Robert agreed. "It's not."

"I'm not trying to annoy you, you know?" Mongkut softened his tone. "I hope you can be happy - with or without Gloria. But if you are truly going to elope, we've only 24 hours left in this freezing cold country so you need to have a game plan."

"Alright, big fella. Let me say three things: One, when did you ever have a game plan? The closest you ever got to a game plan was getting hold of the ball and tanking down the pitch until you reached the touchline or someone was stupid enough to get in your way."

"That's still a plan."

"Well I hope mine will be better than that."

"So do I." The giant smiled and Robert grinned sheepishly back.

"Two: when did you become some font of wisdom as

to whether there is anything I can and can't do? Gloria and I love each other. We want to be together. And this country may be the home of Rugby Sevens but it's far too cold and stupid for us."

"Is that you talking or her?"

"Both! She's been here years and still can't get used to it. She has no ambition to stay here when she can be back in her own climate and own culture. And with me!"

"Well, then, you need that game plan. How is she going to give her husband the slip and get to Thailand?" He pondered his own question for a moment. "You could do it separately. You come home with us, as planned, as part of the team. She just makes her own way to Bangkok."

"What, abandon her to get on with it on her own?"

"You're not abandoning her, you are leaving her to solve her own problems in her own way - and in her own time - and meet you in Bangkok when that time comes."

"Oh, wait a minute. Are you implying it might be a long time. She might take ages?"

"No."

A panic spread across Robert's face. "Or that she won't come at all? She'll change her mind - or allow her husband to change it for her - and I'll die alone in Bangkok waiting for a woman who never comes?"

"No, I'm not saying anything of the sort." Mongkut frowned. "Mind you…"

"No. Absolutely not. We've spent years apart and have magically - through the guiding hands of destiny - found each other again. I am not going to lose her now. Whatever we do, wherever we end up, we will do it together."

"Ok."

"Ok."

"So you need a plan."

"Ok. I'm working on it."

Mongkut watched the sluggish waters run deep and slow downstream and out of sight. "What was the third thing?"

But Robert was lost in thought.

THE SEVENS GET UNDERWAY

Kate took her seat and surveyed the match-day scene. Everyone but her seemed to have forgotten that this was her first Sevens tournament and she was amazed by the scale and attendance of what she saw.

The pitch, emblazoned with the main sponsors logo, lay right in front of her. Behind that were rows of pitch-side benches, and behind these was a railing which separated those with simple ground tickets from those with seats. This grassy standing area was gradually filling up with people laying out picnic rugs and camping chairs. There was a low slope at each end of the pitch and two large corporate stands, erected just for today, directly opposite her.

Overlooking the halfway line was the TV gantry - a British Racing Green cargo container with windows, up on scaffolding. Inside, the director could monitor the views coming in from the cameras dotted around the ground and coordinate them into a single televised stream. And in the far right corner of the ground was a makeshift TV studio, also raised on scaffolding. All curved glass and chrome furniture inside, where the pundits and anchor sat, watched and pontificated.

Behind the goalposts to her right was a huge TV screen atop an outside-broadcast juggernaut, battleship-grey, next to a giant electronic scoreboard. Behind the goalposts to her left was another packed grassy bank and a wall separating the Greenyards from the main road. This was currently a maze of chain-link fences guiding spectators into the ground via security bag and ticket checks. On the other side of the road, separated by more fences, was a massive beer tent.

Kate looked down into the hive of activity in front of her. The tunnel apron which led from the stand out onto the pitch swarmed with stewards, players, coaches, physios and match officials. Behind the stand, out of view, a partially screened walkway, floored with duckboards, led through a stone archway to St Mary's School which hunkered down right next to the Greenyards. The two establishments were jammed together in places, like large grey teeth in a crowded mouth, and this archway gave access to the school playing field, appropriated for today as a practice ground

The only thing which didn't impress her was the apparent overmanning. Every male pensioner within a five mile radius who owned a moustache or a walking stick seemed to have some role to play in blocking a corridor, holding a cordon, manning a doorway or hogging a seat in the stands.

The whole place was heaving like an insect mound - the termites avoiding each other nimbly, as their clockwork schedule was monitored by blazered soldier ants and touchline official wasps in dayglo kit. Snaking amongst them, making occasional forays on and off the pitch, were the lone hornets of the assembly: the pitch steadi-cameraman, his boom-wielding acolyte scurrying after him.

All around was the laughter and good-natured chatter from an ever-growing crowd, intent on enjoying the day. And above it all, capping the scene, the bright blue sky of a glorious April afternoon, fluffy white clouds bobbing on the breeze, wafting the smell of fried onions and dubious cooked meat over the Greenyards.

What bliss it was to be alive on Sevens day.

"Bit of alright, innit love?"

"Hmm." Shirley bit her lip and looked around at the other people in the queue, and their destination at the end of it. "Do you not think perhaps we're a bit, you know, under-dressed?"

They were inching forward in a line towards a large white marquee with floor-length clear panels down one side. A red carpet outside was guarded by uniformed officials performing a thorough VIP ticket and bag check. To compensate for the delay, the queue was being watered with free champagne by a waitress carrying a silver tray of flutes.

"Nah. What's it matter? VIP's innit?" Paul beamed and fluttered his tickets proudly in front of his face, like Lady Windermere's fan.

"Yes, but - " Shirley tugged at his elbow, wobbling his flute alarmingly.

"Steady, love." Paul warned. "Not sure how many of these we're gonna get!"

"Sorry." She whispered. "But look at everyone."

"So?"

"Well, they look like they're going to Ascot or Henley…" She looked at their own attire: Peebles rugby tops, bold red-and-white; he in black jogging bottoms, her in matching velour Matalan trousers. "We look like we're going to Farmfoods."

"Listen, Shirl. These tickets…" Paul brandished them again. "Good as anyone's. Better even. Didn't get 'em because I know the bosses daughter or 'cos I gave a backhander to the council to turn the other way when some regs get overlooked. No. I got these 'cos I did a great public service to this fine Rugby Club and town tradition." She knew he was parroting from the letter he had received from the Club President but she was proud of him all the same. "We *earnt* this. Anyone turns their noses up at us, they can answer to me." He sniffed proudly. "Like to see 'em say it to my face when they've got a champagne flute stuck up their arse!"

"Shhhh!" Shirley nervously looked behind her as they neared the head of the line, but she smiled to herself at the warm glow which ran through her whenever Paul expressed the lengths he would take to defend or protect her. She wasn't the naturally nervous type, but finding herself out of her normal milieu was something new to her and she was on edge.

Shirley did not regard herself as a social climber, but her mother had been, so some of this automatic desire for self-advancement and implicit snobbery came with the territory. She may only work in a bakery, but she was the Shop Manager, and that position carried with it some automatic status which she cherished. Here, amongst what seemed to be a crowd of genuine middle-class Hoorays, she knew she was out of her depth. She didn't play golf, had never owned a German motor car and if asked if she'd ever travelled would have to admit that the extent of her trips abroad had been Torremelinos for a hen party and Dublin on a one-day booze cruise.

It had been in her job, as managers of Greggs, that she had first met Paul and it had been lust at first sight over the glazed doughnuts. She'd been bustling about taking rolls from the oven while checking the cleaning roster when she'd heard this booming voice over the counter. Turning, she'd caught a glimpse of this bronzed hulk with slick black hair and a trim goatee who looked like a cross between The Rock and the owner of Al's Toy Barn. In short, just the man for her.

Shirley knew what she liked and she liked chunky monkeys. She herself was no featherweight and, at 5'10" she was tall and intimidating. Finding someone who could sling her around the dance floor without throwing their back out was something high on her agenda - Salsa was her thing and a fellow devotee was third on her list of attributes in her Match.com profile (the first two were teetotal and vegetarian). She sadly discovered that Paul unambiguously failed all three of these, ten minutes into their first date. And later, found it was a clean sweep of her top seven, if you threw in occasional soft drug use, tardiness, personal hygiene, and lack of homeownership - but by then she was smitten by this gentle giant who had a smile like a tooth-whitening commercial and a grip like a Volvo on winter tyres.

Together they made a grand couple. Or, more accurately, *venti*.

She cast her eyes around the marquee once they had been ushered inside. It was an enormous white space, bright and airy, but not without the smell of damp grass which pervades any attempt to protect a space from the elements in a Scottish summer. Large round tables and red velour gilt-edged chairs were arrayed around the space, twelve seats to a table, each laid with silverware and a central display of black and yellow tulips (the Melrose colours, she knew).

"This way please." The blazered official who had taken their tickets, threaded them down through the tables to the most central one, laid out directly in front of an oversize flat screen TV currently showing a pipe band marching up and down the pitch, massacring *Mhairi's Wedding*. The music from outside drifted in through the canvas slightly ahead of that from the marquee speakers, combining to create a discordant cacophony of out-of-phase tunelessness. Much like the sound of any normal pipe band.

They were the first at their table and, when they were seated, Shirley looked at the display of silverware in front of her, the multiple glasses of different sizes to her left and right, the place markers with their names inscribed in gold script and then looked anxiously and needily up at Paul to her right. Paul was necking the last of his champagne and reaching on the turn for another as a waitress passed with a full tray. Shirley jabbed a finger into his belly and he turned whelping, a full flute in each hand.

"Hey!" He objected, then swept his hand in front of her and placed a flute of orange juice on her plate. "For you, my sweet."

"That's very kind of you, honey." She flashed a brief smile and looked at the strange orange-coloured drink in his own flute. "What's yours?"

"Bucks Fizz." Paul grinned. "It's got fruit in it!"

"That doesn't mean it counts as one of your five a day."

Paul grinned again. "Who said I'm stopping at five? This tournament goes on all day, you know. Got hours of drinking to get in. This free bar's not going to drain itself."

"Yes, honey." She patted his hand, just heavily enough for Paul to catch her full meaning. "We're both here to enjoy ourselves though, aren't we?"

"Aye." Paul reasoned, putting his glass down. "No worries. I getcha."

Shirley sighed, looking around nervously for their table companions to start arriving, when a waitress suddenly appeared with a tray of Cadbury's Creme Eggs. Paul fell on them like a Doberman on a chuck steak.

"What on earth?" Shirley's eyebrows shot up. "You'd have thought they'd lay on a better class of *hors d'oeuvre* than that, wouldn't you?" She whispered.

Paul grinned sheepishly with a mouthful of chocolate. "Special request."

Shirley regarded him like a parent indulging a small child. "So much for diet, health and fitness."

"Diet? This is a creme egg! Cream. Egg. Dairy times two. Health? Strong as an ox. Look at me!" He flexed an impressive bicep beneath his rugby shirt. "And fitness? I'm all about fitness." Paul munched. "Fitness this all into my mouth in one go!"

Paul had a clear plan and, unlike most of Paul's plans, this one was going to go *to plan*. He had given this so much thought he couldn't quite believe he was finally here now, executing it. He'd even run his plan past Cullen and taken every suggestion he'd given on board - well, almost every suggestion. Paul drew the line at military precision. He was planning a proposal, not a state funeral.

But, boy was he nervous. He didn't want to let on to Shirley, so was trying hard not to give anything away. And he didn't want to forget what was left to do - there were still some vital tasks to be undertaken, still plenty that could go wrong. He was drinking not to get drunk - even if that was what Shirley thought - but to steady his nerves and steel himself for the job in hand. If Shirley thought his current behaviour was simply *Paul being Paul* then so much the better. The subterfuge was complete. So far.

Munching through the chocolate, he studied the fixture list and timings in the centre pages of the programme. According to the draw, Melrose looked like they should get to the quarter-finals at least, maybe the semi's and - who knew - perhaps the final itself. They had finished runners' up for the past two years so they were in-form and maybe this would be their year? But, if he aimed for the final that wouldn't be until 6:20 which meant… Christ, five hours to wait. Five hours in which he had access to a free bar and nothing else to do but watch rugby. What could be more perfect? But he couldn't have too much to drink because he would then be incapable of carrying out the very plan he had constructed so painstakingly. What could be more cruel?

Paul smiled at Shirley, trying not to let his worries show.

"Let's go for a wander." He suggested.

"Hmm?"

"See if these passes do what they said they'd do." Paul waggled his laminate on the lanyard around his neck. "VVIP. Access All Areas is what they said. We could meet the teams, all that! Whaddyasay?"

They stepped out of the tent into the broad sunshine, bright white clouds scudding across this pale blue bowl, rimmed by the Eildon hills in the distance. The red carpet led them down to the rear of the corporate stand and they ascended the steps up and came out at a middle row. Hard plastic seats were empty to both sides of them and the pitch, a glorious patch of dark green, sat ahead of them, heavily watered by the previous week's April showers.

All around them, people were pouring into the ground, taking their seats, or carving out their places before the real crowds started arriving. The beer tent across the road, and the bar in the main stand, were already doing a roaring trade judging by the number of plastic pints being carried; so too were the food trailers which dotted the perimeter.

Paul scanned the setup, taking note of the TV crews and paraphernalia. The first step in his plan was to arrange some separation from Shirley so he could put the necessary arrangements in place.

"Fancy a pint?"

Shirley furrowed her brow. "There's a free bar back in the tent."

"Aye, but it's all wine and cocktails innit? I fancy a proper pint." He scrunched his face up, making a decision. "I'll go find the bar, have a mooch, meet you back at the table?"

Suddenly, Shirley looked uncomfortable. "You want me to go back in there on my own? Sit there and make small talk with strangers without you?"

"Um. Yeah." Paul shrugged.

"No." Shirley resolved. "I'll stay here, if that's all the same to you. When you come back, we can just sit and enjoy the rugby. That's why we came after all."

"Right you are. Won't be long." And Paul breezed away, waiting until he was clear of the stand before breathing a sigh of relief. The game was afoot.

"Who was that bloke?"

"Hmm?" Up on the TV gantry, Steve was trying to hear what the director was saying over his earphones and held one hand over his headset mike as he did so. He may have only been three meters above the ground but wind noise up here was definitely a thing.

"The bloke with the roll-up and the pint?" This was Carl, the gopher, who wound cables, connected stuff up and generally got in the way. Large, smelly and hairy - the cameramen referred to him as Neander-Carl - although not to his face. Carl had just climbed up as the man with the pint had climbed down, and was now leaning on the top railing idly watching as the man wended his way through the gathering crowd on the grassy bank.

"'I was just telling Nigel." Steve sighed. "Wants some kind of kiss-cam job doing during half-time in the final."

"You wot?"

"Kiss cam. You know, like in American Football. Or is it baseball? Dun't matter. Any road, wants me to zoom in on where he's sitting with his girlfriend. Flashed his VIP badge at me like he was some kind of Marvel's Agent of Shield or summat." He leant into his headset again. "What's that? … Ok, right-o. Roger that." Steve covered his mike again and turned back to Carl. "Well, look's like this bloke's gold or summat. It's happening."

Carl hmm'ed a mild surprise and watched the large man with the goatee thread his way back past the corner flag, along the side of the pitch and then disappear behind the director's gantry block.

"Keep an eye on him, will ya?" Steve prodded.

"Me?"

"Yes, you. I need to see where he's going to sit."

"Why?"

"'Cos he says he'll be in the same seats come showtime." Steve looked at Carl who seemed to be having difficulty all of a sudden with the English language. "I need to zoom in on him. So I need to know where he is."

"Right. Gotcha. Say no more" Carl tapped the side of his nose, conspiratorially, and returned his gaze to finding the bulky figure, scanning the area beyond the right touchline as if his life depended on it. "He's going into the Corporate Hostility stand."

"I know that!" Steve was swinging his camera around towards the location in question, looking into the viewfinder and adjusting the zoom. "He told me. Whereabouts?"

"He's just sitting down… hang on… near the middle, about halfway up…. next to some bit that looks like Miranda."

"Aha! Got him." Steve pulled off his headset and leant back in his seat. "Remind me nearer the time will ya? Plenty to do." He fiddled with his controls and scrutinised his viewfinder carefully.

THE SEMI-FINALS

As the afternoon wore on, Wingnut and his sons had become more and more excitable. Galashiels were actually progressing in the tournament, doing well in fact, and Wingnut couldn't restrain himself.

"Told ya you were talking bollocks, didn't I?" He prodded Sam's arm with his elbow, sloshing beer onto his shirt sleeve. "Fucking brilliant we are."

"It's a miracle, right enough." Sam nodded. "We've been lucky with the draw, mind."

"You make your own luck." Wingnut grinned. "Look at me. A free man and the world at my feet. 'Ere! Maybe my luck's rubbing off on them!"

"Well we'll soon see, won't we Dad?" Sean chimed in anxiously. "It's this Thai lot in the first semi. They're bloody good. I think our luck might be about to run out."

"Bollocks!" Wingnut railed. "Fucking jungle bunnies. Where the fuck is Thailand anyway?"

Long before the final whistle, Wingnut had flung his half-empty pint onto the ground and gone in search of something stronger. Galashiels hadn't just been beaten, they had been flattened 42-0. Who had let these bastards even enter the country, never mind the tournament? Now they were in the final! Thatcher's fucking Britain.

And flattened was the appropriate verb. All of their points scored from tries had come from this man-mountain figure who had simply picked up the ball wherever he was in the middle of the park and charged for the goalposts. Nothing had stopped him, and it looked like nothing could.

Apart from, maybe, Hulk.

The main bar had been so busy that he had ordered three separate shorts - you just couldn't tell how long it would be before you could get served again - and then, on downing them in succession, quickly regretted it. Staggering and weaving, he made his way through the crush and out into the foyer, looking for the toilets. The corridor was packed with blazered stewards chattering and laughing, and Wingnut slid past them into the toilets and promptly threw up in the far-right cubicle. He emerged gingerly, wiping his mouth on his sleeve and, turning left instead of right, found himself suddenly in the middle of the players' corridor.

Bulky sweaty, muddy players filled its width, jostling this way and that to get by. Wingnut was in the process of hazily turning around to retrace his steps and get out into the open air when he saw a couple kissing, standing in the corner. They were oblivious to their surroundings and Wingnut couldn't make out any detail about the girl but the man was one of the players wearing the dreaded Thai strip. Instinctively, Wingnut strode over then suddenly came up short as he saw the woman pull away and catch sight of him.

"Gloria?"

Gloria looked worriedly at the Thai player, who put his arms around her protectively and pulled himself up to his full height. Wingnut hesitated. This man was almost as tall as him but was broader, chunkier and younger.

And sober.

The coward in him decided that discretion was the better part of valour. Pushing past the amorous couple he made it to the door and took a gulp of fresh air only to find himself standing in the way of a heavy scurrying missile which was Duffy, head down, almost ploughing into him.

Duffy hadn't wanted to attend the Melrose Sevens but couldn't keep away. Gloria had told him she was going and he wanted to know - had to know - why. He didn't say anything to her and waited until she had left that morning before making his own way there and paying at the gate for one of the last available pitch-side seats. For several hours he sat and watched - not the rugby, but Gloria. She had a seat in the stands. How had she obtained that? He sat and watched while she sat and watched, unaware he was there.

Despite his lack of interest in the sport, he found the knock-out nature of the competition compelling. He started keeping careful, neat notes of the scores in his programme, making annotations against each game, and tracking the winners through as the tournament progressed. Eventually he noticed that one of the teams making most headway through the contest was the team from Thailand. Of course - what a fool he was! When they won their semi-final against Galashiels, he saw Gloria rise from her seat with some finality and disappear down into the belly of the stand.

He sat, still, for several minutes, staring at her empty seat - a tiny black hole amid a maelstrom of noise and activity. Where had she gone? Why was she here? What should he do? His mind raced through a galaxy of thoughts and emotions, his fingers and thumbs orbiting each other like spiralling planets until they collided and mashed the pages of his programme to a pulp.

His heart thumping in his chest, he rose from his seat and surged along the pitch heading for the main stand.

"Whoa, bruv! You can't come in here. Alien-hunters and time-travellers not allowed." Wingnut sneered, his teeth displaying remnants of vomit. Duffy looked up, his way blocked, shock and hatred in his eyes.

"You! What are you doing here? Get away from me. Get away from her. Get away from us!"

Wingnut laughed and shook his head. "Oh, my poor wee man. Too much for you is it? Reputation in tatters, and me an innocent man."

"She was never happy with you. Never."

"Fucking was. You should have seen the way we humped and humped, Duff. Sweat on glistening skin, fingernails clawing at me to go faster, harder. Moaning and writhing. She fucking loved it. Realised what a real man was like and how she'd been missing it."

Duffy started agitating his head, beating his temples with his palms, trying to push the words and images from his head. "Shut up! Shut up! Shut up!"

"Can't. Won't." Taunted Wingnut. "Fucks like a whore, your missus. Couldn't get enough of my dick. Always wanted more. Always."

"Stop! Stop this now! Right now!"

Wingnut thrust his face into Duffy's, a lascivious grin contorting his features like some grotesque Punch mannequin. The fact that Wingnut had an IQ higher than Duffy's sperm count flattered neither of them.

"Loved the fucking taste of it, Duff." Wingnut taunted. "Wanted every last drop. What good is that when you're trying to get pregnant, huh? Beats me, but I fucking loved every second of it."

"No!" Duffy poured all his energy and force into his shoulders and heaved into Wingnut, his low centre of gravity and bull-like strength pushing them both backwards into the corner of the corridor.

"Oh, but yes!" Wingnut grappled with his brother-in-law, trying to wrestle him back towards the door, while Duffy kept on pushing and barging, his rage adding to his raw strength. "And even now, even with me to service her - she's still not satisfied! It's still not enough. Now, she's off shagging some rugby player from her homeland. What a slapper!"

"What? What?" Duffy was flapping and thrusting into Wingnut's torso while trying to come up for air and look to see whether his brother-in-law was being genuine or not.

"Oh yes, just seen them now. Tonguing each other in plain view. What must they get up to when the bedroom door's closed, hmm? Your bedroom door? While you're out scanning the skies for aliens, she's getting her tyres rotated by an illegal alien. Ha!"

Mongkut heard some commotion outside the changing room, had looked around to ask Robert what it was and found he was alone. He stood up off the bench and poked his head around the door frame. Robert was standing with his back to him, some way down the corridor, Gloria leaning in to him, her hands over her ears as Robert tried to shield her bodily from something Mongkut couldn't see. But he could hear a torrent of angry words spurting from somewhere and he wasn't the only person who's attention had been drawn to this unexpected commotion. A few elderly stewards had started to gather and hesitate on the periphery of whatever was taking place.

Mongkut pulled himself up to his full height, towering over everyone else in the corridor even in his stockinged feet and padded curiously towards the disturbance. By the time he had reached Robert he could see a tall drunk man swaying and gesticulating wildly, shouting at a small hairy barrel of a man. The short man had his hands flying up and down his body, one moment beating his head with his own fists, the next moment arms rigid by his sides, his hands clenching and unclenching. Mongkut had seen enough angry people in his time to recognise someone whose volcano was about to erupt. He put his hand on Robert's shoulder and, when Gloria looked around at him, smiled gently and then stooped to ask him softly, in Thai:

"What's going on?"

Robert glanced anxiously at Gloria, her eyes wet and imploring, and then met Mongkut's gaze. "That madman is insulting Gloria." Robert said. "He is telling everyone she is a whore…" He stopped and listened to another few words of the tirade, translating for his friend. "… that she needs sex… lots of sex… with lots of men… lots of times… and that she cannot be trusted to stay loyal to one man… especially him." Robert pointed to the hairy fist-forming man. "He is her husband."

Mongkut looked from Robert to Gloria, from her husband to the ranting madman, and then back at Gloria. "He says: She is a slut… a common whore… who will sleep with anyone for money… suck their, er, engage in oral sex… take on a whole rugby sevens team… at once. Why would she be happy with him?" Robert looked up at Mongkut. "He is a very bad man."

It is at times such as this that executive decisions are made and fates hang in the balance. Robert looked at Mongkut, hesitating, then at Gloria ashamed and fearful, trembling in his arms, and at her husband - a man being driven to despair by a stream of invective, giving himself a tremendous beating while a madman ranted on and on. He saw all this and decided that some slight mistranslation of the drunk's words might be in order. "He is saying: Gloria is a… lady's part… and of low moral fibre… she is typical of all Thai women everywhere… all they want is to find real men… white men… with fat penises and fat wallets… who can give them what they want… All Thai women are like this… what did he think he was doing when he bought her from Thailand?… It isn't so much a country as a meat market where women can be bought… for pennies… and used as vessels for a man's pleasure…." Robert could see Mongkut starting to raise himself up and straighten, his face becoming a freak wave of indignation and ferocity. Robert pressed on "He says: all Thai women are like this…. All of them… wives, daughters, mothers…"

That did it.

Wingnut was ratcheting up his insults but starting to flag. He'd been really enjoying himself, becoming quite impressed by his imagination, vocabulary and turns of phrase as he searched for ever more extreme images to conjure and fling into his victim's face. So why wasn't Duffy all over him? How much verbal punishment was the idiot prepared to take, in front of a gathering crowd? He was going nuclear in terms of his physical reaction but turning most of it on himself. Wingnut had barely a scratch.

The uniformed stewards, cowardly elder statesmen to a man, were gradually summoning up some will to act, encouraged by their swelling numbers, they were creeping ever closer to him down the corridor. Presumably at some point they would pounce, but right now they were like hungry lions on the Serengeti stalking their prey through the long grass - waiting, waiting, waiting until there was no doubt of the outcome. Wingnut didn't want to hang around and didn't think he had the verbal ingenuity to string this out until they caught him.

He started to invent one last slew of insults, emptying both barrels at Duffy to see if could ultimately provoke him to retaliate or implode. Then he felt a shadow fall across him. Like the darkness that passes over the face of the earth when a cloud obscures the sun, there was suddenly a noticeable temperature drop and a stillness, as if a lightning storm was about to hit. Wingnut turned to look over his left shoulder and the last two things he saw, in order, were:

1. A gigantic form, blotting out the light - like the endless Imperial Star Destroyer crawling remorselessly across his field of view.

2. Off to one side, half-seen as the blackness encroached, a silhouette at the end of the corridor, backlit by the spring sunshine beyond. Wearing a cowboy hat.

Paul couldn't believe his eyes - and not just because his beloved Peebles team were now five points ahead against Melrose in the second semi-final. His eyes had almost parted company with his sockets because his phone bore a text message from Cullen.

From Cullen! The man had entered the 20th century and learnt how to text just as the rest of the world was embracing the 21st and giving texts a wide berth. Mind, even this wasn't the most unusual aspect of the whole thing: this was an unsolicited message, from Cullen to him, sent using a mobile device which Cullen very rarely charged, and seldom used.

As emergency priorities went, this was up there with Defcon 1 and Paul looked incredulously at the screen.

WHERE ARE YOU?

Ah. Well, as urgent appeals went, this wasn't quite up there with the beacons signalling the arrival of the Armada. Cullen had fallen inevitably into mobile phone speak - where every conversation started with "I'm on the train" or "I'm watching Heartbeat."

IN MELROSE. AT THE SEVENS. Paul replied, breathing heavily as Peebles once more drove forward with what looked almost like urgency.

YES. WHEREABOUTS. Was the immediate reply.

It was funny, Paul thought. Even without punctuation, he could hear the tone. Maybe Cullen didn't need punctuation? Maybe he ordinarily spoke without it and Paul just hadn't noticed before? He recalled when they had first met, years ago, and Cullen had simply stood in his way issuing bald statements as though they were simple facts which anyone should know and you were stupid if you didn't and he didn't have the energy or breath or time to waste explaining it to you. *"Surgery's closed." "I wouldn't." "Whatever it was, you missed it."*

YES. WHEREABOUTS

Never mind wasting time on prepositions or adjectives. He wasn't even bothering with verbs now.

HALFWAY UP TEMP STANDS. BY BIG TENT.

Two can play at this game, Paul thought. Let's see who

uses a verb first.

GOTCHA.

Aw well, he hadn't expected to come out on top in this battle of wits anyway. Then:

BUSY?

Christ! What was going on? This was almost a conversation! But come on, man! This was his big moment. Plans were afoot. I mean, just not now, ok?

KINDA.

Now it's a one word contest is it? Seconds away, round two.

NEED SOME HELP HERE.

A-ha! A verb, and a sentence. Paul had won! He smiled to himself victoriously and then groaned. Peebles were still five ahead and there could only be a minute or two before half-time. There was some kind of charity game on next, there to give the winners of the second semi-final a breather before the final - Paul's date with destiny. He had a window of half an hour, he reckoned.

NOW.

Paul set his jaw and scanned the capacity crowd, flicking over faces and somehow, magically, inexplicably, finding a still centre. Amidst the cheering and laughing, jostling and drinking, stood a single figure wearing a cowboy hat and a serious expression. Not entirely embedded in the crush that surrounded him - a small but detectable space between him and everyone else, like an invisible force field which he carried with him. Some pheromone he emitted which everyone detected and translated as meaning *personal space - do not invade.*

Their eyes met and Paul realised he was caught. Bollocks. He sneaked a look at Shirley, sitting forward in her seat next to him all caught up in the tension as Peebles came under pressure from the home team.

OK.

He looked over to catch Cullen's eyes again but the man had disappeared. Paul scanned the crowd in that same area between the far edge of the main stands and the corner flag. He could just make out the back of a brown leather cowboy hat threading its way through the press of people.

"Need a waz, love." Paul rose from his seat. "Back in a mo."

"Ok, sweetie." Shirley reached to stroke his hand as he stood, eyes still on the pitch.

The portakabin used as the St John's Ambulance station for the tournament was usually the Rugby Club merchandise shop. Inside were shirts, shorts, socks and scarves draped across the windows, hanging from suspended rails and stacked in shelves against the far wall. A riot of black and gold. Amidst all this paraphernalia, the SJA volunteers had done their best to fit it out to meet their needs.

They had erected a folding courtesy screen on castors across the middle of the portakabin and pushed as much of the merchandise as they could behind it. On the other side they had erected two stretchers, one treatment couch, and a small table and chairs which would be used for making tea and biscuits for anyone overcome by heat exhaustion, tiredness, or drunkenness. The two tabarded medics on duty were playing cards at the table while the pre-final charity game took place.

No-one had been expecting any actual serious injuries. Certainly not this late in the day.

"I'm just fecking saying, you must be cheating or summat, 'cos that's the fourth fecking blackjack you've had on the bounce." Gerry threw his cards down in disgust and rooted in his pocket for some more money. "All I've got left is notes and I'm not fecking giving 'em to you if you're gonna just cheat like that."

"I'm not cheating!" Mike seemed genuinely indignant. "Just my luck, is all." He waxed lyrical and angelic, clutching the cards to his chest as he looked up at the mucky portakabin ceiling. "Today, of all days, my luck is most definitely in. Forty quid each way win on the National and now twenty quid off you at Blackjack. The takeaways'll be on me in our house tonight."

"Well, that's me done. All I've got left I was gonna bet on the winners here."

"Oh yeah. How much?" There was an interested gleam in Mike's eye.

"Why? You want to share some of your winnings with me, is that it?" said Gerry.

"No. I want to strike while the iron's hot. When your luck's in, it's in. On a hat-trick now, I fancy my chances against you if we're gonna bet on different teams in the final."

"I'm not betting you!"

"Why not?"

"'Cos I want to know I'll get paid if I win." Gerry sneered. "When I win."

"If you want to win, you need Lady Luck on your side and today… she's with me." Mike could not have looked more self-satisfied if he had just won a bet for kissing his own chin.

"Oh, yeah?"

"Yeah."

"Right. Well, I tell you what. I've got…" Gerry rummaged in his trouser pockets for the last of his money.

"Twenty quid here. Twenty quid says Melrose are gonna choke and these Thai visitors'll nick it."

"Get out! You're throwing your money away." Mike grinned. "I mean I want to win, naturally, but this is taking candy from a baby."

"Yeah? Well, give me odds then." Gerry taunted and Mike suddenly looked less cocky.

"Now, hang on-"

"No, come on! Lady luck, candy from a baby, and all that." Gerry leant forward, scenting some kind of moral victory. "What odds'll give you me, huh? Two to one? Three?"

"Look, I'm not a bookie. I don't know how to calculate odds."

"So what? You're gonna win aren't you? Why does it matter what odds you give me? If I lose, I lose. The odds only make a difference if I win - like you reckon I won't." Gerry was smiling beatifically now, sitting assuredly atop a pillar of impeccable logic.

Mike chomped his teeth quietly together, mouth closed, as he thought. After a short pause, interrupted only by Gerry taunting him by waggling his head from side to side like some kind of slot-arcade clown, Mike relented.

"All right. Melrose to win by a country mile. Three to one, if those Thai blokes manage it."

"Done!" Gerry spat on his hand and slapped it into Mike's before he could change his mind. "Right, let's go and watch. See if Lady Luck can shine on me."

They both stood and Gerry opened the door to be met with a pair of officials carrying in the limp body of what looked like a human scarecrow who'd come off second best with a farm vehicle.

"What the-?"

"Where shall we put him?" huffed one of the blazers, blood stains all down his sleeve.

"What?" Mike recovered first. "Er, over there. On the stretcher."

"What the feck happened?" Said Gerry, closing the door on the warm early evening sunshine. "Was there a war on and we missed it?"

"Bit of an altercation. Two guys in the main building." The first blazer said with substantial understatement.

"Altercation? Looks like the fecking Somme! Who's this guy?"

"He was the main, um, altercator."

"Uh-uh. And the other guy?"

The blazer looked at Gerry and shrugged. "Not a scratch."

"What?"

"Aye. Big guy. The one from the Thai team?"

Gerry's eyes widened. "Here Mike, mind if I put another twenty on?"

Duffy had watched Wingnut being carried out and the crush disperse as a referee had trotted in looking for the players for the final. Once all parties had been led out through the tunnel, Duffy was shepherded out into the daylight by a steward - which had come as a shock, the events of the past few minutes had felt like an afternoon spent wrapped in a movie, and he now emerged blinking into the unexpected sunshine.

The energy and noise around him, and the clean fresh air in his lungs, neither engaged or involved him. He was walking as if through a dream - or, more accurately, a nightmare. Gloria was gone - no longer his. Any doubts he might have clung to, had now evaporated like early morning mist over the Tweed. The way she had wrapped herself around the rugby player and clung to him. Clung to *him* while Duffy had wrestled with the demons in his head; while his foul contemptible brother-in-law had thrown every insult and weapon at him, over and over, until he could barely stand. Like a comic-book superhero, Duffy had been pinned in place by an inexplicable energy and forced to suffer as all his powers were plucked from him and he was returned to feeble human form. All he was now, was a shell of a person.

As he made his way back to his seat on autopilot he wondered what he should do now. His sister had left him, now his wife. His reputation lay in tatters and he had simply stood and suffered while his brother-in-law had insulted and belittled him. His ruination was complete and he wanted to go home and hide. He didn't want to stay here any longer but didn't know what else to do. He needed some indication, a sign.

Duffy meandered blindly through the standing crowd behind the goal and plodded back to his seat amongst the benches running along the far touchline. His seat was unoccupied, but not empty. On it was an A4 brown envelope, thick with contents. Duffy looked enquiringly at the people sitting either side, but they all had their eyes on the teams lining up for the match start. He picked up the envelope and dumbly sat down as the whistle blew and the charity game got underway with a cheer.

Inside the envelope was a buff folder and a handwritten note:

Read the yellow highlights.
Meet me inside the main gate.
Your sister's fate rests on it.

Bring the boys.

It was signed: *A friend from the future.*

Duffy stared at the note and a shiver went down his spine. He flipped through the folder looking for the passages marked in yellow and when he read them he raised his eyes in wonder. Looking through the action on the pitch in front of him to the touchline opposite he made out the figures of Sam and Sean sitting with arms crossed sternly watching the game. He kept watching them until one of them glanced in his direction. It was Sean, and Duffy held his gaze for a few seconds wondering what to do. Then he stood up and marched off around the touchline towards the pair.

Paul hurried out through the back of the stands and along the walkway to the main exit gate. There was no crush here, all eyes and bodies crammed into a five-meter deep press all around the pitch. Outside the ground, along the main road, the pedestrian barriers and makeshift tables had been cleared away and the only occupants now were idling security men and drinkers ferrying three pint handfuls from the large beer tent.

Paul showed his laminate at the main gate, popped back into the ground and looked around the empty car park. Cullen stood watching him from inside the door which led into the main stand building. A couple of moustachio'ed veterans were half-manning the door and half-watching the female rugby players cavorting on the pitch. Split priorities. The stewards waved him through with barely a glance.

"How'd you get in here?" Paul frowned, miffed that his friend was inside this blazered security cordon without a pass.

"Kate."

"The police lady?"

Cullen nodded curtly. "I need the necklace."

"What?"

"I need to borrow it."

"Well, yeah. But I need it. Gotta to give it to Shirl. The plan, remember?" Paul appealed.

"You'll get it back."

Paul looked at his watch, for perhaps the first time in his life seeing punctuality as a valued attribute. "But I only have half an hour." He whined.

Cullen considered this for a moment. "That'll do." He lied.

"Why? What's going on?"

"You'll see." Cullen glanced at his watch. "Oh, and one more thing."

THE FINAL

Wingnut came round lying on the stretcher in the portakabin. Alone - the medics had left him to watch the final and see whose money was safe and whose at risk. They'd reckoned he wouldn't be moving any time soon and, as Wingnut soon discovered, they were right.

The man with the cowboy hat had other ideas. He was standing in the doorway looking at Wingnut impassively while the crowd roared and applauded the activity on the pitch. All eyes, for now, were elsewhere. The man in the hat closed the door behind him. Wingnut lifted his head, with some difficulty and not a little pain, and surveyed the damage to his body.

His left arm was broken, that was a given. No way could it have held that shape under any other condition. The blood-soaked arm of his fleece didn't really add anything to the available information. Moving on. He was having great difficulty breathing so deduced that he'd either broken some ribs or had massive bruising around them. His lips were sore, his right eye hurt like hell and the image from it was distinctly dark and blurry. The other eye seemed okay but that wasn't much to go on. He figured they'd given him something to relieve the pain because he didn't seem to be in as much discomfort as his injuries might suggest. Although the other explanation for it might be simply shock. He tried to recall what had happened but found he could not. Some vague recollection of being picked up like a ragdoll by the giant and then all was black until just now. He tried moving his feet and found he could, but when he tried to swing them off the stretcher, nothing happened.

A blurry gold thing swam into Wingnut's vision. He was forced to pull his head back so his eyes could focus. When they did, they grew large and he felt himself sober up involuntarily. The gold thing was a necklace. It was being dangled from the cowboy's hand, this stone-faced man with wisps of greying curls poking from underneath his leather hat.

"Yours I believe?" The man said calmly.

A sweat rose involuntarily to Wingnut's brow and he felt the adrenalin fight-or-flight surge course through him.

"Who the fuck are you?" He snarled.

"That can wait." The man hadn't flinched. "This can't."

"Fuck off! And take your piece of junk with you."

"You saying this isn't yours?"

Wingnut nodded stiffly.

"Got your prints on it." The man leant into his face, bending to do so. "Got your prints all over it."

"Never seen it before in my life."

"S'funny. It belonged to your wife." The man waggled the necklace and the disc spun lazily in the thick airlessness of the portakabin. "You remember her, don't you?"

Wingnut felt his mouth go dry, unable to swallow.

"Now, then Derek." Wingnut flinched at the mention of his name. "Where do you think I found it, hmm?"

"Up your arse?"

The man smiled thinly while the necklace continued to dangle in front of him.

"No. Would you like to guess again?"

"Fuck off. I'm an innocent man. Leave me alone."

"Innocent, hmm?" The man leant into Wingnut conspiratorially. "Would you like me to tell you a story?"

"No. Fuck off."

"Are you sitting comfortably? Then I'll begin."

Wingnut, sitting about as uncomfortably as he could ever imagine being, glared into the cowboy's grey eyes, but the man just returned his gaze calmly.

"Once upon a time, there was a young couple. Let's call them… Derek and Heather. Heather was a lovely kind, beautiful young woman with a cheery smile. But her husband was a grumpy, mean and bitter man who would spend all his money on drink. And one day, Heather met a man who showed her kindness, paid her compliments, made her feel loved. And she realised what she'd been missing and how unhappy she was with Derek. This new man - let's call him… Archie. He was a nice man and he loved her. And Heather fell in love with him. And they decided to get married."

"Bollocks!" Wingnut spat and twisted in his restraints, pain spasming up his arm.

"But Derek wasn't happy about this. At all. And when Derek was unhappy, he drank more and he threatened to kill Heather - and Archie - if she ever left him. So Heather and Archie made a deal. A deal that meant they could stay together and be together, just not all the time. Because in order for them to be together, Heather had to stay married to Derek. That was the deal. So she accepted it. And she lived a life with Derek, snatching moments with Archie when she could. But Archie was unhappy with the deal, and begged Heather to leave Derek and be with him. But Heather would cry and say she couldn't because her husband would kill her. And though Archie couldn't bear to see Heather cry, and he didn't want her to die - because he loved her - he was scared. Afraid of Derek. So he went along with the plan. For years and years and years."

Wingnut made another agonising effort to wrestle free, but the man simply thrust his face anew into Wingnut's, angry frown lines appearing over steel-cold eyes.

"I'm sorry, Derek. Perhaps you've heard this story before?" The man continued. "One day - in 2010 - Derek came home from the pub early. Maybe he'd run out of money, or the landlord had thrown him out for being drunk one time too many. Who knows? It doesn't matter. All that matters is that Derek came home early. And found Heather and Archie together. In the marital bed. And Derek was terribly angry. He shouted and he raged and he punched and kicked poor Archie. Over and over, until there was blood everywhere and Archie could hardly see out of one eye. And do you know what? He widdled on him. That's right, when Archie was lying helpless on the bedroom floor and Heather was crying, screaming and trying to pull Derek away, Derek took out his willy and he wee'd on poor Archie."

"This all a complete-"

"Shut up." The man's face was a mask of stone now, his voice cold and harsh. "This is not a complete anything. This is a true story. All true. For anyone to read. Here." He pulled a folder from nowhere and waved it in Wingnut's face. "In the court report. Because they prosecuted Derek, and he was found guilty. And he went to prison for a long, long time."

Wingnut lay still for a while. The man slowly pulled away and watched him silently until he spoke up.

"I did my time. Paid for what I did."

"Yes. Yes, you did." The man nodded, slowly. "For some of it."

Wingnut stared at the man, a combination of naked hatred and visceral fear trembling within him.

"See, that's where this necklace comes in. Remember that?" The man didn't wait for an answer. "Now, wherever do you think I got it from, hmm? It wasn't up my arse."

"With the court report." Wingnut muttered.

"Nope. The necklace wasn't submitted as evidence at your trial. Don't you remember?"

"Long time ago now."

"Yes. Yes it is. But why would it have been submitted as evidence? It had no bearing on anything did it? So…" The man leant back into Wingnut's face. "One last time, with feeling: where do you think I got it?"

"Her mother's?"

"Ah, a new answer. Not, unfortunately, a good answer. Why would I have found it at Heather's mother's?"

"Because that's where she went."

"Is it, though?"

"Yeah."

"That's what you told everyone."

"S'what Archie said 'n' all."

"Yes. Yes, it is. That's what everyone said, in fact, except for Heather herself. And no-one knows what she said, because she simply disappeared. Off the face of the earth."

Wingnut froze, his eyes locked with those of the cowboy. There was a sudden knock at the door and the cowboy smiled thinly.

"It's time."

Wingnut let out his best try at a laugh but instead coughed up some blood and managed a weak grin. His teeth and gums mashed and bloody. "Time for what?"

With a casual shrug, the cowboy grabbed the stretcher

trolley and glowered over him.

"To have your day in court."

For the second time that afternoon, Wingnut's world went black.

"Fuck off, Uncle Duff." Sam's greeting was too much like Wingnut's recent retort for Duffy to ignore and his head went down and his right hand stiffened and clenched by his side. He gripped the envelope tightly in his left.

"Sam!" Sean protested. "I'm sorry, Uncle Duff. He's still smarting from the beating this Thai lot gave us in the semi."

"And the rest." Sam grunted but he wouldn't pull his gaze away from the activity on the pitch.

"We need to go." Duffy said flatly.

"Huh?"

"We need to go. I have a message. We all need to go. All of us. Now." He waved the envelope wildly in front of them.

"What?"

"Very important. No time. Need to go now. "

"Go where, freakshow?" Sam sniped.

"Main gate. Inside. Inside the main gate. Now. Quickly."

"Fuck off!"

"We have to be there. I have a message. All three of us. We need to be there."

"Or what? And who's the message from: aliens is it? No, wait - a time-traveller? Did you get a message from the future, mindmeld?" He gave Sean a dig in the ribs but Sean bristled and edged away.

"Come on, Sammie. Give it a rest, huh?" Sean turned

to Duffy. "What's this about Uncle Duff? Why have we got to go? What about the final? What about Dad?"

"Never mind your Dad, this is about your Mum!" He raised his voice sharply and both boys looked up at him. He was in a state of maximum distress. "Have to go. Have to. Come on!"

"Mum?" Sam choked. Duffy had both their attentions now.

"Is she… at the gate?" Sean's eyes were blinking furiously.

"No. Yes. I don't know." Duffy groped, desperately. Whatever the time-traveller wanted, Duffy didn't want to risk Heather's future. More than anything right now, he wanted to see her again. So did her sons. "Yes. Yes. She is there. Come on!"

He urged them up with his arms and turned to lead them back along the touchline.

"Be on Miranda in 3-2-"

"He's not there." Steve said into his headset.

"What?"

"He's not there." He repeated. "She's sitting on her own."

"Give me camera four on screen." The director said and the image from Steve's viewfinder appeared on the far right of the bank of four. "Well, where the fuck is he?"

"I don't know. Said he'd be here." Steve pulled his eyes away from the camera and scanned the ground packed with people, craning to find any sign of the large man with the goatee. It was a popular look today, it seemed.

"Is he anywhere else in the stand?"

The director watched as the camera scanned the rows

above and then below the seated figure of Shirley. There were still a few empty seats - presumably the property of the over-inebriated stuck back in the marquee - the remainder were occupied with well-dressed and excited business types.

But the man of the hour was not amongst them.

"Well, he's got exactly... two minutes before the second half. If he doesn't show by then, he's had it. VIP or no VIP."

"We could do-"

"Leave the *we could do*'s to me, would you?" The director replied curtly.

Steve covered his mike with his hands. "I love you too, arsehole." He returned to his viewfinder.

Over on the temporary stand, Shirley was sitting in the sunshine. Alone, watching contentedly the various crowd activity along the touchline and in the banks at either end. She glanced up to the large TV screen to her left but saw only a shot of the talking heads in the mobile studio commenting on replays from the first half. She glanced at her watch and sipped her orange juice, oblivious.

There was only one figure standing inside the main gate and he didn't look much like a time-traveller to Duffy. He was a tall, bulky olive-skinned man scruffily dressed, leaning calmly against a turnstile. He wore a trim goatee and was rooting for something in his mouth with a toothpick. Away to Duffy's right, a whistle blew and a huge roar went up - the second-half was underway.

Duffy led the boys up to the time-traveller warily. "Are you from the future?"

"Oh aye." Paul answered, as off-hand as he could

manage. The minimalist stage directions he'd been given by Cullen had amounted to: *Stay calm. Agree with everything. Just get them there.*

"Is she with you?" Duffy looked around at the sudden emptiness, eyes wheeling around this hushed desert amidst a riot of noise and sporting drama.

"Aye." Paul pulled himself away from the brickwork and pocketed his toothpick.

"You don't look like you're from the future." Duffy mused.

"Oh I am. Definitely." Paul leaned in, confiding. "Blending in."

"Yes. Yes!" Duffy's eyes ignited. "Of course, of course! Have to blend in. No suspicion! Clever. Oh so clever."

Having such an appreciative audience, Paul was beginning to enjoy this role. Perhaps a future on the stage beckoned? He gave a tiny smile. "This way."

Duffy, Sam and Sean followed Big Paul over to a portakabin with dirty mesh on the windows. Paul knocked on the door and waited.

When Wingnut came to, he was soaking wet. The man must have woken him with some water from somewhere. He was also tied much more tightly to the stretcher which had now been angled up in a tilt so that he was positioned like corpse about to be jettisoned feet-first down some slide to hell. He had bandages wound tightly around his shoulders, chest and forehead so that he couldn't even move his head, could only look forward. He felt part victim, part mummy.

"I have bound you over." The cowboy's eyes creased, noticing Wingnut's efforts at reconnoitring his new circumstances. "To keep the peace, so to speak."

"What the fuck?"

The table had been moved into the middle of the room in front of the white screen, now acting as a backdrop for the cowboy who leaned on the table and thumped it quietly with one fist.

"Silence in court. Sheriff Cullen presiding."

"What?"

Cullen smiled thinly. "We're having a retrial."

"Huh?"

"You know, where we revisit your crimes, review the evidence and consider a verdict."

Wingnut squinted at the stupid man in the stupid hat with ill-disguised contempt. "Yeah, well you may be a cowboy but you're no Sheriff." He laughed at his own joke. "And, you know, there's no point you looking so fucking pleased with yourself. You're not the one who can take the credit for my injuries. I was beaten up by the Jolly Green Giant, not you."

"I'm not looking for credit." This man was so calm and contained, he might have been taking a sermon in church. "I'm looking for justice."

"No fucking idea what you're on about, pal. Now, would you mind getting me off this fucking thing and letting me get back out into the real world so I can go about my business as a free man!" Wingnut forced these last two words out through gritted teeth as he strained at the ties on the stretcher which still held him fast.

"Our purpose here today is to establish your innocence. Or guilt. If you are innocent then, of course, you shall go about your business freely. But if you are guilty…"

"And who's going to find me guilty? You?"

"The members of the jury." He said, reasonably.

"What jury? You're fucking nuts!"

"A hand-picked jury. The perfect jury. For you." Cullen smiled again, indulgently. "Court rise."

Wingnut tilted his head this way and that, half-expecting to see some ghostly jury appear through the door. There was a strange surreality about this situation, but beneath his fury was a creeping fear that his time had genuinely come. There was plenty about this man's demeanour that said unhinged psycho.

"Now, I think perhaps we'll resume our conversation about this. Exhibit A." Cullen withdrew the gold necklace from a pocket and dangled it in front of Wingnut's face. The engraved disc sparkled in the striplight as it twisted this way and that in the man's hand.

Wingnut glared at it but didn't respond, If this fool was going to make the same stupid mistake that all villains in movies made - expounding on his theories and imagined slights at extreme length giving the hero time to escape or be rescued, then he - Wingnut - as the hero of his own tale, would be only too delighted to see if he could use this time to get himself out of here. "Help!" He shouted. "Get me out of here!"

Cullen hit him in the face with a fist that came out of nowhere and Wingnut's head bounced back onto the stretcher, his neck rubber-banding. He must have lost consciousness briefly because the man was slapping him across the face, left, right, left, right.

"Fuck off! Stop that you-" Cullen's intense glare wore a mask of menace. Wingnut stopped dead, and he breathed raggedly through a broken nose and reconsidered his strategy. "Ok. If I talk, then will you let me go?"

"I will." The cowboy said, although there something not quite right with the emphasis he used on the two words. He had emphasised the *I* and not the *will.* Wingnut let it pass.

"Go on then. I'm all ears."

"Yes. You are." He waggled the necklace in his fingers again. ""I was asking if you knew where I got this. Remember? The answer is: not far from here."

"There's many places not far from here."

"I mean, yards from here - not miles."

Wingnut stiffened. "Probably one of my sons. They've both got one - must have dropped it sometime today. Sammie probably. A bit pissed, you know."

"No. This one was dug up. Some months ago."

"Dug up?"

"Some months ago. Attached to a dead body."

"Don't know what you're talking about." Wingnut shifted in his restraints, trying to get more air into his lungs. "Help! Someone get me out of here!"

"There'll be no rescue for you." Cullen intoned. "There was no rescue for her."

"What? I don't know what - or who - you're talking about."

"Yes you do. Your wife, Heather."

"She ran away. Who cares?"

"She's dead." Cullen pressed down hard on Wingnut's arm and he shrieked in agony.

"No, she isn't!" Wingnut shaking his head in a vain bid to hide from the pain. "She ran off. Probably with that fucking Archie."

"She's dead." Cullen pressed down again. "And you killed her."

"Bollocks!" Wingnut, tears in his eyes, managing to

barely hiss the words. Cullen pressed down a third time on Wingnut's arm. The pain was unbearable.

"Didn't you?" Cullen bent in closely, his eyes looming, occupying all of Wingnut's field of view. His arm felt like it was shattering anew, tearing his entire world apart. "Didn't you?"

"No." Wingnut moaned. "It was an accident, ok? If it'll fucking shut you up and get this over with. It was an accident."

"What happened?"

He opened his eyes, looking up the ceiling. His voice softened. "She came to me, before the trial. She was furious. She'd seen Archie's wounds. Her eyes were violet, huge. Full of hate. She spat at me, told me she and Archie had been seeing each other for years. That I'd never been there for her. And that even when I was, I wasn't able to…"

"What?"

"Doesn't matter." Wingnut closed his eyes again, wearily. "She was fucking asking for it. Her and that bloody Archie. No surprise - finding 'em together. She hadn't touched me for… a long time. I hit her. Put all my weight behind it. She fell against something. Never got up again. It was an accident."

"What did you do with the body?"

"I brought her here. Used to help the groundsman in exchange for a few beers in the bar after, free. Had my beers, and it was dark. She was in my boot, in some black binliners. There was building work going on - they were putting some footings in, so I just dug into the pit they'd made, one side, and stuffed her in there." Wingnut heaved a heavy sigh. "Didn't realise she still had her necklace on."

Cullen remained silent. There was a big cheer from the

crowd outside.

Wingnut opened his eyes and looked at the cowboy. "We done, then? Can I go?"

"No." Cullen furrowed his brow, confused.

"Look, you got your little confession, right? But you can't do anything with it. So, you've had your fun. Now let me go."

"I can't do anything with your confession?"

"No. Statute of limitations, and all that."

"There is no statute of limitations in this country. You've been watching too much American TV."

"No? Well, it doesn't matter. you're not the law. They could've knocked on my door any time. But they haven't." For the first time during the ordeal, Wingnut smiled. "I think you're lying. I think you've got the square root of fuck all."

Cullen's face tightened. "We haven't finished hearing all the evidence yet. There are still legal arguments to be made."

Wingnut screwed his face up at this lunatic cowboy sheriff and his weirdness. "Christ! I thought Duffy was off his rocker. You and him would make a great pair."

"I'd like to call my first witness. MacDuff Ingoglia."

"What?!?" Wingnut blinked furiously and shook his head as if to test he was awake. His eyes bulged when Duffy calmly stepped out from behind the screen. "What the fuck?"

THE VERDICT

Duffy stood defiantly, red angry eyes burning into Wingnut's own. He was shaking with rage.

"Mr Ingoglia, Could you present the court with Exhibit B, Mr Marshall's medical records." The cowboy nodded to Duffy who revealed a buff folder in his hand from behind his back and waved it solemnly in the air for Wingnut to behold.

"Would you please read to me the section highlighted in yellow on the final page?"

Duffy opened the folder, head down, rocking slightly as he read: "Sperm count: low. Motility: zero."

"Thank you, Mr Ingoglia. Would you care to tell the court what this means?"

"What the fuck's it got to do with him? Who put him in charge? Get me the fuck off this thing!" Wingnut rocked and made the stretcher rattle and skid on the painted floor. His ties held.

"It means he is infertile." Duffy intoned.

"Yeah! And you'd fucking know wouldn't you, Jaffa?" Wingnut spat bloody spittle in Duffy's direction but it just landed on his own bandages.

"Mr Ingoglia, are you familiar with the medical reports surrounding sperm analysis, fertility tests and so on?"

"I am, yes. I have had many tests myself. Many many. Lots. And reports. Lots and lots of reports. Motility - yes, I know all about motility."

"So you are something of an expert in this regard?"

"Yes. I am, yes."

"Who says that's my record?" Wingnut ranted. "Where did you get that? Who gave you that?"

"This is the prison medical record of Derek Arthur Marshall." Cullen said. "You."

"Bollocks!" Wingnut steamed. "I want my lawyer! Get me that smarmy bastard. I want him here right now. This is fucking crazy!"

"You don't have a lawyer, Mr Marshall. You will have to defend yourself. It won't be the first time you've resorted to self-defence, will it?"

"Fuck off."

"No." Cullen said, flatly. "Now, Mr Ingoglia. Can we just clarify again? Given your extensive history and experience in fertility tests, would you say this report clearly shows Mr Marshall to be infertile."

"Yes. Zero motility. Zero. So yes. Infertile. Definitely."

Wingnut shook his head, wearily. "Don't be a dick, Duffy. Of course I'm not fucking infertile. Knobhead." He turned to Cullen. "How can I be infertile, hmm? I've got two strapping sons. Have you seen them? Infertile, my arse."

Cullen paused, then said simply:

"They're not yours."

When Robert went down under a clumsy challenge, clutching his right knee, his first thought wasn't "things really couldn't have turned out any better than this."

But it should have been.

Because when the trainer ran on and was unable to get the magic sponge to immediately repair his reduced mobility, the coach signalled for a substitution and Robert hobbled over to the touchline, leaning on the trainer's shoulder and realised his final might be over but he now had a perfect position from which to expedite an escape with Gloria. It was quite, quite perfect.

Apart from the game result.

Their not-so-secret weapon, Mongkut, had failed to fire. Six times.

Six times in the match he'd been given the ball. Six times he had fumbled and juggled, then allowed the ball to bobble to the ground. Four of those six times, a Melrose player had been able to scoop it up and scamper unimpeded down the pitch to score. Mongkut had somehow failed to notice the ball had slipped from his grasp and the game was now proceeding behind him. He had continued on for some seconds, like a Loony Toon's character briefly defying gravity until it dawned on him. Whereupon, the message seemed to get through to him in reverse order. Like a cooling tower felled by controlled detonation, Mongkut had crumpled from the bottom up: feet askew while his legs still stomped, knees buckling while his hips still pumped. Eventually the message arrived at his face, which registered some awful conundrum as his whole body collapsed onto the turf and he gained a face-full of soil. This lumbering dump truck of a human had accelerated from standing and within eight paces found himself a tangle of limbs in a self-ploughed furrow.

The first time it happened, Robert had stood glaring at him, hands on hips. The second time, he had stormed over to the bemused giant and demanded to know what the hell was going on. Mongkut had looked at him with a face like a collapsed shed and held both hands out, trying to clumsily articulate his fingers. Robert had looked down at his friend's hands and seen the swelling and bruising which had been the result of the beating Mongkut had administered in the player's corridor. They were unfit for their one true purpose - keeping a firm grip on the ball until he reached the try line.

Watching now, from the sub's bench, detached from the action, Robert could see all too clearly that they were going to lose to Melrose.

Wingnut fought, wrestled and kicked with rage against the ties on the stretcher holding him firmly in place. His face was red and sweaty, visibly so, even beneath all the dried blood, and he was furious.

"Archie? Fucking Archie? You're a liar! A fucking liar! Show me that folder! If it's my record, show me. Show me now!"

"The folder just says you're infertile." Cullen said calmly. "Archie told me the boys are his."

"Archie? Fucking Archie?"

The man nodded and Wingnut, vicious thug though he was, knew truth when he heard it. He closed his eyes and heard muted sobbing. Opening them, he saw Cullen pull back the folding screen and Sam and Sean suddenly materialise in front of him, both restrained by a huge olive-skinned man with a goatee. Sam was standing with his jaw locked, his eyes wet but blazing with fury. Sean stood rooted to the spot, holding his brother's hand as though they were small boys again. Duffy stood off to one side, stiff and tearful, his gaze on his feet.

"That concludes the evidence." Cullen announced, extending his hand towards Duffy who handed him the buff folder. "We will retire and let the jury consider their verdict."

Cullen and the man with the goatee walked over to the door and slipped out, snicking it closed behind them. Wingnut watched them leave and turned in disbelief back to Sam and Sean.

"Sammie! Don't believe him." Wingnut wailed. "Your my boy. Look at you! Look at me!"

Sam's eyes blazed raw hatred and he pulled back his fist to punch the man he'd known all his life as Dad.

"Sam!" Sean cried out and Sam glared back at him, his fist frozen in mid-air.

"Seanie!" Wingnut cried. "Son! Tell your brother. Sam - listen to Sean. You don't believe this crap do you Seanie?"

The brothers held each other's gaze for a moment, a silent message passing between them. When Sam looked away, Sean followed his eyes to a black-and-gold rugby shirt emblazoned across the window mesh.

"Hand me the lighter, bro." Sam's voice was dead and final.

Sean looked at the rage in his brother's eyes and then at the pleading face of the man he had taken to be his father. He fingered unconsciously for his absent necklace and tried to remember his mother's face. Time oozed out ahead of them like a black, treacled smear. After what seemed like hours, he put his hand into his pocket and brought out the lighter.

Sam grinned as the Zippo flickered a shadow across his face.

"These jerseys, you know? They go up really nice."

Wingnut's eyes widened in horror as the flame caught.

When the final whistle blew, Melrose had won and the

Greenyards went spare. The Thai team, now no longer a threat, were swamped and lauded to the skies and people from all points of the ground poured onto the pitch. Match officials and players were herded back towards the tunnel at the halfway line and a gaggle of organisers bounced onto the pitch carrying a long blue rope which they used to cordon off a large rectangle of space as the crowd encroached. The distorted voice ringing out over the tannoy was jubilant and the atmosphere was euphoric. The sun winked through the clouds and the warm spring evening resonated to the applause and chants of the revellers who, by this stage, were 87.8% inebriated.

The steadicameraman and his sound man darted in and out amongst the players who, tired and muddy though they were, stood - some shell-shocked, others exhausted, many circling incessantly amongst themselves slapping each other on the back and giving each other a hug. An interviewer with a microphone appeared from somewhere, summoned the cameraman and pulled the Melrose captain to one side for a chat - the enormous close-up of a muddy, sweat-stained grin loomed over the ground from the large TV screen on the rear bank, now empty of supporters.

Eventually, the players lined up to get their medals. Kate had shaken Mongkut's hand, his chest heaving - she presumed, with pride, it couldn't have been through effort since he had spent most of the time on the floor. But she was pretty sure Robert hadn't been up to collect his medal and shake her hand. She looked out across the melee on the pitch and couldn't see him now. Perhaps he was too injured to come up for his medal? She would go and see if he was in the treatment room - dismayed at the prospect of not being able to say goodbye to the two players who had briefly shared her home. It had been a rare - very rare - event, having anyone else inside her own private cocoon and she realised now that, despite herself, she was going to miss it. Miss them.

Both teams had gathered into groups for team photos and Melrose had understandably been the focus of attention, brandishing the Ladies' Cup. The home side cheering and singing, the crowd all joining in, and the constant praise and bragging from the tannoy replaced by We Are The Champions blaring distortedly out across the slowly growing shadows.

She stood patiently and smiled for the last of the photographers wanting pictures of the honorifics and VIPs then whispered briefly to Des, next to her.

"I'm going to slip away, if that's all right. Want to say goodbye to my two lodgers before they leave."

"Are they off tonight?"

"Yes. Cheapest flight they could get. Shame really, would have been nice to have a little celebration with them tonight and have them travel tomorrow but… they're on a budget."

"Aren't we all. Gets more and more expensive every year this, you know?"

"Hmm?" Kate was distracted, still running her eyes over the players down on the pitch, looking for Robert.

"Expensive." Des repeated. "I mean, don't get me wrong. It's a great tradition, great event. Proud and honoured to hold it. All that. But staffing, policing and security cover, cleanup afterwards. I mean look at it."

Kate scanned the rapidly emptying ground. Now that the trophy and medals had been awarded, the place was being evacuated with amazing speed. The pitch side benches had all been abandoned and the grassy banks at either end of the pitch were now littered with abandoned programmes, plastic pint glasses and assorted detritus. Even the corporate hospitality stand was now empty, save for an arguing couple seated halfway up - the woman berating her partner who looked, even at this distance, like an awfully cowed Paul McInnes.

Out by the roadside, pedestrian barriers and traffic cones were already being piled onto the back of slow-moving trucks; the food outlets, pulling down their shutters and being hitched up to the back of 4x4's, leaving black bins overflowing with styrofoam and wrappers.

"Yes. It must be a big and expensive job."

"Aye. And with exquisite timing I got this today." Des pulled a letter out from his jacket pocket. "Letter from the insurers saying that our premiums for public liability will be going up next year. They say our ground can't handle the capacity, it's unsafe in its current form. The sooner we can finish our fund-raising and rebuild this place the happier I'll be."

Kate looked at him sympathetically, suddenly seeing a tired man tucking a letter back into his jacket.

"Well, let's not think about that right now shall we? It's been a complete success and a tournament to remember. And the weather's been top notch."

"Aye." Des surveyed the majesty of their surroundings, the last of the day's glorious sunshine turning to shadow over the ground.

"A beautiful end to a marvellous day."

"And our team won!" She smiled.

"Of course." He returned her smile. "You know, I had this awful feeling that something was going to go wrong."

"Really? Why?"

"Well, after the Cup being stolen and all." He confided.

"I wasn't going to breathe easily until it was in the hand of the winning captain."

"Well, it's all over now."

"Aye. For another year." Des sighed deeply, then sniffed the air suspiciously. "Can you smell smoke?"

Robert had been able to sit quietly on the bench while the victory bedlam erupted around him, saw everyone's attention drawn to the players milling on the turf, fast becoming hidden by the swarm of pint-swilling people who were pressing up against the rope and trying to get a better view of the trophy-giving ceremony. He looked to his left and met Gloria's eyes. She had been sitting quietly on the edge of an empty seat in the stands. Where she'd come from he wasn't too sure - he had lost her in the aftermath of Mongkut's attack on the raving madman. One minute she'd been in his arms, sheltering from the invective; the next she'd gone and Robert was being shepherded away by officials down the tunnel and out onto the pitch for the final match.

Here she was now, doe-eyed and coy, gazing at him adoringly. He glanced around to make sure no-one was paying him any attention, then he pitched himself slowly up off the bench and limped over towards her. She threw him a look of concern at his uncertain movements but he grinned sheepishly and reached for her shoulder to give him a little support. Together, they slowly sneaked along the stand, the hubbub and clamour fading gradually as they rounded the corner and walked out through the gateway into St Mary's training pitch where the activity and noise had subsided. It was like they had entered a cloister and the very air around them felt fresher and freer.

"Which way now?" Robert asked.

Gloria smiled at him and squeezed his hand.

"Follow me."

"Fecking hell, it's on fire!" Gerry had turned the corner of the main stand to find the portakabin alight and wisps of smoke escaping into the blue sky.

"Shit!" Mike made a dash for the door and grabbed the handle.

"What are you doing?" Gerry demanded. "Don't fecking open it! The oxygen will feed it and it'll go up like no-one's business."

"I don't give a monkeys. All my winning's are in there!"

"Winnings? You're joking? It's only money."

"It's only MY money!"

"Seriously? You're going to risk your life for a few quid? Come on, grab some of the stewards. Let's evacuate the place. Put an announcement out over the tannoy."

Mike watched as Gerry raced over to the back of the stands, out of earshot. "You put an announcement out, pal. I'm getting my fucking money."

Gingerly, he opened the door.

The tannoy wowed and fluttered, urging people to stay calm and leave the Greenyards by their nearest exit. The whole portakabin was engulfed when Des rounded the corner of the stand, and flames were shooting through the open door A smoke-stained St John's Ambulanceman was panting heavily and kneeling over a bandaged figure lying on a stretcher, smoldering.

"Jesus. Is he ok?" Des didn't know anything about First

Aid but he did recognise the smell of cooked meat.

"He's alive." The SJA man said. "For now, any road."

Des stood and watched the flames rising into the blue sky as the smoke blackened against the scudding clouds. A fresh breeze was encouraging the fire, hungry flames beginning to reach out and lick the wooden soffits and bargeboards around the roof of the main stand close by.

Kate came skidding around from the pitch and stopped at Des's side.

"Everyone's out, pretty much." She panted, looking at the figure on the stretcher. "Anyone call an ambulance?"

"I did." Said the exhausted SJA man. "Should be here any minute. Borders General is only up the road."

"What about the Fire Brigade?" She looked at Des who tore his gaze from the under-threat stand, and put out both hands in a calming gesture.

"Now. Let's not be too hasty."

THE END

Mongkut was caught between arousal and disgust. He had the aisle seat and Robert was next to him; Gloria was in the window seat and the pair of them were jiggling and giggling like lovesick teenagers on spiked punch. Every movement Robert made, meant some part of his anatomy struck, intruded or protruded into Mongkut's oversize frame and the loud whispering was clearly audible several rows back - a location Mongkut had tried to retreat to, only to find it offered no refuge from the sound and came with the added disadvantage of a large, heavily-perfumed woman who was clearly interested in what he had between the posts.

It was alright for everyone else - they probably didn't understand Thai - but Mongkut could make out every crashing double-entendre and squirming pun emanating from his friend and companion. Even jamming his earbuds in as far as he could, didn't help. Mongkut screwed up his face in concentration and tried to focus on the movie, imagining the knees jostling and elbows digging him were mere turbulence on a very long flight.

"Oooh." Moaned Gloria. "That's one heavy tackle."

"Hey! You're not allowed to move the ball forward like that." Robert wriggled. "And that… that's definitely offside."

"I'm just twying… for a conversion."

"What?" Robert was so aroused, he wasn't sure he understood what she was saying any more.

"I'm going to convert this loose forward..." Gloria glanced around and the sound of a zip being yanked was clearly audible throughout the cabin. "Into a tight head."

She lowered her face towards Robert's trousers. "It would have been better if you'd come in your shorts."

"I might soon if you're not careful." Robert gritted his teeth, as his trousers grew more and more constricting. Within moments, Gloria had added to the constriction with her own contribution.

"Do you know the correct procedure for a... um, ruck?" Robert cast his eyes up to the overhead lockers as he felt her warm breath on him. "You need to crouch..."

"Done that."

"Touch."

"Hmm-mm."

"Pause." Robert rolled his eyes. "And engage."

"I know." Gloria thought to herself. "I used to be a hooker."

"It's like bloomin' Picadilly Circus these days." Archie moaned as he dropped himself stiffly into his armchair. The TV was showing horse racing on mute and the air in the room was stifling. The windows were all tightly closed even though it was a beautiful spring afternoon outside.

"Cupar?" Kate quizzed.

"No. My house!"

She scrunched her nose a little and looked at him askance. "You've had a lot of visitors then, I take it?"

"Aye. Well, you and that tall bloke in the hat. Counts as a lot when you can go a whole week wi'out seeing any bugger."

"What was his name?" Kate asked, whilst knowing

instantly where this was going.

"Can't remember that, luv. It'd push out vital PIN numbers. Cowboy hat it was. Were here last week. You coppers these days, you don't dress conventionally do you?"

"Did he say he was a policeman?"

Archie screwed up his face, trying hard to recall. "Well, mebbe no. Not sure, now you ask me direct like. But he asked questions like a copper any road. No disputing that."

"I see." Kate made a mental note to reprimand Cullen when - *if* - she next saw him. "We have released the remains. For burial."

"You mean her body?"

"Remains." Kate repeated, softly. Archie was silent for a few moments.

"Do you really need to ask me questions now? Isn't it all a bit late for this?"

"I'm sorry. I like to be able to tidy off any loose ends when I close a case."

"You mean it's been open all this time?"

"Well… no."

"You could always not bother. Just check that other fella's notes."

"Did he make notes?"

Archie did his trying-hard-to-recall face again. "No. You're right, he didn't."

"So, uh, from the top?" Kate prompted.

Archie sighed and paused for a moment. It seemed like it might be a fine line for him: irritation at being asked to repeat himself versus delight at having some unexpected company to talk to. He arrived at a decision and burrowed himself ever-so-slightly further into his armchair. Kate sat down.

"Well, as I told this other fella. No-one ever bothered to ask me anything. Or chase me down. It were all about him and his crimes. No matter about victims in them days. Course, it's all right now - victim support units, women police officers offering tea and sympathy, counselling. Victims these days - they got it easy!"

"You seem very well acquainted with modern police practices, Mr Strachan."

"Aye well, I watch Casualty. Lewis. Only BBC mind!"

"I see. But racing on Channel 4?"

"Beeb lost the rights to everything 'cept the National and Cheltenham. What am I supposed to do?"

"Yes." Kate pursed her lips. "And Derek?"

"Oh, him." Archie's face darkened. "That… gobshite. He never loved her - not like I did. And she knew it! I'd told her over and over that we should get away, take the boys, but she wouldn't. Too scared. Knew what he could do - would do - if she ever crossed him. The fact that the boys were mine and not his - he'd have killed her." His eyes filled with tears. "Turns out she was right."

Kate waited for him to continue. Archie sniffed and tried wiping his eyes with the heels of his hands. "Sorry. I'm sorry."

"It's ok." She said. "Grief takes time. Let it have the time it needs."

"That fella in the hat, he didn't seem so… sympathetic. Just came out wi' it. I didn't know. Never knew." He started sniffing again, finding it hard to push out his words. "Shoulda gone back… such a coward… hiding away here, all these years… shame on me."

"It wouldn't have mattered." Kate came over to him, her voice softening.

"Would've mattered to me!" Archie whirled his face up at her, defiance in his eyes. "Mattered to my boys. MY boys. Damn him and his life behind bars. I could've given them a home, a future. Love."

"Mr. Strachan?" Kate put an arm around his shoulder. "You still can."

"The feeding frenzy for two, please." Paul said to the young girl who was their waitress in The Lamb & Flag.

"And for yourself?"

Shirley smiled sympathetically at the girl. "I think he's ordering for both of us."

Paul looked at her and shook his head. She handed back the menu.

"Caesar salad for me, please."

Shirley scanned the pub and its inhabitants sadly, realising that the natural order had been restored. Her sojourn into a world of champagne and glamour and heels had been an all-too-brief glimpse into another life, another existence - certainly not one she was likely to inhabit any time soon. If at all.

"Do you know what day it is today?" She prodded.

"Tuesday." Paul said confidently.

"Thursday, actually. But what I meant was, what *date* it is. Today."

Paul looked her in the eye. She stared him down, waiting. Hoping.

"Nope." He finally managed. "I got nothing. I know it's April."

"Yes. Yes it is. A very significant date in April, in fact." She crossed her hands in her lap, rearranging her napkin, straightened in her seat and waited.

Paul took a heavy swig from his pint glass, trying to buy himself time. Eventually, he had to put it back down on the table. He looked at her like Alfred Hitchcock watching his dog drown. "I'm sorry to say, my sweet, that all I can think of…"

She raised her eyebrows, prepared for the worst.

"… is our first anniversary."

"No, actually. Wait, what?"

"It is exactly one year since our first date!" Paul burst into an enormous grin, his tombstone teeth shining in the table lamp. For a moment, Shirley was too stunned to be happy. He had remembered.

"How…?" She stopped and smiled broadly. "Why didn't you say something?"

"Surprise!" Paul pulled out something small from a pocket and popped it on the table in front of her. "Happy anniversary, Shirl."

"I am.. astonished." She said, feeling her pulse quicken at the size of the plush ring box. She was suddenly afraid to touch it.

"I had something a bit more… extravagant planned but-"

"You did?" Shirley wasn't really focussing on what he was saying any more, unable to take her eyes off the box.

"Uh-huh. But… well, there was a slight problemette."

"I see."

"Yeah, you see, at the Sevens-"

"Can I open it?"

"Hmm? Yes, that's what it's for. It's a present. You won't see what it is unless you open it."

"Of course." Trembling, she picked up the box and opened it.

"See, at the Sevens I'd asked the-"

"Oh." Shirley's disappointment was crushing.

"What do you mean: oh?"

"Nothing." She recovered, rearranging her features into a half-hearted smile. "What is it?" She thought she knew what it was; she was certain she knew what it was *not.*

"It's a necklace." Paul beamed. "I got in engraved on both sides, see? You spin it round…" He flicked the delicate disc with a giant finger "… and it says PM ♥ SS."

"It's…" Not what I wanted, thought Shirley. The words were hard to squeeze out. "… lovely".

Paul wore a proud grin a mile wide and Shirley forced herself to do a mental self-correct. This was her world - the real world - not some movie scene. She wasn't in a relationship with George Clooney, she was in a relationship with a homeless-in-all-but-name joiner. With a heart of gold.

"I don't think I've ever seen one of these before." She picked it up, opened the clasp and draped it around her neck. It was a snug fit and the tiny disc seemed rather small against her expansive collar bone. It's the sentiment, she told herself. Not the substance. "Where did you get the idea from?"

"Er…" Paul reddened. "Just… came to me."

"It's really sweet." She smiled at him again, this time more considerately, and placed her hand on top of his. "It's a lovely thought, sweetheart. Thank you. I shall always wear it."

"Cool."

Their food arrived and Paul tucked into his mega-plate with unconcealed glee. Shirley's chicken had the mouth-feel and taste of a candle that had been sneezed on.

"You know, for our anniversary next year…" She

paused, concerned, as Paul choked on a mouthful. "Maybe we could go somewhere a bit more… upmarket?"

Paul recovered and adopted his serious-thought face.

"I was thinking, you know, after our VIP treatment at Melrose? Somewhere nice. Maybe this time we could dress up?"

Paul unconsciously felt for an imaginary collar around his neck.

"Of course, my sweet." He said and tucked away an idea for twelve months' time: Wetherspoons.

"So the SHS stands for… ?" Kate brushed a strand of hair from her face, blown there by the strong breeze whipping in through the trees. She and Cullen were standing on the open top of the Seventies house, watching the sun come up over Selkirk.

"Sam and Heather Strachan."

"Who's Sam?"

"Archie." Cullen thrust his hands into his pockets, hunching slightly against the brisk wind. "Archie's his middle name. Christian name's Samuel. Samuel Archibald Strachan. Heather used to call him Sammie - which is why their first child was called Sam."

"And Sean?"

Cullen shrugged. "Archie just likes names that begin with S."

"You get all this from talking to him?"

"Some. I knew of him way back. Before your time."

"So you just… found him?"

Cullen shrugged again. "I knew he was a Fife lad."

She studied him closely: the lines on his face, the light in his eye, the set of his jaw, the broken nose.

"Don't you miss it? This? Police work?"

"No."

"Really?"

"Really." He turned towards her and there was a sadness in his face, just for a moment. "Memories. I don't need them anymore."

They stood in silence for a while, listening to the pine trees swishing in the wind.

"The stand's being demolished." She said. "Well, what's left of it."

"Huh. Wingnut?"

"First degree burns. Doesn't look good." She glanced around at the barren rooftop. "Is this you then?"

"No. I'm done here."

Kate took a deep breath and long drawn-out sigh.

"You didn't need to do this, you know. Any of it."

Cullen pursed his lips and gave a final shrug, avoiding her eyes. "It needed to be done. Got to do what's right."

"Says who?"

"Me."

"And who decides what's right?"

"Me again." His brow creased in thought.

"I see. Judge, jury and executioner then, is it?"

Cullen turned and his face opened briefly into a smile.

"Guilty."

Sam and Sean stood by the graveside, heads bowed. Archie stood beside them.

The earth was newly turned and the gold engraving on the granite headstone sparkled in the clean, fresh air. They each placed some flowers on the plot, in turn. Archie crossed himself and kissed the gravestone. Sam and Sean both had tears streaking down their faces.

"Why didn't you ever come and get us?" Sam asked. "All these years?"

"I didn't know she was… gone. I thought she was with you both. That you'd all be happy."

Sam looked at this stranger - his newly identified parent. The only parent he now had left. He didn't see much of a resemblance, although there seemed a clearer match with Sean. Something around the eyes and perhaps the nose.

"But why not come and be with us then? Be a family?" Sam was starting to raise his voice. Sean tried to quieten him by putting a hand on his arm but Sam shook it off.

"He threatened to kill me if he ever saw me again." Archie said. "Said he had eyes and ears all over Gala. If I ever set foot there again, he'd make sure it was the last thing I did."

Sam sulked and looked down at the headstone. This man was his father? Some father. More like a chicken.

"We've all lost years, son. We can't get them back, but we can use what we have. She lost everything. We don't have to."

"Don't call me son. I'm not your son."

"Yes. Yes, you are. Son." Archie reached for him but Sam shrank away. "I'm sorry. Both of you. Sorry you didn't have me, sorry I didn't have you. Sorry, none of us had your Mum."

"It's not your fault." Sean said quietly.

"Yes it is." Sam sniffed but kept his gaze on the headstone. The engraving swam in and out of focus through his tears.

Archie cast sneak glances at the two boys - men now - by his side and trudged off down the gravel path towards the cemetery gates. Sean elbowed Sam in the ribs.

"Sammie. Come on. He's our Dad. Our real Dad. We should be happy - we have a Dad."

"Been doing just fine without one for years." Sam protested, thinking of the stranger who was supposed to have always been there for him but had flitted in and out of his life like an incontinent moth; who should have loved and honoured his own wife, Sam's mother, but had killed her instead. "Don't need a Dad."

"Don't you? I don't know if I *need* one, but I want one."

"Rather have Mum."

"Yes. But she's gone. She's been gone all this time, we just didn't know it." Sean unconsciously drew his hands up to chest, fingering his repaired necklace. "Look, they're his initials."

"Yeah. Not ours."

"No. *And* ours." Sean insisted. "Sammie, come on! You're even named after him. He loved you, wanted you. Still does."

"Does he?" Sam squinted at his younger brother, blonde fuzz silhouetted against the sparkling sky.

"Yes. But you've got to give him a chance."

Sam fingered his own necklace and cast his eyes down the path to the shape of his father, waiting patiently by the gatepost. "Doesn't even follow rugby."

"Well then." Sean gave his brother a friendly punch on the arm. "Let's show him what he's missing."

Duffy sat on the hill and started a new entry in his notebook:

```
DATE: APRIL 20 2018
TIME: 2230 HRS
```

He waited, pen poised over the paper, unable to write. He watched his hand as it started to shake more and more violently, until he had to still it with his other hand. He held his head up to the darkening sky and his eyes began to moisten.

What was the point? He needed to remind himself hourly, right now. His sister was dead, and had been for years. He had lost his wife - he wasn't sure where she was but he guessed she had run off with that rugby player. He figured he might never see her again. His reputation was ruined - the local paper had reported the trial collapse and lampooned his evidence and status as an "unreliable witness". The boys, Sam and Sean, had also vanished - perhaps afraid they would be identified as the culprits behind the burning down of the Greenyards. He looked down on it now, an unsightly incinerated ruin, blackened and twisted tangles pointing up from rubble at the starry sky.

Now, here he was, back on the hillside like some Alzheimer pensioner who had simply forgotten how to die. Duffy hung his head and flung his pen over into the gorse on the edge of the slope. His movement bobbled his chair which, in turn, knocked over his opened flask of Bovril. The hot liquid bled into the ground and disappeared.

Duffy sat and started to cry. All he had left was a tiny molecule of hope, formed from three minuscule fragments of unexplained data:

1. The flaming H, the sign the time-travellers had given him

2. The olive-skinned goatee'd man from the future, whom he had met and then had vanished.

3. The note on his seat at the tournament: *A friend from the future.*

This last item was his only piece of physical evidence. He took it out now and read it again, tending the embers of this flickering hope. Nurturing it to see if he could fan it into life.

"Hullo."

Duffy started and hurriedly crumpled the note into his jacket pocket. *Stranger on the hill, stranger on the hill!* It was a young woman, wearing a blue waterproof, black trousers and walking sandals. She carried a small rucksack on her back and wore a buff on her head which swept all her hair back and away from a pretty, heart-shaped face. She smiled at him warmly.

"I'm Lois."

Duffy cast his eyes back to the ground and started waggling his fingers, shaking his head. "Stranger on the hill. Stranger on the hill. Disrupting observations. It's a disturbance, Big disturbance. Major disturbance."

"I'm sorry. I'll be quiet." Lois said. "I don't want to disturb you. I wanted to join you, actually."

"Join me. Join me. Join me. Join me." Duffy chanted, rocking in his chair.

"Look, it's ok." Lois approached delicately and stood over him as he swayed backwards and forwards. She risked a gentle hand on his shoulder and Duffy stopped. "I understand. I want to find them too."

"Find them. Join me. Join me. Find them." He mantra'd like some mad riddle.

"The people from the future. Us. The future us."

Duffy stilled and managed a look up into her face. She was smiling, her eyes twinkling. She cocked her head to one side, as if sizing him up. "Can I join you?"

Duffy gazed at her, part in wonder, part in confusion.

"Have you seen them?"

"No. Not yet. Have you?"

"Yes. Once. They are very hard to find. Very, very hard. Deliberately hard." He looked anxiously around the deserted hillside. "They don't want to be found. Not by anyone. Not crowds. Definitely not crowds."

"We're not a crowd, are we? You and me?"

"No." He thought for a moment. "No. We're not. We're not a crowd."

"Can I sit?" She gestured to the spot next to him and Duffy nodded vacantly.

"I watch for them often. Most days. Nights. Not days. Nights."

"I know."

"Do you? How do you? Do you watch too?" He had a startling thought. "Do you watch me?"

"I was on the jury. When you were in court. I heard your evidence."

"No! No. No." Duffy leapt up and started pacing back and forth, beating his head with the heels of his hands. "It was wrong. All wrong. That man. He made me sound stupid. I'm not stupid. I am smart. Very smart. Very very smart. Smarter than that man. He was wrong. Very wrong. Very very wrong."

"Hey. Hey. Shhh. It's ok. Honest. It's ok. Please." She rose and approached him, putting her arms around his shoulders. "Come and sit back down. It's ok. I believe you."

"That man didn't. He didn't. He laughed. The papers laughed. People laughed. Everybody laughed." He knelt his elbows on his knees and ran his fingers through his hair.

"I didn't laugh."

"Everybody laughed. Everybody."

"Not me. Nuh-uh." She drew a small X over her breast with an index finger.

"Really?"

"Really."

Duffy waggled his head, unsure, then looked into her face. "Why?"

She thought for a moment, looking up to her left and then back at him. "I don't know. At first, I just did. But then I got this." She reached into a pocket and pulled out a small folded piece of paper. Duffy took it and opened it. It said: *Duffy is an honest man.*

Duffy recoiled and dropped the note. "Where did you get this? Who gave you this? Where did you get this?"

Lois seemed startled by his reaction. She picked the note up and looked at it, wondering what was so shocking about it. "It appeared in my pocket. After the trial."

"Who put it there? Who did it? Did he have a goatee? Who did it?" Duffy stood up and resumed pacing, but this time rather than beating his head, he was violently scanning the skies, wrenching his head this way and that.

"I don't know. Please! Please don't do that. What's wrong?"

"They're real. Real. I knew it. The sign. The note. I knew it. They're real. I knew it."

"My note?" She stood up again and went over to him. "My note? Is my note proof? Is that it?"

"My note." Duffy repeated, shaking his head. "My note."

"My note?"

"No. My note. Mine." Duffy dug into his own pocket and brought out his own note, the one from his future friend. "Show me. Show me." He urged her to bring her note out again and she did so.

He held them up, side by side:

Duffy is an honest man and *A friend from the future*

The handwriting matched.

Duffy looked at Lois, and Lois looked at Duffy. Let them laugh. Let everybody laugh. What did they know?

Duffy and Lois, they knew.

POSTSCRIPT

The destruction of the **Greenyards** stand by fire was a big news story worldwide. As a result, hundreds of thousands of pounds of donations from fans and well-wishers flooded in. Together with the insurance money, this allowed the rugby club to complete its **1883 Legacy Project** funding. They break ground on the new stand on Tuesday. Colin, Roger, Des (and Audrey) are all delighted.

Derek Arthur Marshall died from first degree burns in Borders General Hospital. His remains were cremated by Scottish Borders council after no relatives came forward to claim the body. Some council employee scattered the ashes somewhere. Probably.

MacDuff Angel Ingoglia still lives in his cottage in Housebyres. **Lois Rutherford** moved in with him last January and has helped refine and improve his whiteboard and paper filing systems. They camp out on the Eildons four times a week looking for time-travellers, where they both enjoy Bovril and crisp sandwiches. Cheese And Onion.

Gloria Phatipatanawong divorced her husband and married **Worrawut "Robert" Pornpipatpong** at a charmingly rural wedding in the Phetchaburi foothills in northeast Thailand. Building on Robert's growing reputation as a dashing star in the Far East rugby circuit, they have founded their own rugby academy. Gloria is expecting their first child.

Mongkut Utamporn was best man at Gloria &

Robert's wedding. He is hoping to become a huge TV star after being chosen for the Thai edition of Gladiators. His stage name is *The Wok.*

Sam Marshall was fired from his job as a car mechanic for abusing and damaging a company vehicle. He decided to switch to pushbikes, where his percussive maintenance abilities would be less damaging and far more effective. He now works for a popular mountain bike repair shop in Galashiels called *Braking Wind.* Every weekend he takes his father, **Archie**, to watch rugby.

Sean Marshall is in the final year of his degree course at Queen Margaret's University and has started applying for jobs in the Peebles area. Last month he got engaged to **Janine Crombie**. She insisted.

Kate Lorimer was promoted to Detective Chief Superintendent but her toilet is still full of shit. She has moved in with her sister, **Sarah**, in St Boswells and is still considering retiring and helping run the Jack Russell kennel business with her. She resigned from the Melrose Rugby Club board after the construction of the new stand was given the go-ahead.

Samuel Archibald "Archie" Strachan moved back to Galashiels from Fife to live with his sons. He is slowly beginning to appreciate rugby union and attends all home matches at Netherdale. He is currently looking for a new suit to wear at Sean's graduation ceremony.

Paul McInnes saved up the money from his Melrose "big job" and took **Shirley Harriet Stevenson** on holiday to the Dominican Republic, where he planned to pop the question. Unfortunately, she spent the first few nights alone - due to an incident at the airport involving a sniffer dog, which required the intervention of the British Embassy and an early return to the UK. Paul is still working on his plans for a suitably impressive proposal and, meanwhile, plucking up the courage to ask Shirley to move in with him. Shirley has no intention of doing so, until she has a ring on her finger.

Mungo James Cullen lives alone. Somewhere. After the last of his cans of orange spray paint were destroyed in the bothy fire, he switched to lime green.

AUTHOR'S NOTE

Thanks to all those at Melrose Rugby Club who answered my foolish questions, gave me a tour of the Greenyards and provided me with some excellent local colour, which I hope I have not spoilt by deploying it clumsily here. Any mistakes or bloopers I have made are entirely my own - although some errors are deliberate. For example, I know the goalposts at the Greenyards are concreted in and cannot be removed, but there is only so far I will allow the facts to get in the way of my plot, and a blazing letter H seen by Duffy from a hill was too good to just throw away. And a fire in the portakabin probably wouldn't set light to the stand. And there was no building work where a dead body could be buried. And… well, you get the idea. It was all bloody unhelpful, to be honest, so I had to make all that up too. Facts, eh?

And obviously, the Greenyards did not burn down and the 1883 Legacy Project is still running and attracting funds for the eventual rebuild. It is a very worthy cause and if you are tempted to offer a contribution you can do so at **melroserugby.org/1883-legacy-project/fundraising**. And before you ask - no, the Club President is nothing like Des at all.

The description of the jurors (and the conversations they had during the trial) is entirely invented. Anyone who has been selected for jury service will know this, since members of a jury hardly ever talk to each other and the whole process is a terrible and lengthy bore. They don't use the word *trial* for nothing, you know. Having said that, this whole book was inspired by a story I saw from a German newspaper (about a man who paid his neighbour to impregnate his ex-beauty queen wife only to discover that his neighbour was infertile - so he sued for breach of contract!) and a stint of jury service I did myself in Selkirk Sheriff Court some years ago, where the case involved a fight in a pub after the Boxing Day Gala/Melrose fixture. For those people who have ever asked me: where do you get your ideas from? Well, this answer will have to do.

My thanks, also, to the staff at Selkirk Sheriff Court for allowing me to sit in on jury selection, and to Tom Porter for giving me invaluable insights into courtroom proceedings - and the seeds of another idea for a book. But that's another story.

A shout out to Big Paul, for allowing me to draw a completely fictitious representation of him and his life. If he ever reads this, I'm sure he'd agree with me that he and Shirley make a grand couple, though. I wonder if it'll last.

Penultimately, I'd like to thank my beta readers: Deidre M, Mike M, Pete B, John K, Mike BG, Jane/Fallacious Rose and Jacqui B. They were incredibly helpful in pointing out errors, inconsistencies and identifying the bits where I'd dropped the ball. I hope the finished book is worth the effort they spent helping me with it. It means a huge amount to me to know that I have a team of Beta readers prepared - even eager - to read my stuff and help make it better. Thank you all.

And last, but by no means least, my deep gratitude to my partner and Alpha reader, Claire. She listened to me prattle on for months and months with half-explained bits of the story and heard my anguish as the book developed. And, when she asked me for more details, I would say "Can't say - spoiler alert." I must have driven her mad. I can do that. But she pointed out things that jarred and I changed them and, in doing so, improved the finished article. The jokes are all mine though.

Any and all other inaccuracies or omissions are intentional and not meant to represent a lack of research or thoroughness on my part. Honest.

Finally, an appeal to you: dear reader. This book took me nine months to complete and that's a long time and a lot of work. It would mean so much to me if you could drag your sorry mouse over to Amazon, click on this book and leave a review. If you've read down to here, you either liked it a lot or are just a stubborn completist. Regardless, show me you care: let me know what you thought. My next book will be all the better for it.

mjf

1.10.2018

Tell others what you thought…

As an indie author I am highly reliant on user reviews to help other readers decide whether my books might be for them. If you enjoyed this book, please tell your friends and leave a review on Amazon .

Read more Cullen and Big Paul adventures!

Follow their adventures in

DIRTY BARRY

-or-

WHERE SEAGULLS DARE

-or-

A FISTFUL OF COLLARS

About the Author

You can learn more about Mark Farrer at www.markfarrer.com, like him on Facebook here or follow him on Twitter @mark_farrer

Printed in Great Britain
by Amazon

47481206R00224